MI-SA

Her dreams promised a man: powerful, faithful, and protective, his flowing hair as dark as night. The brave and beautiful shaman seeks a partnership that could save her world ...

COTA

Proud chief of a rival people, he was joined by destiny with Mi-sa. But do their paths run together—or will their partnership spell doom for both their peoples?

KEEPER OF DREAMS

Praise for Lynn Armistead McKee's
Touches the Stars:

"A MEMORABLE WORLD ... when man lived by his skill, his courage, his emotions, and his faith. Mi-sa is an extraordinary heroine whose remarkable life story is destined to hold readers enthralled. The unusual backdrop and unique culture of Mi-sa's tribe are enough to keep readers turning the pages ... Splendid."

—*Rave Reviews*

Diamond Books by Lynn Armistead McKee

WOMAN OF THE MISTS
TOUCHES THE STARS
KEEPER OF DREAMS

KEEPER OF DREAMS

LYNN ARMISTEAD McKEE

DIAMOND BOOKS, NEW YORK

This book is a Diamond original edition,
and has never been previously published.

KEEPER OF DREAMS

A Diamond Book/published by arrangement with
the author

PRINTING HISTORY
Diamond edition/August 1993

ISBN: 1-55773-921-8

Diamond Books are published by The Berkley Publishing Group,
200 Madison Avenue, New York, NY 10016.
The name "DIAMOND" and its logo
are trademarks belonging to Charter Communications, Inc.

PRINTED IN THE UNITED STATES OF AMERICA

10 9 8 7 6 5 4 3 2 1

*For my family—you help me
catch my dreams*

ACKNOWLEDGMENTS

There are those who deserve particular thanks. My gratitude to the great hunters: Denise, Angela, De, and Penny. Also, to Verda for her support beyond the call, and to Aminah for her friendship and unending assistance. My appreciation to Joan for advice on those special parts. I also want to thank Susan Protter, my agent, and Judith Stern, my editor—both are top of the line!

PROLOGUE

The small young body tossed on the mat, his little brown arms flailing in the heavy air as he turned over. The night was moist, hot, and stifling. But that was not what made the boy so restless. Inside his head, images flashed, blurry, fuzzy, accusatory faces with angry piercing eyes and drawn, hollow cheeks—the elders. His good dreams, especially the ones with the nice woman, always slipped away too quickly. The bad dreams that frightened and tortured him stayed with him most nights.

A quarrelsome, weathered face lurched out of the fogginess of his dream. "Have you had a vision yet?"

The boy shook his head.

"Atula," came another harsh voice. The boy shrank back. It was his father's voice. "A vision?"

"No, Father," he answered.

"When?"

"I do not know, Father." He could feel the tears forming and the pain in his tight throat as he held back his crying.

All of the elders gathered in front of him, no longer only faces, but full bodies assembling to stand in judgment. Atula's small hands tugged at the bottom of the flap of hide that covered him from waist to mid-thigh. His mouth grew dry, and his heart pounded in his ears. The People awaited a sign, his first vision. He was the fruit of his father, the shaman. The Gift flowed in his blood. When would he fulfill the prophecy?

"Atula," a soft, kind voice called. The woman's voice. The images of the elders faded. The woman held him close, his small arms clinging about her waist, and all the fright, all the shame, disappeared. Though he held on tightly, she was only a dream, and the dream slipped away. He wished he could catch the dream, hold it in his head a little longer, just to see her face, to know who she was.

Atula opened his eyes. His mother's sister, her husband, and their children were still lazy and warm with sleep. He sat up and looked out from the platform. The sun was rising, a stain of pink and gold tarnishing the eastern sky. Was the woman in his dreams his mother? Was that warm sense of sanctuary a mother's love? If that was so, he missed her. He wished he could remember his mother, but the spirits had taken her when he was only a baby.

Atula climbed down the ladder and sat next to the cold hearth below. When Chulee, his mother's sister, awoke, she would take a coal from the ever-burning central hearth to start her own fire. His stomach grumbled with morning hunger. Maybe he could catch a turtle or even a marsh rabbit. His father would be proud when Chulee invited him to join in the morning meal that his son had provided.

Atula jumped to his feet and sprang into the brush. Above him, in the twilight of dawn, the earliest birds wheeled and swooped, their bellies hungry like his. Atula sprinted through the thicket of the lush hammock with the lightfootedness and enthusiasm of his youth.

Without warning, his foot landed in a hole, his ankle twisting, bringing him down hard on the damp black soil.

"Ooo!" he cried out, pulling himself up to sit, grabbing his ankle. Then he eyed the hole, a gopher tortoise hole. Perhaps he'd find the morning meal here.

Atula took a stick and probed inside the hole. He had heard

that gophers sometimes shared their holes with snakes. Convinced there was no snake, the boy reached in and pulled out a handful of dirt, widening the hole. On his knees and forearms he knelt and peered inside. The sun had come up, warm on his back, shining down over his shoulder and into the hole. Something glinted in the light.

Atula reached in, walking his fingers along the bottom of the slanted hole until he felt something hard. He curled his fingers, scraping the object into the palm of his hand. He withdrew his fist and sat back on his bottom, pushing his thick black hair away from his face with his upper arm. Quickly he uncurled his fingers to see his prize. His mouth fell open in wonder when he saw it.

In the morning sun, the pale yellow calcite crystal glittered. It was in the perfect shape of a shell from the Big Water. What spirit had made this wondrous sparkling thing?

Atula poked it with his finger, then rolled it in his hand. The sun glanced off it and into his eyes. He looked up as a sudden cool wind blew in his face. The sky was a blinding blue. The trees rustled around him, and the fallen leaves swirled.

"Atula," a voice called. It was the woman. "Do not be afraid. The time has come."

The boy huddled in the wind, the voice seeming to be part of it. But he was not dreaming. He rubbed his eyes with the knuckles of his first fingers, then felt his scalp for lumps. Had he hit his head when he fell?

"Are you afraid?" she asked.

"Yes," the boy whispered, immediately regretting his confession of cowardice. He closed his eyes.

"It is all right to admit fear to your mother. But why do you not open your eyes, look at me, and see if you are still afraid?"

Reluctantly the little boy opened his eyes. Standing before him was a glorious apparition, a woman born of the air, soft and made of the clouds, her long dark hair caught in the wind.

"You are my mother?" he asked, thinking how ethereal and beautiful she looked.

"Yes. Come, Atula, and let me touch your face."

The child stood and moved toward the woman as she reached out her hand. Atula felt the warmth of her fingertips as they brushed his cheek. She smiled kindly at him. "The dream of the elders will come no more."

Suddenly her warm hand disappeared, and she faded into the air. The wind was still, and the leaves settled to the earth.

Atula ran back into the village, eager to tell his father. He passed Chulee and her husband, who looked up as he ran by.

"Father," he shouted, out of breath from the run and the excitement. "It has happened! I have seen her! A vision!" he cried.

Ochassee, his father, grinned. "Ah, indeed it has happened."

Atula told him the story, beginning with the bad dreams and the dreams of his mother that were always so fleeting, never staying long enough. He told of the gopher hole and, suddenly remembering the calcite shell, he opened his hand and showed his father.

"What is that?" Ochassee asked.

The little boy looked at the incredible object he held. He stared a moment. Then with a wide, fascinated smile he looked at his father. "A dream-catcher."

CHAPTER

— 1 —

The silence was broken by the sound of men sucking in their breath in disbelief. The women of the Tegesta village stood still, holding their children against their moss skirts, clutching infants to their breasts. They stopped their tasks, and those who had been seated stood to watch. They stared, dark eyes wide, mouths agape, stricken by what they saw.

Mi-sa approached from behind the crowd. She wished she had a man to stand beside her. Not her father. Not her brother. A man like the one who came to her in her dreams— powerful, faithful, protective, with long flowing hair, dark like the night.

She walked into the gathered Council, moving and weaving her way between the seated men, a silent startling form, until she stood by Cherok, the cacique, the chief. Next to him she sat cross-legged. The air was so dense with mugginess and tension that it could nearly be touched, sculpted between the palms of a man's hands.

She had not entered the Council ever before. No woman had. But she was the new shaman, and it was time. The young woman looked out into the focused black eyes that stared from carved and creased faces. Brows dipped, fissuring

5

their foreheads. Jaw muscles flinched, tightening the lines of
their mouths, drawing their lips thin with misgivings.

"Is this not the place of the shaman?" she asked, indicating
her spot, holding her hands out in front of her, palms up in
question.

The eyes still peered at her with incredulity.

Atula stood, quickly drawing the crowd's attention. "It is
the correct place, Shaman," he answered in a clear, firm
voice, and then sat down.

Cherok nodded. "Yes," he said, agreeing with Atula.

The small village broiled beneath the sun. The air was
thick, heavy with gnats, heat, and humidity. Perhaps the heat
would inflame tempers. Cherok hoped not.

At first the Council's elders focused on the mundane things
about which they always parleyed. But this time the discussions seemed limited, the men intimidated, strained. Mi-sa sat
quietly listening, not joining in. She was observing different
perspectives, grasping dispositions and personalities.

The air boiled with swarms of pests, tiny insects in flight,
spots and specks of annoyance and nuisance. The gathered
men swatted and fanned the bugs away from their faces.

At last the Big Water journey was brought into the dis-
course. Cherok tensed, knowing what was coming. If only
Mi-sa could give the People more time, he thought, as with
a new food, allowing time for the clan to taste it slowly, time
to make sure that it agreed with them. Trails of perspiration
dripped down the sides of his face, and he felt another stream
trickle down his back. Cherok mopped his forehead with the
back of his hand, then nodded at a man who wished to speak.

"Soon the moon will be right for the Big Water journey,"
a man in the rear reiterated.

In Council they began to lay out their plans, discuss responsibilities. Had every man checked his stash of harpoons,
spears, nets, weights, shell hooks? Those articles would become communal weapons and tools once they were out to
sea. Except for a man's knife, which he kept for himself, all
the other gear was shared. Knowing that others would use his

tools and weapons, the maker took extra pride in his work. Respect for his craftsmanship, his manhood, was at stake.

"I have no weapons or implements to contribute," Mi-sa said, speaking out, surprising them.

"Women do not touch such things," an irritated man remarked, not waiting for Cherok to call upon him.

"But I wish to contribute," Mi-sa continued. "All of you contribute, and so should I."

"There is no reason," the man argued, hearing rumblings of agreement circulating through the group.

"Is it not true that everyone is expected to contribute and share on a Big Water journey?" she asked. "Perhaps I am too ignorant because this is new to me." Mi-sa lifted an eyebrow. "Perhaps it is acceptable that someone may use the communal weapons and devices without offering some of his own."

The men quickly understood her meaning and fidgeted uncomfortably. She intended to go with them!

"Cherok!" demanded a short man whose round chest glistened with sweat. "What is this, a woman on a Big Water journey—using weapons?"

"I think you should address Mi-sa," Cherok returned.

"I do not recognize a woman in the Council," the short man said, wiping the beads of sweat from his upper lip, then folding his arms across his chest. Thinking of something else, he leaned forward, squinted, and pursed his lips to emphasize what he had to say. "She may be the shaman because the spirits have recognized her as the seed of Atula, but only men go on Big Water journeys." He sat up straighter, affecting a lofty pose. "Men fashion and use weapons. The spirits have not taken it upon themselves to change her from a woman into a man." The man sat back, pleased with his short oration.

"May I speak?" Mi-sa asked Cherok.

The hammock exhaled in great transpiring huffs of steam. Like the men, the leathery leaves of the strangler fig formed wet beads and rivulets. Everything oozed moisture, the sun drawing the hidden sogginess out of the muck and the flesh, and into the air. The men shifted with aggravation and discomfort. This was not a good time, Cherok thought as he acknowledged Mi-sa with a wave of his hand.

Atula lifted his head with pride. Mi-sa, his daughter, was one to be admired. Nothing could alter her streak of pride. A shaman's pride.

Mi-sa saw her father's expression, and it gave her strength. "I know that it has been difficult for you to accept a woman as your shaman, but that is the decision of the spirits," she began. "The spirits decided that the Gift was to be passed to me through my father. And so I speak to the spirits on your behalf. I have been called by many of you to heal your bodies or the bodies of those you love. When you come with such eloquent requests, you always speak with the respect a man gives his shaman. You have asked me to see into the future, to interpret your dreams, to ask the spirits to bless you. I have done this with eagerness. It is my responsibility and my pleasure to serve the spirits and the People. I fear for you—for all of us. A clan without a shaman is a clan that will die. We all know and understand that. If you allow me to serve you only as a woman, to serve you in such diminished ways, then you have no real shaman. I have power, and my power is not limited because I am a woman. Mine is a great power that comes to me through the Gift. This is my charge. Let me be whole and bring to you the light of the spirits." Mi-sa looked back at Cherok. "I will leave the Council so that every man's voice can be heard without my interference."

Cherok watched her leave. He knew Mi-sa, her substance and determination. She was not afraid of controversy. She had been fearful and uncertain too often as a child when the People did not understand that she was the chosen one. She would not be afraid now.

The rest of the Council also watched Mi-sa leave. Her slim female body, formed of provocative curves, moved gracefully and proudly among them. The men looked at her face—the clean straight lines of her nose and cheeks, the fire that burned beneath the black coals of her eyes. Acknowledging her as the inheritor of the blood gift had caused rifts within the clan. She was indeed an enigma, the essence of a woman, the marrow of a shaman. Mi-sa's body spoke with the suppleness and softness of a woman—heavily lashed dreaming eyes, promising full lips, sensual rounds and arches, smooth tender hollows. But she spoke of such strange notions. She had ideas about taking part in the work and duties of men. She stirred ambiguous, confused emotions as she passed them. She could feel their eyes at her back—eyes that languorously wandered to her narrow waist, the crown of her hip, the length of her shapely legs.

She had joined with no man, although she could choose any male she desired. The spirits had not denied her satisfaction of a primal need. But she would never have a man as a husband. A shaman did not have someone live at his hearth— her hearth—and so Mi-sa had known no man. Unlike other women, she had a choice, and she protected her maidenhood. Because she had the choice, she valued it. She had never met a man extraordinary enough to make her entertain the thought of ending her celibacy. That was something she did not want to think about now, but one day she would need to produce an heir to carry on the line. But what man would want a shaman, a woman within a man's world? The spirits had been asking her to make sacrifices since the night she was born. Dealings with the spirits had never been a matter of choice. She had no power or control over the Gift.

Mi-sa left without looking back. As she passed the women, they returned to their chores, looking away quickly and timidly, ushering their children off to play. They had listened to the discussions. They had heard the men. But they had also heard Mi-sa. They wondered how she could fulfill her obligations as shaman if she was limited to a woman's world. They were glad they did not have to make the decision.

Mi-sa decided that she would wait alone for the men to come to an agreement. She wished to visit with her mother, talk with her about what had happened in Council, but she did not want to burden her. Instead she walked to the edge of the village, on the north side.

At night the men hung their medicine bundles near their heads. They slept with their feet pointing to the south and their heads to the north. There, behind the medicine bundles, on the north side, the Trails of Men began, threading out across the vast saw-grass prairie. She stood at the edge, daring herself to step past the invisible line, the boundary that separated the territory of men from that of the women. The men believed that women, especially menstruous ones, would ruin the hunt if they touched those northern grounds.

Mi-sa looked across the tips of the undulating scored blades of the sedge. In her platform she kept two long bones from an animal that she had heard of in legends. Her father had given them to her to use in certain rituals. She thought about that animal, a tall four-legged beast, larger than a deer but built much the same. According to the legends, it had hooves, a long tail, and a shock of hair at mid-forehead in its long face. The creature also had a mane of hair, more like a man's than an animal's, along the ridge of its neck. Sometimes when she was holding those bones she could almost see the world as that animal had seen it. She could almost go there, move back into ancient times. She came so close sometimes.

Now, as she looked across the saw grass, she thought of the animal again. What had this place been like when the legendary animal lived here? What had that creature seen? She wondered if the People would one day suffer the same fate and vanish. Would nothing be left but their old bones?

The wind brushed her face, whipping her hair to her back. Above her the sky began to churn; eerily luminous gray clouds were moving in, gathering together, clustering and brooding. Her small hand captured a maverick strand of hair that crossed in front of her eyes. She swept it back, letting the wind seize it.

Mi-sa breathed in deeply. This was one of those times that overcame her, creeping in on her from another world. She recognized the feeling and concentrated on clearing her mind, relaxing, becoming receptive. The purling wind embraced her as if it might lift her. A voice rode on the wind, finding its way to her, calling her. Cautiously she raised one foot. She held it up, hesitating. She could feel the land pulling her, drawing her, expecting her to step onto it. And the wind spoke her name.

Mi-sa put her foot down, feeling the tooth-edged saw grass swipe at her leg. The storm echoed, rumbling, threatening. Again through the swishing and lashing of the saw grass she distinctly heard the unearthly voice beckon. Words, sounds, spun from her tongue in a quiet song, and in a moment she felt the wind move her. Beneath her feet she could feel the spongy island of peat vibrate with the crack of thunder. Even through her closed eyelids she saw the lightning flash.

After taking a few more steps—or was it many?—she opened her eyes. Slashing rain stippled her with rolling drops until one blended into another. The young woman turned, facing each of the four directions, watching the rain and wind thrash the stubborn swords of sedge. The strong, dank smell of the peat rose to her nose. The voice of the wind summoned her, directed her, and Mi-sa raised her hands to the black sky, lifting her face to the rain. She stood mired in the soggy peat, singing to the clouds.

Miakka had seen her daughter walk toward the north edge of the mound. When she did not return and the storm seemed to grow fierce, Miakka went to see. Still standing within the village, she saw Mi-sa in the distance, her arms raised, not in supplication but in honor.

A loud crack of thunder followed a brilliant jagged bolt of lightning. Miakka shuddered. She didn't like the lightning. "Mi-sa," she called out, a little uncertain as to whether she should interfere. Mi-sa didn't seem to hear her. Miakka wished her daughter would get out of the storm. She worried that someone would see that Mi-sa had entered the territory of men. She didn't want any more altercations or squabbles surrounding her daughter. There had been enough. This was a new beginning, marking the fragile acceptance of Mi-sa, a woman shaman.

"Mi-sa!" she called again, louder this time. Miakka turned, shielding her eyes from the rain, looking back to see if anyone else had heard her call or had seen Mi-sa. She was relieved that she saw no one.

Miakka trotted closer, standing at the edge of the north line of the platforms. She raised one hand to her mouth to help channel her call, but just as her lips formed her daughter's name, she froze.

Above the howl of the wind and the splattering of the rain, she heard a thrumming, a buzzing, a vibration. As the sound filled her ears, she witnessed a bright blue-white light surround Mi-sa. The halo of light fanned out, and flickers of brilliance broke free like sparks from a green-wood fire.

Miakka stood awestruck. She watched as the light faded. Mi-sa looked down from the sky as she lowered her arms. Finally the young woman stood still, her body appearing taut and tense. Miakka watched the transformation as Mi-sa's shoulders relaxed and her body slackened.

The rain turned to drizzle, and the wind quieted. Mi-sa turned around and looked at her mother, then took a deep breath and walked closer to Miakka, closer to the invisible border that separated the men's exclusive land from the common land.

Miakka was anxious, fearing that someone still might see. "Come," she said, trying to hurry Mi-sa.

At last Mi-sa was close enough. The mother reached for her daughter's hand. Mi-sa stood on neutral ground, ground that was appropriate for women to occupy.

Miakka looked deep into her daughter's eyes; every time she did so she realized that there was a dimension to her daughter that she would never know. A part of her child belonged only to the spirits. And a part of her daughter would always be a child, the child born beneath the shooting star, the child whose father, the shaman, had named Mi-sa, Light in the Darkness.

Mi-sa's hand was cold. Miakka removed a skin she had wrapped around herself to keep dry and draped it over Mi-sa's shoulders.

"The Council has decided," Mi-sa said.

2

CHAPTER
— 2 —

The time had come—the day to begin the Big Water journey—the journey to the sea. Mi-sa stood in the opening of her platform. The sun was rising, splattering the low sky with gilt-edged clouds. The moon was round and full, yet to grow timid in the light of the daystar. The night had been long and still did not seem to want to let go.

Mi-sa had awakened several times during the night, anxious and startled. She had stood looking out of her platform, searching for the sunrise, but there had been only the moon and the stars.

At last she inhaled the morning air, still damp with the night sweat of the earth, the musk that was much like the earthy smell of the man who appeared in her dreams. The wonderful dreams. The nights of contentment and peace.

She started early today, checking the basket that sat by her sleeping mat. Strong and woven from rushes, it could hold many things. Packed inside was more of the mossy air plant in case she needed to reweave her skirt or make a new one, but that was all. What else should she take with her? Food would be provided by the clan. She had no useful tools to contribute. The basket looked empty.

"Mi-sa."

She had been concentrating so hard that she had not heard Cherok, her brother, come up the ladder behind her and into the platform. She was glad to see him. She immediately wrapped her arms around his neck as she had so many times when they were children.

"I have brought you something," he said, smiling as she ended the embrace and stepped back.

"A gift? What have you brought?"

"First you must listen to me," he said, reaching out and holding her hand. "Hear all that I have to say. Do not interrupt to object. Do you agree?"

"All right," she said, sitting on the floor, tugging on his hand.

Cherok sat across from her. "Remember that you have promised to listen."

Mi-sa nodded. What curious thing could Cherok have brought that would demand such serious talk?

"You are the shaman. I have known it all your life, from the first time our father bent low before the fire with you in his arms as he named you. In your eyes I saw that you touched the stars, that you were with the spirits and with the People. But all the people of our village have not known this for so long. Accepting a woman as a shaman has been difficult for them."

"I understand, but—"

"Mi-sa, do not speak," he said with a smile, chastising her for interrupting. "Even though this has been difficult for them, it is the will of the spirits, and you must carry on, dismissing their reluctance. Their skepticism must not inhibit or intimidate you. Do you understand so far?"

Mi-sa nodded but did not speak.

"The Big Water journey can be filled with dangers. It is a man's work and requires the tools and weapons of men. You cannot go unprepared. Each man carries his own knife. I cannot let you go on this journey defenseless." Cherok paused and squeezed her hand. "I love you, sister."

Mi-sa's eyes clouded, and she wiped at the tears.

Cherok handed her something wrapped in a rabbit fur. "Open it," he said.

Mi-sa slowly unfolded the small pelt, stopping to look at her brother before unfurling the end. What would she have done all her life without him? It did not matter that they had different mothers; the blood of their father was strong.

She uncurled the end of the fur wrapping and looked at the object she held in her hand. It was a man's knife, the edge of the macrocallista shell ground sharp. A fighting knife. A weapon.

"Cherok," she said, nearly whispering with surprise. "I cannot—"

"You must. I am haunted by the possibility that you might someday need to defend yourself and be unable to. Take this—for me."

"But the men will be angry with you. This will be hard for them."

"So it will be hard. The Great Spirit has made his will known to us, and we must do as he wishes if we want to walk the sacred path."

"But as you have said, the men need time to adjust. A woman carrying a man's knife may cause more dissension."

"Mi-sa, the aged ones tell us that everything they see changes a little in a man's lifetime—from when they were suckling babies until they became aching old men who stand with the aid of walking sticks. They say that when change comes to a living thing, we must accept it. That is the wise thing to do."

Mi-sa reached over and again embraced her brother. She whispered his name as she felt tears roll down her face. They were a part of each other, bound by something from another time. There was a power, a connection, perhaps because they shared a father, a holy man, a man whose seed carried a spiritual covenant. Whatever this special bond between them was, why ever it was, it ran deep.

Mi-sa placed the knife in the basket, lifting the moss and shoving the blade underneath it. But then she stopped, withdrew the knife, and walked to a peg in one of the platform support posts.

"What about this?" she asked. "Could I use this as a sheath for the knife?" She took down from the post a pouch that was used for gathering herbs and roots and other medicinal plants.

"That will be good," Cherok answered.

Mi-sa tied the pouch around her waist and slipped the knife inside it, watching the blade slide against the leather. She closed the flap and kneaded the outside of the pouch, feeling the shape of the weapon inside as it dangled at the top of her thigh.

"Are you comfortable with it?" Cherok asked.

She walked about the platform, feeling the new weight bump against her. "Not too awkward," she answered.

"How quickly can you get to it if you need it?" he asked her.

Mi-sa threw open the flap, reached inside, and withdrew the knife, then held it out in front of her in a defensive stance. The shell blade felt cold and smooth in her hand. She felt her stomach crawl into an anxious ball as she put Cherok's gift back into the pouch. What if she really did need to use a weapon? Could she effectively defend herself with the knife?

She slid her hand out of the pouch and patted it. This was a good place to keep the knife. She was not hiding the weapon inside the basket, but she was not flaunting it. She did not wear it as openly as the men, who slipped their knives boldly through the belt of their breechclouts. Perhaps this way the weapon would not be too offensive to them. She had no intention of swaggering about, parading the knife. They would not have to stare at a woman donning a man's weapon. She also knew that she could not let them see her awkwardness or the gut uncertainty she felt. She could only show herself as confident and consummate.

Cherok went to the ladder. "Make your preparations," he said before he left.

"I love you, too, Cherok," she whispered.

Atula also came to see her. Her father helped her select herbs, roots, and leaves to pack. Then he handed her something from his own pouch. "These you must keep with you," he said, poking at some plant parts and mushrooms he had placed in her hand. "These are powerful things that open your mind to the spirits. Use them if you must."

Mi-sa nodded and folded the plants inside a small piece of hide. Atula had taught her other ingredients for vision teas, but not these. They must be most powerful, she thought.

Atula reached out and touched her arm as she placed the packet in the basket. "You will do the best that you can. The spirits have given you more power because you were denied a lifetime of training. They compensate. We are not to understand their ways. Trust the instincts they have given you. Hear what they say, and do not cloud your visions with worldly concerns. The spirits speak to the People through you."

Mi-sa looked at him, perplexed by what he was trying to tell her.

Atula saw the bewilderment on her face. "I have not been able to teach you all the things. The spirits know this. Be receptive to their voices, their messages. Do not grieve over your mistakes. Let me carry that burden because I let you grow to a young woman without teaching you. It is my fault that I did not recognize you as the heir to the shaman's gift. The spirits tried to tell me. I was blind because you were born a girl child."

Atula took her by both shoulders and looked deep into her eyes. Mi-sa stared back, lost for a moment in his gaze. There was still magic inside her father.

"You need the face of a shaman," he said. "Hand me the paint."

Mi-sa reached for a pot of dark red pigment mixed with fat. Atula took it from her and dabbed his fingers in it. With one hand he lifted her chin, and with the other he stroked the slick color across her cheekbones and out to the edge of her jaw. A coal provided the dark smudges he chalked over her eyelids.

Mi-sa stared at her father, who was deep in concentration. She was curious how the colored marks made her look. She had seen Atula with these same marks. Why had the spirits chosen a woman?

She remembered her childhood, her growing up, and how difficult that time had been for her, how the People misunderstood her. Would her childhood have been easier if the spirits had chosen to keep the custom of bestowing the Gift upon a male child? And when the spirits had seen her distress, why had they not intervened?

Atula pulled back, cocked his head, and looked at her face. "Now you look like a proper shaman," he told her.

"I have so many questions," Mi-sa said. "So many things I wonder about."

Atula looked at his daughter. "Tell me," he said, folding his arms. "How can I help?"

"Dreams. Do you have dreams?"

"Of course. Dreams are meaningful to a shaman."

"That's not what I mean," Mi-sa said, shaking her head. "Do you have dreams that are empty of meaning—just dreams?"

Atula looked at her, feeling sorry that she was so troubled and confused. "Dreams that come to a shaman come from the spirits. Sometimes a shaman understands the meaning immediately. Sometimes not for a long time. A shaman's dreams are visions."

Mi-sa hesitated before speaking again. Her words came out haltingly. "Mother . . . Did you dream . . . have a vision about her? Did you know you would love her before you did? Did the spirits tell you?"

"No. Your mother was enough in the flesh." He laughed.

"Father, I want to know." Mi-sa did not smile.

Atula's face turned serious. "No, Mi-sa, I did not have dreams about your mother. The spirits did not tell me in a vision. We fell in love like any other man and woman, though such a love must surely be the work of spirits."

"Oh," Mi-sa said, sounding disappointed. Who, she wondered, was the man in her dreams?

"You look so unhappy."

"No. I am all right," she answered.

Atula stood and walked to a corner of the platform. Propped up in the corner was a tall staff with the carved head of a hawk with shell eyes and painted feathers. Beneath the head, the wooden staff was twisted into the shape of a snake, its mouth agape, fangs exposed, ready to strike. Farther down, where the staff straightened, the wood had been worn smooth through the generations by the shamans' hands.

"This belongs to the shaman," Atula said, handing it to his daughter. "Carry it proudly."

Mi-sa slipped her hand into the impressions. The fingers that had held it before were large and had left depressions that swallowed hers. She held on tightly, defiantly, and in her heart the spiritual fire burned bright. She knew that despite her uncertainty now, she would one day pass on that staff, and set deep inside those old worn grooves would be new, shallow but significant depressions made by a woman's fingers—her fingers.

Mi-sa gently moved the staff. The feathers and shells that dangled beneath her hand swished and tinkled. The sound was musical, the soft spiritual tone making her close her eyes. Her lips moved, but she made no sound as she said a silent prayer for strength and wisdom.

She held her staff, took a deep breath, and let it out.

"You are ready," Atula said before descending the ladder.

Mi-sa looked at the basket that almost looked too small now. Her own fetishes, made with the counsel of the spirits, jingled and clacked as she lowered them inside the basket. The prayers came easily, spoken from somewhere inside her. They came naturally, bubbling from a fountain of insight and wisdom. When she was a child, those spontaneous prayers had sometimes frightened her mother. The words and chants had flowed from her so unexpectedly and in such quiet, mystic ways.

Mi-sa walked to the opening of the platform and looked out. The moon still hung there, insubordinate and resolute, though it must have known that it would eventually lose to the sun. Men were already beginning to move toward the gathering place in front of the trails. Almost time to go. She would walk alone to display courage and confidence.

Mi-sa watched a little longer. She did not want to appear overanxious by arriving too early. Women began to follow the men, carrying baskets laden with food. She saw Miakka coming her way.

"Let me carry your basket," Miakka called up to her. "I will go ahead with it."

Mi-sa smiled at her mother. It was a good idea. Mi-sa brought down the loaded basket and staff. The weight of the basket made her lean to one side.

"A shaman should arrive with dignity," her mother said, taking the basket from her daughter.

Miakka was right. She should arrive at the canoes unencumbered, ready for the ceremony. Her struggle with the heavy basket would have undermined her dignity.

"I am glad you walk with me," Mi-sa said, smiling at her mother.

Miakka looked ahead at the gathered crowd. "The warriors of your people await you."

The men could not take their eyes off her. It was a strange sight for them; a woman in the accoutrements of the shaman. There was something powerful and sensual about the contrast between the harsh colored lines on her face, the feathered cape around her soft shoulders, the severity of the staff encircled by her long slender fingers. The crowd grew quiet.

Mi-sa planted the staff firmly in the soil. She had given a blessing the night before to each warrior who was going on the voyage. The men had slept away from the women, keeping their weapons and tools at their sides. Today they were rested and eager.

The last of the baskets was placed inside the two large Big Water canoes. Other villages often banded together to go on such journeys. But those Tegesta villages were close to one another. This village was built upon a lonesome hammock, far from the many villages built upon the ridge of land that stoically rose from the marsh. The nearest neighbor to Cherok's clan was too far away for frequent communication, but still the people of the isolated village carried on with the Tegesta traditions. They knew and respected their heritage.

The men of the village boarded the canoes and waited. Suddenly Mi-sa's voice rang out. Her face was glowing in the morning sunlight, the sleek painted lines shining. Her long black hair dipped past her waist as she tilted her head back and called the spirits. "See us. See us who embark on this journey. Let the water whisper our names. Let our weapons be sharp and our aim true. Guide our hands and our eyes. See us. See us who embark on this journey," she called.

As she had on the day she had walked into the Council, she could feel the men's eyes on her, wandering, searching, staring.

The shaman and the cacique, the two most powerful clan members, traveled in separate dugouts as a safeguard in case of trouble.

Cherok smiled as he saw Mi-sa lean forward and force her staff into the bank and push off. Cherok's canoe followed. She relinquished the job of moving the canoe to a man standing ready with a long pole.

A sudden shiver ran through Mi-sa as she watched the men with the pole ease her canoe farther along. Her mother stood close to the water, but as the canoes gained distance, Miakka's face began to fade.

Mi-sa suddenly stood up in the canoe, causing the dugout to rock, startling the men as she held on to the last glimpse of her home. As the mound became smaller and smaller, Mi-sa stood tall, unmoving, inside the canoe, staff at her side, her other hand clutching the skull fragment of Ochassee, her grandfather, that hung around her neck. The shiver had been like the sensation at the beginning of a vision. But the vision never developed. That was odd.

A few great egrets flew above them like escorts as Mi-sa took her seat. The shiver again. Perhaps she felt the peculiar sensations because this was something new for her. She would talk to Atula when they could be alone. She looked back at him and then at the other men. All the men were smiling, chatting, enthralled with the beginning of the Big Water journey—but Mi-sa was not so thrilled.

She took her last look at her village, a deep green hump, like the algae-covered carapace of a turtle, in the brown sea of saw grass. The great egrets, streaks of gliding white, good omens, veered to the south. The silent flurry cleared the sky without much notice. Mi-sa shifted, feeling uncomfortable already. The peculiar feeling came not because the seat was too rough or too hard. Nor was her uneasiness due to heat or glare, or even due to the fact that she was an unwanted participant in this journey. She could not quite understand the source of her disquiet and restlessness.

Mi-sa looked up, wanting to sight the egrets again, but they were gone. A more ominous form had taken their place. A dark bird with a large wingspan was riding the thermal currents in the air, circling the small flotilla. The turkey vulture watched from high above.

A sudden rush of fear surged through her, filling her with a strong sense of foreboding. *Stop*, she wanted to say. *Turn back!* But she did not want to show alarm. She did not want the men to see how frightened she had become. They would think she was weak—a woman afraid of this men's journey.

She looked again at Atula. Had he also seen the egrets leave and the vulture appear?

CHAPTER
— 3 —

The canoes moved more swiftly as the water deepened. By the end of the day, the dreary stretches of saw grass had disappeared, but the sky had turned gray, occasionally whipping up a quick rainstorm. Gradually the Tegesta made their way into a river banked with trees, vines, brush, and ground cover—a dense jungle with wet green fingers that hung over the edge of the water. The river was dotted with springs, clear, dazzling blue water that gushed to the surface.

The sun set over their right shoulders as they headed southeast. "There," Cherok said from the front of his canoe, indicating the overnight camp they often used.

Mi-sa strained to see everything. The change of surroundings had kept her attention the entire day. The dramatic variations in light and color, in depth and dimension of landscape, had engrossed and captivated her as the canoes moved from flat wetland, and what seemed like an eternal lens of water, to outcroppings of limestone with all forms of life clinging to them in congested thickets. The only time the women experienced a change in scenery so sensational was when they went to the coontie grounds, the high dry pinelands. She wished her mother could witness this.

The men beached the canoes on a slope in the bank, a

ramp they had made over time. They then began to clear away the opportunistic brush that had sprung up since their last visit. Mi-sa set aside her staff and feather cape and joined in, pulling the tall weeds by hand. The men took out their knives and fastened them to sticks, then slashed stalks down to their roots. The extended knives made the work easier, with no need to bend over, but Mi-sa thought it better to keep her knife concealed and use it only if she had to.

The men dripped with sweat as they worked, their bodies gleaming beneath the angled rays of the sun. The gnats massed around them like swarming clouds.

"Talasee," Cherok called. "Start the smoke fire."

Talasee took a coal from the insulated pouch he carried and placed it in a nest of cattail fluff. Gently he blew on it as he rested the prize on the ground, bending over it and nurturing the flicker until he had a strong blaze. Mi-sa brought him an otter-stomach pouch filled with water.

The men had cleared the area, set aside the long grassy weeds to be used as beds, and piled the leaves in heaps. Though the leaves were already damp from the frequent rain during the day, Mi-sa poured more water over them and stirred them with a stick, making certain they were saturated. Satisfied, she carried an armload of the wet debris to the fire. Talasee nodded, and Mi-sa dumped the leaves onto the fire, creating a heavy gray smoke.

The men took refuge in the gray cloud of smoke, which offered immediate relief from the retreating insects. They rubbed a repellent on each other, a salve made from fish oil, alligator oil, and bear grease. Mi-sa had not thought to bring salve when she packed her basket.

Several of the men noticed as she swatted insects and crept closer to the fire, staying in the thick smoke, but no one offered to share his ointment.

One of the men dabbed himself with the oil as he stared at her, fantasizing what it would be like to rub the oil on her body and feel the fleshiness of her breasts slip beneath his hand. Mi-sa could feel his unwelcome eyes wander over her.

She turned sharply, her disapproval and contempt flashing in her eyes. The man looked away.

As the late afternoon settled over them, the air became heavy with humidity and acrid smoke, and the insects became more aggressive. Mi-sa stayed near the smoke, close to the fire, tolerating the heat.

"Mi-sa," Cherok called, seeing her discomfort.

She looked up to see him beckon her with his hand. The heat had made her feel sick. Her head was light, and her body was drenched with perspiration. She wiped at her brow, smudging her face with dirt.

"Here," Cherok said by the edge of the water, handing her a pouch. "Fill this one for Talasee."

He motioned for her to step into the water and flashed his supply of the repellent at her.

The young woman waded onto the small shelf in the river and splashed water on her overheated body to cool down. She scooped up handfuls of water and gulped it.

"Well," Cherok began, "are you going to fill the pouch?"

Mi-sa nodded at him, taking the pouch from her shoulder and dipping it in the water. "Now you will share your ointment?"

"Here," he said, discreetly exchanging the ointment for the pouch. "I have another. Keep this one. You are so stubborn I knew you would never ask."

"How do you get inside my head?" she asked him with a grin.

"You taught me, remember? Are you not a part of me?" he asked, referring to their special kindred and spiritual link.

"Thank you, Cherok," she said as she passed him. "I will sleep with my back to the ground."

Cherok chuckled again, understanding what she meant. She could spread the repellent everywhere but on her back, and she would not ask anyone to do it for her.

As the evening progressed, the Tegesta shared baskets of dried fish as well as strips of deer meat and alligator. Bellies full, they stretched out by the smoke of the fire. Talasee threw more wood and wet leaves on it for the night. The brush they had cut served as their beds.

"I am glad you are here," Cherok said to her. "It is your place."

Mi-sa looked up and smiled at him. There would never be a man in her life as important as Cherok. He was more than her brother.

Cherok moved on, preparing his bed.

The wind stirred the leaves, whisking all kinds of debris across the clearing. The rain quickly began to fall in heavy, furious drops. Talasee grabbed a deer hide, and with the help of another man, held it over the fire to protect the coals. The hide flapped and snapped as the men grappled with it in the gale. The rain had come like this all day, in violent bursts, lasting only a short time. This squall proved to be no different, moving on before too long.

Soon they all returned to their soggy beds and slept—even Mi-sa.

Her first dreams feathered in and out, nonsense wanderings. But deeper in sleep she heard music, a song she did not know. Then she heard a deep voice call her name.

"Come closer so that I might see you," she said, turning and looking for him.

No answer came, but she could feel his warm hand move from behind her and caress her cheek. She leaned back, settling into him. "Who are you?" she asked. "When will I know you?"

Mi-sa could feel him nestle in her hair, feel the warmth of his breath on her neck. Then he began to drift away. She could feel the coolness of the breeze against her cheek where once his hand had rested. She felt the cold vulnerability of her back as he moved away.

"Wait, please," she called as she turned around, wanting to hold on to the dream a little longer. But he was gone.

Her eyes opened, and the wink of the tiny red cinders in the fire made her remember where she was. She stood and walked to the fire for comfort, staring into the burning coals.

She broke a stick that lay nearby and, finding it dry enough to burn, held it in the flames, watched it catch, listened to it crackle. As she peered into the glow, she heard a whispering—or was it just the sound of the wind? Mi-sa tossed the stick into the fire and looked up at the sky. Clouds moved swiftly across the moon. The wind had picked up again, swirling the leaves, kissing the fire, bringing it more life. The smoke blew away from the sleeping men before it could discourage the insects. The rain would not be far behind.

Mi-sa gazed into the fire. Perhaps the eerie whispering was really only a lingering fragment of her dream. She had so many questions. She wanted to ask Atula about her dreams and about the dread she had felt at the beginning of the journey. She found herself wishing he would awaken.

In a moment Atula sat up. He saw her sitting by the fire and went to join her. "Something troubles you," he said, squatting next to Mi-sa.

"And you?" she asked.

Atula pitched a small twig into the blaze, then folded his legs under him as he sat down.

"Do you not feel it?" she asked.

"I do not look for things anymore. That is your job now. Tell me what troubles you."

"When we left the village," she began, "I had the same feeling I get when a vision begins, but it stopped with only a shiver."

"Then perhaps there was no vision to come," he said.

"Perhaps. But I was left with this ominous feeling. A sense of dread." Mi-sa stopped for a moment. "If only I knew what to expect, how to react. What does this mean, or that? I feel so blind, as if I were walking in the dark, with no light, no direction."

"The Gift is burdensome," Atula remarked. "Especially for you."

Mi-sa closed her eyes. "I saw more signs. Surely you noticed them, too."

"Tell me. I will try to help."

"The egrets. White egrets flew above us, but then they left. When I looked again, a vulture circled us, watching from high above."

Atula's face was solemn. "Everyone could see the egrets. Everyone could see the vulture. But you are shaman. You could see more than birds. What was in your heart?"

"I wanted to turn back."

"And why did you not direct us to do that?" he asked.

"I did not want the men to see me afraid."

Atula breathed deeply. "It could be that the spirits have shown you something, and you have ignored it because of your pride. You must have faith in yourself as well as the spir—"

He did not get to finish. Mi-sa interrupted. "But I must be so careful," she defended herself. "If the men see me weaken, see me falter, that would undermine their confidence in me. This is a fine line that I walk."

"Then you must listen more keenly. If the spirits have given you a vision, a message, you must deliver it."

Mi-sa stood up and started to pace. "But you did not notice the birds. You would have understood their meaning," she said, leaning over to him.

Atula patted the ground, asking her to sit again. "The spirits do not speak through me anymore. They recognize you as shaman."

"Surely you hear the voices of the spirits. Before I was shaman, even as a little girl, I saw and knew things. The spirits showed me, spoke to me."

"And they do so now. Trust them. Trust yourself."

A blast of wind howled in the trees, blowing the flames off the fire so they escaped into the night air.

"I have dreams," she said hurriedly, anticipating the rain.

"Do you wish me to help you interpret them?"

"Well," she began, "they are of a man."

Mi-sa went on to explain the dreams and the man who came to her, the man she did not know. Was the dream or vision only a fantasy, or did it have meaning? Atula listened intently, watching the lines of her face change from curiosity to puzzlement.

"What do you think it means?" he asked.

Mi-sa looked into the distance. "I do not know. I am afraid that it is only a mockery, that there never will be a man."

"This causes you great trouble?" he asked, looking up at the branches of the trees. The wind was growing stronger. "Was there anything else?" he questioned.

"Here by the fire, moments before you joined me, I heard my name whispered, as in the dream."

"Have you seen his face?" Atula asked, speaking louder as the wind rushed past.

"Never. The dream is fleeting."

Atula smiled and reached for his medicine bag. He fumbled with the drawstring but was suddenly distracted by the angry howl of the wind. He let go of the medicine bag and looked up. In the moonlight he could see the clouds racing by. Bad sign. Three levels of clouds, all moving swiftly across the sky. "Open your mouth. Taste the air," he said, standing up, his face wrinkling with worry.

Mi-sa stood next to him, opening her mouth, tasting and smelling the wind. The air was filled with the essence of a storm—a storm bred at sea.

Atula closed his eyes and started a chant. Mi-sa watched in awe. Her father was so powerful, the wind in his hair, the moonlight on his face, the sound of his voice echoing with its mystic rhythm. The wind began to roar.

Suddenly Atula turned to her, his eyes filled with a revelation. "This is what the spirits—"

He did not finish. The wind crashed through the trees, tearing a large limb from its trunk, sending it hurling through the air. It caught Atula on the side of his head and slammed him to the ground before he could tell her what he had seen. Blood trickled down the side of his head.

"Atula!" she screamed, feeling the first bites of the wind-driven rain. She touched her fingers to the side of his neck,

then turned him on his back. Kneeling over him, she waited
to feel his breath on her cheek, but there was too much wind.
Her hair blew frantically across her face, tangling in front of
her eyes and flying into her mouth.

The wind screamed, becoming louder and louder, as if it
were a living thing. The men had awakened, surprised out of
their sleep.

"Help me," Mi-sa called to Cherok. "Atula has been hurt!"

The rain whirled through the air, mixed with leaves, sticks,
and dirt. "Help me," she called again, looking up to see the
moon disappear behind a great cloud. More limbs were flying, cracking and crunching as they banged into trees.

Cherok tied his hair in a knot behind him to keep it out of
his eyes. He felt Atula's chest and looked at his face.

A loud cracking, then a creaking sound startled them. An
old gumbo-limbo pitched toward them. Cherok grabbed
Atula's feet and dragged him out of the way. Men scurried for
cover. The tree fell, pinning one man beneath it. The man
screamed with pain, blood dribbling from the corner of his
mouth. Some of the men tried to lift the tree, to no avail.
More trees began to crack, splinter, and fall. The men scattered, running from the ferocious storm.

"There is no place to hide," Mi-sa screamed to Cherok.

"The canoes," they heard Talasee yell. Mi-sa and Cherok
struggled to see the bank. The large canoes were rocking, beginning to lift and ride the flooding river. They looked back
for others who might help, but the storm had terrorized them
all; men ran in all directions in search of someplace safe.

Cherok and Mi-sa ran to help Talasee secure the canoes.
They tugged at one of the dugouts, squinting in the rain, trying to pull it farther up on shore. Already water slapped at
their ankles. It was difficult to see, for the clouds covered the
moon, and the rain created a nearly opaque curtain that
plunged down in stinging, battering sheets.

"Pull," Talasee screamed, trying to coordinate their efforts.
It was becoming nearly impossible to hear over the tumultu-
ous roar of the tempest. Even the earth seemed to rumble.

Another extraordinary gust caught the stern of the boat and whipped it around, knocking Talasee to the ground.

"Cherok," Mi-sa shouted, "Talasee is down."

Cherok hurled himself into the violent wind, fighting his way toward Talasee. The fire keeper stood up, holding his shoulder, trying to immobilize it and stop the pain. He reeled, attempting to keep his balance in the wind.

"I am all right," Talasee managed to say, staggering toward Cherok.

"Stay back," Cherok warned.

Talasee didn't seem to hear him. He continued to fight, leaning into the wind, pushing forward until he reached the canoe. He let go of his shoulder, groaning at the loss of support.

The canoe spun around, its bow crashing into another dugout. Splinters fanned out from its side. Mi-sa's feet slid under her as she wrestled with the canoe. A green twig stung the side of her face, smacking her with the stem and the leaves. She brushed it away. The twig caught in the wind, flying on. She felt the water at mid-calf. The river was rising dangerously fast. They had to forget about saving the canoes and get away from the water.

"Come on," she called to Cherok and Talasee.

"Where?" Talasee screamed.

"Just run! We have to get away from the river."

Cherok ran to Atula. Talasee stood helpless, unable to assist because of his injury. Mi-sa lifted Atula's shoulders and heaved as Cherok hoisted his father over his shoulder. He locked his arm under Atula's buttocks. Atula's limp torso, head, and arms dangled down Cherok's back.

"All right," Cherok said. "Go!"

The three of them began to move at a sprint, nearly blinded by the rain and wind, abandoning the boats, covering their heads with their hands, guarding themselves from flying debris.

CHAPTER

— 4 —

Cherok stumbled in the mud, twisting his ankle but managing to stay upright. They moved against the wind, fighting to maneuver forward. They had to hurry. They had no destination, but the river was rising so swiftly that if they didn't get enough distance between it and them, they would all be swept away.

Talasee stopped and called to the others. "Do you hear?" he screamed above the clamoring wind, wobbling as he tried to stand still.

"Yes," Mi-sa answered, cocking her head to listen again. She looked at Cherok who was nodding; he, too, had heard a whoop, loud and shrill, miraculously sounding above the wind.

"Answer," Cherok yelled to Talasee.

Talasee called back. Two or three more calls echoed in the distance. Good, they all thought. They were able to keep in contact with some of the others. When the storm let up, they could reassemble.

As soon as Talasee had answered, they pressed on. Cherok buckled under Atula's weight but did not go down. The mud sloshed under them, sucking at their feet; their chests burned with each breath. Mi-sa could feel the heavy thud of her feet

as she tramped through the woodland. Her ears throbbed with
the sound of her pounding heart. The wind still whipped and
thrashed everything around them. The rain struck like hard
pellets, pummeling them without mercy.

Suddenly Cherok went down, sprawling in the mud, dropping Atula.

"Talasee," Mi-sa screamed.

Talasee turned and ran to help. "Are you hurt?" he yelled
to Cherok.

"I am all right," he answered. "Mi-sa, help me. Guard your
shoulder, Talasee," he said, pushing himself up on an elbow.

Talasee extended his healthy arm to help Cherok stand.
Mi-sa knelt in the mud and propped Atula up again, surprised
to hear him moan as she lifted his shoulders.

"He is waking," she said excitedly.

Cherok saw Atula's eyes open for a moment. "Keep
strong, Father," he said as he picked him up, draping him
over his shoulder. Atula moaned again.

The three of them kept close, afraid that the darkness would
separate them. Staying together was important. They followed
Talasee. How high would the water come? They kept on and
on, losing track of how far they had gone. They had to stop often, but only for a moment, while Cherok jostled Atula into a
better position and recovered a bit of his energy. They had run
for so long that the pounding of their hearts and the wheezing
of their lungs were the only sounds that filled their ears, silenc-
ing the wailing wind and the battering rain. They kept moving
throughout the night, stopping and plodding, catching their
breath and moving on.

Finally they had penetrated the thick jungle far enough that
the forest became a barrier, blocking some of the wind. Small
branches flew through the air, but most of the big ones could
find no clear course.

Cherok stopped by a tree, panting, heaving for air. He
gently laid Atula on the ground. "Wait," he called to the other
two. "We have come far enough," he said through gasps,

leaning against the tree and closing his eyes. Carrying Atula and fighting the wind had taken all his strength.

Talasee whooped loudly. It was amazing that they had heard the others before. They must have been close. Mi-sa, Cherok, and Talasee waited for an answer.

"Try again," Mi-sa encouraged, squatting down to catch her breath.

Talasee bent over at the waist, placing the hand of his good arm on his knee for support. He took a couple of deep breaths and then let out the special cry again. Far in the distance they thought they heard one reply. But maybe they only wanted to, he thought.

"We have all gone in different directions," Mi-sa said.

"Which way should we continue, Shaman?" Cherok asked, looking up at her.

Mi-sa stood and looked around, wiping away the rain that dripped down her face. She listened and looked for a guiding sign. "We will stay here," she finally announced. "I agree that we have gone far enough."

Cherok slid down against the tree, finally sitting in the mud. Slowly he regained his breath. Atula coughed, and Cherok lifted his father's head onto his thigh. Atula looked around blankly, as if unsuccessfully trying to orient himself.

"Call again," Cherok told Talasee.

Talasee rubbed his hand over his face, wiping away the rain and pulling down the lines of his face. He stood up straight, cupped one hand around his mouth, and whooped. They all listened.

"Did you hear an answer?" Mi-sa asked.

"Maybe one," Cherok said. "The wind is too loud, and they are too far away."

The rain did seem to slacken, and the howling of the wind subsided. "I think the storm is easing," Mi-sa said, almost afraid that when she spoke, the wind and rain would return with violence.

Cherok leaned his head back against the trunk of the tree.

"The storm will let us know if it is not over. . . ." His voice trailed off with fatigue.

Mi-sa again wiped the dripping water from her eyes and looked up. A glimmer of moonlight sprinkled through the heavy foliage, and she glimpsed a black swatch of night sky set with a few stars. She walked over to Cherok and sat next to him, closed her eyes and patted the pouch at her side, checking the knife. The constant rustle of the branches in the wind no longer deafened her. The sound was soothing, and the mud soft and warm against her. She would move in a moment, she thought, and gather some branches to make a bed. But first she would wait a little longer to be sure the storm had moved on.

Talasee let out one last whoop. There was no answer.

The sun shone through the boughs before they had time to dry. Every tiny drop glistened with the light as it grew larger and heavier, until it finally weighed too much and was forced to glide down the scored channel of a leaf, cling to the edge, and then fall to the ground.

Mi-sa shifted. She sat up and bent her head to her chest, stretching her stiff neck muscles, massaging them with her hand. The sun was bright. The only reminder of the storm was the cluttered ground and the steady breeze that now blew from another direction. Limbs and twigs and downed trees covered the area. Some trees stood with missing crowns that had snapped off and blown away. She realized that this had been one of the terrible storms that came from the Big Water in the hot weather. But she also knew she and her companions had not suffered its full fury. They had only endured some of the squalls. She had lived through many Big Water storms, some worse than others. This storm had only grazed them. They had been spared.

"Cherok," she called as she tapped him.

Cherok's head was resting on his chest. He opened his eyes and looked down at Atula. He could see his father's chest moving. He was alive.

"Look up, Cherok. The sun. The sky is clear," Mi-sa told him.

Cherok looked, then closed his eyes as he thanked the spirits. He carefully moved Atula's head off his leg, then rose and called to Talasee.

The fire keeper was quick to awaken. He started to move, then grabbed his shoulder and groaned with the pain.

"Easy," Cherok said as he moved next to him. He pulled a strap of rawhide from his waist and began removing the different pouches and sheaths that hung from it. He would have to restring them with some vine.

"Hold your arm over your chest, your hand higher than your elbow," Mi-sa directed as Cherok looped the strap under Talasee's forearm and then around his neck, adjusting the length before tying it.

"This will give it some support," Cherok said.

Mi-sa looked around and found some vine. She cut two long cords of it with her knife and then picked up a swatch of gray moss from a fallen limb. She stripped several thick leaves from a strangler fig and walked back to Cherok and Talasee.

"Here," she said as she placed the leaves on Talasee's upper arm. "Hold this." Over the leaves she wadded some of the moss, making a cushion. "Now hold here," she directed, moving Talasee's hand on top of the moss. "It will keep the vine from cutting into your arm." She wrapped the vine across his upper arm and over the pad of leaves and moss, binding his arm to his chest. She did the same thing closer to his elbow. "I hope this will keep your shoulder still—keep it from being jarred," she said, inspecting her work.

Talasee moved about, testing the sling and bindings Cherok and Mi-sa had made. "It helps."

"Have you heard any of the others?" Talasee asked.

"No," Mi-sa answered.

Cherok cupped his hands around his mouth and hollered out the whooping cry. "My voice does not echo like yours, Talasee," he said, giving up the call.

Talasee took in a deep breath, tilted his head back, placed his good hand next to his mouth to direct the sound, and cried out. "Ayeee-ya! Ayeee-ya!"

The three of them waited silently for an answer. "Again," Mi-sa whispered. Talasee let out the call, turning in each direction and sounding it again. The air was silent except for the wind.

"We have scattered too far," Cherok concluded.

"Then we should decide on a direction," Mi-sa said. "We must make some decisions before we move on."

"We cannot go back to the camp on the river. It is flooded," Talasee remarked.

"And we cannot travel back to the village through the water. It is too deep now. The shallow trails are washed over," Cherok stated.

"The beach," Mi-sa said. "We have to go on to the beach. The others will realize that, too. We are closer to the beach than to the village, anyway. They will all head to the beach and then get as close to the mouth of the river as possible. We will all meet there."

Mi-sa's plan seemed like the best strategy, and the three of them agreed to move on. If they headed east, they would eventually reach the Big Water. There on the white sand, where the land ended and the water began, they hoped to meet up with the rest of the men who had started out on this journey.

"I fear for the village," Cherok said after they had been silent for a few moments. He voiced what they had all been thinking.

Mi-sa thought of the last time she had seen her mother. She remembered watching Miakka grow smaller and smaller in the distance as they left the village yesterday. Their departure seemed a long time ago. It upset her to think that she might never see her mother again, that the village might have been destroyed and all of the Tegesta drowned. If the water had risen over the mound, maybe some of the People had escaped in canoes. But the wind had been so furious. Surely it had ravaged the platforms and swamped the canoes. But her people were ingenious and would find a way to survive. They had to, she thought.

"Once we are all reunited, we will make our way back home. The water will recede. Only a little time will pass before we can head home," Cherok said to them.

"If we had not lost everything to the storm, we could make a travois to carry Atula. But we have no hide," Mi-sa said.

"But we have limbs and branches," Talasee said and faintly smiled as he looked around at all the debris left by the storm. "We can use vines to lash the smaller limbs across two of the larger ones and pad it with some palm leaves. There is plenty of vine, and if it breaks, we have much more."

They set to work, moving quickly, and when the travois was complete, Mi-sa and Cherok lifted Atula onto it. She looked at her father's head. A large lump and a small gash stood out on the side where the branch had struck him. Mi-sa treated the injury with some medicinal leaves she gathered. The available plants didn't make a very good medicine, but they would have to do.

"Can you think of anything else we should do before we leave?" Cherok asked.

"Nothing," Talasee answered.

"All right," Mi-sa said. She began walking toward the morning sun.

Cherok squatted inside the apex of the travois, grasped the two poles, and lifted them under his armpits. He held on to the poles that extended out in front of him and stood, stepping and leaning into the poles, dragging the travois behind him. Talasee followed. The earth was muddy in some places, and in others the bedrock stood out of the ground, bald and scarred, craggy and deteriorating. Some of the pinnacle rock was so eroded that it broke away in yellow and orange grit as the travois scraped over it.

The land became dotted with tall old slash pines. The young pines stood at many heights, pointing their candles skyward. Silvery green palmettos that grew in thick clumps

shared space with the pines. This was good coontie ground.
In open spaces, blue porter weed, coral sumac, and creeping
bitter gourd with its sticky bright red arils grew vivid in the
sunlight. Animals had beaten down several paths through the
wild grass, crisscrossing one another. Mi-sa and the others
watched carefully for the rattlers and coral snakes that thrived
in this territory.

"Water," Atula whispered.

Talasee saw his lips move and heard him speak. "Stop," he
called.

Cherok lowered the travois. There were enough puddles of
standing water on the ground and in depressions in the rock
to get a drink easily. Mi-sa used a large leaf to scoop some
from a small transient pool. She kept the leaf curled as she
lifted it to Atula's lips. He sipped the water and then closed
his eyes.

Cherok used the time to check the travois. Some of the
vines had broken; others had come untied. He repaired them.

"Let me help," Talasee said.

"Your shoulder," Cherok protested.

"But I have one good arm. I feel useless. I need to help."

Cherok nodded, and as he lifted the travois, Talasee and
Mi-sa helped guide and support the weight farther back on
the rails.

They moved on again, suffering the heat, humidity, and the
insects. The beach would have been only half a day's travel
by canoe from the camp. Already most of the day had gone
by. They wondered how much longer this hike would take.

Mi-sa noticed that the ground was sandier, covered by myr-
iad fine, tangled, leafless orange vines. The pines thinned out
and were scrubbier, shorter, and seemed to lean to the west.

"We will be there by nightfall," Talasee said, sniffing
the air.

"Smell, Mi-sa," Cherok said. "The Big Water is on the
wind."

Mi-sa lifted her head and breathed in, taking note of the
scents. Yes, she thought, she had been here in visions, flown

here with the birds before. Cherok and Talasee were correct. The Big Water was near.

The land changed again as the shadows became long. Sea grapes, coco plums, and locustberry appeared. The thick palmettos became sparse clusters. The sun began to set.

"Look," Talasee called to them all as he noticed a fern-filled depression in the earth. "A spring." They lowered the travois, and Talasee trotted over to the water. He knelt, cupping his hand as he dipped it into the water. "Fresh. No salt," he said after tasting it.

"Good," Cherok said, sounding relieved. They had all been concerned about where they would get their water if they stayed away from the river.

In the distance the dunes rose in front of them, great drifts of sand. The sea oats atop the white hills waved in the wind, and the spikes of the yucca stabbed at the sea breeze. They quickened their pace now that their destination was in sight.

Soon their heels were kicking up sand behind them. Mi-sa stood on top of a dune, looking out at something she had seen only in her visions. Before, she had flown above it. Now she stood in front of it, tasting the salt, hearing the waves crash onto the shore, smelling the Big Water. As far as she could see, the blue-green sea that deepened in color stretched onto the horizon. How far did it go? she wondered. Did the men take their canoes to the far edge of the Big Water?

Cherok stood beside her. He leaned over and took a handful of sand. He straightened and faced the wind as he held his fist out to his side, then opened his fingers and let the wind have the crystal grains.

Mi-sa stood entranced. This was the creation of the Great Spirit. She could feel the life of the Big Water rushing inside her. Her eyes widened, her body tingled, and her mouth slipped open in awe. Cherok smiled, appreciating her amazement, understanding the overwhelming reverence she had to feel.

"Do you go to the far edge?" she asked.

"No," he answered. "No man can go that far."

Cherok squatted and drew a large circle in the sand, then made a small pile in the center. He pointed to the pile. "This is the earth, an island surrounded by the waters." Cherok pushed his finger into the sand in four equally distant spots around the island. "Great cords suspend the earth from the heavens—attached here, at each of the four directions."

Mi-sa watched in wonder.

Cherok connected the opposite finger holes, east to west and north to south, with lines extending out to the edge of the circle. When he had finished, he had created a large circle with a cross inside and a small hump at the center of the cross.

Mi-sa shivered in the ocean wind. She still had so much to learn. Again she shuddered. The sensation she felt before the spirits showed her something suddenly overpowered her. The ocean breathed in her ears, and the wind stroked her face. The spirits were going to speak to her. Mi-sa's eyelids fluttered, and then she stared blankly at the marvel of the Big Water.

Cherok had seen her look this way before. He knew he must not speak; he stood quietly and waited for her to tell him what she had seen. But he wished to be with her, to see what she saw, to go where she went, above the earth, out of his body, to the domain of the shaman. Cherok closed his eyes, hoping that Mi-sa would come for him, reach into his mind, and take him with her as she had so often when they were young. He cleared his mind, emptying all the clutter. He waited.

CHAPTER
— 5 —

Mi-sa sped through the white clouds inside her mind. The vision was coming. She heard Cherok's voice calling her, and though she often let him share these experiences with her, something told her she would not do so this time.

She freed herself from earthly tethers, leaving Cherok behind, becoming as light as the air, as pure as the sun. The vision began. A soft breeze blew gently through her hair, warm and delicious. But then she began to suspect that the puff of wind was not a natural current. Someone's breath was on the back of her neck. Shouldn't she be frightened? But she wasn't. She welcomed the breath. Without having to turn and look, she knew the person behind her was a man—the man who came to her so mysteriously in her dreams.

He moved even closer, nestling his face in her charcoal hair, and she could hear him as he drew in and let out each breath. He moved her hair aside with his fingers, kissed her neck with damp lips, then rested his hands on her bare shoulders. Mi-sa leaned her head to the side, giving him more access to her neck. She could feel the movement of his hands as they began to slide down her arms and then cross in front of her, moving over the swell of her breasts, drawing her to him, pressing her eager body against his. His hard muscles rippled next to her skin. Who was this man she welcomed so wantonly, who touched her so tenderly and so hotly?

Mi-sa turned slowly to face him, but the spirits closed her eyes. The dream had never gone this far before, and now she was afraid that it would stop. His hands cupped her buttocks, pulling her against him, and then they moved up her sides, gliding along her smooth soft skin, following the arch of her hips, up her sides and into the gentle curve of her waist. She was adrift, concentrating only on the sensations that his touch brought. His firm hands paused as he tasted the hollow of her throat. She trembled inside, feeling the heat between them, the need to pull him even closer. She was certain that he could feel her quaking—feel the weakness in her legs and the dizziness in her head. She bowed her head, spilling her hair over him in a lover's curtain as he suckled her breasts.

But being close did not satisfy her. She wanted to feel his weight on her, wanted him to cover her flushed body with his. The man understood, and placed his hand in the small of her back, supporting her as he eased her down. Mi-sa felt the soft grass being crushed beneath her, and she could smell its bouquet mingled with his scent. She waited to feel the force of his strong body, the lush heaviness of him. But he teased her, rolling his tongue across an erect nipple, nipping delicately at her neck, touching her with his fingertips, bringing her flesh alive. She murmured softly, imploringly.

Finally the man pressed his warm body against her and pushed her deeper into the bed of grass. He brushed the back of his hand against her flushed cheek, and she turned to it, her mouth open, answering his touch instinctively, searching to fulfill a drive and a need. His hand wandered up the inside of her thigh, feathering along to cup the silken rise that hid her sweetness. His palm and fingers stroked her, touching and urging her to open herself to him. Mi-sa twisted her fingers in his hair, taking handfuls in her small fists. She felt him strain against her, heard him moan as she gave him entry. And then he became one with her, taking her slowly and deeply. She opened her mouth to call his name as he so exquisitely filled her.

Abruptly she emerged from her vision and stood on the dune, looking across the Big Water, the name lost. "Wait," she called out. "Tell me who you are."

The vision had been so real that she still panted and her heart still raced. She knew that if she spoke, her voice would falter, for she still fluttered with the agreeable tension. Never before had she experienced anything like that. What incredible pleasure the man had brought her, and yet somehow she knew that she had only stood on the brink of something much more powerful.

So that was joining, she thought. A man could do that to a woman. Had he also felt the same? Perhaps there *would* be a man so extraordinary that she would surrender to him. Perhaps there *would* be a man, just as the vision had shown her.

"What did you see?" Cherok asked, opening his eyes.

Mi-sa looked at him, smiling mysteriously. She did not answer him.

"Tell me. You did not come for me. I was prepared."

"It was nothing," she finally said, her voice throaty and full, her face hot and rich with a deep red glow.

"Mi-sa," Cherok asked curiously, "what did you see?"

Again Mi-sa looked into his eyes, her own eyes flashing. "There will be a man," she said, walking down the dune toward the sea.

Cherok followed. "Are you all right?" he asked from behind her, speaking loud enough to be heard over the sound of the Big Water.

Mi-sa turned around so that she walked backward and could look at her friend, her half brother. "Oh, yes," she answered, her lips curling into an unfamiliar smile. "Come, Cherok." She prompted him to catch up, turning away. "I want to feel the water."

Mi-sa had never touched the Big Water before, never seen it or heard it, except in visions. This was much more astounding. The experience satiated all her senses—the sound of the waves, the smell of the sea, the feel of the clear air, and the sting of the windblown sand. She realized how much more intense a real encounter was than a vision. And if this was true for the Big Water, what would joining be like compared to the vision she had just had?

Cherok took a few steps into the water as it spread out across the sand at the end of a wave. In a moment the water fled back to the sea, taking with it the sand beneath his feet, leaving deep impressions. "Are you afraid?" he asked, seeing that she had hesitated just short of the waterline.

"No. I want to be ready. I will do this for the first time only once." Mi-sa took a deliberate step, her foot coming down onto the hard wet sand. Cherok moved farther into the water. She stood still as she watched the waves come in, crashing and flowing toward her. Warm water moved over her feet and then shyly retreated.

"Deeper," Cherok encouraged her, holding out his hand to her.

"Yes, deeper," she said, taking his hand as they both moved until the water came up to their waists. Small fish darted through the clear turquoise water, playing above the white sandy bottom.

Mi-sa sank under the water, making certain that the Big Water covered all of her. In a moment she stood up, leaning her head back and squeezing out her hair. "It burns your eyes," she said.

Cherok laughed. "Yes, it does. And every small scratch and abrasion. It works like medicine."

"I believe you are right," she said, looking at all the small cuts and scratches that now stung from the salt. Mi-sa licked her lips and pondered the taste. Then she took a handful of the water and lifted it to her lips. She sipped, but spat it out. "Medicine for the outside of the body. It is not good for the inside," she remarked.

"How do you know these things? Do you hear a voice?"

Mi-sa looked up at him. "Not a voice, an understanding. Have you ever drunk this salt water?"

"All the men know that it upsets the stomach—that it is not good for drinking. That is why we were so pleased to find the spring so close."

Mi-sa looked back toward the dune. Talasee stood atop it. "I think we should stay here for the night. Tomorrow we can move down the shore toward the river."

Cherok agreed with her. They walked back up onto the beach, the red sunset teasing the dunes.

Talasee wanted to start a fire but could not find dry kindling. How easy it had been when he carried a coal. Tomorrow everything would be drier.

The insects ventured out in droves. In a few more days they would come in even greater numbers to breed and hatch in the stagnant water left by the storm.

Mi-sa sat next to Atula. He did not look good. He should have been more lucid by now if the head wound did not threaten his life. But Atula seemed to drift in and out of sleep, never really grasping where he was.

Talasee's stomach grumbled with hunger. The only ready food was the coco plums. In the failing light, he gathered the pale yellow fruit from the bushy plants. It was a small round fruit with thin skin and cottony but juicy flesh surrounding a center stone.

"Ahh, Talasee," Cherok greeted his friend when he returned with the coco plums. "The evening meal."

Talasee dropped the armload of fruit onto the sand as the three of them sat down. Mi-sa took a coco plum and bit into it. Having never tasted one before, she discovered that the pulp tasted sweet but somewhat astringent. "It tastes like the smaller coco plum that grows on the hammocks, but the color is different. Those on the hammocks are deep purple."

"They are much the same," Cherok agreed.

"I think I saw some purslane and maybe some sea grapes," Talasee added, "but it was getting too dark to see properly."

Mi-sa's stomach was not full, but with every coco plum she became more content. What was ahead? she wondered, looking up at the stars. The unknown man of her visions haunted her.

Mi-sa squatted near Atula, singing a chant and calling the spirits. Talasee and Cherok watched her in the light of the moon. In her heart she wondered if the spirits had deserted them. She worried that Atula would not recover. Then, in the midst of a very plaintive chant, she realized that the spirits did hear her, but sometimes she did not like the answer they gave her.

She knew that Cherok would understand, and she hoped that Talasee would also know that if Atula crossed over to the Other Side, it would be because the spirits called him, not because she had failed as a shaman.

Again she sang out, calling the spirits in the shaman's secret tongue. "Hear me," she called. "Do not desert your faithful servant."

The beach served as their bed, and the song of the ocean became a lullaby sung by the spirit of the Big Water.

When morning came, their bodies itched from salt and insect bites.

Talasee called from behind the dunes, near the water. A porpoise had washed up on the beach.

"It is dead but fresh," he said as the others came closer.

Mi-sa was sure the spirits had indeed provided for them. They had heard her, sending a clear sign that she remained in their favor. And if they saw her, they also saw her people.

Cherok said a quick prayer of thanks as the hunters always did when they took an animal. The People believed they should always express their gratitude to the animals. When they fed upon animal flesh, the animal's spirit could go on.

Using his knife, Talasee split open the belly of the porpoise, the blood flooding onto the wet sand and mixing with the next wave that seeped under them. His hand searched the inside of the porpoise, pulling and prodding. When he loosened the stomach from the surrounding gut, Cherok cut it free.

Mi-sa watched, intrigued by their expertise.

"Take this and wash it. Clean it out. We will use it to carry water with us," Talasee instructed Mi-sa. "Cherok and I will cut some of the meat. If I can find enough dry wood, I will start a fire. The porpoise meat will fill our bellies before we leave."

"And the rest?" Mi-sa asked.

"It will have to go to waste," Talasee answered.

"Not so," Cherok said, pointing to the long, dusky shadows in the water near the shore: the dorsal fins broke the waterline as the sharks moved in closer. "The blood has brought them."

Mi-sa was captivated by the contoured bodies as they moved sleekly through the water like pacing, anxious men.

"Move down the shore, away from the sharks, to wash the stomach," Talasee advised her. He cut a chunk of meat and tossed it out to the sharks. The water quickly churned with activity.

"They could take your leg off," Cherok told her. "Stay shallow and be careful."

Mi-sa walked along the edge of the water. One dark shadow seemed to follow her, moving parallel to her. She looked back to see Talasee and Cherok pushing the porpoise carcass out into the water. In an instant, the water roiled with feeding sharks. Mi-sa looked for the dark form that had followed her. It was gone.

"Now," Cherok called to her. "They are busy with the porpoise."

Mi-sa nervously edged into the sea. After each step she searched the water, afraid that she would see one of the sharks coming for her. Another step. The water slapped her thigh as a wave broke ahead of her, then rolled on toward the beach.

Mi-sa dunked the stomach under the water and sloshed it back and forth, then forced water through one end and out the other. Again she filled the stomach partway with water until it was heavy. She lifted it, holding the open ends shut. Mi-sa shook the stomach, moving it from side to side, gyrating it, bathing the inside with salt water.

Something bumped her just above her ankle, and she

jumped, nearly dropping the porpoise stomach. She looked around her, the glare worse now, almost blinding her as she tried to see into the water.

She quickly moved backward, looking toward Cherok and Talasee who stood on the beach watching the sharks feed. Finally, when the water barely covered her feet, she stopped and shook the remaining water out of the stomach. Clean enough, she thought.

Mi-sa trotted back to the two men. As she got closer, she could see the violence around the porpoise carcass. There seemed to be even more sharks than before. "How can they see in all that confusion?" she asked.

"They will bite one another," Cherok noted. "I have seen some with shark bites in their fins and tails." He took the porpoise stomach. "Come back with me to the spring. We will fill the stomach with fresh water and tie off the ends. Then we can travel along the shore and not worry about finding water to quench our thirst. That will be easier, especially with the travois."

The sun was already hot, the sand warm under their feet.

As Mi-sa leaned over the spring, she could see into the still water. Her hair was tangled and disheveled, her face streaked and smudged with what had once been painted lines of honor. There was no hint of a shaman's dignity or sanctity in what she saw in the water. Her image forced her to confront things she did not want to think about. Perhaps the reflection went deeper than the skin, a representation of what was really inside her, the image of a shaman who was demeaned, maybe even inept—the lines of honor and dignity smeared disparagingly. She had not interpreted the signs, not understood the warnings that the spirits had shown her of the impending storm. She had to make up her error to the People. She had to prove her worth.

Deep in thought, Mi-sa gazed into the water, staring at her image. She saw Cherok appear behind her.

"We are finished," he said.

Mi-sa looked up at him and then back into the spring. She splashed water on her face, rubbing furiously with her hands. She wiped her face on her arms and again looked at Cherok. "You did not tell me," she said, forcing a smile.

Cherok laughed, relieved at the departure of the pensive expression he had seen on her face a moment ago. He had watched her and waited quietly. Sometimes Mi-sa retreated from the rest of the world, seeing, hearing, and thinking things. He respected that. He loved her, not as a lover, but even more than a brother loves his sister—more spiritually. Their connection was profound and intuitive, and he did not like to see her troubled.

"What should I have told you?" he asked, so glad to see that her mood had lightened.

Mi-sa grinned at him. "I could have scared away the sharks," she said and laughed. Again she washed her face. Some of the greasy colors still stained her skin. The spring continued to ripple from the intrusion of her hands. She couldn't see if she had made progress.

"Better," Cherok said when she looked up at him again.

He tied off the ends of the porpoise stomach with a strip he had taken from Talasee's sling. Both of them had to carry back the heavy full stomach.

Talasee had not been able to start a fire. He'd waited for Cherok to return, suddenly realizing how impaired he was with the use of only one arm. Cherok helped him start a small fire. Talasee stabbed at the meat and eventually speared it. Then he held the skewer between his knees and moved the meat to the middle of the skewer. Cherok took it from him and rested the skewer ends in the crotches of the sticks he had set at either end of the fire. Now and again Talasee turned the skewer, sometimes having to hold it to keep it balanced.

The meat was warm and tasty, especially satisfying to such empty stomachs. Mi-sa held a piece of it under Atula's nose. No response. She held his head up and dripped a small amount of water into the corner of his mouth so that he wouldn't choke on it. "Drink a little," she whispered. Atula swallowed. Mi-sa lowered his head. "Good," she told him as she squeezed his hand.

When they finished eating, Mi-sa stood and said, "It is time to go."

Talasee and Cherok tied the water pouch to the travois, and they pulled it down the beach to the harder wet sand.

"We will walk along here," Cherok told them. "It will not be so difficult and tiring. The wet sand is cooler, also."

As the sun moved overhead, the white sand became blinding. Gulls dived and darted in the sky, their cries shrill above the sound of the Big Water.

Suddenly Mi-sa stopped. She heard another sound—a special call.

"Did you hear?" she asked.

It was so hard to differentiate sounds with the noise of the birds and the sea and the wind interfering. Talasee cupped his hand by his mouth, ready to call out.

"No! Wait," Mi-sa said, stopping him. "Listen again."

They set down the travois and stood still, listening. Nothing.

"What do you think, Cherok?" Talasee asked.

"The sound was odd, do you not think so?"

"Perhaps it came from a bird or animal," Talasee said.

"Perhaps," Cherok agreed, looking up toward the dunes and the thick brush behind them.

Mi-sa listened carefully. She stepped away, moving toward the dunes. She closed her eyes and motioned for Cherok and Talasee to be still. In another moment she turned and went to the travois and knelt next to Atula. He opened his eyes and looked at her. Incredibly, he understood what she was going to ask.

"Trust yourself," he whispered feebly.

Mi-sa stood, scanning the sky and then the water. She turned again and faced the dunes. Finally she stared at Cherok and Talasee. "Do not call out," she said, her black eyes filled with fear.

CHAPTER

— 6 —

Cherok stared across the dunes, trying to look over them. He knew what Mi-sa thought before she told Talasee. The sound they had heard might be from an A-po-la-chee.

Mi-sa's stomach balled into a nervous knot as she remembered when the A-po-la-chee warriors had last attacked her village. The homes of her people had been set ablaze, the roar of the fire louder than the growl of an angry bear. She remembered seeing the People's blood spilled on the soil, hearing the cries of the children as they hunkered down next to the dead or wounded body of a loved one.

"Wait here," Cherok told her.

"No, let me go with you," she answered, patting the pouch in which she carried the knife he had given her.

"I will argue with you later," Cherok said, waving her back, showing the strength of his words in his expression and movement of his arm.

Cherok and Talasee began to slink toward the dunes, stalking, moving quickly but crouched, becoming one with the sand and the wind, moving to the same rhythm, making the same sound.

Mi-sa knelt next to her father. "Can you hear me?" she whispered, running her hand over his forehead, wiping away the sand that clung to his skin, pushing back the hair that hung in his face.

Suddenly she heard another suspicious sound, something like a bird but perhaps a man. A-po-la-chee? Mi-sa stood, clutching what was left of her tattered, shredded skirt. "Father, do you hear?" She watched as Cherok and Talasee crept over the dune and disappeared behind it.

Atula did not respond. She waited a few moments, expecting to see Talasee and Cherok reappear. When they didn't, she became anxious. Mi-sa realized how vulnerable she and her father were. They were too easy a target, too easily seen out on the beach.

Mi-sa stooped between the poles of the travois and lifted it, pulled and heaved, taking big breaths with each effort. She turned the travois and dragged it away from the waterline, every step a struggle in the hot sand, leaving deep furrows behind. But she had to conceal them, use the dune as a shield!

Mi-sa leaned the travois into the sand ridge, and she, too, huddled against the hill. Slowly she crept up the dune on her belly until she reached the top. She kept her head tucked low, beneath the crest, breathing hard. She gathered her confidence before she looked. Cautiously she eased herself a little higher and peeked over the crest of the hill. She held firmly to a cluster of sea oats, using them to pull herself up higher. Now she could see into the brush. No Cherok. No Talasee.

Mi-sa pressed herself against the sand, lowering her head again. It would not be wise to stay exposed too long. Where were the men? How far had they gone into the woods? She dared not call out. She couldn't take a chance of giving them away. If the sound had been an A-po-la-chee, Talasee and Cherok could be upon them right now!

The sun was scorching, wrenching sweat from her so that the sand stuck to her skin. Her hair hung in long tangled strings with bits of leaves and broken twigs haphazardly clinging to the dark strands. She brushed it back, only to have the wind blow it in her eyes again. Mi-sa tucked her face into the crook of her arm, resting it on the side of the sand dunes.

A touch on her shoulder made her jump. Cherok. He and Talasee had come over the dunes farther down the beach.

"Nothing," he said right away. "We saw nothing."

Mi-sa sat up straight, twisting to face him. "No A-po-la-chee?"

"We did not see any," Talasee answered.

"But that does not mean that an A-po-la-chee is not there," Mi-sa said. She couldn't believe her instincts had been wrong. She had been so sure.

"You are right," Talasee agreed.

"We cannot risk walking far out on the beach. We should use the dunes to protect us," Cherok added. "Just to be cautious."

The walk was difficult, the labor hard, especially in the heat. Talasee and Mi-sa helped bear the weight of the travois. Mi-sa had to lift her side a little higher because she was shorter than Talasee. Keeping the timing and the balance was important or else they would become more of a burden than a help to Cherok.

The day was torturous. Their bodies were sticky and irritated from sweat and salt. Their stomachs grumbled with hunger. They ached so badly sometimes that they had to stop and massage a sore and strained muscle or shoulder. The cramping, the exhaustion, the tension, slowed them down.

Mi-sa's legs and arms screamed in agony. Moving the travois up the beach alone had been punishing. Continuing to help pull it brought more pain. She winced with each step, her nostrils flaring. But she said nothing, made no complaint.

Talasee often checked the coal he had put in his pouch. Starting the fire, even with Cherok's help, had been a laborious task.

Occasionally they stopped and drank water from the stomach pouch. Sometimes Mi-sa got Atula to drink, but she was certain he was not taking in enough water. His skin sagged, and his eyes had dark circles beneath them as they sank deep into their sockets. His lips cracked, and when she touched him, his skin was not resilient.

As they moved slowly down the beach, Mi-sa continued to watch the rise of the dunes ahead. Frequently she turned to look behind them. She had felt strongly that Talasee should not answer the call they had heard. She believed it was the cry of an A-po-la-chee. She did not feel they were safe, even though Cherok and Talasee had not seen anyone. There was reason to be afraid.

The plumes of sand they kicked up behind them grew smaller as their tired legs trudged on. They looked at one another but didn't speak, afraid to ask how far off course they might have run during the storm.

When the sun sagged in the western sky, Cherok suggested that they stop. Talasee built a fire after Cherok tightened the binding on his injured arm. Mi-sa sat next to Atula, encouraging him to drink. There was no meat to eat, only coco plums and sea grapes. Talasee searched the shallows, looking for crabs or small fish that he might catch with his hand.

Mi-sa wandered. The shoreline had changed, the white sandy beach shrinking to a narrow strip, the ocean surrendering to broad tidal flats. Even the scent in the air had changed. Once a fresh sea breeze, the wind now carried a salt reek, a stench of rotting plants and mud. Leggy mangroves encroached on the Big Water. Birds gathered on the ground and in the water. In the air they wheeled and swooped, rode the currents, glided with outstretched wings. There were pelicans, sandpipers, gulls—birds she recognized, and birds she had never seen. Saltwater crocodiles hid in the elaborate and knotted aboveground roots of the mangroves.

Land crabs scurried into hiding holes as Mi-sa moved about. Oysters and mussels that the raccoons loved to eat clung to roots at the edge of the water. Mi-sa stepped carefully, picking off one of the mangrove leaves. She touched the salty leaf to her tongue.

The shallow water was brown beneath the mangroves, the leaves constantly yellowing and falling. Sea-foam sloshed between the arches of the labyrinth. Mi-sa fingered one of the long ropy roots that dangled from the top of the tree as it reached for the water where it would branch out into roots. Long, slender seeds bobbed upright in the water. She searched the trees, finding some still heavy with seeds.

Cherok called to her as he came up behind her. "We will move in the shallow water tomorrow. There is no way to move through the mangroves, especially with the travois."

Mi-sa nodded in agreement, still looking over the intriguing watery forest.

"Here," Cherok said, snapping some mussels off the roots. "Good to eat."

Mi-sa helped gather more mussels before she and Cherok returned to Talasee and Atula.

"I think the spirits will call him soon," she said quietly, speaking of their father.

Cherok looked down. "I know," he said, sorrow tempering his voice to a near-whisper.

They slid their feet through the water. Mi-sa took one last look back into the trees. "What is that?" she asked, stopping.

She could see something wedged in the roots farther down the shoreline. Cherok followed her pointing finger; then he, too, saw it. A canoe!

They dropped the mussels and ran, splashing through the ankle-deep water. Talasee stood, watching them curiously.

Cherok tugged at the canoe, trying to dislodge it. It was tipped to one side but not swamped. If they could right it, the canoe would glide out of the tangled roots.

The two of them leaned over the high side of the canoe, trying to force it down with their weight.

"How could it have gotten stuck like this?" Mi-sa asked.

"The storm. The wind and waves. Ready?" he asked. "Now."

Both of them pushed down with all their weight. The canoe creaked.

"Almost," Cherok told her. "Again. On my signal."

Mi-sa slid off the side of the canoe. She braced her hands on the edge, ready to heft herself atop it. Cherok said, "Now."

The canoe rocked and was suddenly free. He walked to the other side of the dugout.

"Hold it still," Cherok said, moving around the boat. His eyes had suddenly lost their glimmer.

"What is it?" she asked.

Cherok ran his hand along the inside of the canoe and up toward the bow. "It is A-po-la-chee."

Mi-sa's head shot up, searching the thick mangroves, the distant stretch of beach where Talasee stood. "Where are they?"

"Lost from the storm. The dugout came from much farther north. The storm must have carried it."

Mi-sa said nothing. Cherok must be right, she thought. The storm. The A-po-la-chee who had manned the boat probably lay dead at the bottom of the sea. North. Much farther north.

Talasee trotted out into the water to meet them, bracing his bandaged shoulder with his other hand. As he got closer, he realized what Cherok had noticed. "A-po-la-chee?"

Cherok nodded.

"No matter. This canoe will still take us down the coast and up the river. Home."

Cherok smiled at Talasee. Mi-sa tried but failed.

"I dropped all those mussels," Cherok remembered. He looked at Mi-sa. He saw that she had also discarded hers. "But my belly feels better with excitement. I hope that we have been right and the others will come to the mouth of the river."

"They will," Talasee said.

Their bodies did not ache so much anymore. Their limbs felt more powerful, and their spirits lifted. They ate more coco plums and sea grapes. Cherok returned to the mangroves and brought back mussels.

At nightfall Mi-sa tended to Atula and then stretched out on the beach next to him. "Father," she whispered, hoping that no one but Atula could hear her. "What lies ahead?" Her father reached up to his throat and feebly loosened the medicine bag around his neck. He reached inside, and from the pouch he withdrew something. He held his shaking hand out to her. Mi-sa took his hand and felt him drop something into her palm before he pulled his hand away.

"Dream-catcher," he whispered.

She looked to see what he had given her. Resting in her palm was a beautiful crystal shell. "Father," she said, wanting him to explain, but Atula had closed his eyes. She put the calcite crystal in her own medicine bag, closed her eyes, and wished for sleep.

A noise, a rustling, startled her. The fire was dying, now only a glow from the coals. She did not move, holding her breath to hear better. Talasee and Cherok lay still. They were sleeping, she was sure.

The sound grew louder, the rustling becoming a rumbling in her ears, like distant thunder. The sky was clear. The stars were twinkling. There was no storm, no thunder. The spirits were making her aware, making the sound louder to her ears—to the shaman's ears.

Mi-sa touched her father's hand. It was limp and cool. The spirits had called him. He had crossed over. The sounds came again. There was danger. Not being able to properly grieve made her angry. Mourning would have to wait. Quietly, slowly, she rolled onto her belly and then used her forearms to drag herself forward on the ground. She crept toward her brother.

"Cherok," she whispered. He did not open his eyes. "Cherok," she said again, tapping his arm. "Listen. Do not move."

Cherok heard but kept his eyes closed. He slid his hand along his side and withdrew his knife, holding it close to him. Mi-sa opened her pouch, moving slowly, very slowly and carefully. She ran her finger over the blade, cutting a fine line into her flesh.

Cherok was not far from Talasee. He turned to his side and touched Talasee's shoulder. Talasee immediately opened his eyes. He felt for his knife also, then shuffled his feet, kicking sand over the coals of the fire. The three of them lay very still as a cloud slid over the moon.

Cherok listened, then moved into a crouch.

"Father is dead," Mi-sa whispered to the men.

Cherok looked at his father in the pale moonlight and a deep pain welled up inside him.

"I am afraid," Mi-sa confided.

"The mangroves," Cherok said quietly to Mi-sa, wanting her to hide there. He and Talasee stooped low, moving off the narrow strip of sand and into the woods. Mi-sa watched, then looked at the mangroves. She crept behind Cherok and Talasee. She had her knife also, and held it tightly.

Suddenly a scuffling began ahead of her. Loud whoops. Cries. She stood and ran forward as the cloud moved away from the moon. A-po-la-chee!

Cherok stood face to face with one. Both bent their knees, held their hands in front of them, and moved in calculated circles, jabbing their knives at each other, dancing to escape the enemy's knife.

Cherok made a quick strike, cutting the warrior's side, leaving a line of blood. The warrior flinched, then came back, slashing at Cherok.

Another warrior whooped and ran toward them, jumping onto Cherok's back. With his good arm, Talasee pushed one of the A-po-la-chee and tripped him, making the enemy fall to the ground. Then, before the warrior could recover, Talasee pounced on him, kneeling on the man's chest. The man waved his knife, nearly catching Talasee in the upper back. But as the warrior lifted his arm, Talasee plunged his knife into the enemy's throat. The man's eyes bulged as he reached for his wound and gurgled. Talasee jumped up to face another.

"Go, Mi-sa!" Cherok screamed.

Mi-sa stood with her knife in her hand, arm extended.

"Run!" Talasee screamed at her as he continued to fight.

Two more A-po-la-chee appeared, running and whooping,

one with a knife and one with a club, a strombus shell hafted on a stick.

Mi-sa backed away.

"Run!" Cherok yelled. A warrior grabbed Cherok around the neck and dragged him off into the bushes.

Two warriors now had Talasee pinned to the ground. They were binding him with something—tying him up. "Hurry!" he screamed before a warrior kicked him in the side.

One of the A-po-la-chee stood, letting the other finish binding Talasee. He looked around to see who his enemy had called out to. His piercing eyes suddenly met Mi-sa's. He flashed his white teeth at her.

Mi-sa turned and began to run back to the beach. She would have to outrun him. She passed Atula as she started to run for the mangroves. Then she spotted the canoe grounded on the beach. The tide had come in.

She grabbed the bow and pushed the canoe into the water, running deep, giving the boat a good shove. She hurled herself inside, and the dugout pitched violently as it quickly moved to deeper water. The warrior followed until he had to swim. The canoe was not moving fast enough. She had no paddle.

The A-po-la-chee swam faster. He was catching up, his long arms swooping through the air and then down into the water, pulling against the sea, moving him rapidly toward her. A fountain of water splashed at his feet as he kicked. She could see it clearly in the moonlight. Closer! He was gaining on her!

She could see his face now. He reached up and grabbed the stern of the canoe, perversely grinning at her. In an instant he had the other hand on the back of the canoe, ready to hoist himself aboard.

Mi-sa kicked at his hands, but he held fast. In a moment he had heaved himself waist high. She rammed her fist into his face. The blow took him by surprise, making him let go with one hand, drop into the water, and shake his head. But then he laughed aloud. Again he caught the canoe with both hands and was suddenly inside, wet and smelling like the mangrove mud.

She kicked at him, her foot landing on his chest as he maneuvered himself into a squat. "Get away!"

The A-po-la-chee warrior laughed at her, grabbed her wrist, and wrenched it until she grimaced. He said something to her, but she did not understand his words.

She kicked at him again, but he was too close for her to land a good blow. He grabbed her other arm and twisted it until she groaned with the pain.

Then he had her on the bottom of the boat, his weight keeping her still. She arched her back to push him off.

She raked at him, trying to scratch with one hand as her other hand tried to push him off. She could feel his hardness against her as he grabbed one of her arms, squeezing, hurting her, making her whimper. He breathed hard in her ear, his mouth wet and hot. He seemed encouraged by the sounds of her struggle. The man reached between their bodies and held himself, attempting to guide himself into her.

Her knife! Where was the knife? Mi-sa used her free hand to search the bottom of the canoe, frantically running her fingers along the coarse wood.

The man breathed in giant gasps and moans, and for a moment she thought she was going to be sick.

Suddenly she felt the smooth blade of the fighting knife beneath her fingertips. She curled her fingers around it, and everything seemed to grow quiet. She could not hear the warrior. She could not hear the sea as she picked up the knife and held it above her attacker. With a quick, strong stroke, she plunged it into his back.

The man thrust his head back. Mi-sa froze, seeing the fury in his eyes. His hands went around her throat, tightening, choking off her air. Then his head fell on her chest. She felt his warm blood spread out across her as his grip loosened.

Mi-sa lay still, the warrior atop her, as the canoe drifted with the current. The sound of the sea returned. She closed her eyes, shaking.

She shoved at the body, crying out and grunting with the effort. She slid to one side, being careful to keep the canoe balanced. She lifted some of his weight with her arms, and finally she was free.

Mi-sa sat up and reached under his shoulders. His blood felt warm and slippery as she raised him up. After much manipulation and work, keeping her weight to the opposite side from his, using her feet, she heaved him overboard, nearly tipping the canoe. She remembered the porpoise carcass and the sharks.

She sat in the bottom of the canoe, rocking, her bloody arms crossed over her chest. She still trembled, her whole body shaking.

Was this the man in her vision? How could the spirits have thought she could enjoy such a thing? No, she realized, this was not what she had experienced as she stood on the dune. The man in her vision had been welcome, unlike this warrior. Nor had this man taken her. He had only tried.

Mi-sa curled up in the bottom of the dugout and cried, but not for herself. The tears streamed down her face, but she didn't make any sound. She cried for Atula. She cried for the People, knowing what the storm must have done to their village. The A-po-la-chee had Talasee. They had Cherok!

The grief and tears had to end, she decided as she looked at the moon. No time for that now. She had to think of what to do—had to think. Perhaps the spirits would speak to her in a dream. She was so tired, and like her mind, her body cried in its own agony. Tomorrow she would think of what to do.

Mi-sa lay down in the dugout, pulling her knees up to her chest, folding her arms in close to her body. The waves slapped at the canoe like a mother's peaceful song.

CHAPTER
— 7 —

The Kahoosa village had not suffered the brunt of the storm. The violent weather had come ashore much farther north. The Kahoosa had experienced wind and rain, but nothing severe.

Olagale, the shaman, had stood at the entrance to his platform and watched the clouds as they sped past. They moved from the northwest to the southeast in a great curving swirl. North, he had thought. The Tegesta would know this storm.

While he watched, smelling the dank scent of the wet muck as the first rain fell, the spirits gave him a small glimpse of the future. Something was riding on the wind of this storm. Something was coming with it—coming to the Kahoosa.

The canoe traveled on the southerly current. Mi-sa slept in the bottom, still tucked up into a ball. A black-tipped fin passed the dugout, then circled it. The shark saw better in the moonlight than in the bright daylight. The canoe was a curious shadow moving slowly on the surface. Again he circled, not satisfied with his first pass. He bumped the rough wooden side with his nose and swam away.

The canoe rocked with the waves and the small push it had taken from the shark, but Mi-sa did not notice. In the darkness, the canoe came close to shore, passing the mangroves, the feeding raccoons, and the small strip of beach that seemed to suddenly widen.

Quietly the canoe traveled on, passing the mouth of the river, rocking gently with its discharge, moving on south more quickly as the wind built up. Following behind, a porpoise arced in the water.

The sun made Mi-sa open her eyes. In a moment she realized where she was, remembering the A-po-la-chee, Cherok, Talasee, Atula, and the warrior she had heaved over the side. She sighed, turned to her other side, and tried to sleep again. She wanted to sleep and to forget—for everything to go away—to escape.

But the sun was relentless and merciless. She sat up, feeling the strong breeze. The shore was too distant to see a river mouth. She realized how unwise it had been to sleep.

Mi-sa uncoiled her body, feeling the ache of her sore and abused muscles. The canoe had moved far out in the water. She squinted and looked to the west. Nothing but sea, and sky, and a dark blurry line that was the land. She turned and faced the east. Cherok had said that no man could go to the edge.

Mi-sa got to her knees and put one hand in the water, paddling against the sea, trying feebly to turn the canoe toward land. The dugout did not respond, still drifting with the current and the wind. She peered over the side but couldn't see the bottom. This Big Water was so deep.

A shiver of fear ran through her. She knew nothing of the sea—not how far it went or how far she would float across the Big Water with no food and nothing to drink, no way back to the land, no one to come for her.

Again she used her hand and arm as a paddle, stroking furiously, but the canoe did not turn. Mi-sa leaned toward the other side, and the canoe began to roll. She shifted back, centering her weight, stabilizing the boat. There was nothing she could do to save herself. She dipped her hand in the water again, lifting it lazily, letting the water trickle off the ends of her fingers. The sea was wonderful—so magnificent, so dangerous.

Her thought was interrupted when she saw the first fin—then another. She knew what they were; she had seen them swarm in the shallows, feeding on the porpoise. Mi-sa stiffened and quickly withdrew her hand.

The spirits would provide a solution. They had seen to it that she could not do anything for herself—they willed her fate. Whatever they decided, she would accept. She needed to speak with them and feel their presence.

Mi-sa closed her eyes and breathed deeply, calming herself, putting her body and mind at peace so the spirits could speak to her. She quieted, feeling her heart slow down and her muscles relax. When she was ready she began her song, a beckoning song. She called upon the spirits to see her and to hear her. She asked them to give her strength and guidance. She prayed for forgiveness. When the spirits showed her signs, she had given in to pride, not wanting anyone to think that she was weak and easily frightened. She did not ask the spirits not to punish her. She asked them to help her accept her fate so that she would not feel so fearful. She asked them to prepare her for what was to come.

Suddenly Mi-sa felt the canoe shudder with an impact. Her eyes flew open. She grabbed both sides of the dugout and held tightly. Again she felt a bump.

What she saw surprised her. A silvery gray body rolled on the surface of the sea. It was a porpoise, like the one they had found on the beach. She didn't know anything about the animals and wondered if she should be frightened. Again the animal surfaced, nosed the canoe, and pushed it, then looked up at her. It had kind eyes, Mi-sa thought. Strangely, she knew she did not have to be afraid.

The animal nudged the canoe repeatedly. The dugout was turning, moving toward land, the dolphin propelling and guiding it. The shoreline became clearer—white beaches, clusters of mangroves, tall salt weeds, scrub plants, great sparkling dunes. Mi-sa closed her eyes and thanked the spirits.

When the dugout floated over the shallows, she got out and pulled the canoe until she beached it. The porpoise hovered nearby. The young woman stood in the shallow water and watched the animal. She lifted her arms and held out her hands, palms up, closed her eyes, and let her mind cross the water so that she could see the eyes of the porpoise. The porpoise stared back, its tender eyes full of warmth. And then it was gone, and Mi-sa stood on the beach, looking out across the vast ocean.

The sprawling Kahoosa village was quiet.

Naska pulled the woman's back closer to him. His naked body was sweaty. The woman edged away.

"You begged for me just a while ago," he said.

The woman did not answer. She turned to face him. She stared hard into his eyes, her face not betraying her thoughts.

Naska fondled one of her breasts and then bent his head to nuzzle it. He felt Ursa shiver as his tongue teased her taut nipple. He smiled to himself. "You are ready for me again," he mumbled, his mouth full and occupied.

"Naska," she started, her voice gravelly. "I am always—"

She did not get to finish. He turned her and moved over her. She held him against her. He dropped his head along the side of her neck, thrusting against her until he found passage.

"Naska," she said again.

But he didn't even pause. His breath came in short frantic gushes. He knew that she wanted him to confess his feelings for her, tell her that she was in his heart. But he did not want to discuss it now. Definitely not now.

Ursa moaned from his deep penetration, more pain than pleasure. "Tell me what is in your heart," she murmured.

"Yes," he answered hoarsely.

His response did not make sense. He had paid no attention to her. Ursa loosened her embrace and stopped moving with him, turning her head to the side, away from him.

Naska groaned, driving into her, but she remained limp and apathetic. He could feel his passion quickly vanishing, his manhood softening inside her. He rolled off her and onto his back. "Why do you do this?" he asked in a raspy, frustrated voice.

Ursa propped herself up on her elbow and leaned over him. "You know how I feel about you. That is why I am always ready for you. As you said," she whispered, nipping at his lips.

"Leave," he said softly.

She couldn't believe that he meant it. Shocked, she sat up. Then she leaned forward and touched her mouth to his stomach, coaxing his manhood back to perfect hardness with her hand. "I am sorry," she said, regretting how she had pushed him.

Naska remained passive, letting her fondle him with her hand and her mouth, pretending to be indifferent. At the last moment he nudged her mouth away, moved her beneath him and entered her. Instantly he shuddered and moaned, stiffening and relaxing.

He lay on top of her, nearly dropping off to sleep before he finally moved off. In a few moments he drew a deep breath and stood, took a handful of berries from a basket, then shoved them in his mouth.

Ursa sat up and wrapped herself in the deerskin that had covered their grass mat.

"If you take the blanket, clean it," he said, looking through the basket for some other succulent fruit. He was hungry this morning. Ursa had given him an eventful night and a doubly exciting early morning.

Quietly she picked up her skirt, wrapped herself in the skin blanket, and backed down the ladder.

Mi-sa sat looking at the canoe. Since she had no paddle, she decided to leave the dugout. She didn't want to risk being carried far out into the ocean again. The Big Water was not like a river. She could not see that it flowed in any direction, except for the waves that lashed the shore. She did not understand the sea. She would be safer if she walked.

By noon she was certain her directions were confused. She should have reached the river by now. She paused. She was hungry and very thirsty. Even the salt water looked inviting to drink.

Again the beach seemed to change. There had been tufts and forests of mangroves. Sometimes there was a strip of beach and saltwater flats. Other times she had to negotiate around the mangroves by moving out into the water. But now she saw other trees and plants appear—the kinds of trees and plants that grew near fresh water.

Mi-sa stopped, wishing for the sound of the Big Water to be still. She was sure she heard something else. She heard the sound of moving water—like a river. She trotted in the shallows, following the slow curve of the shore, filling with excitement. The river—water to drink, her link to home. She would meet up with the others, and they would go back for Cherok and Talasee. She felt like crying because she was so happy.

Suddenly she stopped. There it was, the mouth of the river! The clear fresh water gushed from it, breaking into small white falls and then flowing into the Big Water. Across the river stood a huge stone object. The thing looked like a giant turtle sitting at the end of the point, glaring out at the Big Water.

Mi-sa didn't run, but moved out of the water and into the brush. She approached cautiously, eyeing the strange thing she had seen. Finally, peeking between the dense green foliage, she saw it clearly—a huge rock carving, an enormous stone turtle that overlooked the sea.

She stood still in amazement. She had never heard of this, never heard the men speak of this thing. She moved closer, carefully pushing back the hanging vines and branches.

Naska stretched and grinned. Cota, his brother, was the cacique, but he did not live any better than Naska! There were

many things to do this day. Maybe kill a deer and provide a
new skin for Ursa. He had been a little aloof and insensitive.
Perhaps some mussels plucked from the buttresses of the
mangroves might appease her. He could make the trip
quickly, returning before twilight. He did not want to estrange
Ursa. She did know the ways of pleasure. How did some
women come by it so naturally? Her body never failed to stir
him. Her breasts were full and did not sag. Her hips curved
gently. And she did know the ways of moving and
touching—ways of tempting and arousing. He had sampled
other women, but Ursa did know those things best. Yes, he
should do something special for her. If he did not, she might
choose to spurn him. Women were different from men, he
thought. They required so much more than men. Why could
they not just enjoy the pleasure of joining and leave it at that?
Never mind. Such thoughts never led anywhere. Taking a little extra time to get her something would be worth the trouble if it meant having her again. He needed to woo her. That
was all.

Naska took a coal from the central hearth and ignited his
own fire. Over it he warmed some elderberry tea. Fresh sea
turtle eggs came to mind. This was the season for such a del-
icacy. Ursa would like them. He smiled, put down his shell
ladle of tea, and decided to head to the beach.

Mi-sa hid in the thick jungle along the river. Her body was
tight, her ears and eyes sharp. Cautiously she worked her way
up the riverbank, searching for the makers of the stone turtle.
They would be able to help her. The sun went with her, moving west in the sky, heating the afternoon.

The day passed slowly, the passage along the river difficult
to traverse. Finally a familiar smell made her stop, lift her
nose, and sniff. The dull smell of smoke wafted in the air—
not wildfire, but smoke from cook fires, sweet coontie bread
warming, teas brewing, fish grilling. A village was nearby.

Slowly and cautiously Mi-sa moved through the low underbrush. The ferns tickled her legs; vicious vines made fine cuts

as they raked her calves. The insects were thick under the shelter of the wet green canopy. They fouled her vision and her breathing.

She edged toward the bank of the river, finding it easier to travel there. Her foot stepped into something hot and moist, a nest made of decaying plants and grasses. An alligator's nest. The decomposing plants were steaming in the midday heat, incubating the eggs. If the nest was here, the mother was surely nearby and irritable. Mi-sa scampered up the bank, watching for a provoked female alligator. She knew that they were not only fast in the water but quick on land as well.

Naska took a small pirogue and paddled downstream. Ursa might also like some grapes, he decided. He knew where they grew in abundance, just across the river. He grounded the canoe and started to walk. He felt particularly vigorous today as he snatched a few sparkleberries and popped them into his mouth. He stopped as an alligator cruised the bank, crawling up on the shore to sun itself. He knew that the large animal would have difficulty spotting him if he did not move. The alligator appeared especially irascible, snapping at flies and thrashing in the mud of the bank.

Must have a nest—a female, Naska thought. When the alligator settled, facing another direction, he cautiously moved on. During this season the alligators were unpredictable and dangerous. When he reached the beach, he would be even more careful. Crocodiles did not need to be provoked. They had a cantankerous disposition. They snarled and snapped their long narrow jaws at anything. They built their nests in the hot, dry sand. The recent rain might have made them exceptionally agitated; the moisture threatened to destroy their eggs.

Naska moved deeper into the thick woods looking for grapes.

Mi-sa crept through the plush greenery. She reached for her pouch, touching it to make certain she had replaced her knife. The hardness of it gave her confidence.

As she moved from behind the plump trunk of a short cabbage palm, the village came into view. She could see only small sections at such a distance, depending on the density of the trees and the movement of the foliage by the wind. She would have to move a little closer to see the village more clearly.

Mi-sa crept close to the ground, hiding behind every trunk and branch. Finally she could see people moving about. The village was immense. She watched closely.

Her hand went over her mouth as she realized this village was not Tegesta. This was not her river! After a few moments she deduced that the village was Kahoosa. She had heard descriptions of the Kahoosa. She cringed, trying to remember everything she knew about them.

They were a powerful tribe, but they had come to an agreement with her people. The peace had come through a Tegesta woman. Teeka was her name. That was the story told around the fires. At one time the Kahoosa had been feared, a tribe that was the enemy. Not anymore.

Mi-sa still felt uncertain. Her village was so isolated from the rest of the Tegesta. Perhaps the Kahoosa could not be trusted. Perhaps things had changed and there was no peace between her people and the Kahoosa.

She hunkered down, hiding among the thick ferns. There was a noise behind her. Someone was coming!

CHAPTER
— 8 —

Naska stopped, listening to the thrum of insect wings, the twitter of birds, the natural sounds, searching the air for that one noise that did not belong. His brown body blended with the woods. He thought he saw something move in the brush ahead. He sank into the undergrowth, crouching as he moved, nearly invisible. Slowly he drew his knife from the leather sheath that hung at his waist. He circled back to the river, anticipating a better look. If he had been spotted, he would be expected to come from the direction in which he was last seen, but he was cunning; he would come from behind.

Mi-sa looked toward the noise. She saw nothing. The rustling could have been a rabbit or a raccoon. She sat quietly, hidden in the thicket of ferns with her knife in her hand, straining to keep the sound of her breathing quiet.

Suddenly there was a burst of noise. She jumped, tried to turn, but someone wrenched her arm behind her back and pressed something against her throat.

Naska jerked her arm up high behind her, holding his knife firmly to her throat. If she lowered her head, the sharp blade would nick her skin.

Mi-sa tried to turn her head to see him, but quickly felt his strength. He said something to her, but she didn't understand the words. Again he spoke, aggravation thick in his tone. She did not know his language. Obviously he wanted a reply from her. He repeated the same thing over and over, sounding angrier each time. She held still, hoping he would realize that she could not speak his language.

Naska stared at the back of the woman he had captured. Her skirt was shredded strands hanging from a narrow rawhide strip that settled beneath her waist and rested along the crest of her hips. Her hair hung in clumps, and the back of her calves were smeared with dirt. Her other arm dangled next to her, and in her hand she tightly clutched a knife—a man's knife.

"Let go of the knife!" he told her. She did not respond. In Kahoosa he again ordered her to drop the knife.

Mi-sa swallowed air, her mouth dry with fear. She could hear the anger mounting in his voice. Naska nudged her arm up higher. She groaned.

"Then drop the knife!" he commanded.

"Tegesta," she mumbled through the pain.

Naska's face was alive with curiosity and surprise. "Tegesta?"

Mi-sa nodded carefully, afraid of the knife at her throat.

"Let the knife fall to the ground!" he said in her language.

Mi-sa loosened her grip on the knife, uncurling her fingers. She felt the knife slide out of her hand and heard it land on the ground with a soft thud.

"That is better," he said, reducing the pressure on her arm. "What do you do here? Why do you spy on my village?"

"I am not spying."

Naska pushed on her elbow, jamming her arm even farther up behind her. "Why do you spy on my village?"

"I was not spying," she insisted, taking a deep breath, ready for more pain.

"Then why do you hide across the river?"

"Let go of my arm, and I will tell you," she said.

Naska kicked the knife away. "Why should I let go of your arm?"

"Because I will not answer your questions until you stop hurting me!"

Naska laughed, rolling his head back. He loosened her arm and spun her around, keeping hold of her wrist. He looked at her face, her flashing eyes so full of spunk. "You are insolent," he said, grinning at her.

"I am shaman of my people. I am not easily intimidated," she said, hoping her voice would not tremble and give away the fear she felt.

Now Naska laughed even louder. "A shaman? You are bold," he said and chuckled.

"Do not ask me any more questions if you do not believe my answers."

"You are an arrogant one." Naska put his knife away and tugged on her wrist. "I will let you tell this to my brother, the cacique. I am sure he will find this as humorous as I do."

"I want my knife." Mi-sa planted her feet, resisting his efforts to pull her along.

"You think that I would give you your knife?"

"Yes. Are you not Kahoosa?"

Naska could not believe that she would ask him to give her the knife. And what did being Kahoosa have to do with anything? "You are strange, woman."

"Are not the Kahoosa and the Tegesta friends? Is there not a peace between the two?" She paused a moment, then said, "Give me my knife."

Naska shook his head in disbelief. He pulled on her arm again.

Mi-sa edged forward. "Then you are not going to retrieve my knife?"

Naska twisted her arm back behind her and jolted her forward. "You are making this walk a difficult one."

Mi-sa moved through the woods with Naska pushing her. He shoved her toward the canoe. "Get in," he ordered.

He pushed the canoe off the bank and jumped inside, taking the pole. "The alligators are nasty this season," he com-

mented, delivering the message that jumping into the river
would not be wise.

They crossed the river, and when Naska beached the canoe
he ordered her out. Mi-sa stepped free of the boat, taking her
first close look at a Kahoosa village. As they moved up the
mound, she was astounded at what she saw. There were
many, many platforms, many hearths, baskets of food, drying
meat, smoking grates, and skins stretched between trees.

"What have you found?" came a voice from the group of
people who watched her pass.

"Where is my brother?" Naska asked the man who had
called out.

"He sits at the central hearth. He seeks the advice of some
of the elders. Your father is there also."

"Move," he said to her, pushing her forward.

Mi-sa felt the eyes of the curious staring at her as she
passed. Everyone paused for a better look. She could feel
Naska smiling behind her.

The central hearth had a raised plaza on which the older
men were sitting. Some men stood and watched Naska bring
Mi-sa.

Cota stepped forward, moving closer to his brother and the
woman he escorted. His eyes met hers. What had Naska
done?

Mi-sa gazed into Cota's dark eyes. There was something
about him—something that she knew. At any moment she expected him to reach out and take her hand. In her imagination
she rested her tired head on his shoulder, and he led her away.

"Look what I have found," Naska said, shoving her toward
his brother.

Mi-sa stared at Cota. Just as unexpectedly as it had come,
the sense of familiarity was gone. She studied him. He was
tattooed like a king, and his breechclout was dyed with regal
designs. Around his neck he wore strands of glistening shell
beads and pearls interspersed with sharks' teeth. He wore a
small braid in one side of his otherwise loose shoulder-length

hair. A strip of sinew with white feathers attached was woven into the braid. Mi-sa had no doubt that he was the cacique.

"Are you this man's brother?" she asked, as if she were in charge.

Cota's lips turned up into a smile at the woman's forwardness. She spoke in Tegesta, and that was how he answered her. "Yes, Naska is my brother. He has neglected to make the proper introductions."

"She was hiding across the river, spying on the village," Naska said. "She carried a fighting knife."

"A woman carrying a knife?" Cota questioned.

"I am shaman," she retorted clearly.

Naska laughed nearly as hard as he had the first time she told him that. "Yes, brother, I forgot to tell you that part. She claims to be a shaman."

Cota was fascinated with this mysterious, dauntless woman. "Where do you come from?"

"Your brother does not like my answers, and so I will not tell you any more."

Cota examined her, looking hard for clues that would reveal something about her. Her eyes shone like black pearls. Her hair hung tangled in her eyes. Her face was abraded, as were her arms and legs. Her skirt was nothing more than a waistband and a few curling gray threads of moss. Her hands looked torn and rough. Her trip to his village had not been an easy one.

Cota looked across the mound at the many who watched inquisitively. He spotted Chalosee, a good woman, a young woman, a woman who interested him. "Chalosee, come here."

Chalosee emerged from the crowd, moving close to Cota. "Take her and clean her up. Give her all she wants to eat and drink. Maybe she will feel like talking later."

"Wait," Naska said. "Brother, make her tell us her secrets. We will reward her with Chalosee's hospitality if she complies."

Cota looked back at the proud young woman whom Naska

had brought to the village. He stared quietly a moment. "No, that would not be hospitable. Take her, Chalosee."

Naska grumbled, obviously disappointed in his brother's decision. Cota never listened to him. Naska could feel his belly tighten. Cota was cacique only because he had been born first, not because he was wiser. Actually, Naska thought, Cota did not have the guts to make tough decisions. Naska resented the respect that was showered upon his brother. He, Naska, should be the cacique. He was more like Kaho, his father, when his father was young—when his father had first led the Kahoosa—when all the neighboring tribes, including the Tegesta, had feared him and paid tribute to him. Naska had that kind of strength inside him. Cota was going to rule like an old man—as their father had, once the peace was established with the Tegesta. His mother was the stronger one, he had always believed. He had heard the tales about his father, about the charismatic young leader who swept through the region, claiming it all for the Kahoosa. But then Kaho took Naska and Cota's mother, Teeka, as his wife, and he mellowed under her influence. The Kahoosa no longer commanded the respect they deserved, thought Naska. His mother was a good woman, but nevertheless a woman. Kaho had become soft. Cota was soft.

Mi-sa followed Chalosee to the river to bathe. "Mind the alligators," Chalosee warned.

While Mi-sa cleaned herself, Chalosee made her a new skirt from moss that she had smoked over her fire to kill the mites and other insects that hid in it. As Mi-sa tied the skirt around her, the movement of the moss through the air sent a whiff of the smoky smell to Chalosee.

They returned to Chalosee's hearth, and Mi-sa gratefully drank the Kahoosa woman's tea.

"The wife of our last cacique, the wife of Kaho, Cota's mother, was Tegesta," Chalosee said, initiating conversation.

"Teeka?" Mi-sa asked, recognizing Kaho's name.

"You know of her?"

"She is a legend among the Tegesta. She was the one who

brought the peace between the Tegesta and the Kahoosa."
Mi-sa paused, contemplating the circumstances. "Will she
come to visit me?"

Chalosee looked up from her basketry. "There," she said,
pointing to the charnel house that sat gloomily over the
slough.

"She is dead?"

"Not so long ago. A terrible illness claimed many of the
Kahoosa."

Mi-sa was disappointed, and her face showed her dejec-
tion. "I know the illness. It also took many Tegesta lives. The
sickness killed more Tegesta than the A-po-la-chee ever did."

Chalosee's eyes sparked. "A-po-la-chee? They attack the
Tegesta?"

"They are a warring people. I have seen them come into
my village to kill, to pillage and destroy."

"They do not come this far south. I think I should thank
the spirits."

"Yes, you should be thankful. But I saw some A-po-la-
chee not too far from here. One day ago. We found their
wrecked canoe. They took my friend and my brother. I was
the only one to escape!"

Chalosee looked shocked and frightened. "Have you told
anyone?"

"No one."

"Come with me," Chalosee said, getting to her feet. "Follow me."

"I do not wish to speak with the one called Naska. Teeka's
husband. I will speak with him."

"I will take you to him."

Mi-sa walked behind Chalosee, watching the way the
woman's hair bounced with her quick steps. Her legs were
long, and Mi-sa had noticed that her fingers were also long
and slim. She was built like a Kahoosa, not a Tegesta.

Chalosee glanced at the central hearth. The men had dispersed. Kaho would be found near his own hearth. He was
quiet and kept to himself since Teeka's death.

Naska looked up as Chalosee and Mi-sa passed. Ursa was speaking to him, but he had lost interest.

"You do not need to apologize for not bringing me turtle eggs," Ursa was saying to him. "I understand."

Naska put his hand on her shoulder, but looked past her at the two women as they went by.

"Naska?" Ursa said to him. "Naska?"

Naska did not answer, preoccupied with Mi-sa. He eyed her hair, still damp from the bath. Her face was not filled with the animosity he had seen earlier, and she appeared quite pretty in a very confident way. He wanted to know more about this woman.

Ursa removed Naska's hand from her shoulder.

"What did you say?" he asked, returning his attention to her.

"You find her beautiful?"

Naska smiled at Ursa and stroked her hair. "Never as beautiful as you, Ursa."

But Ursa saw that he still followed the Tegesta woman with his eyes, even as he spoke to her. She knew it was unusual for a man to take as his wife a woman who came from the same clan, the same village. But there were exceptions. Ursa's mother was not from this clan, and so Naska's courtship of Ursa was acceptable. Olagale would have to sanction the marriage, but that would be no problem. Naska was the son of Kaho and the brother of the current cacique. Certain privileges were due to members of the noble line. The Tegesta woman worried her, though. She was something new and different—a sure challenge to a man like Naska.

"Naska," she whispered, "I wish to be with you now. I want to bring you pleasure."

Naska looked back at her. He had heard her proposal. "I will see you later," he said, taking a step to leave.

"Naska," she said, calling him back.

"Later, woman," he answered without looking back. He had had enough of Ursa over the last night and this morning. He did not feel hungry for her right now, but he knew that he would welcome her to his bed when the moon rose. Now he wished to follow the Tegesta woman.

Chalosee found Kaho at his hearth, as expected. He was smoking rabbit meat on a grate. "The Tegesta woman has something to tell you," Chalosee began.

"Are you from the clan of Teges, as my wife was?"

"No," she answered. "I come from a remote Tegesta village. But I have heard of Teeka. I have heard of you. The story of the king of the Kahoosa and the Tegesta woman is a favorite tale told around the Tegesta fires."

Kaho smiled. "It is a good story, a true story. Come and sit with me," he said, lowering himself to the ground. "What is it that you wish to tell me?"

Mi-sa crossed her ankles and lowered herself to the ground. The smell of the smoking rabbit reminded her of home. "I come from a village that is far away. We were on a Big Water journey when a storm came from the sea."

Kaho looked at her inquisitively. "What was a woman doing on a Big Water journey? Kahoosa women do not go on those journeys. Neither do Tegesta women."

Mi-sa breathed deeply. "But I am the shaman of my village—the daughter of Atula and the inheritor of the Gift."

"Your father was a shaman?" Kaho questioned.

"Yes."

"Did he have no sons?"

"He had several sons," she corrected.

"He came from a pure line of shamans?"

"Yes, and therefore I do, also," she said without hesitation.

"But the Gift is passed on to a son, through the father's seed."

"Always before. The spirits worked differently this time."

Kaho stood up and paced. "This is difficult for me to believe."

"My own people had difficulty. I understand your skepticism, but that is not what I have come to you to discuss."

Naska walked up to them. "So, she insists she is a shaman. Why do you not ask her to prove it? Have her do something."

Mi-sa looked at the younger man. What would he have her do?

"Quiet, Naska," Kaho said. "Tell me the rest," he added, sitting down again.

"I have not come to speak with this man," she said, looking at Naska.

"He is my son. Whatever you have come to say, he may also hear."

"Then send for his brother also," Mi-sa said.

"Why should my father send for Cota? I am the one who found you. Why does Cota need to be included?" Naska protested.

"Is he not the cacique?" she answered.

Kaho smiled at her sharpness and the daring way she handled Naska. Perhaps she really was a shaman. She was certainly full of spirit. He called to Chalosee who lingered nearby. "Bring Cota."

Chalosee was happy to oblige, for she enjoyed being near Cota. She had come here with her family from another village when her small hammock became overcrowded. Some of the families had volunteered to move away. Cota had made her heart flutter from the start. She knew that many women in the village had hoped to attract him, but lately he had shown more than just a casual interest in her. They had enjoyed some flirtatious moments. Even while talking about plain things, their eyes spoke about something else. Others had noticed, and young women poked Chalosee and giggled behind their hands whenever Cota came near. If the cacique chose to court her, their union would be quite acceptable to the villagers. In fact, they expected it.

Chalosee hurried off to find Cota.

Mi-sa turned to Kaho, lowering her head to show him respect.

Kaho smiled.

Naska clenched his teeth.

CHAPTER
— 9 —

Cota posted guards around the village. Two of the sentries were sent far down the river to build a large fire next to the stone turtle guardian. The turtle was worthy of such a statue. The turtle provided an abundance of good food and a beautiful shell for a shaman's rattle and adornments for the People.

Near dusk, Chalosee prepared her evening meal. Mi-sa watched Chalosee working near the fire. Against the sunset and in front of flames, Chalosee was sometimes only a silhouette. Mi-sa looked up at the early evening stars—fires that burned brighter than Chalosee's. Those fires in the sky, the hearths of those who had come before and the lights of the spirits, guided her and governed her life. They burned in the heavens and in her heart.

Mi-sa was sure the spirits could hear her thoughts as she stared at the stars. What should she do next? she silently asked. Should she ask the Kahoosa for a paddle and go back for the canoe? Then she could take the canoe into the Big Water and go back north to find her river. But paddling against the current that flowed along the shore would be difficult for one person.

When the other men from her village arrived at the river—her river—they would wait. When she, Cherok, Talasee, and

Atula did not show up, the others would eventually give up on them and make their way home. Surely she could get some help from the Kahoosa. They would take her home. The men of her village would recuperate, and as soon as they were strong again, they would go after Cherok and Talasee. In a few more days she would bring the matter to Kaho's attention—or maybe even to Cota's. It would be impolite to make demands so soon. If the Kahoosa became offended, they would never help her.

Chalosee had planned to share her meal with Mi-sa, but then Cota stopped at her fire. He carried a terrapin by the tail. "A woman must have a hunter to provide her with food. I have brought your evening meal," he said to Mi-sa.

She was hungry but did not want to be obligated to anyone. "I can take care of myself."

"I am certain that you can," he said. "This is a gesture of friendship—of Kahoosa hospitality." His jet eyes were bright with firelight.

"Then I thank you," Mi-sa answered. She looked up at him and smiled. For a moment her tongue seemed jumbled, and her heart was beating so loud that she was sure he could hear it.

He waited for her to speak again, also turning his mouth into a smile, noticing her self-consciousness, finding her reaction to him most attractive.

"Would you like to stay?" Mi-sa finally asked.

"Yes," agreed Chalosee, feeling her cheeks grow warm, "that would be nice."

"I take my meal at the central hearth," he answered, still looking at Mi-sa, intrigued by the duality of her—her sauciness and poise—her vulnerability, and the ease with which she displayed her emotions.

Chalosee's face wrinkled in disappointment.

Mi-sa forced herself to look away at the dangling turtle that so conveniently stuck out its head. In a quick movement, Cota slung the turtle on the ground and cut off its head with his ax. He strung the turtle by the tail over a low branch.

Chalosee placed a pot beneath the turtle to catch the blood so that it would not foul the earth around her hearth. She would dispose of it and the entrails later.

"Welcome, Tegesta woman," Cota said, his voice smooth and deep, his expression sober. Then he smiled faintly. After he walked a few steps away, he paused and glanced back to see that she was watching him. He wanted to know more about this woman who claimed to be of the spirits. He changed his direction and headed toward the fire of Olagale, the Kahoosa shaman.

Mi-sa's eyes were fixed on the man who walked away. There was a compelling arrogance to his gait, a commanding assurance in the way he moved. Now she was angry with herself for noticing, especially since he had turned and seen her staring.

Chalosee also watched Cota leave, and Mi-sa noticed her enchantment.

When the turtle finished bleeding, Mi-sa scrubbed the shell in a large bowl of water. Then she laid it on its back and cut away the plastron, the bottom shell, and slit the skin from the neck to the tail.

"Will you share this with me?" she asked Chalosee.

"I have my own meal to fill my stomach."

Mi-sa explored the insides of the turtle and removed the sandbags, stomach, intestines, heart, and lungs. There were no eggs.

"You save the liver?" Chalosee asked.

"It is good. It flavors the broth. Do you not use it?" she asked, carefully cutting away the small green bag to the left of the liver. The contents of this organ could contaminate the whole turtle.

"No," Chalosee said, wrinkling her nose at the thought.

"Maybe you would like it," Mi-sa suggested as she rinsed the turtle and then, with the liver, placed it on its back in a clay pot, which she suspended over the fire. She covered the turtle with water.

Chalosee held out a handful of fresh and dried herbs. "Use these."

"Yes, add them," Mi-sa gladly responded before she added hot stones to the pot. Soon the water boiled.

When the meat slipped from the bone, Mi-sa lifted the turtle out of the water with a shell ladle and a cooking stick. "There will be plenty," she said, but Chalosee shook her head.

Mi-sa waited until the turtle was cool enough to handle. Then she removed all the bones, the claws, the shell, and the black skin.

"May I use your knife again?" she asked Chalosee. The woman handed her cooking knife to her guest. Mi-sa chopped the meat into chunks, then returned it to the water and let it steep with the liver and herbs a little longer.

The aroma was making Mi-sa's mouth water. Chalosee handed her a prickly pear speared on the end of a forked twig. Mi-sa brushed off the spines with a handful of grass, then took it off the spear.

Mi-sa wished for the fine knife that Cherok had given her. She thought about him and struggled with tears as she sliced off the ends of the prickly pear with Chalosee's knife. She slit the fruit down the middle and folded back the outer surface to expose the juicy pulp. She closed her eyes after tasting it. *I will come for you, Cherok. I will come.* Unconsciously she massaged the medicine bag that hung around her neck.

The sun had already set, and night had come by the time her turtle was cooked. Others prepared for the night as Mi-sa ate. Tired as she was, she still wondered if she would be able to sleep.

Earlier she had told the story of the A-po-la-chee encounter, the storm and the journey, and her happening upon the Kahoosa village. She was glad that the peace between the Tegesta and the Kahoosa remained intact. The Kahoosa men had smirked when she spoke of being shaman. They had appeared to welcome her, but she was exasperated by their skepticism, their patronizing smiles, when she spoke of the

Gift. She did not want to be humored. She did not need to be indulged. She had told them the truth.

Chalosee took a step up the ladder to her platform. "You may share my shelter. I have another mat."

Mi-sa was pleased but did not want to intrude. "Your hospitality is kind, but I can make my bed on the ground."

Chalosee stopped climbing. "Tegesta woman, do not insult me by refusing my offer."

"I am sorry," Mi-sa apologized. "I did not mean to sound ungrateful. I do not want to impose. Please call me by my name, Mi-sa."

"You are my guest, Mi-sa. Cota has ordered it." There was a stillness before Chalosee continued speaking her thoughts and climbing the ladder. "And my own heart wishes it so, also," she said, turning away and stepping up.

Mi-sa smiled and followed Chalosee up the ladder. She stopped at the top and looked out over the village. "Which one is his?"

"What do you mean?" Chalosee asked, not understanding her guest. She walked closer and looked out with Mi-sa.

"Your village has so many platforms. Which one belongs to the cacique?"

Chalosee hesitated before looking back at the village and pointing. "There, at the edge of the mound." Chalosee's stomach turned over. The Tegesta woman was pretty, and Cota had surely noticed—and Mi-sa had taken notice of him. She swallowed back the fear that Mi-sa would take Cota's heart.

The moonlight filtered through the trees and joined the dying fires. There was enough light to make out the shadowed form of the platform that Chalosee indicated. Mi-sa would take a better look tomorrow, up close.

Mi-sa lay on the mat and stared out. She felt like a child again, vulnerable, alone. Atula would have continued to guide her and teach her the ways of a shaman. Perhaps he would even have told her who the man was who appeared in her dreams, the man who had touched her in her vision on the dune.

She had learned the fetishes, the words, some from Atula and some from the spirits that came to her. Now she had no medicine bundles, no fetishes, no magical herbs, no accoutrements at all, except the skull piece of her grandfather that dangled around her neck. She was in the darkness as she had been as a child. She could feel the spirits pull at her, wanting to communicate with her, and yet she did not know how they expected her to acknowledge them without her fetishes and herbs.

Mi-sa looked over at Chalosee and was sure she was sleeping. There was a divine urgency inside her. The spirits wanted to speak.

Quietly she crept beneath the platform and stirred the last coals of Chalosee's fire. She eyed the village. The Kahoosa slept.

She started to hum a song she had often sung as a child. She didn't know where the song had come from, but she had always known it. There were materials and devices that a shaman used, teas and special articles. She had none of them, and she was afraid. She remembered the special mushrooms and plants that Atula had given her—lost in the storm with everything else. In her heart, her failure to interpret and deliver the messages sent by the spirits was not excused or forgiven just because she had not been trained in the ways of a shaman since childhood. She was certain she would have to pay a price for not heeding the signs of the great storm, and she would suffer without complaint. The spirits were disappointed in her.

In a moment her eyes closed, and she was caught in the rhythm of the song that she sang from her soul.

Inside her mind the white fog blew away and she looked down upon her own village. She was a child, sitting under a great strangler fig with Cherok. Cherok held her hand.

"You are special, Mi-sa," he said. "You do naturally what they expect of me."

"You are the special one, Cherok. You show me things."

"Take me with you, Mi-sa. Take me high into the clouds."

The white fog came back, clouding the vision. She wished it away, but the mist only became thicker. "Wait," she heard herself say.

She sat quietly, thinking about the vision the spirits had given her. The meaning was clear. She had to find a way to help Cherok. He was alive and waiting for her, depending on her. Cherok was the only one who had befriended her, who had recognized that she was the one with the Gift. Now she was the only one who knew Cherok was alive and needed to be delivered from the hands of the A-po-la-chee. She had to get home.

As Mi-sa stared into the glow of the coals, she did not see the man who approached in the shadows. His dark shape moved quietly and discreetly.

"What keeps the Tegesta woman from sleep?" came the voice behind her.

Mi-sa jumped and turned around. The voice had come from Naska. "You startled me. Why do you sneak up that way?"

"I did not sneak. You were not watching. What keeps you from sleep?"

"I am far from home."

"Have the Kahoosa not made you comfortable?"

"I am grateful for the Kahoosa's kindnesses, but this is not home."

Naska sat next to her. "A different mat, a different platform. Do you miss a man—your husband?"

"I have no husband. I am shaman of my people."

Naska grinned, which made her angry. He saw the indignation in her eye. "Ah, I had forgotten," he said.

"I have responsibilities that weigh heavily."

"A woman should have a man, even if she is a shaman."

"The custom does not change because I am a woman," she said, standing up.

Naska rose next to her and firmly held her shoulder. "A man's touch would soothe you."

Mi-sa pulled away and grasped the ladder. "I do not need a man."

Naska laughed, then reached out and touched her buttocks as she ascended the ladder. "You should let me show you what a man is like with a woman."

Mi-sa stood at the top of the ladder. She could feel her face hot with anger. "Just any man is not good enough," she said, disappearing into the darkness of the platform.

As she lay down on the mat, her thoughts whirled. She thought of so many things that she should have said to Naska. If only she had thought more quickly. Then she heard Naska's loud raucous laugh as he walked away.

Again she thought about those things she had lost on this journey. In the morning she would look for her knife. She'd pack a basket and persuade someone to help her find her river and take her home.

Chalosee turned on her mat and opened one eye. The Tegesta woman lay still.

When morning came, Mi-sa rose quickly and followed the trail Chalosee had taken her on to bathe in the river. Even though a place with so much activity did not usually attract alligators, the women were cautious, standing only ankle deep in the shelf along the river. One of the women took a large tree branch and repeatedly struck the water, making loud slapping sounds while she screeched to discourage the alligators from approaching. When the breeding season was over, they would be less of a threat.

The bathing women splashed themselves, rubbed dirty spots with sand, and then rinsed by pouring pots of water over themselves. Mi-sa stood downstream from them. The water rippled about her ankles.

Chalosee leaned over to fill her pot and watched Mi-sa curiously out of the corner of her eye. The Tegesta woman stood still, unmoving, looking down. Chalosee stood up, only half filling the pot, still looking at Mi-sa. She stepped onto the bank and quietly walked toward her. "Mi-sa?"

Mi-sa did not look up. Chalosee was curious as to what had the strange Tegesta woman so absorbed. She moved up behind her, looking down at the water to see what Mi-sa saw. As she stepped right up behind her, she stopped, surprised by the images in the water at Mi-sa's feet.

But as Chalosee leaned forward for a better look, her own face was reflected in the water. Mi-sa's head jerked up, and her eyes opened wide as she turned to Chalosee.

"I am sorry," Chalosee said, moving back. "I did not mean . . . I did not want to startle . . . sorry."

Chalosee turned away from Mi-sa and trotted back to the path that led into the village. The other women looked up and wondered what had happened.

Mi-sa reached into the water with her hands. Chalosee had spoiled the moment. The spirits had come and created images in the water—things she needed to see, but Chalosee had interrupted.

She scooped up some water and splashed it over herself, looking across the river. Her knife was there, and she was going to get it.

She walked back to Chalosee's platform.

Chalosee peeked out at the Tegesta woman as she came close. She pretended to be busy with her basketry, but she couldn't concentrate. She had seen faces in the water— strange apparitions.

"Can a woman take a canoe?" Mi-sa asked.

Chalosee had not heard the question. She was thinking too hard about other things.

Mi-sa touched the woman's arm. "A canoe. Can a Kahoosa woman take a canoe?"

"I know of no woman who has done so," Chalosee finally answered.

"I want to go across the river. Just to the other side."

"The men take the canoes. I have been in one, but never held the paddle or the pole."

"Do you think that Cota would allow me to take a dug-out?"

Chalosee stood up. "Take one of our canoes across the river? Why?"

"Because there is something of mine on the other side that I would like to get."

"Ask Naska to take you. He would take you in the canoe."

"But I wish to go alone."

"No. No, no, no. Men take the canoes," Chalosee said, walking away, shaking her head, carrying a handful of reeds.

Mi-sa had heard Chalosee, but the spirits breathed within her. She walked to the river, moving through the thick brush beside the path. At water's edge, she sat and stared at the heavy mass of dripping green foliage on the other side. The river was not very wide. She could cross in a canoe without much trouble and in a very short time. No one would miss her or the dugout. She would be back before they knew she was gone.

Mi-sa crept along the riverbank, pushing back the branches that became obstructions. The canoes were this way, just a lit-tle farther down the river. She could get to them without be-ing seen.

As she moved down the bank, a ripple of water came up behind her. The nostrils and the eyes of an alligator broke the surface.

CHAPTER

~ 10 ~

Mi-sa stood at the bow of the canoe. The dugout was not beached so high that she would have trouble pushing it out into the water. A paddle and a pole lay inside.

She looked back toward the village, up along the gray dirt path. No one was coming. Quickly she pushed the canoe, hearing it grate on the sandy ground. A few more grunts and shoves and the stern of the canoe entered the water. She pushed the pirogue farther until only the tip of the bow was precariously balanced on shore. She climbed in, pushed the pole hard into the bank, and felt the canoe slide into the quiet water.

The boat rocked, and Mi-sa spread her feet to keep from falling until the canoe stopped rolling. She knelt, picked up the paddle, and dipped it into the water, drawing it toward the canoe, turning the bow around.

The canoe moved silently. The water swirled around her paddle as she stroked it from side to side, taking the canoe across the river, moving downstream with the current. When she drew close to the opposite side, she redirected the canoe parallel to the bank, looking back toward the village to judge her position. She rested the paddle across her knees. This was

the way the village had looked when she first saw it. This
was the angle and the distance.

She put the paddle back into the water and pulled hard,
nosing the cypress dugout onto the bank. She hopped out,
feeling the soggy earth squish between her toes. She pulled
on the bow, tugging the canoe firmly onto the land.

Her search led her through the tangled aerial roots, the
creeping, strangling vines, pools of decaying leaves, brown
fallen Sabal palm fronds, reclusive scorpions and spiders. After a few moments she realized her approach was wrong.
Mi-sa backtracked to the river, looking for the alligator nest
she had found before.

Finally she saw the piled-up leaves and debris of the nest.
Now all she had to do was locate the route Naska had taken
with her. Small broken branches, crushed grass, and fallen
leaves helped her find the way. A tiny wisp of gray moss
clung to the end of a limb of a small sapling, waving in the
wind. Moss from her skirt. Mi-sa touched it with her fingers
and looked ahead. There was the spot. The ferns were flattened where she had hidden.

She stooped to see the ground better as she waded through
the underbrush, moving the ferns, grasses, and vines away.
This was the direction in which Naska had kicked her knife.
On her hands and knees, Mi-sa ran her fingers along the
ground, beneath the damp, rotting leaves, the scrawny, leaf-
barren ground vine, the stems of the ferns. Suddenly she felt
something. She spread the living cover away so that she
could see. Her knife! She picked it up, sat back on her heels,
and ran her fingers across the smooth blade. She wiped it
clean on her skirt and then stroked it again.

The pouch that dangled at her side accepted the knife as if
it had been made for it. She remembered when she had felt
the heaviness of the knife on her thigh for the first time. The
awkwardness had since disappeared.

She should hurry back now. At the water's edge she looked
across at the Kahoosa village. From this distance she could
again see how large the village was. Through the trees and

brush, splashes of color stood out, spaces filled with posts
and platforms, vague brown bodies moving.

The return trip was more difficult. She had to cut across
the current, moving upstream. She hoped no one would
choose this time to stare through the woods. In a moment she
would be back on the other side of the river with her knife,
and no one would know that she had been gone. Let Naska
wonder when he saw her knife, she thought with a smile.

At the landing, Mi-sa stood up in the canoe. She tilted,
shifting her weight. The canoe rocked, and she teetered,
spreading her arms out for balance. She hopped out of the canoe. The jump made the canoe pitch. Mi-sa wiped her face
from the splash and turned to catch the dugout. It was drifting
away. She reached for the protruding end of the paddle, dragging it with tension, pulling the canoe back to her, but the
paddle suddenly snapped free.

Mi-sa held on to the paddle and moved deeper, swimming
toward the sailing dugout. She swam a few strokes and
stopped, then reached out to the canoe with the paddle, hoping to snag and draw the dugout back to her. But the paddle
edged the canoe away. While Mi-sa watched, helpless, the
dull black scutes of an alligator surfaced in the wake of the
dugout. Its long tail swung from side to side, propelling
the animal toward her. She instantly realized that the canoe
was lost; she turned toward the shore, stroking with one arm
and pulling the paddle with the other. The bank seemed so
close, but it was taking so long to go to it. And what if the
alligator followed her onto land? What would she do then?
Climb! Shimmy up a tree!

When her knees struck the bottom of the narrow shelf, she
scrambled toward the bank, trying not to look back, afraid
that if she did, she might fall. But she did look back, and as
she did, the alligator came up behind her. She saw its cold
eyes and hard, cold skin. Mi-sa's heart lurched. Her legs
moved, but she seemed to gain no distance, as in a nightmare.

Stumbling, her one hand scraping the bank, she felt the alligator's cone-shaped teeth as they drilled into her calf. She

fell flat, her face in the mud, muffling her scream. She grabbed the paddle. In one motion she twisted, leaving the attacked leg still, sat up, and raised the paddle in the air with both hands. She held her breath and slammed the paddle down as hard as she could on top of the alligator's head, explosively blowing out her breath at impact.

Stunned, the animal unlocked its jaws. Mi-sa felt the bite loosen. She drew back the paddle and shoved it at the alligator's eyes. Immediately the beast released her leg and retreated into deeper water

Mi-sa struggled to higher ground, lifting and scooting her backside, dragging her leg, watching the alligator back into the river. The veil of water on her injured leg became awash with blood. Strangely there was no pain. She had heard stories of men losing limbs and suffering other serious injuries and remarking that, oddly, they felt no pain. She looked to see if the animal had taken her calf or if her lower leg was dangling by thready tissue. Four dark red holes marred one side of her calf. The animal had caught her leg at an angle, the other side of its jaw missing her flesh. The beast had not mangled or taken her leg, though it had bitten deep. She let out a sob of relief and checked the water again. The alligator submerged, leaving only a small ripple. Mi-sa put one hand under her knee and bent the injured leg, pressing the other hand against the wound.

The canoe was drifting downstream, riding the current to the Big Water. She would have no explanation to give the Kahoosa, only that she had wanted to retrieve what was hers.

Blood oozed between her fingers, thick and dark red, like fluid ribbons. When she lifted her hands, the holes in her flesh filled with blood that quickly trickled out. She clamped her hands back over the wounds and pressed hard.

Mi-sa leaned back and looked at the rich green canopy above her. The blue of the sky was caught there in small patches and flashes. Tawny light splintered through the leaves like brilliant sharp needles. "Spirits of my ancestors, be with me."

When no more blood seeped through her fingers, she carefully let go. At the release, a little blood dribbled down her leg, a slow-moving line, viscous and murrey.

Guardedly she stood, keeping most of her weight on the uninjured leg. She hobbled up the sloping path. As she limped, the wounds reopened. If she could just get to Chalosee's hearth!

Each time she stepped, even though she only used the injured leg to steady herself, hot pain shot through the limb, making her dizzy. She braced herself against the slender trunk of a gray wax myrtle.

Her head spun. Mi-sa blinked slowly with concentrated effort. Even her good leg felt barely attached. Her arms and legs seemed heavy. She slid her back down the tree, resting against the base of the trunk. Someone would come. Someone had to come.

Blood pooled, soaking the grainy soil. Light-headed, she looked at her leg, finding it hard to focus her eyes. Her leg looked blurry. All her thoughts were fuzzy. She was confused.

Mi-sa felt support behind her back and under her legs. She was being lifted. Warm, strong arms carried her. She rested her head on Cota's chest, uncannily recognizing his scent, oddly feeling content. Her thoughts tumbled in fragments and questions. Like an echo in a dream, she heard his voice.

"What have you done, Tegesta woman?"

"Mi-sa? Child?" The woman's voice was harsh with age.

Mi-sa attempted to open her eyes, but they were too heavy.

"Drink more," a man's voice echoed.

She wanted to sleep, wished they would leave her alone. She felt the shell ladle touch her lips. Reflexively she opened her mouth and let the liquid spill in, shuddered at the taste, then forced herself to swallow.

"Change the poultice before the sun sets," the man said.

Mi-sa squinted. An old woman with a wrinkled, ashen face drawn tight over sharp bones looked up at someone. Mi-sa's eyelids sagged as she followed the old woman's gaze. A man was standing nearby, looking down at her. His face was painted with streaks of color, and he held rattles and fetishes. His head was crowned with a bristling dyed-red roach that trailed down his back. A shaman.

From her other side came another man's voice, deep tones and masculine qualities tempered with gentleness. "Olagale, will she be all right?"

"She lost much blood. But she drinks. She is fortunate that you found her. And my medicine will keep her body at rest as it builds strength. I have prepared medicine packs."

The old woman spoke. "I will watch her carefully."

"Do that, Hala." The deep voice came closer, and a face appeared. "Olagale, do whatever you can. Stay with her," he said as he leaned closer, his face becoming clearer. Cota. She felt his hand on her cheek.

The old woman's lips grew thin as she spoke again. "Olagale does not need to stay. The wound looks serious, but she will heal. I will tend to her."

Cota spoke again, staring down at Mi-sa. "Her journey here was difficult. A woman on a man's journey, the storm, the A-po-la-chee. Her body is tired. Bad spirits may find her weak and susceptible."

"If you wish me to stay with the Tegesta woman, I will," Olagale said.

"Give her your best medicines," Cota said, touching Mi-sa's cheek again, looking into her cloudy eyes. He straightened up and moved back where she could not see him any longer. But she could feel his footsteps on the ladder until he reached the ground and walked away.

The old woman looked at Mi-sa, leaning into her face. "Drink some more," she said. Hala opened her mouth, as if she meant to drink, as she touched the ladle to Mi-sa's lips.

Mi-sa turned her head, but Hala turned it back and lifted it. "You must drink. Olagale's medicine is good. It will make you rest and heal."

Mi-sa sipped and closed her eyes. Hala eased her charge's head back to the floor.

Mi-sa did not need any more of Olagale's sleep medicine. She was already too groggy. She held the elixir in her mouth, waiting to hear the old woman and Olagale move away. The taste was bitter, and she wanted to spit it out, but if she did, they would make her drink some more. If she could wake up, get some strength, gather her wits, she could prepare her own medicines.

At last she heard Olagale and Hala step down the ladder. "Do not be in my way," Hala groused. The old woman's voice trailed off.

Mi-sa turned her head to the side and let the medicine trickle out of her mouth and into the weave of the mat. She tried to sit up but did not have the strength. It was hard to think or see clearly. Olagale's medicine was strong.

She closed her eyes, giving in to sleep. Next time she would feign sipping the shaman's medicine, not even allow it into her mouth.

Naska stood at the base of the ladder that led up to Hala's platform, checking behind him to see if anyone watched. It was dusk, the early stars finding their places in the night sky as he climbed the ladder. At the landing he waited for his eyes to adjust to the darkness of the shadowy platform.

Mi-sa lay outstretched, one of her arms bent, her wrist curled so that the back of her hand touched her temple. A silver stripe of moonlight cut across her face.

Naska's eyes wandered over the length of her body, pausing at the swells and curves of her femininity. Her face was flushed from the heat of the night, but he wished to imagine it flushed with passion.

"Get out!" came a grumbling call from below. Hala banged the ladder with her walking stick. "Get!"

Naska looked back at the sleeping body one more time. He would have this Tegesta woman.

"You heard me," the old woman complained, ending her chiding with a rattling cough.

Naska descended the ladder.

"You did not do anything, did you?" she asked grumpily as Naska stepped away and she started to climb up.

Naska laughed. "Now, what would I do with a sleeping woman? My women know when they are with me."

"Arghh," she mumbled, shooing him away with her hand.

Naska walked away, chuckling to himself. The fires were dying down. Looking at the Tegesta woman had stirred him. His blood coursed warmly through his loins. Where was Ursa?

CHAPTER
~11~

Chalosee brushed the dirt floor beneath her platform with a cabbage-palm broom. The long, slender brown leaves stirred the dust and cleared the breeze-blown debris, the thready fibers floating on the air. When she finished sweeping, she threw out some tea from a pot beside the fire, accidently dropping the pot. She sighed, a little angry with her carelessness as she picked up the broken pieces of her fine pot.

In her hand she held one of the shards. The fragment was as black as soot, but the Big Water sand she had used to temper the clay sparkled in the moonlight. To break a pot was wasteful, she thought, still scolding herself.

Chalosee tossed the pieces of her broken vessel into her dying fire. She looked up to see Naska leaving Hala's platform. She wondered if Ursa was aware that he had an interest in Mi-sa.

"Who do you wait for?" Naska asked, walking up to her, looking around.

"No one. I am slow and clumsy tonight."

Naska grinned. "I think you wait for my brother."

"No," Chalosee protested. "I broke a pot and I have to clean it up."

"Maybe you wait for me," he said, feeling his own teasing

remarks rouse his appetite for a woman. He stepped closer, deliberately provoking her.

"There, I am finished," she said, finding the last piece of broken pottery and dropping it into the fire. She moved back until her shoulder touched the ladder.

"You think my brother could . . . ?"

Naska did not finish. Cota had come behind him. "Naska, why do you pester her? You have a woman. Go on. Ursa probably awaits you."

"I am sure that she does. Perhaps if you had a taste of me," he said to Chalosee, "then you would also await me. Ursa will tell you."

Cota moved close to Naska. "Go now, brother. Tomorrow is the Scattering of the Fire. It will be a long, exciting day."

"Yes, it will be." Naska gave Chalosee one last cocky smile. "I think you waste your time with her," he whispered loudly to his brother, patting him on the shoulder. "You should get yourself a woman." He turned his back and walked away.

"Perhaps he is right," Cota said.

There was a pause, full of awkward silence. "Do you agree that it is time I had a woman?" he asked.

Chalosee smiled. "Perhaps."

"Sometimes you can find some truth hidden in my brother's talk. He will not be back to bother you. Do you feel safe?"

"I am not afraid of him. He only likes to make me feel uncomfortable. He enjoys the game."

"I will have a guard watch your platform."

"There is no need."

"I am glad you realize he means no harm. That is just his way. The other women know it. You are new to the village, and so he seeks you out and teases you. You should be flattered. He would not do these things if he did not find you attractive."

Chalosee looked down, feeling the heat flood her cheeks.

"You blush," Cota said, smiling at her embarrassment.

"You are an easy target for Naska." Cota walked closer and lifted her chin so that he could see her face. "Do not be embarrassed by the truth. Look at you," he said, letting her see his eyes wander over her. "Do I make you uncomfortable?"

Chalosee's voice trembled. "No."

Cota brushed her arm with his hand. "Naska is brazen and ill-mannered. He says whatever he thinks."

"And you?" she asked, barely able to get the words out, nearly crumbling as his fingertips lightly stroked her arm.

"I weigh my words carefully. I think them through."

Cota leaned his head closer, and Chalosee could feel his breath on her. For a moment she thought that he would touch his mouth to her, but then he spoke.

"Tomorrow will be long. You will need a good sleep, too."

He backed away, and she felt a cool draft as the warmth from his closeness was withdrawn. "Good night," she said, blanching at the tiny quaver in her voice.

"Tomorrow," Cota answered and then walked away, his outline proud in the moonlight, his blue-black hair catching the light of the stars and dying fires.

In the distance Chalosee heard Olagale softly beating on his drum, his voice warbling in song.

Daylight broke through the thatch and the open side of the shelter. Mi-sa felt its warmth on her back before she opened her eyes. She wanted to stay awake. Olagale sat propped up in the corner, his head sagging on his chest, his breathing noisy. She looked for Hala, but the old woman was not in the platform.

Mi-sa scooted closer to the opening. When she moved, her leg hurt. She looked at the injury. She could tell that Hala had changed the poultice during the night.

Hala sat on the ground outside, feeding lightwood to her new fire. The old woman twisted and looked up. She raised her hand and waved Mi-sa away. Mi-sa backed into the platform.

His own sharp snore jarred Olagale awake.

"It is a good morning," Mi-sa said to the shaman as he stretched.

Olagale grabbed his shoulder and rotated it, working out the stiffness.

"Hala is below. I watched her at her fire, but she seemed irritated by my observation," Mi-sa said.

Olagale rose. "There may be a peace between the Tegesta and the Kahoosa, but we are not the same. Our customs come closer with each generation, but we still live differently."

"Then I broke a custom?"

"You intruded on Hala. Every soul meets the new day, the rising of the sun, alone, in his own way."

"I should apologize. I did not know."

Olagale squatted next to her and held her leg in his hands, gently turning it, feeling for heat or swelling.

"What medicine did you use?" she asked.

"I do not know all the names in your language."

"Tell me about them. Describe them."

Olagale rocked back on his haunches. "For the bleeding I used the juice of a plant that has soft leaves. Grows this high," he said, holding his hand near his bent knees. "You may know it from the seeds. Black, they are, and stick to everything. Tiny spines at the tips."

Mi-sa's eyes brightened. "I know it. The leucantha. I have even eaten the cooked leaves, and I have drunk it in a concoction. Some like it. I do not. But the juice is good for bleeding. What are the words you said over it?"

Olagale stiffened, shifting his weight. "The words? They are sacred words. Words for the spirits, not for men. Not for a Tegesta woman."

Mi-sa saw Olagale's agitation and decided not to pursue the question. The time was not appropriate.

"And to prevent the bad spirits? What did you use?" she asked.

"Why do you ask these questions? Do you doubt my medicine?" he asked, his brows dipping bitterly and his lips pinching hostilely.

"No, you misunderstand. I am impressed with your medicine. You must be powerful and know many things."

"I do," Olagale said, rising, his ego bolstered. "I know the Kahoosa magic and some of the medicine of the line of Teges, a pure shaman from the Tegesta."

"My father was also from a pure line of shamans. He had the Gift born in him, passed from his father, and his father before that."

"Then you should know that it is not only the medicine that heals. The power is in the words, the prayers the shaman knows. The shaman is the link to the spirits, and the spirits decide for all of us."

"That is so," Mi-sa answered, smiling up at him. "I have heard my father say the same. That is why I asked about the words."

Mi-sa bent her injured leg and looked at the medicine-soaked swatch of soft hide that was tied to her calf. "I would like to see the wounds," she said, loosening the ties.

"You have no faith in my medicine?" Olagale said gruffly.

Mi-sa could see the resentment in his eyes. "Shaman, do not be offended. I am merely curious. It is, after all, my leg," she said, continuing to untie the rawhide binders as she looked up at him.

Olagale did not respond, but he looked down so that he, too, could examine the uncovered wound.

Mi-sa pulled away the pad of hide. Stuck to the underside was a collection of plant parts—Olagale's medicine. Some of the medicine clung to her leg. She could not recognize all the plants because Olagale had shredded them. She picked a piece from her leg and smelled it.

There was little swelling, and the wounds did not look angry. "Yes, your medicine is good and strong," she said, lifting her head to see his eyes.

Olagale looked squarely at her, holding his breath before he spoke. Then, without a flicker of a smile, he said soberly, "Pulp of the prickly pear, leaves of the yellowseed, flowers of the moonvine, bark of the gumbo-limbo, and leaves of the leucantha."

Mi-sa smiled. Olagale had shared his medicine with her. "Do you know the dove plum?"

"Of course. The fruit makes a good tea."

"But dove plums will also dry a weeping wound if you use them fresh."

"Ah," Olagale remarked. "We let them sit for days before brewing. Too bitter. Too astringent. I can see the value of the fresh fruit for wounds as you describe."

Again Olagale squatted next to her. He examined the wound, turning her leg so that the light fell on it at a favorable angle. "Alligator. Not crocodile."

"What is the difference?" Mi-sa asked.

"How many crocodiles have you seen?" He shook his head, drawing his lips to one side and wrinkling his forehead. "Not enough. You live to the west. You would not know. Crocodiles are uglier. Pointed nose and teeth that hang over the jaw. Not everyone can tell just by looking at a wound, but I can. They look different, they bite differently."

"Does it matter?"

Olagale lifted his head. "I suppose not."

The shaman dipped another soft swatch of hide in a pot filled with the medicine and held the fresh poultice to her leg, chanting his Kahoosa prayers. Mi-sa did not know the words, but she knew the rhythm and could predict the drops and rises in his voice. The melody was the same as that of a healing prayer she knew; only the lyrics were different. She waited to feel the power of the shaman surround her, tingle along her spine, warm her blood. But the words were empty, the song stark. She watched for the vigor of the shaman's words to strike the very air and fill it with the intensity of the spirits' healing. She waited for those things to happen, as she had seen them happen when her father healed—and when she healed.

But the air stayed thin and ordinary. When Olagale finished singing, he shook his rattle over Mi-sa's head.

"I am thankful, Shaman. What can I offer as payment, to show my appreciation?"

Olagale eyed the pouch at her side. "What do you have in there?"

Mi-sa flinched. "Nothing that you would want."

"Show me," he said, his expression and voice awash with inquisitiveness.

"Think of anything you might like. When I return to my people, they will send you gifts. Name what I can use to thank you, and it will be yours."

Olagale's eyes remained fixed on the pouch. "You are ungrateful if you do not show me what is in the pouch."

"Shaman, I am most grateful, but in this pouch I carry a gift from my brother. It has no value to anyone but me."

Olagale leaned over and touched the pouch, his fingers pressing, outlining the contents. "It is a knife," he said after poking and prodding. "The knife you crossed the river for. Retrieving this knife led to your injury." Olagale reared up straight. "Perhaps the spirits frown on a woman carrying a man's knife."

"It is a knife given to me by my brother, to protect me."

"Naska says it is a fighting knife."

Mi-sa hesitated but then took the knife out of the pouch and held it in her open hand. She gingerly traced the shape of the knife with her finger. "My brother is the cacique. He is very wise. As I have said, we were on a Big Water journey. He would not let me go on the journey without a way to protect myself, even if it broke tradition. My brother is very special to me."

Olagale stared at the knife. "Mmm, it is a good knife," he said, reaching out to touch it.

Mi-sa extended her hand so that he could see it even better. "Yes, it is. And it means very much to me. My brother is gone, stolen by the A-po-la-chee. The knife is his way of still protecting me. I ask that you not take this from me."

Olagale looked up at her. He studied her face—looking for honesty or deceit—searching for signs of woe and sadness.

He looked into her eyes, finding his answers there. "That would be too high a price," he finally said, to Mi-sa's relief. "But I remain troubled that a woman was on a trip to the sea. That is men's work."

"I did not accompany the men as a hunter. I went as their shaman."

"Put it back," Olagale said, pushing away Mi-sa's hand. "I have decided on a payment."

"What is it?"

"You will spend time discussing this strange story with me. But first I want to think more about what you have already told me. Then I will have questions."

Olagale finished tying the poultice to her leg. "You should walk on it. Trick the evil spirits. Let them think the leg is well, and they will go and look for another wound." Olagale stepped down the ladder. "You will want to see the festivities today," he said as he departed.

When Hala came back inside the platform, she offered Mi-sa some fish and tea. "Olagale says you do not need any more sleep medicine. He says your leg will heal. He brags about his medicine," she grumbled.

Mi-sa pulled at the fish, tearing small bits away, carefully picking out the bones. The fish was delicious. She had not realized how hungry she was. When she swallowed the bite of fish, she could feel it travel all the way to her empty stomach.

"I have not been polite," Mi-sa said. "Thank you for the meal."

"It is not from my portion of food. Cota provided it for you," Hala said. She watched Mi-sa eat, then asked, "After your leg is healed, how long do you intend to stay?"

"I want to leave right away," Mi-sa answered after swallowing another bite of fish. "I need to get home."

"How?"

"I hope the Kahoosa will extend their hospitality and goodwill a little further."

"You want a Kahoosa escort?" Hala obviously didn't like the idea.

"If it is permitted. If not, then I will go on my own."

"How far is your village?"

"I do not know. I need to discuss this with the Kahoosa men who travel the rivers."

"You do not know how far away or even where your village is, and you will travel there alone?"

"If I must, I will do it."

"Are all Tegesta women so venturesome?"

"Tell me about your cacique," she said, blatantly declining to continue the same conversation. Mi-sa took another mouthful of the fish. She had already told these people that she was not just any woman. She did not feel the need to offer any more explanation to Hala. More talk of being the shaman of her people would only lead to more of the old woman's grumbling and muttering. Mi-sa did not need to justify her heritage to this woman or to anyone. She answered only to the spirits.

Hala looked up. The Tegesta woman was uncompromising. A worthy attribute, but she did not like Mi-sa's infatuation with Cota. "He is a fine man. The People look to him for fair arbitration, helpful advice, good judgments, and wise decisions. He will guide the Kahoosa and the Tegesta into a permanent union."

"Does he have a woman?" Mi-sa asked.

Hala's face contorted. "You come into our village and immediately take an interest in our cacique. Let your leg heal and go home."

"I have no interest. Only curiosity. Why does that annoy you?"

"He looks at my daughter, and she looks at him. I do not want you to interfere. Stay away from Cota. Do not go after his heart. You would not keep it anyway. You wish to go home, and Cota must stay here. Do not distract him from Chalosee just as a whim."

"Chalosee is your daughter?"

"Yes, and she is all I have; my husband died shortly after we came to this village." Hala busied herself inside the platform. The Tegesta woman had gotten her point.

CHAPTER
~ 12 ~

"Here," Hala said, handing Mi-sa some tubers of nut grass to put on her mat to keep the insects away. "Save one of them to clean your teeth," she added. "It is time to walk."

Mi-sa took Hala's extended hand and pulled on it. The older woman steadied herself, helping Mi-sa to her feet.

Mi-sa looked down at her leg. She kept the weight off it, but still she could feel the throbbing near the wounds.

"Do not be weak," Hala criticized.

"I am not weak, but I am not stupid, either. I will not ask the leg to do anything that will cause the wounds to open. And only I can judge that. Do not be so impatient."

"Only the well are so argumentative." Hala smiled.

Mi-sa's lips turned up at the change in the old woman's expression. "I am ready. You go down first so that if I fall you can help me up."

"Then do not start until I clear the ladder."

Mi-sa grinned. "Then talk nice to your guest."

Hala did not smile back, but Mi-sa could see the light of a hidden smile in the woman's eyes. The smile was in her heart; it did not matter if it was not on her lips.

As Mi-sa started down the ladder, she realized that she was

weak. Her arms shook as she grasped the rung. Her hands grew clammy, and her heart beat very fast.

"The sun will go down before you touch the ground," Hala said, goading her.

"I am coming, old woman. I told you to be patient."

In a few more moments Mi-sa reached the ground.

"I knew you could do it," Hala said, sounding proud of her prediction and handing Mi-sa a walking stick.

"I walk like an old woman," Mi-sa commented as she took a few steps.

"You walk like me."

They followed the path to the river. People stopped and stared as they passed.

"Go about your business," Hala scolded them. "Leave the Tegesta woman some peace."

Mi-sa looked behind her as she and Hala cleared the core of the village. She knew he was there, could feel his black eyes.

Standing at the central hearth, Cota watched, his brown body glistening in the morning sun, his black hair blowing in the gentle breeze. Though she thought she should turn away, she couldn't. His image held her as firmly as if he held her with his arms.

"You lag behind," Hala complained. "Never mind them." The old woman thought that Mi-sa was offended by the curious stares of the villagers as they passed.

The spell was broken, and Mi-sa followed Hala to the river. At the water's edge, she sat down.

"Clean your teeth," Hala said. "I will wash you. You do not want to get the leg wet."

"I can wash myself."

"No, you cannot. Do your teeth."

The nut grass did make her mouth feel fresher. Hala sang as she washed her, and Mi-sa realized that the old woman's gruffness was only a bluff.

"What song is that you sing?" Mi-sa asked.

"One that I sang Chalosee when she was a child. A mother's song."

"The sound is sweet. Is it a Kahoosa song or one of your own?"

"Mine—for my daughter."

"It could be a love song," Mi-sa said.

"It is," Hala snapped.

"I meant—"

"I know what you meant. But it is a song of love that a mother sings to her child."

Mi-sa recalled the many songs Miakka had sung to her. So many times, alone in their platform, misunderstood and feared, frightened and alone, Mi-sa had cried at her mother's breast. Two things she had always been able to count on—her mother's love and Cherok's loyalty. Mi-sa breathed out, almost sighing. How she missed them both.

Hala gathered Mi-sa's long hair and dropped it over the front of one shoulder. "What is this?" She stared at two scars on Mi-sa's back.

"From long ago."

"Who did this to you?" Hala asked, leaning around Mi-sa to see her face, realizing that the injuries were stab wounds.

"It is not important."

"Are you afraid to tell?" Hala asked, squeezing water from the piece of hide she was using to wash Mi-sa's back.

"I was only a child."

"Who would hurt a child? Why?"

"A woman was afraid of me. I was born under a star that streaked the sky on the night that the A-po-la-chee attacked our village. This woman thought that on the night of my birth, my sign, the star, was connected to the terrible attack of the enemy. She believed that I was a power of the Darkside. The woman was not alone. Many believed that to be true."

"And so she stabbed you?" Hala said unbelievingly.

"My father was the shaman. He believed that my brother, Cherok, carried the Gift. The woman thought her own son had the Gift. She was angry that my father did not recognize the spiritual powers in her son. She believed I influenced our father in his decision."

"But you were only a child!"

"She thought I was a servant of the evil spirits."

"She meant to kill you," she said, sounding convinced.

"Yes. While I slept."

"What happened to the woman?"

"I never told that she was the one. You must understand that she was not wicked—her mind was not right. There was something wrong with her son. Keeping him alive was very hard for her. Eventually her mind gave in to the constant demands. She was obsessed with caring for her son."

"You excuse her and call it a mother's love!"

"She was an older woman with no husband. She had borne the son of the shaman, and so the clan provided for her. What would she have done with no man to hunt for her? Think of the humiliation. Her son saved her from disgrace."

Hala shook her head in disagreement. She saw no excuse for this woman. "The Kahoosa would have—"

Mi-sa stopped her. "But she also repented. The spirits forgave her. She helped the People to see me as their shaman. All of this was part of the spirits' plan, and I accept their wisdom."

Hala patted dry Mi-sa's back. "You really are a shaman."

"Yes."

"All the while your father was training your brother, you were really the one with the Gift?"

"Yes."

"How did they come to recognize you?"

"My brother and my father became ill—with the same illness that ravaged the Kahoosa. There was no one to save the People. My father had a recurring vision that he finally understood. He called me to his side and sent me out to heal the sick."

"Was the woman who stabbed you ill?"

"No, but her son was. It was not easy for her to ask me for my help."

Hala sat back, quizzical lines squirming across her face and eyes, crimping her mouth. "Why did you help her son after what she had done to you?"

"The spirits have given me the Gift. They did not ask me to judge others. That is for them alone. They did not tell me to pick and choose those whom I should help. They gave me the Gift to help all the People."

"You tell a sad story," Hala said softly, totally engrossed in Mi-sa's tale.

"My life has always been at the will of the spirits."

"A true shaman's words."

Mi-sa turned and smiled at the old woman. "Beneath your disagreeable crust, you are really a kind woman."

"Do not tell anyone." Hala laughed. "No one would ever listen to me again."

"I am certain that I am not the only one who has noticed."

"Get up, Tegesta woman. We will walk some more, then go back. You can help me with my work."

"What work do you do today?"

"Tonight the cacique will scatter the ashes of the fire and kindle a new one. Today we will feast and deplete our own fires. My cooking pot and roasting pit will be busy all day."

The walk back was slow, but Hala prodded Mi-sa on, fussing and mumbling most of the way.

"Prepare this." Hala handed Mi-sa a basket of wild savory.

"For tea or soup?"

"Tea," she answered.

Mi-sa began to tear the fragrant plant into small pieces.

Hala removed the warm stones from her roasting pit. She picked up a sharp cooking stick and poked at the starchy roots of the breadroot and spurge nettle. "Longer," she said to herself and started replacing the warm stones with hot stones from the fire, pushing some beneath the roasting tubers and then piling more hot stones on top.

Hanging from the outside of her platform was a basket of red coontie meal. The large tubers had been chopped, pounded, mixed with water, and strained. The result was a fine reddish sediment meal. Hala grabbed the basket, licked a finger, touched it to the meal, and then tasted it.

"Feed my fire," she called to Mi-sa.

Mi-sa added wood and coaxed it into a blaze.

"Let it burn to hot coals," Hala said. "Then call me." She climbed up the ladder and went into the platform.

Mi-sa finished tearing up the wild savory. She took a large pot, filled it with water, and suspended it over the fire. She dumped the herb into the water and stirred it.

Across the mound, she saw Cota. He was walking in her direction. She felt her stomach flutter. She wiped her face and ran her fingers through her hair.

Cota nodded as he passed. Mi-sa was disappointed. She had hoped that he was coming to talk to her.

The cacique stopped at Chalosee's fire and then sat next to her. Mi-sa could not hear the conversation, but she could see the way Chalosee smiled, the way she lowered her head and eyes, apparently blushing from flattery.

Mi-sa heard Hala's shuffling footsteps behind her. She looked away from Chalosee and stirred the brewing tea, watching the bubbling mixture and the crackling fire.

"The fire is hot," Mi-sa said.

Hala appeared with a wooden slab on which rested small cakes. She had mixed the red coontie meal with rendered bear grease and formed patties. Also on the slab was the pot of remaining bear grease. "Give me that pot," she said, nodding her head at another pot as she sat down.

Mi-sa picked up the cooking vessel and moved it over near Hala, then looked back toward Cota and Chalosee.

The old woman scooped up some of the bear grease in a shell and with her finger pushed it out into the clean pot. Then she handed it to Mi-sa. "Hang it low, close to the fire."

Mi-sa hung the pot over the fire, adjusting the length of the rawhide straps.

"Do you hear it?" Hala asked, leaning toward the fire.

"Hear what?"

"The bear. When you hear his scratching and snapping and spitting, it will be time."

Mi-sa looked into the pot. Soon the grease was hot and began to sizzle.

"There. Hear him?" Hala said.

"Oh," Mi-sa answered. She had never heard sizzling grease described that way before.

"Out of my way," Hala said, moving closer to the fire. She lowered one of the red coontie cakes into the hot grease. The grease spit and spattered, bubbling over the cake. The old woman watched the cake grow crisp, then used her sharp stick to turn it over.

"It smells wonderful," Mi-sa said.

Hala removed the cake and continued to cook the others. The whole village filled with aromas from all the cook fires. By late afternoon the hard work was done.

"Take a nap," Hala said as she watched Mi-sa yawn.

"I am fine."

"Everyone will rest. The festivities will continue late into the night." Hala stood and motioned Mi-sa to follow her up the ladder. "Just rest for a while. You do not have to sleep."

The central hearth was ablaze, the flames lapping at the night air. The men sat around the fire, and the women served them, crouching low as they approached the men, showing respect for the hunters, the providers.

Mi-sa sat alone, privileged to take part in the Kahoosa ceremony. She watched as the men ate, laughed at one another's funny exaggerated tales, told stories of hunts and brave deeds. She watched as some of them whispered about the women who served them, clapping each other on the back to show approval. The Kahoosa men were not much different from the Tegesta. When men gathered, these were the things they did and this was the way they acted.

Ursa stooped before Naska, a bowl full of steaming turtle

meat in her hands. Naska grabbed her hair and pulled it back over her shoulder. "Straighten your back and look up at me," he said to her. Naska tapped the man sitting next to him. "Believe me," he said, looking at her breasts, "they are as succulent and warm in the mouth as this meat she brings." He took the bowl from her and dismissed her with a wave of his other hand. The man next to Naska slapped him hard on the back. Some of the turtle meat and soup sloshed out of the bowl. Naska quickly spread his legs so he wouldn't get burned.

"And do they get away from you as easily as this meat does?" the other man asked. Both men laughed riotously.

Ursa pulled her hair back over her breast as she walked away, looking over her shoulder. She hoped that Naska would not fill himself with cassite and go to sleep before coming for her.

When the men appeared full and satisfied, the women ate what was left, sharing with one another as the music makers assembled around the large drum. Cota stood at the fire, and the village became silent. Mi-sa stared at the cacique, the king of this powerful tribe. When his eyes met hers she looked away, hoping he had not noticed.

The central fire had burned down to coals. Each man came to the fire and took a glowing coal, carried it to his own hearth, and laid it in the center of the cool hearthstones. The spirit of the eternal fire was dispersed to the People.

Cota stirred the ashes of the central hearth, burying the last of the cinders with ash and soil. For a few moments the village was black; only the tiny dots of the single coals glowed in the night. The Kahoosa were silent.

Cota called out, "Aya-aya-yah!" The rhythm of the drum began, then the clacking of the deer-hoof rattles and the clinking of the shell bells. Olagale's voice rang out, high, vibrant, quavering. The villagers began to feed their fires, bringing their hearths to a blaze, lighting the village with their small fires. It was a symbol that the tribe was made up of individuals. When their fires were burning brightly, one by one they brought a new burning ember to the central hearth, signifying that unity of the tribe made them strong. Cota nurtured the central fire until its flames danced in the night and its soul popped and snapped.

Olagale threw a handful of magical powder on the flames. The fire spat and belched a stream of blue smoke. "The smoke from this fire will cover the earth, reaching even to the heavens. Be like the smoke," he said to the people.

The women formed a line that circled the fire, then began shuffling their feet, bending their knees, taking small steps to the rhythm of the drum. The men followed, weaving among the women and forming an outer circle. They took bigger steps, more complicated steps, as they mimicked the flickering flames. The voices grew louder, and the anklets and armbands of hooves and shells all rang out in time with the drum. Sparks from the fire spiraled into the black sky.

Cota, with a fox skin crowning his head and trailing down his back, sang out, wobbling his head, rotating one shoulder at a time, deeply bending his knees, leaning forward as he danced, caught in the magic rhythm of the drum, the heartbeat of the earth. His eagle-feather collar fluttered, lifted by the air that stirred beneath it.

Mi-sa sat immobile, but not because of her injured leg. Watching him dance took her breath way. As he moved past her, she could feel the breeze that he stirred, feel the rhythm of his steps vibrate in the earth.

Chalosee moved about the fire, taking small proud steps. Her eyes also stayed on Cota.

At the end of the dance everyone smiled, whooped, yelped. Chalosee offered Cota cassite and small bits of mushroom that only the men were allowed to have. He held his hand beneath hers, guiding it to his mouth. Her hand paused, lingering against his lips. Cota chewed and swallowed the small bit of hallucinogenic mushroom.

Again the music makers beat the drums, and Olagale's voice rang out. Another dance. The music, the sound of the shells and hooves, the rhythm of the drums and rattles, the peal and harmony of the voices, reached inside the dancers, found their spirits, and directed their moves.

After several dances Naska moved close to Ursa, placing both hands on her shoulders as he faced her, still moving his body to the beat of the drum. Gradually he led her away from the circle, whispering into her hair, running his hand down her back as he walked her to his platform.

Cota came up beside Chalosee, and Hala backed away. Mi-sa stared. Even at a distance she could feel the heat of his body, hear his words, feel his breath.

Cota moved in front of Chalosee so that he walked backward, placing his hands on her small waist. He slid his hands down, feeling Chalosee's thighs beneath the moss skirt.

Mi-sa reached for her own thigh, sure that she could feel his hands touch her there.

"Will you come to my bed?" the cacique asked.

Mi-sa hoped that she would dream of the man this night.

CHAPTER
— 13 —

Mi-sa watched as Cota danced in front of Chalosee. He touched her gently, teasingly, moved so close to her that there seemed to be no space between them. She watched Chalosee's eyes close as his hand brushed across her face. Mi-sa stood in the shadows beneath the tall oak, her heart beating to the rhythm of the drums, the sound of the music.

Cota touched Chalosee's lips with his fingertip, drawing an outline. "Come," he said, putting his hand behind her neck and pulling her toward him.

Chalosee did not speak but followed him away from the dancers and the festivities. She had never been to his bed, to any man's bed. Suddenly she felt awkward and terribly inexperienced.

At the foot of the ladder Cota touched his mouth to her hair. "Do not be afraid," he whispered.

"I am afraid I will disappoint you," she said, looking down.

Cota drew back to look at her then, took her trembling hand and led her up the ladder.

Mi-sa backed farther into the shadows and wound her way to Hala's platform. She lay on the mat and stared into the darkness. She asked the spirits to let her hold her dream a little longer if the man came to her in fantasy tonight.

"Sing to me a lullaby," she said to the spirits.

Near dawn the first dream came. Mi-sa curled her legs up and pulled her arms in, sighing in her sleep.

Hala turned over and looked at her, then settled into a comfortable position.

The dream began with a touch, a light caress down the side of Mi-sa's face, under her hair and out to her shoulder. He had come to her.

She was watching the sun rise, admiring the colors, and as always he was behind her, where she could not see his face.

"Why do you not tell me who you are? Why can I not see your face?"

She felt his warm breath in her ear, making her shiver. He wrapped his arms around her waist, overlapping them, drawing her more snugly against him.

"Please," she whispered, not sure if she was addressing the man or the spirits. "I long to know who you are and what you mean in my life."

Suddenly the man was gone; the comfort of him, the warmth of his arms, and the sound of his beating heart vanished. Mi-sa tossed in her sleep and sighed.

Hala did not sleep well. Never did anymore. Seemed she only dozed on and off through the night. She heard the Tegesta woman's sighs and opened her eyes. Mi-sa made a sound like a whimper, a pitiful cry.

Hala, the gruff old woman, came and sat next to her, humming a sweet song, as she had done for Chalosee when Chalosee was a child. "Do you want to tell me?" Hala asked.

Mi-sa heard her. "No," she whispered.

Hala returned to her soft humming, lightly rubbing Mi-sa's back.

But after Hala returned to her mat, Mi-sa found herself in another dream. Atula was calling her. She was happy to see him.

"The dreams still come?" Atula asked, in a tone that told her he already knew they did.

"Yes, Father. I am puzzled by them. I know this is the work of the spirits, but why do they send such vivid visions and still hide him from me?"

Atula's image paled, and in the distance she heard a small boy's voice. The vision changed, and her father was only a little child groping in a gopher tortoise hole. She saw him reach in and pull out a sparkling, glittering object. He held it up so that it captured the light of the sun. Then suddenly her father was a grown man again, and he held out his hand, offering her the crystal cast. Just before he disappeared she heard him say, "Dream-catcher."

Chalosee was sitting next to her mother, talking softly below the platform, brewing some berry tea. The village had begun to stir with early morning activity.

Mi-sa looked out of the platform, the thread of her dreams quickly unraveling. "Dream-catcher," she whispered. That was what her father had said.

She was perplexed by the word only a moment before she recalled her father, near death, saying the same thing as he slipped an object in her hand. So much had happened she had forgotten about it. She removed her medicine bag, loosened the ties, and shook the contents into her palm. She singled out the calcite crystal and put the other objects back into the pouch.

Mi-sa poked the crystal shell cast and watched it rock and gleam in her hand. Beautiful. She held it up so the sunlight shone through it, catching and glinting at beautiful sparkling angles so brilliant that she was blinded by them.

"Mi-sa," a voice called behind her, but no one else was in the shelter.

She sat still, captured by the brilliance. She felt a hand on her shoulder, a firm warm touch that finally made her look up. At first the face was blurry, her eyes adjusting from the radiant light of the crystal, but she knew who it was—the man in her dreams.

He took her hand and urged her to stand. When his face became clear, Mi-sa realized this was truly a vision. A loud buzzing drowned out the sounds of the village, and everything except his face was doused in blackness.

"Cota," she whispered, the rest of her paralyzed.

Suddenly he was gone—instantly—as if he had never been there.

Mi-sa sat on the mat, astonished and bewildered. She looked down at the magical crystal. Her face fell. All this time she had asked the spirits to make the man known to her. Now they had done so, and she was greatly troubled. Cota could never be anything to her or she to him. He was the cacique of his people, and she the shaman of hers. Their paths had converged only briefly, and soon they would part. How bitterly unkind. It seemed that the spirits were still displeased with her.

Mi-sa placed the crystal back in her medicine bag. She knew what she must do. The sooner she left the Kahoosa village, the better it would be for all. The quicker she arrived home, the more swiftly Cherok and Talasee could be rescued. The Kahoosa would have to forgive her seeming lack of gratitude. They would have to understand her urgency.

Again Mi-sa looked out of the platform. Chalosee appeared quite happy. She should have. Cota had chosen her.

"Come down," Hala called, looking up into the platform. "Have some morning tea."

Mi-sa nodded.

"The cacique chose Chalosee last night," Hala said as Mi-sa sat.

"That is wonderful, Chalosee," Mi-sa said, feeling the small barb of a lie catch in the back of her throat. "Does it make you happy?"

Chalosee was smiling, her black eyes sparkling. "It makes me very happy."

"Would not a Tegesta maiden be happy to be chosen by a cacique?" Hala asked, seeing that Mi-sa lacked enthusiasm.

"The Tegesta ways are different."

"They could not be so different that a maiden would not be pleased to become the woman of a king," Hala grumbled.

Mi-sa smiled and sipped some tea from a shell ladle that Chalosee handed her.

"Tell us how it is different. Tell us the Tegesta ways," Hala continued, brushing a hank of coarse gray hair from her eyes.

"Our disparities are not that important. Just small differences in customs."

Hala became aggravated. The Tegesta woman never liked to talk much. When Hala had wondered about the scars on Mi-sa's back, she had had to probe and question. "We want to hear about the differences. We think they are important."

Mi-sa took another sip of tea. She did not want to seem secretive. She could see that Hala was becoming agitated. "This is a delicate subject for me, but I do not want my friends to misconstrue my silence."

"Then on with it," Hala prodded.

Mi-sa rested her ladle of tea on the ground, then looked up at Hala and Chalosee. "Tegesta maidens do not join with a man until he is her husband. Such things are not even talked about. Young Tegesta women are innocent."

Chalosee and Hala looked at each other. Finally Chalosee asked, "Then how does a man know if the woman pleases him?"

"She pleases him in other ways. The joining is saved for the marriage bed. The only exception is that the shaman may join with anyone without a marriage."

Hala rocked back and giggled. "Do you sample the Tegesta men?" she chortled.

Hala's indiscreet question made Mi-sa smile also. "I have the privilege, but I do not think there will be a man. That would be too much for the Tegesta. I am a new river for my people. I must keep the current smooth and steady for those who come after me."

Chalosee was not laughing. She found Mi-sa's situation sad. How tragic that she would never know a man. "There is not much for you to look forward to, is there?"

Mi-sa sat tall. She did not want anyone to feel sorry for her. "Being the shaman is an honor. I do the work of the spirits for my people. I have other things to look forward to. Very fulfilling things."

Mi-sa noticed the men beginning to gather about the central hearth.

"They will discuss the future of the Kahoosa today. Today is a new beginning—a new fire," Hala explained.

The men who were gathering had brought their young sons with them. "Boys sit at Council?" Mi-sa asked.

"Today is special for boys and men. The men take their youngest sons, those who have lived four summers, and tell them what is expected of them as they grow to be men. Each must take a wife, have children. If the People are to survive, every man must be a good provider, a good hunter. When he fashions his weapons he must pay attention to detail, and he must use them skillfully, making his kills quick and clean."

Mi-sa nodded, understanding. She thought of similar traditions practiced by the Tegesta.

Cota's voice caught her attention. He stood in the center of the seated males, his brown shining body painted with fine black designs. His straight black hair hung loosely to his shoulders except for the one braid intertwined with a leather lace and a few white feathers. He spoke in Kahoosa. She could have concentrated and picked up a few words but instead she only watched, entranced by the handsome cacique.

The little boys' eyes grew wide with admiration as the cacique spoke to them. The older boys stood back, jousting with each other, showing off for the smaller ones, demonstrating their superior strength and agility.

Soon the few small boys scattered, fleeing across the

mound, squealing and whooping. The men stood back, laughing and talking, speaking to the fathers and uncles of the young boys.

The older boys rattled and shook the bushes, cheered the little ones on.

"What are they doing?" Mi-sa asked, standing for a better look.

"They have been sent to catch a butterfly. It is their first task on the long trail to manhood."

This was an interesting custom, Mi-sa thought, one more thing she would share with her people when she returned.

Finally, after quite some time, one of the boys returned with a beautiful brown butterfly spotted with yellow and blue.

"I have one!" he cried. "Look, I have caught the first one!"

He stood proudly in front of the men, his chest heaving from pride and the long, exciting chase.

Cota stooped so that he could see the child's prize up close. Mi-sa saw the gentleness of the man. "If you hunted for another butterfly like this one, would you know where to find it? Do you know how it lives?"

The small one shook his head.

"Study the butterfly. See how its wing splits into a fancy tail. Know it again if you see it. And what are the habits of this creature?"

Again the child shook his head, his excitement dwindling.

"There is more than just the hunt—things all hunters should know. Good hunters must know their prey."

The little boy looked down at the butterfly in his hands.

"This butterfly loves to take the sweet nectar from the pickerelweed," the cacique said. "That is how you will know where to find another." Cota smiled at the boy and tousled his hair. "Now listen to Olagale."

The shaman took the butterfly from the boy's hand and rubbed the wings on the child's chest. "The creature gives to you its swiftness and grace. Be thankful. Be grateful for the relationship between man and animal."

The child looked at the smudge on his chest, then found his father's face in the crowd. Surely he was proud.

"Now let us wait for the others," Cota said.

The day passed slowly as Mi-sa took care of her tasks, then wandered the village. She stopped at a secluded spot at the edge of the river. She looked down at her bandaged leg. Vaguely she could remember Cota carrying her, her head resting on his chest and his strong arms under her.

She brushed away a place and sat down. She needed to be alone, to talk to the spirits. She wanted to find Cherok. Mi-sa closed her eyes and breathed deeply through her nose and blew the air out through her mouth. She began relaxing her body, thinking of each part, beginning at her toes and working up to her scalp, finding the place in the crown of her head where she gathered her spirit, making ready for flight. Suddenly she burst free in a white cloud and brilliant light, rushing on the wind through a tunnel that sucked her into another world.

Abruptly she was still, shrouded in a cloudy haze. "Cherok," she called. "Come to me."

Mi-sa looked for him, walking through the mist, calling his name. She was afraid he would not come to her. That might mean he was dead.

"'Hear me, Cherok. Hear me call your name."

Finding him, calling him with her spirit, had been so easy when they were children, but they had never been this far apart. She wondered if the distance would make a difference. No, she decided. This dimension was not governed by those kinds of things.

Then came a whisper, a faint voice hidden in the mist.

"I hear you, Cherok," she said. "I am coming for you soon. Be strong," she said.

Cherok did not answer, but she saw scenes of her brother and Talasee carrying heavy loads, doing hard work for the A-po-la-chee. She saw them being struck with clubs and lashes. But they did not cry out. The Tegesta would be proud of them.

"We will come for you, Cherok. Do not give in!" she called out.

The mist began to disappear, and Mi-sa heard the rushing of the wind as it passed her. The vision flight was ending.

When she returned to the village, the men were seated at the central hearth, the fire burning in the late heat of the day. They were thinking and discussing important things. The torture of the heat kept them reminded of the seriousness of their responsibilities.

Mi-sa also had responsibilities, and hers were as pressing as their concerns. She needed to go home, to help her village through this difficult time . . . to be away from Cota. And as soon as the Tegesta warriors straggled back into the village, as soon as there were enough of them, they would strike the A-po-la-chee and bring home Cherok and Talasee. They depended on her. She could not be distracted by a man who came to her in her dreams.

Cota saw her walking toward them, her back straight, her eyes unblinking. The woman's hips swayed with all the nuances of seduction, but he knew that was not her intention.

Naska turned, and he, too, saw her coming close.

The other women kept their proper distance from the meeting Council. There were to be no disturbances, no distractions. The men's business was solemn.

The Kahoosa gawked and gasped when she approached the Council of Men, just as the first Tegesta had.

Naska rose to his feet. "This is not a woman's place," he said.

"I am a shaman."

"Perhaps what you say is true," said a hefty man with a scar running down his arm, "but you are still a woman, and you are not Kahoosa."

"That is so," she answered. "But I have the right as a Tegesta shaman to seek a seat in the Kahoosa Council. Is that not part of the peace between our people?"

The men began to grumble.

Kaho had seen her coming long before the others. He smiled to himself. This was a woman of strong fiber and depth—like his wife. He stood and greeted her with respect. "Shaman." Then he sat back down.

"Let her speak," Cota said, gazing out at the faces that now looked angry.

"Brother, I cannot believe you allow this," Naska said.

"Quiet," Cota ordered. "We will honor the Tegesta shaman. Speak. The Council will hear you."

Mi-sa looked at the faces that dared her. She risked having them deny her request because she was so brazen. But going to the Council was the way the request should be made.

"I humble myself before you," she began, hoping to soothe some of the men.

Naska seated himself squarely in front of her. He picked up a stick and tapped the ground with it, creating an irritating background noise and distraction, displaying his displeasure. Suddenly he stood up, stared hard at her, broke the stick in half, and walked out of Council.

CHAPTER
~ 14 ~

The Kahoosa Council was still. Naska had rudely expressed what many of them felt. The presence of a woman in their midst seemed like a sacrilege.

Their bodies dripped, sapped of fluids by the sun and the fire. They scorched and boiled inside and out. The breezes that usually stroked the branches had stilled, and everyone fell silent in amazement and curiosity. Mi-sa used the quiet to look into the faces of the men. She struggled to keep her eyes from fixing on Cota, for she knew that if she looked at him she would be lost. She would again taste his mouth on hers, fill with the aching and the hunger that he brought her in her dreams. If she looked deep, she would surely feel his wet mouth along the column of her neck, hear his hot breath, and feel it sear her within, spread through her like the waves of the Big Water, crash through her and rage into those hidden, unexplored places. She would feel his touch shatter her into prisms of ecstasy and raw, ravenous need. She would crumple before the remembrance of her dreams, her visions of him, and forget why she had come, what she was about to say.

She moved a glossy tendril of hair away from her eye, brushing it back as she began to speak, afraid she would collapse if her eyes met Cota's. "The Kahoosa have been charitable hosts, and I am indebted to you." Her voice sounded surprisingly smooth and soft. The men leaned forward to catch her words. "But it is time for me to return home. Though I am a shaman, I am not a man and have not traveled the rivers. I need a guide. I am asking the Kahoosa to extend their kindness."

The men shifted, their pendants of perforated bone and shell clinking, the luster of pearls shining in the light. They had tied their hair up in knots set with finely carved and polished bone pins and arrowheads. Their rugged faces offered her no comfort.

Cota watched her speak. She held herself proudly, confidently, but Cota studied her, seeing the slight trembling in her hands, the vulnerability behind her clear eyes, and most curiously, the rich flush of her face. He remembered how soft and delicate she had felt in his arms as he carried her to Hala's. And he could recall the scent that had wafted up to him from her hair as her head rested against his chest.

"You are requesting an escort?" he asked.

"Only a small group—for a short time," she answered, hearing the sound of his breathing in her ear, the feel of his callused hand running along her shoulder.

Cota breathed deeply. "I am certain that we could find your village quickly. We know the rivers and the points along them where the Tegesta villages are."

"Then you will provide an escort?" she asked anxiously, trying to concentrate, seeing his bronzed skin pebbled with perspiration.

Cota stared at her and found himself not wanting her to leave his village yet. He longed to know her better, to discover what the woman, not the shaman, was made of. Ambitious passions and desires welled up inside him. She piqued something unpredicted inside him. He could not let her leave yet. And there was good reason to deny her the escort.

"You brought us the news that the A-po-la-chee are near. I cannot recommend that warriors of our clan leave the village to accommodate you. At least not at this time."

"But I must go now. My people have suffered from the storm. They have no shaman. My brother and Talasee have been abducted and enslaved by the A-po-la-chee. I must return home, gather my people together so that Cherok and Talasee can be freed. There is no time to waste." *And you must leave my dreams. Do not come again and whisper into my ear, press your taut body against mine. It can never be. Let me go.*

"We do not have the warriors to send," an irritated man in the crowd argued.

"We will take you when the threat of the A-po-la-chee ends," Cota said. "If three more cycles of the moon pass and there has been no attack, we shall reconsider."

"No!" she objected. "Can you not see how urgent—"

"I will take her," a voice from the back of the crowd called. Naska boldly reentered the Council. "One warrior is all you need to send. I know the waters."

Cota flinched, his strong hands balling tightly. "An escort of three would be appropriate. There is too much risk for one to travel alone."

"But as you have said, my brother," Naska continued, approaching Mi-sa with a faint corrupt smile, "we need our warriors here to defend our village. Surely this strong clan can send just one man to help this woman. I am sorry," he quickly apologized. "This shaman."

Mi-sa looked at Cota. She could not go with Naska alone! But she could say nothing. She had made the request.

"I anticipate dissension among us," Cota said. "I think it best if the Council adjourns and reconvenes tomorrow after the thoughts have settled in our heads. A little time often makes things clear and helps us avoid discord. Do you object, Naska?"

Naska raised his hand. "I have no objection." Those whom he could have gathered to his way of thinking would reject him if he openly challenged his brother. It would appear to be rivalry and jealousy if he did so.

Kaho spoke. "Cota offers us good advice. I believe we should listen to him."

"Does anyone else wish to speak?" Cota asked.

The men were quiet, but the buzzing of the insects, the flutter of the breeze-blown leaves, and the call of a distant hawk once again filled the air. Naska had nothing else to say. Not now. He would be patient.

"Council is adjourned," Cota said.

The men milled about for a short time, then dispersed and busied themselves with their daily chores. Naska gave Mi-sa a slow, sardonic, and vain smile.

Kaho watched the charged looks that shot between his sons and saw their impassioned glances at the Tegesta woman. Naska was blatant about his intentions. There was nothing covert in the way he spoke or looked at Mi-sa, his eyes beginning at the top of her head and slowly wandering down along her body, his lips curling into a smile.

But Cota was different. When Cota looked at the woman, a fire burned in his core and shone in his eyes.

And the Tegesta woman had no trouble looking back at Naska, her face reflecting her distaste. But when her eyes fell on Cota, she struggled to look away, to regain control.

Chalosee waited by her platform. She had watched the curious exchange and hoped that Naska would be allowed to take the Tegesta woman away. That would be best for all. She saw Cota coming toward her, his brown, oiled, muscled body shining in the white-hot rays of the sun.

When he stood in front of her he took a handful of her hair and pulled her toward him. He did not ask, and she did not have to answer. She followed him to his platform.

Kaho stood back and knew that it was not Chalosee who had stirred the need in Cota. He nodded his head knowingly and looked for Mi-sa.

"Come to my hearth," he said when walking up behind her. "There are things we should discuss."

"I believe that only you understand," she said, snapping a twig from a sapling as they walked along.

"Perhaps that is so. I think maybe even you do not understand," he said, smiling at her, looking for her reaction.

"That could be," she answered. "But I do know that I must return to my village. If the Kahoosa refuse to help me, I must try to get there on my own. I will only ask for a canoe."

"Do not be so hasty," he said, sitting on the ground that was shaded by his platform. "Sit across from me. I want to watch your eyes. They speak for you."

Mi-sa obeyed. "Nothing will persuade me to stay longer. For many complicated reasons, I must leave quickly."

Kaho tilted his head and studied her face. "You remind me of my wife. Do not be offended if I stare."

"I am honored," she replied.

They sat quietly for a few moments, as was the custom, so that no subject was brought up too quickly.

Kaho finally spoke. "There is a plan to all things. Do you know that?"

"Yes," she answered.

"Have you ever thought about the father sun? He lives beyond the Big Waters, and behind his platform he keeps secret medicine bundles. But every day he makes his journey from the east to the west, where he passes the night. The moon is his wife and the morning star their child. The Breath Giver designed the sun, the moon, and the morning star, just as he gave us life."

In the distance thunder rumbled. A late afternoon storm was brewing out in the dark water. Kaho quickly mumbled a prayer.

"I know what you have told me," Mi-sa said.

"Does the Breath Giver make a mistake? He gives great thought to his creations and design."

"Yes," she said, agreeing with him, but puzzled by the conversation.

"Did the Breath Giver create you, give you life?"

Mi-sa nodded, still confused.

"Then you must trust that he will make the right decisions. Have you considered that he brought you here, had all those events happen so that you would come to this day in the Kahoosa village?"

Though she was confident the spirits guided her and chose her destiny, she had never thought of it quite as he expressed it.

"The course of the sun was carefully plotted. Let the Great Spirit point out the trail you are to follow."

Mi-sa suddenly felt humble. How did this man understand the spirits so much better than she, a shaman, did?

Again the thunder boomed. Kaho leaned back, sniffing the air, puffing out his chest as he inhaled. "The wings of the Thunder Bird beat the wind."

Mi-sa looked to the west where the storm gathered. "The sky grows dark."

"Mm," Kaho agreed.

Mi-sa sat watching the blackening sky, the distended clouds swelling with rain. She thought about the things Kaho had said.

"Are you telling me not to be so anxious to leave?"

"I understand why you hurry, but your swiftness will not alter the great plan."

Mi-sa drew a line in the dirt with her finger. "I am sorry, Kaho, but I do not understand your direction."

"You will liberate your brother when the time is right, when the spirits decide. You are here because the spirits want you to be here."

Mi-sa looked up. "Then you say I have no will?"

Kaho smiled gently. "No. I only suggest that you listen to the spirits. They will help you know how to proceed. Perhaps they show you things, but you do not see."

Mi-sa felt her stomach turn over. How could he know about her ignoring the signs of the big storm?

"Your face shows you are troubled," he said.

Mi-sa could not respond.

A sudden breeze, thrown by the distant storm, blew through the village. The two of them remained silent, noting the approaching storm, the way the wind sang in the branches, the way the leaves swirled in spirals in dry places.

"I have seen the way you struggle to look away from Cota. It is as if you know him."

The color drained out of Mi-sa's face, her eyes widened, and her hands grew clammy. "How would I know him?"

"You are a shaman."

"I have known you and your sons and all the Kahoosa only since I arrived."

"You have no difficulty looking at Naskâ. He makes you angry, but you look straight at him, even if it is in displeasure. But Cota. Your eyes dart, look away, and then find their way back."

"It is not so," Mi-sa said, uncrossing her legs, pulling them both to one side, and sitting on the opposite hip.

"It makes you uncomfortable even to talk about him. I believe that you have great abilities as a shaman, that visions come easily to you."

Mi-sa rubbed her forehead as her head began to ache. "I need to go back to Hala's platform before the storm comes," she said.

"Of course," Kaho said, seeing the storm in the sky and also the storm that roared within her. He stood and extended his hand to help her up.

As Mi-sa walked back to Hala's shelter, she passed the young boy who had captured the first butterfly. His chest was still dusted with color from the butterfly wings. His father handed him a piece of meat. The lessons were not over for the day.

"Do not eat the most tender parts," the father said, "or your body will grow soft like the meat. Leave that for the old ones."

Mi-sa smiled. She understood the meaning. The young boys were to leave the tender portions for the old ones, not because their bodies would grow soft but because the old ones' teeth were not so good.

When Mi-sa reached her destination, Hala was pushing a few things beneath the platform to protect them from the imminent storm. Mi-sa felt the first prickle of rain on her back and in her eyes.

"May I help?" she asked.

"Go up. I am finished," Hala answered.

Mi-sa climbed inside the platform and soon heard the old woman ascending the ladder.

"You had many dreams in the night," the old woman said, finding herself a place to sit.

"I am sorry if I disturbed you."

"I do not sleep so well anymore. You did not disrupt my rest."

The conversation was cordial but stilted. Finally Hala said what was on her mind. Her face was strained with furrows and dipping, sloping lines.

"I watched you enter the Council. The Tegesta ways are very different."

"If I were a man and a Tegesta shaman, there would not have been any disapproval."

Hala shook her head. The Tegesta woman did not understand. Hala's eyes were hard. "Look at you. Your body is ripe with young curves. Even the way you walk and move distracts the men. They cannot think of you as only a shaman. You are a woman."

"I will always be a woman. I have been told that the elders believe all living things must accept change."

The rain was coming down hard, pummeling the thatched roof of the lodge, splattering and splashing on the ground. The sunlight paled to a dirty gray.

"I am your friend, Mi-sa, but it will be good when you leave. Go with Naska. He is all talk."

"That is up to the Council. But I will not wait three cycles of the moon, even if it means I must go alone."

Hala grumbled to herself, then looked at Mi-sa. "Do not be foolish because you are so stubborn."

Mi-sa was tired of arguing with everyone. No one cared about Cherok, about her people and their suffering. If she were a man, she could simply have left. And to have to see

Cota again and again . . . Suddenly she felt that she might cry. She held her face in her hands and turned away from Hala, feeling every muscle and sinew inside her tense.

Suddenly she whipped around and looked at the old woman. "I cannot afford to make mistakes or do anything wrong. My people are waiting. They depend on me. For now they are alone, with no connection to the spirits. They will perish. My brother also waits, suffering every day. Do you not see?" she started to sob.

Hala was taken by surprise. So much was going on inside this woman. How strong she was. She bore the burdens of her people, alone, struggling against a world of men. She walked up to her and put her arms around her.

"Cry, child," she whispered. She patted Mi-sa's back.

Chalosee lay on her side, curled up against Cota, looking out at the rain that had turned to a drizzle. The cold storm wind felt good as it slipped through the platform and over her warm body.

Cota's arm was draped over her shoulder, and his hand hung loosely over her. She turned her head and touched her mouth to his arm, then cupped his hand in hers so that he more firmly held her breast. He felt so warm and comfortable, heavy with sleep. She wished the rain would not end. The storm would keep her cuddled against him even if he woke.

Naska stood in the rain across the mound, looking at Hala's platform. The rain dripped down his face and formed small streams running down his chest. A jagged bolt of lightning cracked the sky and lit the village. Naska didn't blink. The light had given him a glimpse inside Hala's platform.

He knew how he would sway Mi-sa once they were out alone on the river. He would comfort her, listen to her, touch her gently at first. Naska's face glowed with a smile as the rain trickled off his nose. His brother would not have everything he wanted.

CHAPTER
━ 15 ━

The rain kept falling. Kaho stood beneath Olagale's platform and called out to him.

"Come," Olagale answered, waving his friend up and then stepping back into the dry shadows.

He offered Kaho a deerskin to dry himself. Then they sat down and looked out at the rain, passing a few moments of silence.

Kaho turned and looked at Olagale, signaling that he was ready to begin speaking. "Do you remember long ago, when I brought my wife to the village?"

"Of course," Olagale answered, smiling, happy to reminisce with his old friend.

"I have thought about it often," Kaho said. "I remember the first time I saw her in the Tegesta village. I had had many women, but the instant I saw her, I knew she was different. Who would have thought that a Kahoosa cacique would take a Tegesta bride?"

"There were those who did not think you should. But Teeka won them with her ways."

"Yes, she did. Now, as I grow older, I realize the demands I put on the Kahoosa."

"'Breaking traditions is the way of the young. You did it so well." Olagale laughed.

"And as I look back, I am convinced that it was all part of a greater plan. Proud and vain as I was, I had nothing to do with the design of things." Kaho's expression turned solemn.

"You grow melancholy."

"It is always painful for me to think of her and know that she is gone."

There was silence as the two men looked out at the rain. The pause ended when Kaho spoke again.

"The agreement with the Tegesta. The agreement for unification—Cota is part of that. He is the child of the Tegesta woman and the Kahoosa man, the incarnate flesh of the peace, meant to rule the Kahoosa and the Tegesta as one."

"Cota is the cacique. The obligation is fulfilled." Olagale squinted at his friend. "What troubles you?"

Kaho looked at the thatch over his head. "There is more." He sighed heavily, then looked back at Olagale. "Some things were nearly forgotten as time passed."

"More?"

"Do you recall, Olagale, that it was the wish of the Tegesta and the Kahoosa for Cota to take a Tegesta wife when he grew to be a man and became the cacique? Could the spirits have willed the Tegesta woman here?"

Olagale fidgeted with the thong that held his medicine bag around his neck. "Perhaps," Olagale said. His bony fingers slid back and forth along the thong. "Do you forget Chalosee?"

"How many times have you told me that the spirits have their own designs? I believe they have brought the Tegesta woman here—for Cota—for the peace."

"I think you are sentimental—remembering Teeka. The idea of a union between another Kahoosa man and Tegesta woman brings back memories." Olagale smiled. "It is all right to reminisce."

"Old friend, there is more than just memories. You are a man of the spirits and understand more than I. But I believe that the appearance of this woman is the work of the spirits, just as my finding Teeka was. They have brought Mi-sa here for my son—for Cota."

"But she cannot stay," Olagale reminded him. "She says she is a shaman."

"And I believe that she is. Do you not?"

"It is difficult to accept, but I detect a quality in her, a special essence. I believe that she is a shaman." Olagale raised both hands in the air. "So you see . . ."

Kaho stood, walked to the opening, and leaned against the post, looking across the village. "Everything changes. We do not know where the spirits lead us."

"That is so," Olagale agreed.

"I want you to consult the spirits before the morning," Kaho said without turning to face his friend.

"I can do that. This weighs heavily on you."

Kaho turned his back to the rain and looked at Olagale. "If the spirits have brought her here, then—"

"I do not know how it can be, since she must leave soon."

"I do not know either, but I must trust."

"I will have an answer for you tomorrow morning."

"After the boys' instruction, the Council will reconvene. If the Tegesta woman is meant for Cota, Naska must be stopped." Kaho looked hard at Olagale. "He cannot be permitted to take her away from the village. She must be delayed."

Olagale stood. "The spirits will guide us, old friend," he said, reaching out and putting a hand on Kaho's shoulder.

"Cota's mother would be pleased if he ensured the peace by taking a Tegesta bride," Kaho said.

"I understand."

Kaho left without further conversation. He walked to the edge of the slough and sat under a tree that dripped with rain. He sang a simple song, his voice tremulous and low as he looked toward the charnel house.

* * *

In the morning the instruction began for the young boys. These were not the same ones who had been taught the lesson of the butterfly. These boys were older, farther along on the trail to manhood.

The men began with a dance, their warbling voices accompanying the beat of the drum. They bent deep at the knees as they stepped, their bodies loose, connecting freely with the sound of their song and the rhythm of the drum. They became the blowing saw grass, the slowly flowing dark water. The boys joined in, imitating the men, learning the words, the cadence, the rhythm, getting in touch with their world. Their voices rang in the air and floated out over the village and up into the spirit world.

The dance and song ended abruptly with four final strikes to the drum. For an instant they froze as though paralyzed, taking pride in ending their dance and song at the exact moment the last drumbeat sounded. Then they broke into laughter, and the men congratulated the boys.

The fathers and uncles collected the boys and led them out of the village. Cota took Nakila's child. Her husband was dead, and she had no brother. Cota hoped she would soon find another mate. The clan would not provide for her forever.

"Look," Cota said to Pa-hay-tee, pointing out a small gray bird. He told the boy the name of the bird and told him to remember that it liked to roost in the oak. "Recognize it by the color of the feathers."

Cota stooped and took Pa-hay-tee's hand. "Shh," he whispered. The boy looked at Cota with admiration. He wanted very much to please this man.

"Look at the beak," Cota said. "Can you tell what it eats?"

The boy could see the bird perched on the branch, but he could not easily make out the shape of its bill.

Cota brushed the ground, clearing a spot. With a twig he drew the bird's beak in the dirt. "It looks like this. Good for worms and insects."

The boy leaned over and looked at the drawing and back at the bird. He nodded his head.

"Now listen for the song."

They waited quietly until they finally heard the gray bird sing.

"Is that its only song?" the boy asked.

"You learn fast," Cota said, making the boy smile. "Some birds have many songs. Especially this one, which mimics the songs of others."

Pa-hay-tee swelled with pride and again grinned at his teacher.

They stood and proceeded on. Cota watched the ground and the grasses for signs of animals. "Here," he said, squatting low. Cota kissed the back of his own hand, making a squeaking sound. Again he made the noise.

The boy looked at him in question.

"A fox," Cota told him. The boy raised his hand to his mouth and tried to make the sound, but Cota stopped him. "While you play, you can practice. Next time you will call the fox," Cota whispered. "Be still, listen, and watch."

Cota made the sound with his hand again. A few moments later a fox came near, stopping and sniffing with its sharp nose, its ears keenly cocked forward.

"Do not move," Cota whispered. "He may smell us, but if we are still . . ."

Pa-hay-tee grinned and then looked back at the fox. Suddenly the fox turned, startled, and ran off.

"Tell me what happened to make the fox run away?" Cota said.

"I moved my head."

"It is best to learn the secrets of the animals when they do not know they are being observed. Next time hear my words."

Pa-hay-tee hung his head. He so wanted to make Cota proud of him.

"But you are learning. I will tell your mother how observant you are."

An unsure smile eased across the boy's lips.

"All the animals have something to teach you. You must know how to learn from them and accept their lessons." Cota stood. "Watch the hawk to see how he strikes his prey. His attack is clean, unerring. The watchful birds, the cunning fox—each has a gift to share with us."

Cota led Pa-hay-tee through other adventures, making sure the boy noted the trail. He showed him how to tie tall grass together into a bundle to serve as a marker and how to bend small saplings over and secure them. He made the boy note which side of the trees had the lightest bark.

When the sun was straight overhead, it was time to return.

"Follow the trail, watch for the signs we left, and lead me home," Cota said.

The youngster looked surprised, a little afraid, but he beamed as he turned around.

When they reentered the village, Cota stopped the boy by holding his shoulder. "You did well this day. Be proud, but not so proud that you forget. Tonight when you lie on your mat, close your eyes and follow the trail again. Remember all the things you have learned. Smell the trail, touch it, hear it, see it all again so that it finds a place to stay in your head."

Pa-hay-tee nodded.

"Go, then. Go and tell your mother that you will grow to be a fine hunter and warrior."

Pa-hay-tee ran off, a single whoop blurting from him as he saw one of his friends.

Mi-sa sat with Chalosee and Hala, helping them scrape the hide of a deer that Hala's brother had brought them. Her brother lived in her home village. He had stayed there when she and Chalosee moved, but he did not forget them, and made regular contributions to the Kahoosa village where Hala and Chalosee lived.

Mi-sa looked up, aware that Cota was nearby, even before Chalosee was. She rocked back on her heels and held the scraper in her lap. He was a beautiful man. She could feel the rugged power of him against her as he had been in the vision on the dune.

"Cota," Chalosee said, looking up. She rose and went to meet him.

Easily his arm went around her shoulders, and then he rubbed her back under the fall of her hair.

"Work it here," Hala said, making Mi-sa look back at the hide. "This will be a wedding gift. We will make it very soft, fit for the bed of a bride."

Mi-sa looked up. "Has Cota announced that he will take Chalosee as his wife?"

"Not yet."

Mi-sa watched them walking, laughing, smiling at each other. She saw when they stopped and faced each other, and she saw Cota hold Chalosee's face in his hands for a moment before they continued on.

"Are you going back?" Hala asked.

"What do you mean?" Mi-sa answered.

"Into the Council of Men."

"No." She knew it would be best if she awaited their answer outside the Council. And she did not want to be that near Cota again. It was too painful, too difficult to concentrate, to make her mouth say the words she was supposed to.

Naska strolled past the two women on his way to Council. He hesitated and stared at Mi-sa. His dark eyes danced, his hard face smiling at her.

"I will be back," Mi-sa said suddenly, dropping the scraper and moving away.

Hala looked up surprised. "Where are you going?"

Mi-sa just looked at her. She didn't know where she was going. No place special. She just needed to be alone, to speak with the spirits. She backed away from Hala. Naska moved on.

Mi-sa walked away from the village and stood beneath the canopy of Sabal palms, live oaks, and strangler figs. And then as she had done when she waited for a decision from her own

Council, she held her arms up to the sky and made herself
ready to talk to the spirits.

Naska sat behind the gathered men. He was certain they
would let him take the woman home.

Cota began. "We have had time to let our thoughts and
ideas settle in our heads. We have had time to think through
our choices. Now we will discuss them and make a decision.
Who will begin?"

"I will, Cacique." An angular man with a sharp long nose
stood up.

Cota nodded, giving him permission to speak.

"I think the woman should wait until the A-po-la-chee
threat has passed. We should not endanger ourselves."

"I understand your concern for the welfare of the
Kahoosa," Cota said, showing agreement.

Naska rose and waited for Cota to recognize him.

Cota nodded, giving Naska permission to speak. Naska
looked at all the men, making sure that everyone was listening.

"These are the same Kahoosa who have entered into a
peace with the Tegesta," Naska began. "Why should the
woman have to wait? You have heard her story. She comes
from a Tegesta village that was hit by the big storm. She has
been separated from her people. She is their shaman, and they
need her. Are we so selfish that we would let a whole clan of
our brothers suffer before we helped them?"

The lanky man spoke again. "Your argument sounds good,
but we must use our heads, not our hearts, to make decisions.
The time is not right to provide her with an escort. We would
be foolish. The foolish fall to the hands of their enemies."

Naska wandered through the men, his voice full and commanding. "Then I offer myself as her escort. We can spare
one man."

"Naska," Cota interrupted, "you do not speak from the
heart. Everyone knows why you wish to escort the woman,

and it is not a kindness from your heart. The Kahoosa will not be shamed by you."

Naska laughed. "Brother, why would you think such a thing? I will take her back to her village, and then I will return. What makes you so hostile?" he asked arrogantly.

"Why can he not escort her?" another man asked. "I think that it is the best solution. We can send one man with her. If anyone knows the waters, it is Naska."

Another man got Cota's attention and permission to speak. "No. The journey is too dangerous for one man. We should not allow Naska to put himself at risk, especially with the A-po-la-chee about."

"Actually, one man is harder to catch than many. I think it is much wiser to send only one escort," another man added.

Kaho stood, and Cota recognized him. The men grew quiet; the mumbling stopped. They had great respect for their former cacique. He was a man of wisdom. They would listen to what he had to say.

"The dissension continues, but we must come to an agreement. I have asked Olagale to consult with the spirits. He said to me this morning that he has done so. We should listen to what the spirits have told him."

"Olagale," Cota said, calling on him.

The spirit man wandered to the front of the crowd. He took his time, moving with self-assurance. He made them wait so that when he did speak, there would be more power in his words.

All the men focused on the shaman who stood before them. The lines he had painted on his face before talking with the spirits were still faintly visible.

"Cacique," Olagale began, nodding at Cota. "Kaho came to me during the rain. We sat together a long time and discussed many things—things from the past, things of the future, private matters, and matters that concern all the Kahoosa. We talked about the Tegesta woman and what we should do. We decided that the spirits should advise us."

Olagale paused, making sure that he had captured everyone's attention. He scanned the men's faces, his own features pensive and sober. The crowd was so quiet that the churring of a small rodent and the flapping of a bird's wings as it left its perch were audible.

"Tell us," Cota said.

"The spirits are wise. They know more than we do, and we can never see the whole unfurling of life as they do. They see out of the past and into the future. When we ask them to send us word, to give us answers, we are obligated to heed their reply. This we must all understand before I go on."

Olagale paused again as if expecting a response. The men nodded and mumbled their agreement.

"Sometimes we cannot understand the design of the spirits. If we could, then perhaps we would be as great as they. We are not to doubt or to challenge them. Nor are we to disagree with them. If we do, they may forsake us for not trusting and believing them. This is what you must know and feel in your hearts before I tell you what the spirits have answered."

The men stirred. What was Olagale preparing them for? Why did he need such a strong preface?

Mi-sa felt the light spiral and settle deep inside her. She lowered her arms comfortingly to her chest. The aura around her faded.

She stood still for a few moments, refocusing and regathering, and then she turned toward the village. As she walked back, the last of the power that had soared in her came to rest.

She saw Hala standing alone at her hearth. Chalosee was not with her. The men of the Council had dispersed. Cota stood alone in the center of the plaza, watching her.

Except for the whispered mumblings, the village felt oddly still.

"It is decided?" Mi-sa asked Hala.

The old woman turned her back and walked away.

CHAPTER
— 16 —

"Hala?" Mi-sa asked, starting to follow her. "What is wrong?"

Hala snatched some weaving reeds from a bundle she had prepared, then slowly lowered herself onto the ground, still ignoring Mi-sa.

Mi-sa squatted in front of her. "I thought we had become friends. Why do you act this way toward me? What have I done?"

Hala threw her reeds in the dirt and looked up. "Why did you come here?"

"Hala, you know how I came to your village. I have told you before."

Hala picked through her weaving material and began fashioning a new basket. Her knobby fingers worked quickly with the expertise of many seasons doing the same task. "Be on your way, Tegesta woman," she said softly.

Mi-sa reached out and touched Hala's hand. "I do not understand. Please look at me, my friend."

The old woman drew back her hand and continued with her work.

"Please," Mi-sa said again.

Hala looked up. "The Council has decided. Olagale persuaded them. He is a man of the spirits—like you. Perhaps the two of you ..."

"Olagale? Why are you angry? What did he say?"

"You really do not know?" Hala said.

"No, Hala. What has upset you?"

"Olagale says that the spirits demand that Cota take you to your village. He alone."

Mi-sa looked back at the earthen plaza. Her stomach turned over and balled up into a nervous knot. "Cota?"

"Olagale says it is the wish of the spirits. And so it will be."

The old woman rattled on as Mi-sa scanned the village, her eyes stopping on the striking cacique. There he was, standing close to Chalosee, touching her arm, lifting her chin in his hand.

"When?" Mi-sa whispered.

"One day," Hala answered.

Mi-sa stood watching Cota with Chalosee. "Oh, Hala, I did not wish this. I have no intention of ruining your daughter's happiness. I only want to go home."

"It does not matter what you want. Cota is what you will get, and Chalosee fears that she will lose him to you. Can you not see that she is plainer than you? And the mystery about you. That would entice any man."

"It will not take long to reach my village, and then Cota will return," Mi-sa said, trying to soothe her friend. But in her heart she, too, was troubled. Being alone with Cota would be a painful, constant reminder that she could never have this man who had come to her in her dreams for so long. How unkind of the spirits.

"She also worries about the A-po-la-chee and about Cota traveling alone."

"What if I go to the Council again?"

"And ask for Naska?"

"No," Mi-sa quickly answered. "Would they send someone else besides Naska or Cota?"

"There was a short argument about having the cacique

leave the village, but Olagale insists that it is the spirits' decision. They will not send anyone else. It is done."

"What if I do not wish to go with Cota?"

Hala looked up, surprised. "To say that would anger the men. They have made a sacrifice for you. You cannot be so insensitive."

Mi-sa sat down. "But, Hala . . . I do not wish for the escort to be Cota," she said softly, trying to hide the choking in her throat.

Mi-sa's comment made Hala stare at her. She looked long into Mi-sa's eyes. "No, I suppose you do not," Hala said, realizing that the Tegesta woman could barely hold her emotions in check. "Your spirit is good," Hala said.

"Sometimes I do not know," Mi-sa said under her breath. "My life, this situation, everything, has become so complicated. My intentions are simple. I wish to do what is best for my people, but not at the expense of yours. And now this."

"Cota is in your heart, is he not? I saw your feelings in your face from the beginning."

Mi-sa looked into the trees, afraid even to glance at Hala. There was a long and thoughtful pause. Thoughts of Cota threaded through her life, even when she was a child, wanting so desperately to have someone love her. Then as she became a woman, he had entered her dreams. He had brought her peace and hope long before she knew who he was. Even before she saw his face or heard his name, he had been part of her. She would not be able to give him up easily.

She dipped her fingers inside her medicine bag, feeling for the crystal shell. She withdrew the dream-catcher and held it in her hand, turning it, watching the sunlight sparkle and glint.

"Perhaps it is not always best to catch your dream," Mi-sa said, putting the calcite crystal back in her medicine bag.

"Can you tell me what you mean?" Hala asked.

"I have visions and dreams."

"Is Cota part of those visions?"

Mi-sa hesitated. She fumbled with her medicine bag, feeling the crystal shell inside it.

"Have you seen Cota in your visions?" the old woman asked.

"Yes."

Hala stood and began to pace. "I will not ask you any more questions. I do not think I want to hear your answers."

Mi-sa lowered her head, feeling responsible for Hala's sadness and concern. "I would tell you more if I thought it would help. But, Hala, I do not understand it all yet."

Hala moved toward Mi-sa. The Tegesta woman was not her enemy.

"I wish no one harm," Mi-sa said, rising, her eyes brimming with tears.

"Be still," Hala said, holding Mi-sa's head to her.

Naska was enraged. Olagale should not have interfered. Cota must have persuaded the shaman to step into the discussion. As always, his brother tried to ruin him, discredit him, shame him. How ridiculous to say the spirits had suggested that Cota escort the Tegesta woman back to her village.

Naska tore a dead limb from a tree. Anger burned inside him, exploding into a fireball. He snapped the branch over his knee, breaking it in two.

"Ahhhh!" he bellowed, hurling the longer half of the stick into the trunk of another tree. He liked the thud of it and the cracking sound as the wood split. The noise relieved some of his rage. He pitched the other half into the base of the tree and watched it skitter across the forest floor just before it hit its target.

"You choose an acceptable way to express your anger," came a voice from behind him. Kaho.

Naska turned. "Did you expect me to do otherwise?"

"Your past follows you," his father said.

"All of the Kahoosa think they know me. No one does, really," Naska said, his expression harsh and bitter.

"You must learn to accept decisions made by the Council

even when they do not please you, Naska. Listening to others has always been difficult for you."

"Did you come here to talk to me as if I were still a boy?"

"I came to find my son—my son who thinks I do not know him so well."

"You know Cota, not me."

"You are wrong. I know both my sons, but one of them wishes I did not."

"How are you so sure of everything? Do you not know that you can be wrong sometimes?" Naska pitched another small stick he found on the ground.

Kaho waited until Naska looked at him. "I can be wrong, and I have been many times. But not about this. Not about you."

"But what you think you know about me you do not like. Why do you bother with a son who displeases you? Spend your time with your favored son, the great cacique."

"I have no favored son," Kaho said, tilting his head to study Naska more carefully, searching for some sign of what it was that ate at him, that had made him so irascible and discontent ever since he was a boy. "My heart has a place for both of you. Why do you fight that so hard and so long? I see both my sons' strengths and weaknesses. And I love you equally. You just will not let me."

Naska raised his hands and heaved out a gust of air. He had always yearned for his father's attention and approval. "Do you not remember the boy who brought you his first kill? The boy who ran through the forest, skinning his knees and cutting his face when he fell because he was in such a rush to show his father the brown rabbit—to please his father? How many times did I look to you as almost a spirit, deserving the same devotion?"

"I hope many times, more than I can count. And I gave my approval when you sought it appropriately."

"You always attached conditions."

"But you have always rejected custom and tradition."

Naska laughed. "The stories are still told about the young

Kahoosa leader who swept over the region with his might and his force—the leader who defied custom and tradition when it suited him—the legend of Kaho!"

Kaho looked at his son. "The times were different. I was not angry. I was building a nation, perhaps wrongly, but—"

"I am the fruit of your seed. If you look in the water, you will see that I am your reflection."

"Then listen to my wisdom. Do not make the same mistakes I made."

Naska held his arms out in question. "Then offer me wisdom. Do not ask me to conduct my life based on the words of my brother or to listen blindly to the Council."

"I tell you that you cannot balk at everything you disagree with just because it is not your way. Bitterness will sour your soul. Your gut will grow rancid, and your tongue will speak nothing but the words of a faultfinder. You will rot from the inside out, and everyone will be repulsed by the stench."

Naska's face changed. Kaho hoped that perhaps he had reached him.

"I am finished with this conversation," Naska said. "More pleasurable things await me." He walked past his father and back into the village, teasing the young girls as he passed them, tempting the young women with a quick sensual look or comment. He left a trail of females watching him as he made his way to Ursa.

"Are you repulsed by me?" He laughed, then took Ursa by the back of her head and pulled her to him. His mouth was furious upon hers. Many people stared, and mothers turned their children away.

Naska let go of her and looked back through the village. He hoped his father had watched and had seen how he was not filled with misery, how he was received by others in the clan, especially the women.

Mi-sa sat inside Hala's platform. She watched as the women busied themselves about the village. She wondered what her life would have been like if she had been born without her father's gift. She realized that she had no real instinct for being just a woman. Her mother had not been able to provide a suitable example. Miakka's life had been difficult because of Mi-sa. How she missed her mother.

For a moment she sat lost in her daydreams. Chalosee called up to her.

"Come," Mi-sa answered.

"I have brought you something for your journey," Chalosee said, handing Mi-sa a basket of food.

"Chalosee . . ." She could not finish.

"You do not need to say anything. Somehow, deep inside, I know that Cota will not come back to me. I know also that you are not to blame. I struggle with my feelings. I love Cota, and I do not want to give him up. And last night I had a dream. Dreams are real, are they not? Meant to be listened to?"

"Your dreams are only dreams," Mi-sa answered.

Chalosee's trembling fingers touched her lips. "I was alone," she said.

"Give me your hand, Chalosee," Mi-sa said, reaching out for her. "Close your eyes."

Mi-sa began a soft song, one that she thought would bring peace, one that would lead to reassurance. There would be nothing between her and Cota. He would return to Chalosee.

Suddenly a chilling wave flooded through Mi-sa. She dropped Chalosee's hand and shuddered.

Chalosee looked at her, bewildered. "What is it?"

"Nothing." Mi-sa turned away from her and set the gift basket near the far wall. "You are very kind."

Chalosee was shaken by Mi-sa's reaction. "My dream will come true, will it not?" Chalosee asked. "You know it also."

"No," Mi-sa answered.

"You dropped my hand—stopped your singing. What did you see?"

"The song was done," Mi-sa lied, nervously fumbling with other baskets along the wall. She had not seen Chalosee with her heart broken, but she had seen a quick flash of the future, and it had made her reel.

"My mother has convinced me that you mean me no harm. I believe her."

Mi-sa took Chalosee's hand again. "I am anxious to tell my people what good Kahoosa friends I have made."

Hala had come up the ladder. She smiled. "I am happy that you have talked."

"Yes," Mi-sa said, "I am also."

Chalosee wrapped her arms around her mother, hugged her tightly, then without turning back descended the ladder.

"She is so afraid," Hala said.

"I know," Mi-sa answered.

Hala and Mi-sa prepared some other baskets to take on the journey. The sun hung huge and blazing red on the western horizon, then quickly slipped away, ending its long trip for the day. The earliest stars began to twinkle.

Mi-sa removed the knife from her pouch. "My brother gave me this as I was about to depart on the journey. It is beautiful, is it not?"

Hala nodded.

"He did not care that it might anger the other men. He loves me that much."

Hala did not say anything, letting Mi-sa ramble.

Mi-sa's fingers glided along the smooth blade. "I can never forget how much he loves me." Mi-sa looked up at Hala. "I am glad we leave in the morning. Soon Cota will come back here, Chalosee will be happy, and I will send our warriors to rescue Cherok."

The night floated over the village, wrapping it snugly in shadows and darkness. Cota's head rested against the side of Chalosee's face, their damp bodies pressing against each other. He breathed deeply, getting his breath back. Beneath him he heard Chalosee's soft sigh as she, too, recovered her breath.

Cota started to slide off her, but she held him.

"Not yet," she whispered.

He settled back against her, their bodies still locked together. She stroked his hair and ran lazy fingers up and down his back. For the moment he was more hers than anyone else's—not the clan's, not the tribe's, hers alone, completely.

"Cota?" she whispered.

He did not answer. She closed her eyes and drifted off to sleep.

During the night, Cota awakened and slowly rolled to his side. Chalosee moaned contentedly and shifted. He touched her long black hair as it spilled over her shoulder. He gazed out into the moonlit village. He had a strong feeling that his life was about to change, that the journey with the Tegesta woman would alter many things.

Chalosee turned on the mat. The dream had come again. She was alone. She woke, whimpering, relieved it was only a dream. She reached out for Cota, wanting to curl up against him, but he was not there.

CHAPTER
━ 17 ━

Cota stood next to the slow, low-burning embers of the central hearth. The fire keeper had stoked it well so it would last until sunrise when he would feed it new fuel.

The moonlight washed over the village. The slow breeze whispered through the aged trees, making the leaves flutter, casting fickle shadows that danced to a secret melody.

Hala's platform, nestled close to a tall, spreading strangler fig, stood deep in shadows. He could not help but stare, as if magically drawn. He pictured Mi-sa sleeping, her small body curved gently at rest, her black lashes feathering across her cheek, her lips parted, a strand of her hair riding on a puff of the gentle wind. He could almost hear her breathing, the beating of her heart.

The scent of burning pine needles distracted him. In the distance Olagale's fire burned. Cota walked toward the shaman.

"What keeps you from sleep?" Olagale asked.

"A man must think about many things when all is quiet." Cota sat across from the shaman. "Why do you purify yourself?"

Olagale threw another handful of green pine needles into the fire and leaned into the thick gray smoke. "I must talk with the spirits before you leave—before the sun begins its journey across the sky."

"Olagale, can you tell me what you know? Can you tell me why the spirits say that I am the one who must escort the Tegesta woman?"

"The Tegesta shaman," he corrected. "She is a woman and a shaman."

"But why is it important for me to help her return to her village? I suspect the spirits have more than one purpose in their plan. There is more to this than just being an escort."

"Much more," Olagale said, taking a handful of damp clay. He began covering his chest with the white substance. "Did you not listen to what I said in Council? We are not to question the spirits' decisions. We are not of their world. They guide and direct all we do."

The shaman covered his arms and legs with the clay as Cota watched. "Would you spread it on my back?" Olagale asked.

Cota took the clay, and Olagale turned his back to him. When Cota finished, Olagale took an old charred stick and drew four straight black lines down his cheeks, then blackened his lips. "I should be alone now," he said. "I am ready. The sky will lighten soon."

Cota walked away, taking one last look back. Olagale's ghostly shape swayed behind the thick pine smoke. His hand danced over the flames, and then Cota saw the shaman cast something into the fire that made it crackle and burst with a halo of sparks.

When the sun edged over the night sky, Cota greeted it in his way, beginning the day as he had since he was a child, sitting quietly with his legs crossed and his back straight, his keenly honed senses responding to sounds, feeling the air, smelling what was on the wind. A fire burned somewhere to the west. Then, eyes closed, hands on his knees, he began his morning prayers.

Chalosee stood back, waiting until he was finished. When

she saw his head drop and his back slacken, she knew she could approach. Her hands massaged his wide shoulders.

"I reached for you, and you were not there."

"I could not sleep," he said, without turning around to look at her.

"The night passed too quickly. I am sorry to see the sun," she said.

Cota reached around and took her hand, leading her to sit at his side. "The sun might hear you," he said. "What if it did not come this way?"

Chalosee rested her head on his shoulder. "I remember not so long ago when the sun became black. It did not stay dark long, but I was frightened. Now that I have you, I would not be so afraid."

Kaho walked up from behind them. "Everyone meets the new day early," he said.

Chalosee stood. "I will see you before you leave?" she asked Cota, afraid that she would not have any more time with him.

"I will come for you," Cota answered.

Chalosee turned and left.

"May I sit with you?" Kaho asked.

"It is my honor."

"Sometimes women see only with the eye of the heart." He paused a moment. "Men do this also," he added.

"Seeing with the heart is good," Cota said.

"Indeed. That is the only eye your mother had. I wish she were here today."

"You still grieve," Cota said, looking at his father.

"I will always grieve. A part of my heart is dead. But a part of her is here in you ... and in Naska." Kaho paused. "Arghh," he said, scolding himself for his sentimentality, "old men become too much like women." Both of them chuckled.

"Here," Kaho said, holding out his hand. "I have brought you this."

Cota watched his father's gnarled hand open, his leathery

palm holding a small strip of otter skin. "Put this in your medicine bag—for safe passage on the water."

Cota was pleased. "I will take with me the spirit of the otter."

"My stomach grumbles," Kaho said. "I will visit the hearth of one of the old women. One of them will feed me this morning," he said and laughed.

"Cacique!" a child's voice called. Pa-hay-tee ran toward him. He stopped in front of Cota. "I was afraid you had gone."

"I would not leave without seeing the greatest young warrior in our clan," Cota said, rising and tousling the boy's hair.

Pa-hay-tee glowed. "I have a stick to feed the fire. It is for you. I have said prayers over it. The fire spirit will appreciate the sacrifice and be with you."

"Come," said Cota. "We will share our morning meal."

Mi-sa took another look in Hala's basket. "You and Chalosee have given me too much."

Hala slurped from the shell ladle, then said, "It is rude to refuse a gift. The giver might think you do not like it."

"I am not refusing. I am humbled by your generosity."

"Then take it gladly."

"Thank you, Hala. I will miss you. I am sad that we will not see each other again."

"Yes." The old woman's eyes became bleary with tears, and she rubbed at them with her knobby knuckles. "Here," she said, ladling fish stew into a bowl for Mi-sa.

Mi-sa accepted the food and began to eat it. Hala put down the ladle. "Good-bye, Tegesta woman," she said, walking off.

"Hala? Where do you go?" Mi-sa asked, surprised that Hala was leaving. She did not feel that they had said a proper good-bye.

Hala did not turn around. "To Chalosee."

Mi-sa set the bowl on the ground and stood up. "Good-bye, Hala," she said. "I will remember you."

Mi-sa's appetite was suddenly gone.

* * *

"Come, Naska," Ursa said, ready to leave the platform and join the others to wish their cacique a safe journey.

Naska still sat on the mat.

Ursa looked back at him and then out to the village. "Everyone is gathering now."

Naska reached up and grabbed a handful of her hair that hung down to her waist. He pulled gently, just hard enough to make Ursa bend her head back toward him.

"Naska," she said with discomfort.

He let go of her hair and ran his hand up her thigh, beneath the moss skirt. "There is no need for either of us to go. We will not be missed."

"Do you not want to wish Cota well? And the Tegesta woman?"

"Their journey will not be affected by our good wishes. Why waste the cool air of the early morning?" He kissed the back of her knee and nipped at her thigh.

"It is expected of us. Of everyone," she weakly argued.

Naska firmly turned her toward him, slipped his hands under the moss and held her around her buttocks. He rose up on his knees and kissed her belly. Ursa's legs went weak, and she also dropped to her knees, pressing her mouth to his strong salty shoulder. He put his arms around her waist for support as she arched her back and leaned away, the long line of her neck curving, her hair falling to the floor at her heels. Naska filled his mouth with the warm, soft flesh of her breast. Ursa knew she was not going anywhere.

"Help me take my things to the canoe," Cota told Pa-hay-tee as they finished eating. He led the child into his platform and handed him several articles to take to the boat. "Your touch will bring me good luck," Cota said.

"This?" the boy asked, indicating a long spear.

"Yes, but I will carry that. A man must always be responsible for his own weapons."

* * *

Mi-sa wandered through the crowd and down to the river-bank. The people parted as she passed. She stood by the canoe and put the baskets into it. She grasped the side of the canoe and started to step in. A large hand suddenly covered hers, lifting it from the canoe and offering support. It was Kaho.

"The canoe rocks on the slippery bank," he said.

Saying thank you was not enough, Mi-sa thought. He had made sure that she did not slip or stumble, that she did not risk losing her dignity.

As she stepped into the canoe she heard Pa-hay-tee call out, "Wait! Wait!" The boy dropped what he carried.

Cota picked up the things and took them to the canoe. He nodded to Mi-sa and then turned to watch for the boy's return.

In a moment Pa-hay-tee came running through the gathering. "Here! For you," he said, panting.

He handed Cota a lance he had made. Pa-hay-tee had cut the oak wood in winter while the sap was down so that it would not split while it dried and smoked by the fire. Some moons later the boy had greased the shaft and held it over the fire, working the staff straight. The lance shaft was smooth. Pa-hay-tee had rubbed it with a swatch of sharkskin.

Cota tried to wiggle the antler point, but it did not move. The boy had fit the tip solidly into the slot cut in the shaft, and then he had bound it with wet rawhide. When the rawhide dried, it shrank, tightly binding the antler-tip point to the shaft.

"This is a fine weapon," Cota said, making Pa-hay-tee grin. Nakila, the boy's mother, came up behind Pa-hay-tee. She was grateful Cota had taken the time to help her son. Pa-hay-tee idolized the young cacique. She was glad Cota treated the boy with consideration.

Mi-sa was moved by the boy's apparent adoration of Cota. But even more, she was touched by the way Cota returned that respect and regard. For a man of Cota's stature to treat everyone, even a child, with courtesy and consideration was

the mark of man of integrity, a characteristic of a worthy cacique.

She reached for her medicine bag and held it in her hand,
and her mind began to spin fantasies of what it would be like
to be just a woman, Cota's woman, to feel his touch, hear
him whisper sweet words in her ear as he ached to be one
with her, to share a child, a son, like Pa-hay-tee.

The canoe lurched as Cota pushed it off the bank, ripping
her away from the unreal world. In the back of the crowd she
saw Chalosee standing with Hala, who had wrapped her hand
around her daughter's head and pulled it to her shoulder.
Chalosee willingly leaned her head against her mother and
held her hand to her trembling bottom lip as she watched the
canoe back into the water.

The water whirled in eddies where Cota dipped the paddle.
The canoe moved silently, turning away from the village.
Mi-sa looked to the sky, watching for an omen. But this time
there were no egrets, no circling, wheeling flashes of white to
accompany them. And there was no turkey vulture, no sign
that the venture was ill-fated. No omens.

Pa-hay-tee danced on the bank, waving and singing until
he could no longer see the canoe.

The cool air of the morning quickly became hot and heavy
with humidity. Mi-sa wiped a trickle of perspiration from her
brow as she watched the river unravel before her.

"How many days had you been gone from your village
when the storm hit?" Cota asked.

She turned around and looked at him for the first time
since they had left the Kahoosa village. "One day. The storm
came in the night."

Cota nodded and kept on paddling. Mi-sa knew her village
was isolated, far from the other Tegesta villages, but that was
all. She could give him no other directions or clues.

"We are far west, a small village, not close to other villages."

Cota nodded again. Mi-sa grew uncomfortable. "Do you
not want more information?"

"If you knew more, you would tell me."

"But how do you know where to go?"

"I will take you to the Tegesta waters. Then we will decide from there."

"Oh," Mi-sa said, embarrassed that she had questioned him. She turned around to watch the wide river as it snaked through the lush foliage.

"Tegesta woman," he said.

Mi-sa looked back at him. He tipped his head, gesturing toward the other paddle. "Do you know how to use it?"

Again she blushed with embarrassment. "Yes," she answered, picking up the paddle. "I should have ... I did not ..."

Her thoughts were muddled. She had not thought of offering to help. How inconsiderate. She wondered what he thought of her.

Mi-sa had paddled a canoe alone but never with someone else. She quickly found that teamwork was more important than two paddles.

Suddenly she felt him close behind her, wrapping his arms around her, his body straining for balance as it touched her.

"Like this," he said, kneeling, his arms over hers, his hands over hers, directing the paddle in straight, powerful strokes. The soft, damp skin of her back and her sleek, hot hair rubbed against his chest. "One hand up here," he said, slowly sliding her hand up the hard wooden shaft. Cota felt his voice catch with a sharp reflexive gasp, and he held her still and quiet until he dared to move and speak again.

Mi-sa felt the wind on her face, blowing her hair back, making her skin tingle; she could hear the water rushing along the banks. She shivered. His body was snugly pressed against hers. There, where their bodies touched, she felt no wind, only heat.

"The other here on the throat," he murmured as he easily slid her hand down to the head of the blade. "Yes," he said as the paddle squarely entered the water. "Push forward now, at the top; then pull back down here," he said, his voice tinged with urgency. He led her to move with him. "Nice, smooth, easy, deep strokes."

She could feel his words breeze warmly past the juncture of her neck and shoulder; she could smell his skin as his arm moved past her face and stirred the air.

"Again," he said, feeling her movements meet and match his, gaining speed.

The paddle feathered over the top of the water as they swung it forward to stroke again. Together they thrust it down into the water. The canoe moved faster as they stroked more quickly, in harmony, as if they were one.

Mi-sa faltered when she realized the canoe was not moving straight ahead, but his strong arms tightened around her, forcing her to return to his even rhythm.

She could hear him heave for air, breathing with the tempo of their strokes. "Work with me," he said. "Feel it. Ride the river." Her arms rose and fell with his. Rose and fell. Rose and fell. The canoe swiftly glided through the water.

Mi-sa shuddered again, and he slowly eased his grip, letting her take over. "Good," he said.

Cota moved away and again took up his position, straightening their course, watching her work her paddle. He was glad she caught on quickly. It was not a good idea to be so close to this woman.

CHAPTER
— 18 —

The pink morning sky grew to a blazing afternoon blue. The river narrowed, its flanks overflowing with willow, ferns, tall reeds and grasses, great oaks, and palms that draped and bent out over the water, dripping with moonvine and moss, green and gray fingers reaching for the river.

Alligators ducked under the water as the canoe cruised past. Occasionally coveys of birds nervously burst out of the trees, then settled again, disappearing into the verdant cover.

Mi-sa took her paddle out of the water and laid it inside the canoe. She retrieved one of the baskets, put it in her lap, and began rummaging through it.

Her stomach rumbled with hunger. She found some coontie bread and offered a piece to Cota, taking a smaller portion for herself.

"We will stop if you are hungry," he said.

Mi-sa put her hand to her forehead, shielding her eyes from some of the glare. "Can we not eat as we go?" she asked.

Cota crimped one corner of his mouth into a curious smile. "We are going against the current. If I stop paddling, we will be carried back."

Mi-sa's eyebrows arched. "Then we will take turns," she said cleverly.

Cota's half smile broke into a wide grin. There was a better way than arguing with her. He put his paddle down and moved close enough to take the bread from her hand. As he moved back, he nodded at her paddle.

Mi-sa picked it up and dipped it into the water. Cota tore a piece off the bread with his teeth. Mi-sa paddled harder, reaching into the water on alternate sides, struggling to keep the canoe straight, fighting the current.

He watched her endeavor, her contest with the current, and resisted the urge to go to her aid. The canoe edged forward with her stroke, then rode backward as she moved the paddle to the opposite side. She worked harder and faster.

Mi-sa wiped her forehead with the back of her palm as she swung the paddle to the other side. She was making no progress. Again she pulled the paddle through the water, feeling Cota's eyes on her back, picturing the smug smile on his face.

Cota swallowed the last bit of his coontie, cupped his hand in the water for a drink, then picked up his paddle. As the canoe moved more smoothly, Mi-sa looked back.

"Sweep the water on this side," he said, demonstrating the arc she should form with the paddle to help maneuver the canoe toward shore.

In a moment the bow of the canoe pushed through a clump of cattails, and the perched dragonflies took to the air. Cota used the pole to ease the canoe up through the cattails. Mi-sa stood up.

"Wait!" Cota called, but he spoke too late. The dugout tilted and spilled her into the shallow water. Cota shook his head and stifled a laugh.

Mi-sa felt the soft mud squishing between her toes as she stood up sputtering. She grabbed a handful of cattails to pull on. Cota watched her make her way onto the shore. While her back was turned, his face broke into another grin.

"If you would listen to me and not be so stubborn—" He

fell silent, deciding that this was no time to scold her. Her pride was already wallowing in the river.

Mi-sa pushed away some reeds, hearing skittering beneath the grasses. She flinched, then flattened out a spot to sit. Wet and muddy, she looked back at him, lifting her head high and pulling her shoulders back. She wiped hair and water from her face as Cota moved the canoe forward with the pole, then stepped out onto the riverbank. He tugged at the dugout and secured it before taking out her basket.

"Still hungry?" he asked, fighting a cocky smile. If the woman would listen to him, she could save herself a lot of unnecessary embarrassment.

He handed her the basket and sat next to her, noticing the little stream of blood on her shin. "Let me see," he said, straightening out her leg.

Mi-sa bent her leg in protest and looked through the basket.

"Nasty scrape," he said.

"I am all right," she snapped, slowly recovering her dignity. "It does not hurt. I only caught it on the side of the canoe."

"It is bruised also," he said, noticing the discolored lump that had already formed. "I did that once myself," he told her.

Mi-sa looked up at him, wanting to thank him for the effort to salvage her pride with his admission. But then he added, "As a boy."

She quickly looked back at the basket and withdrew a piece of dried venison. She bit into the meat, attempting to tear it with her teeth, but the venison was too tough.

"Woman, you are going to starve," he said, taking the strip of meat from her. He smiled as he held one end of the venison between his white teeth and used his knife to slice off a piece. With his finger and thumb he held the small morsel close to her mouth.

"Go on, open," he said. "You said you were hungry."

Mi-sa reluctantly opened her mouth. His finger pushed in the venison, feeling the warmth of the inside of her mouth.

He let his finger linger there a moment, just inside, then hesitated again as he touched her lips.

She had felt foolish and inept a moment ago, but that feeling was quickly washed over with a tingling wave. She wanted to look away, but as his thumb brushed over her lips and then slowly traced their outline, she couldn't. She finally raised her hand and took him by the wrist, belatedly pulling his hand down from her face.

Their gazes locked until she made herself look away. He pressed the meat strip into her palm, then rose and walked into the brush.

Mi-sa folded her arms over her drawn-up knees and rested her chin there, staring at the river. These feelings would pass soon enough, once she was home and Cota was gone. That wonderful pleasant sensation when he was near, whenever he touched her, would be transformed into anguish and longing for something she would never know. The overwhelming, euphoric loss of sensibility when he looked at her, those feelings that made her cast everything aside except the look in his eyes, left her empty and lonely once he took his eyes from her. That, too, would end with his departure. Perhaps the spirits would be kind enough to let him continue to come to her in her dreams.

"Eat some more." His voice ended her musing.

Mi-sa searched through the basket. "You finish this," she said, giving him back the remaining venison. "I will find another piece that is not so tough."

Cota took it from her. "You should also tend to other things while you are here."

Mi-sa knew what he meant and slipped into the brush to relieve herself. When she finished and began her walk back, there was a rustling behind her. Not the scurrying of a lizard or a beetle, not even a squirrel or raccoon. Something bigger, she thought. She stood very still, except to take a quick look behind her, saw nothing, and trotted back, feeling comforted when she saw Cota waiting for her.

"I am ready to leave," she said, a bit breathless.

"You are hurried," he commented, noticing her anxious state.

"Yes, I am eager to find my village. I do not want to waste time."

"Are you certain that is all?"

"Yes," she answered, attempting to appear preoccupied with the task of preparing the basket. "Do you want anything else?"

Cota touched her shoulder, making her look up at him. "Yes," he said, "I do."

Mi-sa swallowed, feeling her heart thudding in her chest. Again she was lost in his gaze, unable to speak or make herself seem detached and composed.

"Do you not want to know what I want?" he asked.

Mi-sa felt dizzy, her legs weak, her tongue tied.

He put his hand on her neck, feeling the pounding of her pulse. "Are you afraid?" he asked.

"Afraid of what? No. What should I be afraid of?"

Cota looked at her. All the strength he had witnessed in this woman was suddenly tempered with a gentle, provocative vulnerability. "You are fire and water." He paused. "Bread," he finally said.

"Bread?"

"More bread. I want another piece of bread before you finish packing that basket."

It took a moment for Mi-sa to understand. "Oh," she said, scrambling to find him another piece, certain he sensed how ruffled and flustered he made her feel.

Cota watched her curiously. She had been frightened by something in the woods but did not want to admit it. But there was more, when he had said he wanted something else, when he had touched her neck—and her response had aroused him. It would be best if they found her Tegesta village soon.

Together they paddled the canoe up the river until the sun hung low in the sky, making the horizon run with smears of red, yellow, pink, and violet.

Cota found a spot that was suitable for a camp. He banked the canoe, secured it, and then helped Mi-sa out of the dug-out.

"Your oarsman skills have improved," he said, helping her balance as she stepped out.

"You are a good teacher," she answered.

"Take only the basket with the food. I will get the rest," he said.

Mi-sa lifted the basket that Hala had provided, while Cota selected a few articles from among his belongings. With his knife he cut away low branches and sedge. He cleared a spot and unrolled a skin for his bed. Mi-sa stared at it, realizing that she would have to sleep on the damp ground. With her knife she cut grasses and piled them up to make a bed.

Cota disappeared in the forest.

Mi-sa finished preparing the area, clearing away the thick brush. While he was gone, she stepped into the shallows of the river, stripped off her skirt, tossed it atop some tall reeds, and sank under the water. It felt good to rinse the stickiness of the day's perspiration from her body, and to let her hair soak up the clean water. The river was exceptionally quiet at this time of day. The birds had finished their last feeding, the wind died, and the sounds of the day faded with the sun.

Cota had scouted the area, making certain it was safe. Then he gathered an armload of good dry wood, both kindling and logs that would burn through the night, and headed back to Mi-sa. He could see their camp through the trees. He nearly dropped his cache when he saw the Tegesta woman rising out of the water, twisting her hair, wringing out the thick black tresses. The water slid down her body in a glossy sheen. She shook her head, spraying a fine mist, then retrieved her skirt from the reeds, wrapped it around her, and walked up onto the dry land, where she sat down on the grass bed and watched the blazing sunset, pensively recapturing feelings and emotions, sorting through them.

Cota moved on into camp. The sudden clattering of wood interrupted her introspection.

Carefully he laid the fire, arranging the kindling and dried grasses. From a pouch in which he had protected it from splashing water in the canoe, he removed a small hot coal and slipped it into the bed of dry grass he had prepared beneath the tangle of wood. Gently he blew on it until the grass caught and flamed, catching the twigs. When the fire was hot and aflame, he added the larger limbs.

As always happened with the fall of night, the mosquitoes began to swarm. Mi-sa and Cota rubbed repellent ointment on their bodies.

"My back," Cota said, handing her his supply of the repellent. "Put it on my back,"

Mi-sa dipped her fingers into the salve and then spread it on his skin. His back was hard and ridged with cords of muscle that slid beneath her fingers.

Mi-sa took more of the ointment and dabbed it across his back, then spread it out with her fingertips.

"That feels good," he said, making her start and draw back her fingers. "Have you finished?" he asked.

She did not answer.

"Turn around, and I will coat your back."

Mi-sa obeyed, turning around. Leaning her head to one side, she gathered all her hair and pulled it forward over her shoulder.

His hands were strong; they not only spread the ointment but also massaged her aching shoulders.

"You are sore from so much paddling," he said, working her muscles with expertise.

"Yes," she barely whispered, closing her eyes and bending her head down as he worked close to her neck and then down her spine.

"Tomorrow you will feel the soreness more strongly."

Mi-sa rolled her head to the side as he kneaded one of her shoulders.

"Lie down," he told her. "I am finished with the repellent, but perhaps I can relieve some of that aching."

She stretched out on her stomach on the grass bed and

pulled her hair to the front. He daubed more of the oily salve on her back, this time as a lubricant, and then with the power of his hands he worked each and every fiber of muscle in her back and shoulders.

She had never felt the strength of a man's hands on her this way before. "Your hands are magical," she said without opening her eyes.

Cota laughed. "It must seem so," he said. "You may be a shaman, but you were not raised doing the work of a man, especially in a canoe."

He watched her sigh and smile as he rubbed the tenseness out of the overworked muscles. "The grass is going to itch," he commented. "Hala did not give you a skin or mat?"

"No," she answered. "But I have slept on a grass bed before."

"It will stick to you," he said.

Cota got up and unfolded his deerskin blanket. "It will sleep two this way," he said, "if you do not mind leaving your feet over the edge."

Mi-sa was shocked, and he read her well. "It is only a place to sleep, to keep you off the grass and the ground. Nothing else. I am willing to share my bed with you, but the decision is yours."

"My bed is fine," she answered, sitting up, the tension quickly regaining some of its claim on her shoulders.

Cota shook his head and smiled. The woman never took his advice.

He took the food she gave him from her basket and heated it over the fire.

"Tell me about yourself—something I do not already know," he said, throwing his food scraps into the fire so that the remains would not attract bugs.

"There is nothing else to tell," she said.

"Tell me what it was like for you, growing up. How did your people feel about a girl child being the heir to the Gift?"

Mi-sa sighed. "It is a boring story."

She lay back on her grass bed and looked at the stars. "Is

it true that the same fires burn in the Kahoosa sky as in the Tegesta?" she asked.

"That is what they say. Look. Does not the Tegesta sky appear the same?"

"Yes," she answered. "I know all the stars."

"Then why do you ask? And is that not something a shaman would know?" Cota stretched out on his deerskin and also gazed at the stars.

"Because I wonder if the stars look the same to everyone. Do the fires that burn in the night sky look different to someone of the spirits? Do I see only the hearths of the Tegesta?"

"What do you think?" he asked.

"I have heard the stories of your mother and your father, Teeka and Kaho, and how the two of them brought the Kahoosa and Tegesta stars together by establishing the peace. I think it is a beautiful story."

"It is also a true story," he said. "I am the fruit of that peace. The peace is my mission."

"You carry a heavy responsibility."

"I carry the hope of all the people—the Kahoosa, the Tegesta, all men. The shamans from the time of my mother and father saw a danger to us all, even to the A-po-la-chee. I am the promise. I was born to bring peace, to unite the nations."

In a few moments Cota closed his eyes and drifted off. Mi-sa stared at the sky a little longer and then turned to her side and watched him sleep.

Finally she closed her eyes and tried to sleep. But the grass did begin to itch, and it stuck to the ointment on her body. Small insects wandered through the jungle of her bed and crawled onto her skin, as if Cota's words had made it happen. Never before had a grass bed been so difficult to sleep on.

The stars twinkled, and the moon shone down on her. Even with the sweet songs of night, Mi-sa tossed.

Cota opened his eyes, looked at her, and smoothed out the deerskin. "Come," he said.

CHAPTER
~19~

The grass bed no longer kept her awake; the deerskin was soft and comfortable. But the nearness of Cota, the warmth that radiated from his body like hot, caressing fingers, stirred her own heat. Small things kept her from sleep. She could hear the sound of his breathing so close, and that made her think she could even taste his mouth on hers. The quiet breeze in the trees sounded like his whisperings, and she ached to feel his strong hands on her.

Mi-sa stared at him as he lay on his back, his face relaxed in sleep, his obsidian eyes closed. She wondered what he would do if she reached out and touched him, woke him slowly from his sleep. She wondered if fate could be changed, destiny redesigned by a single event, by choice.

She turned on her back and looked at the stars, praying to the spirits to deliver her from these torturous thoughts. To give her sleep. To grant her peace.

She awakened to the smell of brewing tea. Cota sat at the fire, a small bowl of tea steaming in his hands.

"This will be a good day for traveling," he said, looking up at the clear sky.

Mi-sa sat up, feeling the burning in her sore muscles.

"The river widens, and the current slows. You will not work so hard today."

"I can still help paddle," she said, brushing her hair from her face.

Cota smiled. "If you feel the need," he said, handing her a ladle of tea. "I desire a fresh meal." He walked away toward the river.

Mi-sa sat and sipped the hot berry tea until Cota returned with a fish still wriggling at the end of his spear. The idea of fresh food appealed to her, and her stomach grumbled.

Cota prepared the fish and cooked it. The meat was flaky and white. She fingered through her portion, taking a small bit, checking it for bones, and then eating it.

"Your leg is healing?" he asked.

Mi-sa looked down at her shin. "I heal quickly," she said, noting the closed wounds from the alligator. "This is not even tender today," she said, touching the circular punctures. "I will find some medicine for my shin before we leave. It will cause no trouble."

"It is not safe for a woman to wander alone in strange territory."

"I will not wander far," she said, placing another tidbit in her mouth.

Cota pulled free a piece of fish and sucked it off the bone. "Only some good advice. My task is to safely escort you back to your village."

"I am obligated," she said.

"You are not indebted. The Kahoosa and the Tegesta are allies."

Mi-sa lightly ran her fingers over her bruised leg. "When we are done eating, will you help me find the medicines I need?"

Cota delayed his next bite of fish. He was pleased she had let down some of her defenses. "All you needed to do was ask."

Mi-sa regally lifted her head and took a deep breath. "I am certain the medicinal plants grow in abundance nearby. The search should not take long." Again she slipped back into her proud stubbornness. "Actually I can get along without the medicine. It is not really necessary."

"Are all the Tegesta so afraid to make a friend?"

Mi-sa's eyes shot fire at him. She rose, smoothed out her moss skirt, and adjusted her hair over her breasts. "I appreciate you helping me find my way home. But I am quite capable of taking care of myself. I do not need anyone, and I do not expect—"

He interrupted her. "I wish you would stand at the river's edge so you could see your reflection, the way your eyes flash, the way your face glows."

His taunting smile made her angry. "Just ensure my safe passage, and my people will reward you. I want nothing else from you."

Cota stood up, reached out, and touched her cheek with the backs of his fingers. "I am not the enemy." He paused a moment, then lifted her chin in his hand so that she looked at him. "And I am certain that your people would be willing to reward me. But I do not ask."

Mi-sa tried to lower her head so that she would not have to look into his eyes, but he held her there.

"Are you finished with your meal?"

Mi-sa nodded.

"Then show me where you think your medicinal plants grow."

He let go of her chin, and Mi-sa led him into the woods. A cluster of white-flowered plants grew where a shaft of sunlight penetrated the trees.

"Just the leaves," she said.

Cota helped her pluck some stems, leaving the plant in the ground so that it could provide medicine for someone else.

"How do you know these things?" he asked.

"Some are in my head. Other things my father taught me."

"How do you know about this plant?"

"I have always known some things. They say that is the

Gift passed from father to son." She looked up suddenly and smiled. "From father to daughter this time."

"Olagale did not have a shaman father. He is not from a pure line."

"I know," she said, strolling beside him back into the camp.

"Did he tell you?"

"No."

"Then how did you know?"

"I knew when he treated me."

Cota emptied the last of the tea from the small pot and walked with her to get water from the river.

"How did you know?" he asked again.

"I have seen my father heal, and I have done it also. Olagale's healing does not have the same power. I do not know how to explain this. You would have to see—to feel."

"Is Olagale not a good shaman?"

"That is not what I mean. He is a good shaman. He has had the proper training, but he does not *know* things."

Cota watched her toss the medicinal leaves into the bowl of water and thread it onto the skewer above the fire. There was much about this woman that intrigued him.

Hala had packed a small skin swatch that was just right for bandaging. After the leaves had boiled, Mi-sa put the swatch into the bowl and let it soak.

"Tell me how it was for you to become cacique," she said, wanting to know more about him before she had to let him go. When he was gone, she would be able to savor all the small shreds she knew of him.

He stirred mixed feelings inside her. At times she wanted to let all her defenses tumble down, forget her responsibilities, forget Chalosee. But always there was Cherok, and if total sacrifice would save him, she would not hesitate to deny her own pleasure. So she tried to distance herself from Cota, but now she dangerously flirted with knowing more about him than she needed to.

"I am part of the peace, the product of a Tegesta woman

and a Kahoosa man. It was said that when Kaho and Teeka had a son, he would become the cacique."

"Naska resents that."

"Yes," he answered. "He feels that he has lived in my shadow and that he will never receive the same respect from our father or from our people. He does not see that the way he conducts himself diminishes the respect people feel for him."

"I was afraid to be alone with him on this journey."

Cota watched her use a stick to remove the medicine bandage from the bowl and wave the swatch in the air to help it cool. "Ursa is his woman," he said, "though he does not say so publicly or take her as a wife."

"Were you surprised when Olagale said the spirits advised that you, and not Naska, should be my escort?"

"The spirits also know my brother."

"Naska made it clear to me what his intentions were."

"I apologize for him."

"I do not ask for an apology."

Mi-sa placed the bandage on her shin, but it slipped off her leg.

"You need another hand," he said, holding the medicine-soaked swatch in place as she tied it on with thin strips of rawhide.

"Thank you," she said as she finished.

"The sun is already climbing in the sky. We need to load the canoe."

While Cota carried some things to the dugout, she lifted his sleeping blanket. Before rolling it up, she held it close to her nose, against her cheek. She felt the unexpected sting of tears. Quickly she shook out the deerskin and spread it on the ground, then rolled it up tight and tied it closed with two rawhide strips.

"Are you ready?" he asked, walking up behind her.

"Your bed," she said, turning and handing him the deerskin roll.

He helped her into the canoe and pushed off with the pole. The dugout glided smoothly out into the river.

"We will be in Tegesta waters today," he said, plunging the pole down into the river.

"I wish I could tell you more. I had never left my village before the Big Water journey."

"I know your village is not near the others. That will help."

Cota settled into the canoe, picked up the paddle, and stroked. Mi-sa reached for hers, feeling the strain on her aching muscles.

"The current is not so strong. Rest yourself," he told her.

Mi-sa tried one stroke and then was glad he had suggested she put down the paddle. She laid it in the bottom of the canoe and watched the river in front of her. After a few moments she turned and sat facing the stern so that she could look at him.

Cota smiled and swept the paddle through the water.

She lifted her face to the sun, feeling its warmth. This early the rays were pleasant. Later in the day she would wish for shade.

As the shadows grew longer, the river widened until its banks disappeared, and the earth became covered with the thin layer of water that ran beneath the grasses. Cota paddled along the canoe trails, paths through the tall, toothed sedge, finally putting away the paddle and using the pole in the shallow water.

Mi-sa felt more confident; this was the land of her home, the land she was familiar with.

"Tegesta territory," he said.

Mi-sa looked all around. "Yes," she said, watching the tips of the saw grass swish in the light breeze. "It will rain," she remarked, seeing the gathering clouds in the west.

Cota rested the pole. He took her hand. "Stand so that you can see farther," he said.

Mi-sa surveyed the land. Though to Cota it appeared the same in all directions, she perceived the slight differences.

One of the hammocks in the distance might be a village of Tegesta.

"Will you know your village from afar?" he asked.

"I will know it before we see it."

Cota pointed to a small tree island. "I believe we should stop there and make camp. It is getting late. We will begin traveling again in the morning."

"Can we go on a little farther? There is still more daylight left."

"We could, but finding a place to camp is important. When darkness falls, there may not be a suitable place nearby."

Cota saw her face fall, her eyes glaze with disappointment, her shoulders slope.

"But we cannot be too far from my home," she said, slowly sitting in the canoe again. She dipped a hand into the water, scooped some up, and let it spill through her fingers.

"You are so anxious," he said.

Mi-sa looked at him and swallowed back her need to cry.

She was indeed magic, he thought as he worked the pole. No one else could make him go against his own good judgment, especially with such a weak plea. What kind of spell had she cast over him? he wondered as he plunged the pole into the peat and pushed, moving the dugout on through the canoe trail, away from the good campsite.

How tall he was, she thought as she watched him raise the pole so that it pricked the sky.

"Perhaps we will keep going a little while longer," he said without looking at her.

Cota poled the canoe along. Most of the way they rode silently, passing the time without conversation, only observation. To the north they passed another small island, and Cota glanced at the long shadow of his pole on the water. He could have maneuvered the canoe in the direction of the hammock, but again he looked at her and poled the canoe on. He squinted into the sun and realized how late it was.

"We must stop at the next island," Cota said. Mi-sa nodded. But as the sun began to sink, the panorama before him lacked any hammocks. Far in the distance, to the west, he spotted a dark green shadow against the horizon. He pointed the canoe in that direction, but knew that they would not reach the island before dark. Perhaps there would be enough moonlight to guide him there.

The night came on quickly, and the sky became overcast, clouds slipping across the moon, moving on the upper wind. The small hammock was no longer visible.

"What will we do?" Mi-sa asked, feeling guilty that she had insisted they go on.

"Are you hungry?" he asked, barely able to see her.

"I did not think it would be a good thing to mention."

Cota laughed and poled the canoe into a cluster of saw grass so that they did not drift. "Look through the basket while I find the repellent," he said and motioned her to move back in the canoe near him.

The rain she had predicted earlier began to sprinkle. Cota worked quickly to coat himself with the repellent and then helped Mi-sa before unrolling his sleeping blanket and wrapping the two of them in it as they sat in the canoe, the basket at their feet also protected from the rain.

Mi-sa fumbled in the basket and withdrew some berries. She snaked her hand up between them and outside the cover, putting a few of the berries in Cota's mouth.

"You think that will satisfy my hunger?" he asked.

"There is more. Bread. Meat."

"Take some for yourself," he said.

Mi-sa avoided the strips of venison, but did find other food to satisfy her.

"We should have stopped as you suggested," she said, pushing a piece of coontie into his mouth.

When he had swallowed, he said, "But this is not so bad."

Mi-sa tilted her head up to the rain as it came down a little harder. With one hand she wiped the rain across her face and cleared the hair from her eyes.

"Lie down," he said.

Mi-sa flinched.

"Lie down, woman."

Mi-sa obeyed, slipping beneath the cover and lying on the bottom of the canoe.

"Move to the bow of the canoe so that your feet touch the prow."

Mi-sa slid forward, and Cota stretched out beside her and spread his deerskin bed over the sides and end of the canoe, creating a canopy that helped keep them dry. In a moment, the skin sagged with collected water. Cota pushed up on the belly of the skin, displacing the water, careful to work the water toward their feet, away from their heads, and spill it over the sides.

A sudden brilliant streak of lightning lit up the darkness. It was followed immediately by a loud crash of thunder, and Mi-sa started.

"Are you afraid of the thunder?" he asked.

"No," she answered truthfully. "It just surprised me."

"There is a story we tell the children when they are afraid of the lightning."

"Tell me," she said, loving the sound of his voice so near to her.

Cota shifted to get more comfortable as he began. "There was a boy with no father and no mother. He played by himself and walked by himself. One day he heard a loud noise and looked up to see a snake fighting with the thunder. The snake called to the boy, 'Kill the thunder and I will tell you all the things that I know.' The boy was about to shoot his arrow when he heard a loud noise. The thunder spoke to him. 'Boy, do not listen to the snake. I, the thunder, can make you brave and strong and wise. Shoot your arrow at the snake.' The boy killed the snake, and the thunder kept its word and made the boy brave and strong and wise. He became the best hunter and the best runner in the village. When he spoke, people listened. Always when the boy told his people something, they found that what he said was so. Then there came a time when the men had to go and fight. The women were afraid the enemy would come and burn their village. The boy told them not to be afraid. He found the men and told them to go home to their women, that he would find and kill the enemy. The men watched the boy go, and they saw thunder and lightning as he walked away. The thunder and lightning came down on the enemy, and the enemy was killed. The boy never came back, and no one ever saw him again. But the wise old men know that when they hear thunder and see lightning, it is nothing to be afraid of. They are certain that they hear the boy's voice in the thunder, and they see his face in the lightning. 'The thunder helper is laughing,' they say."

Cota turned his head to look at her.

"I like the story," she said, looking into his eyes. "I will tell it to my people."

"The rain has stopped," Cota said. He pushed the water off their cover and sat up. The stars were out, and the air had cooled from the burst of rain. He shook the water off the skin and rolled it up, then put it under their heads. "This is not the softest bed."

Mi-sa did not answer. The canoe bottom was uncomfortable, but she did not care. Feeling Cota's skin against hers, feeling the gentle, slow rocking of the canoe was enough. She stared at the night sky.

"I hope you recognize something tomorrow that will lead us to your village," he said.

Mi-sa worriedly touched her lips with her finger. "I traveled the canoe trails only that one time. I am not certain that I will recognize anything until we are near. When we reach my home territory, I will know the way."

She started to sit up.

"Be still, woman. Lie next to me. You rock the canoe."

Mi-sa relaxed back into the bottom of the dugout. She stared blankly at the black sky and watched the twinkling stars.

The noise of the frogs was loud. In the distance a bull alligator bellowed. The saw grass swished. Sounds of home. She looked at Cota. He was already sleeping. She tilted her head back and watched the burning hearths against the black sky.

Suddenly she did sit up. The canoe rolled and rocked, threatening to dump them both.

"Woman—"

He did not get to finish his reprimand.

"Look!" she said anxiously, pointing to the sky.

CHAPTER
— 20 —

"What is it?" he asked, slowly sitting up, more cautious than she. "You nearly swamped us."

"Cota, do you see it? The star in the north. Look where I point. The brightest in the sky."

"I see, yes," he answered. "It is always there."

"I know. And the other stars. We must leave now!"

Cota took her by the shoulders and made her look at him. "What are you talking about? You are not making sense."

"I know the stars in the Tegesta sky. I can guide us to my village by the stars. That is why we must go on tonight, not tomorrow. I know the way."

Cota put his thumb and finger over his eyes and rubbed, pinching in toward the bridge of his nose.

"Trust me," she said.

"Woman, you have had some strange notions, and I have gone along with them, but this . . . I am not so certain. In the daylight you will recognize landmarks that will guide us. It is safer that way."

Mi-sa looked at the stars and then back at him. "No, Cota, I will not. I have not traveled like the men. The trails all look the same to me. But I know how the stars should look."

"Traveling in the dark—by the stars? I do not know. My task is to return you to your village safely."

"What is the difference if we travel by night or day?"

"We cannot see hazards at night," he answered.

"If I keep a keen lookout from the bow, we should be all right."

Cota shook his head.

"Please, Cota. This is the best way. We will arrive at my village sooner. Then you can return home. Please. If there is trouble, we will stop."

"Are you not tired?"

"Oh, I am sorry. I will take the pole," she said, reaching for it. "You did all the work today. Of course you are tired. I was thoughtless."

Mi-sa balanced on her knees as she took the pole.

"No," he said, steadying her with his hand. "This is a man's job."

"But I can do it," she argued.

"You listen to nothing I say."

"I only want to make the journey less difficult," she said, feeling her face flush with embarrassment.

"Then do as you suggested. Sit at the bow and keep watch."

Cota took the pole and stood up as Mi-sa moved to the bow of the canoe.

"You will see," she said. "This is a wise decision."

"I hope so." He did not sound convinced.

Mi-sa looked again at the stars. After a moment she pointed. "That way," she said.

As the canoe moved along, they were often swiped and scratched by long swords of saw grass. In other places the saw grass was flattened, beaten down by the storm. Some of it had begun to rise up into arching lines and shadows, hiding the trails, making the narrow canoe channels especially hard to see and follow.

Cota heard the canoe scrape a grass island, and they felt the dugout come to a sudden stop.

He pushed with the pole, attempting to reverse the canoe and move it back into the deeper trail.

"I will get out," Mi-sa said.

"Take the paddle and swat the grass with it. Drive the snakes out first," he said.

Mi-sa was no longer eager to climb out, but she had insisted that they continue on in the darkness. She slashed the paddle through the grass and slapped at the roots, then climbed out. The ground was not solid, and her feet sank into the rotting peat. She shuddered and hung on to the canoe, giving it a shove. The canoe backed off the thick sedge, and Mi-sa scrambled back into the dugout, her legs coated with particles of the stinking peat.

Later on, they had both had to get out of the canoe to move it. Mi-sa did not complain or hesitate, though she hated it, and she felt her stomach knot with fear.

As time passed, Cota questioned her. "Are you certain you know the direction?"

"I am," she insisted. "We are headed toward my village."

"It will be daylight soon."

"You do not believe me?" she asked.

"Would I have poled this canoe all night if I had no faith in you? I only ask if you still have the direction in sight."

"I wish I could explain," she said.

"Feed me," he said, abruptly changing the subject.

Mi-sa sifted through the basket again and found another tidbit. She held it out to him.

"Do you want me to stop poling?" he asked.

Mi-sa looked at him, confused.

"Feed me," he said again.

She slowly stood up and held the food close to his mouth. A guarded laugh pumped up the corners of his lips before he opened. Mi-sa felt him draw the food from her fingers.

"More," he said.

She reached down, feeling her legs wobble unsteadily as the canoe rocked. Cota reached out with one arm, holding her steady, pulling her close to him for balance.

She knew there was no wind, but the sound of air rushing in her ears blocked out the other night sounds as if she had gone deaf. She felt some kind of tingling, nearly a stinging, ripple down her arms to her fingertips and was afraid that if he let go of her, she would crumple.

The deafening pause finally ended. "You must move carefully," he said.

Mi-sa reached into the basket and retrieved another piece of fruit. Very carefully she straightened up and held it close to his mouth. Teasingly, he took small succulent bits of food from her fingers. He looked behind her, and then with one arm he moved her to his side.

Mi-sa turned, relaxing into his arm, which he had wrapped about her waist.

"There," he said. "The sun is rising."

Together they watched the change on the horizon. The blackness turned to deep blue, and then a fine, thin line of fire orange edged over the rim of the earth.

"I wish it would stay that way a little longer," she said.

"Nothing stays too long."

Mi-sa wrapped her hand around her medicine bag. She felt for the dream-catcher. "Especially not your dreams," she said.

The two of them stood watching the sunrise, Cota only occasionally moving the canoe forward.

"I have a confession to make," he said, looking into the distance.

"A confession?"

"I do not think I am as eager to find your village as you are," he said.

"You have no reason to be eager," she answered, missing his meaning.

"I have reason not to want to find it."

Mi-sa looked up at him, puzzled.

"After we reach your village, I will never see you again. I am not sure I like that."

"No," she quickly said. "Do not say that."

She was flustered and surprised. If he confessed that he

had feelings for her, that would make the parting even more difficult. She had finally accepted that she would never have him, and now he was going to complicate the situation.

"Mi-sa," he said, lifting her face with a gentle nudge of his hand.

Was this the first time she had heard him say her name? How wonderfully it flowed from his tongue.

"I only want to say I will miss you."

"And I will miss you," she returned. "You have been kind."

"Your people will be glad to have you home."

"I will be happy to be with them again. Soon the Tegesta warriors will rescue my brother and bring him home."

"Rescuing him drives you, does it not?" Cota asked.

"Cherok is more than my brother. We have a special connection."

"He is fortunate."

"No," she corrected him, "I am the fortunate one."

Cota let his arm slip from her as he plunged the pole down into the peat and shoved.

Mi-sa sat down as the last of the stars disappeared with the light of day. She was familiar with her surroundings. She could point to nothing specific, but she sensed she was right. They were close to her village. The stars had led her home. She was sure of it.

As the morning sun crept up in the sky, Mi-sa spotted something in the distance.

"There," she said, pointing a steady finger at a patch of green in the distance. "Do you see that hammock? That is my village!"

"How can you be sure?"

"I know that is it. I know it."

"Like the medicines you know in your head?" he asked.

"Yes, like that," she said, still looking at the green splotch. Then she turned to him, her eyes gleaming. "Oh, Cota, thank you. Thank you!"

He heard the excitement in her voice, and then the little cracking that revealed the depth of her gratefulness.

Mi-sa knelt in the canoe and began her prayers. To her it seemed that she had been away not only from her home but also from her spirits. They were more forceful here, closer to her soul, and she felt stronger here, more confident. This was her realm, the land and air she knew in her bones.

Cota watched, not understanding all that she said. He did recognize the Tegesta words, but she also spoke the magic tongue, the language of the spirits. Suddenly he felt a strange tingling, first across his scalp, then down his arms. He held the pole still, engaged by the spillover of power that was coming from her.

Cota had seen Olagale do many things, been near him when the holy man said prayers, when he talked to the spirits, but Cota had never experienced this surge of energy, this powerfully alive feeling that surrounded Mi-sa. He felt a flicker of gut fear that rapidly became a feeling of total awe.

When she finished, she slumped in the bottom of the dug-out, exhausted from the intensity of her prayers.

"Mi-sa," he called softly, but she did not respond. Cota laid the pole inside the canoe and knelt next to her. Mi-sa's chin rested on her chest, and her hair hid her face. Lightly he touched her back, moving lingering strands of hair aside so that he could feel her skin.

He stayed there with his hand touching her back, waiting for her to recover. Finally she lifted her head and looked at him. She frantically searched his eyes. "Did I frighten you?" she asked.

He saw the panic in her eyes and gently touched her cheek. "No, Mi-sa."

She let her head drop in relief.

"I am in awe of your power. I know now what you meant when you talked of Olagale." He waited a moment and then dared to ask, "Did your power frighten people when you were a child? Did they misunderstand?"

Mi-sa looked back at him, this time her eyes filled with

painful memories of long ago. She swallowed, unable to speak.

"I am sorry," he said, taking up the pole. "I did not mean to ask you about such personal matters."

"It is all right," she said. "My people found it difficult to believe that a girl child carried on the Gift."

"Your life has not been easy," he said, rising and pushing the pole down into the shallow water.

"No one's life is easy. Everyone struggles in his own way."

Cota looked at the village they were approaching. "We are almost there. Your people will be glad to have you home."

For the first time she had a terrible thought. "Wait, Cota," she said, grasping the pole to hold it still.

"Wait?"

Mi-sa rose and stared at the small hammock. What if the People were not happy to have her return? What if they were angry? What if they thought she had failed them? She had not given attention to the signs, and surely they knew that.

Her heart ached for Cherok. It did not matter what they thought of her. She had to tell them about her brother and Talasee. Then, when all of the warriors returned, they would go and rescue both of them.

Mi-sa let go of the pole and stared hard into the distance, as if seeking a sign. "Never mind," she said softly. "Take me to my village."

Dragonflies, too many to count, darted in the air, their glistening iridescent wings fluttering in the light. Mi-sa was sure she could hear their wings beating. Her ears also picked up the sound of the small wakes that trailed the tall wading birds, great blue herons and spoonbills that stalked in the shallows and turned to look at the canoe that had spoiled their surprise.

Mi-sa sniffed the air to smell the smoke of the cook fires. Too far yet, she thought. Above the hammock she searched the sky for small spirals of smoke, but the sky was clear, a bright, blinding blue. As they got closer, she felt her stomach tighten.

Cota circled the island, looking for the place the Tegesta kept their dugouts. "I see no canoes," Cota said.

"There should not be many. Only the small ones. We took the large ones on the Big Water journey."

"I see no small ones," he said. "Maybe we'll see them as we get closer."

Cota poled the canoe. A large live oak came into sight, twisted and fallen, stretching out into the water.

"Closer," she said, feeling the ball of fear roil deep inside her. The place where the men of her village had once begun great adventures and returned in their canoes was now a tangle of broken branches and splintered trees. She closed her eyes and remembered her mother standing there, growing smaller as they departed on the Big Water journey. She looked at the sky, as if expecting to see the white birds or the vulture again. "Put ashore here," she said.

Cota beached the canoe, and Mi-sa stepped out of it. She stood on the edge of the hammock, her back to Cota as he dragged the dugout farther up onto the land.

He came around her and saw the dazed, faraway look on her face. "Let me go ahead. You wait here."

Mi-sa shook her head. She opened her mouth to speak, but could not. She walked away from the water, toward the hub of the village. Cota followed.

The storm had hit the hammock hard. The trees should have been thick and lush. Instead, many were stripped or lay fallen and dying. A gust of summer breeze swirled the dead leaves and then let them settle. Lizards and roaches skittered through all the debris, rattling the brittle leaves, matching Mi-sa's own crunching footsteps.

She stepped over the trunk of a downed tree; a long strip of its bark had been torn away where a branch had been ripped off. She stopped on the other side and stared ahead.

The shelter that had stood over the central hearth was now a scattered clutter of fallen wood and thatch. The platforms were gone with little evidence that they had ever stood.

Mi-sa walked into what had been her home, looking at nothing but devastation.

"Miakka," she called, even though she knew her mother would not answer. She stood paralyzed in the center of the Council plaza, surveying the destruction.

Cota stood back. He did not want to intrude, but she stood so still and looked so defeated. Finally he called to her.

Slowly she turned to look in all directions, then trotted along the line where the platforms had stood, to the place where her mother's shelter should have been.

The ground was strewn with fragments of platforms, pottery shards, and broken tools. A fine piece of white deerskin waved in the air, caught on the broken end of a jagged branch. Mi-sa touched it as she passed, pausing only long enough to feel how it had stiffened from the rain.

Everything was so quiet. She heard only silence where there should have been sounds of children playing, of men and women doing their daily tasks—healthy, living sounds. But the hammock was still.

She fell to her knees by a small black scarred and burned patch of earth, the only remains of her mother's fire.

Mi-sa dug her hands through the ashy soil and came up with handfuls, which she raised in front of her. She angrily clutched the earth and reeled back on her heels.

"No!" she sobbed. "No!"

Cota squatted beside her.

"Everything is gone. Everything!" she screamed, loosening her white knuckles and throwing the dirt back on the ground. She bent at the waist, slamming her hands into the empty hearth and pounding the ground with her small fists.

Cota touched her back, and she reared up. Her face was streaked with tears that painted frail, clear lines through the dirt on her face.

"It is all destroyed," she cried. "My mother. My people."

Cota reached around her and held her head to his chest as she wept. There was nothing he could say. Her village had been totally destroyed. He could see that the water had swept over the small hammock, taking away with it whatever the wind had not swept away. He was thankful that there were no bodies that she could see.

He held her against him, feeling her shake and tremble, feeling her chest heave as she cried. Finally she grew quiet, left with the small uncontrollable gasps that resulted from crying so hard.

Mi-sa pulled away from him and looked up. She felt her throat pinch with pain as she fought to hold back more tears. "I must decide what to do. I—"

"Not here. There is nothing to do here. I am taking you back."

Mi-sa held her head in her hands. "There are things I should do," she mumbled, wiping her dirty hand over her face in an attempt to clear her thoughts. But her mind was scrambled. She could not think.

Cota rose and took her hand to help her up, but her knees were weak and wobbly, and she appeared confused.

She felt his arms beneath her knees and behind her shoulders as he lifted her. Her head lolled toward him and rested against his chest. The thudding of his heart was like the drums, she thought, drifting back, hearing the drumbeats as the people danced around the central hearth. Her mother was there. Atula, Cherok, and Talasee.

"There is nothing you can do here, woman."

Cota carried her to the canoe and gently sat her inside. He looked at her as he shoved the dugout into the water. Her eyes were glazed and dull. Her face was streaked with dirt and channels where her tears had flowed. Her shoulders sloped down, and her hands lay open and lifeless in her lap.

Cota poled the canoe eastward, following the shallow trails.

Mi-sa's body sat still in the canoe with Cota, but her mind did not. It had found sanctuary. She walked next to Cherok. The day was clear and bright with a smack of cool air. Miakka waved at them to join her at her fire.

Cota did not like the way Mi-sa looked. There was no fire

in her. The sparkle and fortitude were gone. He called her name, but she did not respond. He shipped the pole and sat in front of her. "Where are you, woman?" he asked, taking her face in his hands.

Mi-sa looked past him with spiritless eyes.

Cota scooped up some water and rinsed her face with it, turning the dirt to a thin mud. He looked in one of the baskets and found another swatch of deerskin, like the medicine bandage she had used. He wiped her face with it, then repeated the cleansing until he had removed all the soil.

"Do you hear me, Mi-sa?" he asked.

She stared blankly.

Cota pulled her into his lap. His arms overlapped hers as they went around her. He brushed her forehead with his hand, stroking back her hair. "Stay with me, Mi-sa," he whispered.

CHAPTER
⟡ 21 ⟡

Cota sat holding her as the day grew longer, afraid that if he let go she would be lost. The canoe drifted slowly with the great shallow river, easing over the rock and peat, through the bristle of the saw grass. The sunlight poured through the dazzling blue, glinting off the water.

He finally released her, his body awash with sweat generated by the heat of her body against his. As he stood, he felt the breeze against his skin.

"Tomorrow we will reach the river," he said, pushing down on the pole.

Near twilight Cota spotted a very small hammock. He banked the canoe and got out.

"Let me help you," he said to her.

Cota took her limp hand out of her lap and lifted it. "Stand, Mi-sa," he said, gently tugging.

She turned and faced him, but her expression was empty and distant.

"That is right," he said, encouraging her.

He led her up on dry ground. "We will camp here for the night," he said, taking supplies from the canoe. "Come with me." He trampled some of the small brush and began to clear an area. She did not move to help, only stared off into the deeper woods.

Cota gathered some wood and checked the coal in the pouch. He had ignored it too long, and it had gone out. "No fire tonight." It did not worry him. "Sit here," he directed, taking her by the arm and seating her in a clean spot before he wandered off.

In a few moments Cota returned with fresh berries. "A little extra," he said, laying them next to her as he walked to the canoe and retrieved a basket. "We have not eaten all day," he said, insisting on carrying on a conversation, hoping that she was hearing him.

"Are you hungry?" he asked.

Mi-sa did not answer.

"Of course you are." He fumbled through the basket, taking out coontie and dried fish, offering it to her. He held it out. "Take it."

Mi-sa sat still.

"It is for you," he said, placing the food on her lap. He took out some dried meat for himself. He gripped the end of the strip of venison with his teeth and cut up through it with his knife.

As darkness fell, Cota finally took the food from her lap and placed it back in the basket. "At least a berry," he said, pushing one between her lips until she opened her mouth.

He covered her with the repellent and coated himself as well. He spread out his deerskin and patted it. "Sleep here," he told her, smoothing it out. He took her hands and led her onto the sleeping skin, then eased her down on her back.

As the stars broke through the black sky, he lay next to her. Her eyes were already closed. She had escaped into sleep. He said a prayer to the spirits. Surely they saw one of their own in despair. Certainly they would come to her.

Mi-sa gasped for air in her sleep. In her dream she was drowning, being covered with water that was rising so quickly and forcefully that she could not swim. The fierce current pushed her on, washing her across the hammock. Suddenly she smashed into a tree. She reached for it, hugging it, sucking in a great breath. Twigs and leaves and debris flew through the air, some slapping against her, stinging, cutting, beating her limbs. She scrambled to reach a higher branch, pulling up on it, dragging her body higher, escaping the savage water.

Gradually she climbed above the raging water, feeling the ferocious wind pound against the tree. She huddled in the branches, clutching tightly. Something below her caught her attention. She looked down, seeing the water rush over the land, feeling the sting of the driving rain, the slap of the fierce wind. Then below her, a familiar form—a body. As it passed beneath her, the water rolled it over. Mi-sa screamed when she saw the face of her mother.

Cota sat up, grabbed her, and held her against him. "Shh," he whispered.

Mi-sa trembled in his arms as she opened her eyes.

"It was a dream," Cota said, stroking her cheek, then touching his lips to her forehead. "Just a dream."

Mi-sa wrapped her arms around him. "No, not just a dream." Dreams were different for people of the spirits. They carried the truth. "Hold me," she begged, burying her face in the crook of his neck.

Cota pulled her even closer, wishing that he could absorb her, give her all his strength, take away her pain.

Mi-sa pulled away, leaning her head back so that she could look into his eyes. Her hands fluttered up to hold his face. Cota was her only tether to the earth. Her people were gone, her village destroyed. There was no one to save her brother. She had only this man who held her, comforted her, kept her from dying of grief and guilt. Only Cota. She stared hard at him, locking her gaze to his, knowing how everything had changed. Then her lips parted as she saw him lean toward her.

The touch of his mouth on hers was gentle and quick, and he kept his eyes open. Then he moved his face away, but she put her hand behind his head and urged him to kiss her. His mouth was hungry—tasting, sampling hers, afraid to linger too long, but quickly coming back to sip the flavor of her lips again and again.

Cota tasted salt and drew back to look at her. Tears streamed down her face and slid into the corners of her mouth. He wiped them away with his thumb, then reached up through her hair, feeling the thickness of it as it ran through his fingers. Tenderly he led her mouth back to his. He did not probe or insist, but with the gentlest of touches on the crest of her shoulder, down the arc of her neck, over the curve of her waist, he brought her alive in a way she had only barely known in her visions of him.

He felt the vibration of her soft whimper as he cradled her, easing her down onto the sleeping skin.

Nothing in her life had ever been like this. She had never abandoned all thought, all reason. Never had anything compelled her so. This was some wonderful place to be, to leave behind all caution, all defenses, to surrender the past and the future for the moment. Nothing else mattered.

Cota lowered himself on her, feeling her skin touch his, from the modest swell of her breasts down the flat plane of her belly and smooth thighs all the way to her ankles. His hard body could feel the complement of her feminine shape, the arch of her hips, the curve of her waist.

"I want to touch all of you," he whispered, lifting himself up, removing his breechclout, then loosening and discarding her moss skirt. The task was easy, and when he had finished, he stopped to look at her. Mi-sa lay still, except for her chest, which heavily rose and fell.

Suddenly he felt a sting of guilt. "Mi-sa," he murmured, his voice hoarse with desire, "I am sorry. You are grieving."

She raised her arms up to him. "Lie with me," she whispered.

Cota's heart beat strongly. "You are beautiful, Mi-sa," he said, letting his eyes wander where his fingertips trailed. His big, powerful palm gently enfolded her smaller hand. He twined his fingers with hers and lowered her hand to kiss her wrist. His tongue damply swept along the inside of her arm before he nuzzled her breast. Cota moved over her and heard her soft murmur as he pressed his body against her.

The raw nakedness of him brought her new pleasure, and she wished that she could linger there forever, beneath him, so close that she was certain she had melted into him.

"I do not want to hurt you," he said softly in her ear. "You have had enough pain."

Mi-sa reached for him, her mouth open and starved for his return.

He took both of her hands and pinned them above her head so that every peak of her body could be engaged by his and he could search ravenously for every crevice. Cota kissed her neck, savoring the sweet scent of her hair, and then moved on to the delicate cradle of her throat, the hot fragrance of her skin, the soft fleshiness of those many rounded forms that made her a woman, feasting on her until finally he had to release her hands. Her whole body was embraced by his.

Mi-sa raked her fingers through the back of his hair. Her naive, frantic clutching let him know she had never been with a man before, and so he guided her, showing her how and where to touch him. And slowly he explored her, finding those secret places that brought her the greatest ecstasy.

Through his own passion, Cota was careful to watch her face, see when she mindlessly bit her bottom lip, feel when she trembled, hear when her breathing came in desperate pants. And when she boldly needed him, he filled her, deeply, completely, until he felt her quake beneath him.

Mi-sa felt him stiffen, then the weight of him fall against her, felt the heavy beating of his heart, heard him take a deep satisfied breath as she did. What wonder this man had brought to her.

Both of them lay spent and still. The sound of the crickets and frogs returned. Only then did she realize they had been muffled by the sounds of her own wanting, the sounds of her soft cries and Cota's heavy breathing and whispering.

He lifted some of his weight from her and started to move aside. "No," she whispered, holding him fast to her. "Do not leave me yet."

He sank back into her, relishing the cushion of her soft body.

"Am I not heavy upon you?" he asked, his voice still ragged.

Mi-sa stroked the back of his hair and closed her eyes. "No," she answered lowly.

Soon she knew Cota had drifted off to sleep, but she was not anxious. She cherished this secret world, protected by him. For a little while longer she did not want to think of anything else—or dream. She only wanted to be a woman.

In the early light Cota stirred, realizing that she lay flush against him. Vaguely he recalled waking in the night and withdrawing from her, and hearing her little gasp, as if her breath had caught somewhere inside her. She had softly moaned and moved closer to him, but without seeming to wake. He had pulled her even closer and felt her snuggle against him, curling and relaxing to fill every curve of his body. How contentedly he had slept.

Mi-sa turned, feeling the cool morning air on her back. Slowly she opened her eyes. He was looking at her, his mouth turned up in a satisfied smile.

He felt the sheath of morning dew on her supple skin as his fingers glided down the shallow valley of her spine.

"I am afraid to move," he said, taking his hand from her back and brushing it over her lips.

"Why?" she whispered.

"I will find that it is not true," he said. "Or you may say you have regrets."

"I have many things I regret in my life. Many things I wish I could do over. But last night . . ." She found the words hard to say. "That is not something I will regret."

He touched his mouth to her forehead and held it there while he thought.

"Cota," she said softly, "I wonder how I can go on without you." She held her breath as he nestled his face in her hair. "My life has been taken from me. Ripped away. I am left empty."

"No, Mi-sa," he said, feathering light kisses on her shoulder. "I am here. I will fill the emptiness."

She rolled onto her back. "It is not so simple."

Cota slipped his arm under her neck and pulled her head onto his shoulder.

"What should I do?" she asked him.

"Go back with me."

"Can we forget what has happened?"

Cota raised himself up so that he could see her face. "No, Mi-sa. I cannot forget. This was destined by the spirits. I sensed it the moment I saw Naska bring you into the village. Do you not feel it?"

"Oh, Cota," she said, nearly laughing, nearly crying, "you have been a part of me for so long."

"Then it is simple," he said, smiling and stroking her cheek.

"Chalosee," Mi-sa said in a whisper.

Cota fell back onto the sleeping skin and stared at the great towering white clouds.

"She loves you. And you have made her think you love her." A frightening thought made Mi-sa pause. Perhaps he did. She sat up and wrapped her arms around her knees, resting her chin atop them. "I cannot go back with you. You will have to take me to a Tegesta village somewhere and leave me there."

Cota sat up and put his hands on the backs of her shoulders. "I am taking you home with me. You will be my woman. No Tegesta village will accept a woman who is simply dumped there. They will not know you. Who will provide for you? No, you are going with me."

"How can you say I will be your woman? Your heart belongs to Chalosee." She still would not look at him. "A shaman's dreams bring messages and visions—truths. What I saw in my dream last night was so painful. I needed someone to hold me. To love me. You are a kind and gentle man. When we get back to the Kahoosa village, things will be different."

Cota turned Mi-sa to face him. "Look into my eyes, woman. You are in my heart. I have tried to keep you out, to keep things as I thought they should be. Tried to think only with my head. Do you not see? You, the one of the spirits. This is why the spirits directed that I should escort you home! It is meant to be."

Yes, she knew what he said was true. It was destined. The spirits had shown him to her for so long. And how she had yearned for him.

Cota pulled her back on the skin with him, holding her head on his shoulder.

"What will you say?" she asked. "How can we begin something good if we are causing Chalosee so much pain?"

"I will tell her the truth."

Mi-sa put her lips to Cota's chest and whispered, "Her mother was afraid that I would steal you away. I did not mean to. There was no malice in my heart."

"Nor mine," he said as he felt himself quiver inside at the touch of her lips on his bare skin, the pressure of her small body against his. He knew that he would not be able to let her go, to take his hands, his mouth, his spirit, from her. He would succumb to the irresistible need to be a part of her again. He lifted her face to his. "I cannot speak now," he said.

Mi-sa kissed his throat and welcomed him.

Mi-sa watched Cota use the pole, his arms rising, then plunging. She watched the familiar shallow river grow deeper and change character as he put distance between her and her home. As the morning wore on, she began to unravel all the confusion.

"Mi-sa," he called once, noting what he hoped was only her deep concentration.

"What is it?" she asked, startled by the break in the silence.

"Are you all right?"

"I have many things to think about. Many decisions to make."

"Can I help?" he asked.

"You have given me strength. That is enough."

"Perhaps I can talk things out with you. That is what the men do in Council to come to important decisions."

"No," she said, leaning back and looking at him, relieved by the interruption. "Let me hear the sound of your voice. Tell me how it was for you growing up. I want to know all about you."

"Why do you not tell me more about yourself? You are the one with the mystery."

"Because I want to learn about you. Please," she said.

Cota lifted the pole. "I have told you about the union of the two nations with my birth. That is why I believe I understand the gravity of the decisions you must make. You have obligations, commitments, born in you. Your life is dedicated to your people, to your purpose. I know what that is."

"Perhaps you do," she agreed.

"It is my mission to keep the peace alive. From my mother's belly and my father's loins, I was created for this purpose. I am the seal."

"Was it a heavy responsibility when you were a boy? Was it a burden?"

"My mother sang me songs of great leaders who believed in peace. My father sat many days with me, teaching me the ways of a cacique, the ways of diplomacy, and the ways of commanding, telling me legends. And Olagale told me about the visions. My charge was always a natural part of me, and I understood it. It was never an encumbrance."

"Many believed in you."

"Yes," he answered.

How different that was from the way she had come to her

responsibility as shaman. If it had not been for Miakka and Cherok, no one would have stood by her.

Suddenly a terrible, painful thought bolted up through this momentary diversion. Cherok. The Kahoosa would have to help her get her brother. Immediately she looked up at Cota, but then just as quickly she looked away. Had she not just heard all that he said about being a peacekeeper? She could never ask him to go after Cherok. She could never ask him to go to war for any reason. A sick feeling welled up inside her.

Cota laid the pole in the canoe, sat down, and took up the paddle, not seeing how her face had drained of color and how she had wrapped her arms around her middle as if she felt some horrible pain.

CHAPTER
— 22 —

She could smell the fires, the smoking meat, the brewing teas as they approached the sprawling Kahoosa village, even though she could not yet see it. The rich, thick foliage along the river hung in slow-swaying curtains over the water.

"This is going to be difficult," Mi-sa said.

Cota pulled the paddle through the water. "We will stand together. Who is to deny the will of the spirits?"

"That will not mean anything to Chalosee. The pain in her heart will not allow her to hear that you have left her because the spirits have willed you to do so."

Cota laid the paddle in the boat. "You sound as if you are the one who has doubts."

Mi-sa shifted, running her hand through her hair, drawing it back from her face. "The spirits are not finished." She paused a moment and then said, "I understand the pain that Chalosee is about to feel. I do not like causing someone else pain. I do not believe that the spirits would want to hurt her."

"The spirits speak in strange ways."

"They test me. They always have. I fear that I have made a wrong turn."

Cota reached for her and put his hands on her shoulders, looking deep into her eyes. "We only follow the path the spirits show us. Can you not see how much trouble it was for them to bring us together? This is all part of a great plan. Greater than man can understand."

Mi-sa smiled faintly. "Cota, you untangle such snarled thoughts. I wish you had been beside me all my life. You and Cherok."

Cota sat back and took the paddle again. "You are ready now?"

Mi-sa drew in a big breath and let it out in a sigh. "Yes." It was difficult to look away from him. He gave her strength.

Cota watched her and understood her apprehension. "I will tell Chalosee. But not harshly. Gently."

Mi-sa leaned to the side, craning her neck to see if she could sight anything around the bend. The current carried them swiftly, and the water whirled them along. Cota had to react quickly to maneuver the canoe safely along the course.

"I am glad we travel with the current," she said, turning to look at him. "Paddling is hard work."

The corners of Cota's mouth curled upward, and a grin spread across his face all the way into his eyes.

While he looked at her, he was stunned to see the expression on her face change, her eyes grow bright but distant. Then Mi-sa stood up in the canoe.

"Sit," he said, afraid that she would tumble out. He was not sure, but he thought he heard voices—singing, chanting voices. Cota withdrew the paddle from the water and silently laid it across his lap. An unseen cloak of eeriness drifted over the boat and settled around it. The air became heavy, and he felt that he could reach out and grab a handful of it. He heard a crackling sound, like green wood on a fire, spitting and sparking, and out of the corner of his eye he thought he saw lightning.

The current slowed, but with an unnatural force it captured the tiny boat, turning the bow north, twirling the lone dugout, spinning it. The water coiled into a whirlpool; the canoe caught in the swirl.

Mi-sa's eyelids fluttered, and a charge of energy flowed

through her. A vision was coming—a strong vision—and all the auras and sensations that preceded it were acutely intense. Her spirit eye pierced the thick white mist that guarded the other dimension, the world of shamans, and Mi-sa could hear the air rushing past her like the wind blowing hard in her ears. The fog cleared, and she hung above the earth, hovering there—an invisible visiting spirit.

A-po-la-chee! A village of A-po-la-chee. Their smell was everywhere, and the air was filled with the sound of their voices. A group of men sat in a circle. A young man hunkered low in the center of them all. He was naked and appeared uncertain, turning to face each man who spoke.

An old man with thin spidery strings of silver hair that hung down past his shoulders was speaking. "Yes, I remember my first war party." He pointed a gnarled finger at the young man, veins bulging like ropes beneath the sheer skin on the back of his hand. "It was the time in my life when I was most afraid. You will be afraid, boy," he said and chuckled. Then his face contorted into a serious expression. He leaned toward the boy and squinted, causing layers of skin to sag down over his eyes. His mouth twisted, and his voice was low and breathy. "But you must never let the enemy see your fear. And if you do not show fear, then it is not really there."

Most of the other men laughed softly, but the old man's wisdom went straight to their hearts.

"You have never known such fear," another of the elders said to the young man. "It is important that you meet it before you meet the enemy."

The boy's brown face blanched.

"Prepare yourself, boy," the old silver-haired man said, tilting back with aged confidence.

A man whose hair was black and slicked back with grease got to one knee. His necklaces of beads and shells clinked as he moved. He reached inside a bowl that sat in front of him and pulled out a large chunk of dark red raw meat. "Your first true kill. Not a lizard or a bird. Not a rabbit. A worthy prey. It takes a strong arm and a sure eye. A step on the trail to manhood. The heart of your deer."

The man held it out to the boy who reluctantly took the deer heart in his hand.

The men grew silent and waited.

The boy looked at the eyes of all the men who sat around him. He could hear their voices echoing the old man's command: "Prepare yourself."

The boy wrapped his hand around the heart. His stained fingers dripped with blood. He bit into the meat and tore off a hunk, which he chewed.

The men cheered, and the boy wiped the bloody heart across his chest.

"This is the sacred path to manhood. This is how a boy begins to prepare himself for war and to face his greatest fears," the oldest man said.

The others mumbled in agreement.

The boy was smiling; his mouth and lips, even his nose and chin, were red.

The silver-haired man rose unsteadily, and Mi-sa decided he was their cacique. "You must be brave in war. You must not yield to fear or fatigue or pain. There must not be anything the enemy can frighten you with. It is noble to die in battle while your hair is black, your teeth are sound, and your body is strong. Tomorrow we will see if you can endure pain."

The boy's big smile faded as a warrior pushed a prisoner into the center of the circle. The captive was looking down at the ground. His hair was filthy and matted, and his hands were bound behind him with rawhide that had cut through the tender skin of his wrists. Dried blood crusted the restraints.

The warrior grabbed the man's hair and yanked his head back. It was Cherok!

"See how this Tegesta man resists pain. We want you to see what the enemy can do," the old man told the boy.

The warrior released Cherok's hair, and his head slumped to his chest. He kicked Cherok behind the knees, causing him to fall to the ground. The warrior withdrew his knife from its sheath, cut the bindings, and lifted Cherok's arm. Beginning at the elbow, along the inside of the upper arm, and up to the armpit, the warrior sliced away a narrow strip of skin. Cherok's head jerked back and then forward again. His body grew rigid and shook with the pain, but he did not cry out.

The boy's pale lips showed through the blood that was drying on them.

The cacique stood and walked over to Cherok, facing the boy. The old man dipped his finger in Cherok's blood and tasted it, then told the boy, "Tomorrow you will cut a warrior's gashes in your legs, just as we do before we go to war. Show the spirits your faith and thanksgiving. Show them you have no fear, and the enemy will not find it in you either."

The warrior pulled Cherok to his feet. He was wobbly and disoriented, his eyes glazed, his jaw slack. But then, even as the warrior led him away, Cherok stopped, lifted his head, and looked about.

Mi-sa heard his voice coming from inside him. He knew she was near, sensed it in that special way they had. He called to her to stay away, to be careful.

"No, Cherok," she said. "I am coming for you. Ask the spirits for strength. Be brave, my brother."

Cherok's head dropped as the warrior prodded him on with a stick to his back. Mi-sa saw him join Talasee, who was tied to a post. An old woman stood by, ladling out some water for Talasee.

The warrior called out to her. "Prepare something for this one's arm. He must not become too weak to work."

The old woman nodded, and suddenly the images faded, and the sound of the wind returned with the white mist, and then Mi-sa was back in the canoe.

She clutched at her stomach, fell to her knees, hung her head over the side of the canoe, and retched. She was sick with grief, sick with guilt, sick with worry.

Cota came up behind her, swept the hair from her face, and

supported her, lifting a handful of river water to rinse her mouth. "What was it, Mi-sa?"

She knew she could not tell Cota. She could never force him to make a choice between his whole life's mission and her desperate need to save Cherok. She could not let him know the depth of her pain. Would the spirits never give her peace?

"He returns!" Pa-hay-tee's voice rang out through the village. He was running as fast as he could, jumping every small obstruction, his feet springing as if they were carried by wings. He had been the first to notice the approaching canoe.

Pa-hay-tee had watched every day, often scampering off to the river's edge, squatting on the bank, and peering west. Today his efforts were rewarded. Cota was returning. The youth's sharp eyes spotted the canoe long before any of the elders could see it. Pa-hay-tee was the only one who kept a daily watch—except for Chalosee. He had seen her frequenting the river, finding tasks to do there, and taking more time than was needed. Her eyes often drifted west, as his did, searching for the returning cacique.

The boy wondered if Cota had used the weapon he made for him. He hoped so. It would make him very proud, and would not all the men think he was a fine boy?

Kaho was sitting with Olagale when he heard Pa-hay-tee's shouting. A look of relief passed over his face.

"Your first son returns safely," Olagale said. "The cacique is home."

"I am thankful," Kaho said.

Olagale rose and stretched his legs, shaking out the stiffness. "We must ask right away if he saw any signs of the A-po-la-chee."

"Yes," Kaho agreed, standing next to the shaman. "Come, let us go and greet him."

Naska also heard the news that buzzed about the village, but he was not so anxious to hurry to the river. He would take his time and first have a little fun.

"Chalosee," he called out as he saw her. "Come."

Chalosee stopped and turned toward Naska who propped himself against a tree in the cool of the shade. "Naska," she answered respectfully, nodding her head in a polite greeting, anxious to leave.

"I asked you to come," he said.

"I hurry to meet Cota. Have you not heard?" She knew that he had, but hoped her question would make him leave her in peace.

"Come," he said sternly.

Chalosee knew that it would be disrespectful for a woman to ignore a man's request, especially the request of a man of nobility.

"What is it?" she asked.

Naska raised one eyebrow to a furious arch, and from his mouth slowly withdrew the piece of grass on which he had been chewing. He took his weight from the tree, ending his arrogant slouch with an angry stance.

"I will miss his arrival, Naska," Chalosee said.

"Do you defy me?" His voice was edged with irritation.

Chalosee bowed her head with respect. "Please, Naska," she said softly as she obeyed, moving toward him, taking small, measured steps. He had not bothered her all the time Cota was gone. Now Naska would keep her from meeting Cota at the river upon his return. Chalosee balled her small hands into fists and clenched her teeth.

"What have you done for a man while my brother has been gone?" he asked, running a finger down her cheek to her throat.

Chalosee kept her head down, looking at the ground.

"What kind of dreams did you have? Were the dreams better than the real thing?"

Chalosee felt a shiver of disgust as he brushed his hand over her chest, teasingly close to her breasts. "May I leave now?"

Naska threw his head back and laughed. "Be gone."

Chalosee turned, expecting him to reach out and stop her,

but he didn't. She trotted through the village. Most of the people had already moved on to the bank of the river to welcome their cacique. The crowd and the brush kept her from being able to see. There was such a commotion—people laughing, talking—she could not tell if Cota was still on the river or if he had already grounded his canoe.

"Please," she said, pushing her way past someone. She spotted Hala in front of her. "Mother," she called, standing on her toes and waving her hand above her head. The effort to get Hala's attention was drowned by all the bustle.

Chalosee searched the foreground but still could not see. Then she looked behind her. A cypress stood tall; its limbs began close to the ground and formed a perfect ladder. Quickly she scurried up the tree, high enough to see over the heads of the crowd. Suddenly she stopped, startled. She climbed another two branches just to be sure.

Cota walked through the crowd, accepting the greetings of his people. A man reached out and touched Cota's upper arm, congratulating him on a safe journey. But many of the faces of the people were not fixed on their cacique. They watched behind him as the Tegesta woman again came into their village. There was much whispering and mumbling as she passed. Kaho joined her, easing the awkwardness of her passage.

"Just smile and nod," he whispered to her. "Cota will give them an explanation, and their curiosity will be satisfied."

Mi-sa smiled gratefully at him.

They passed the cypress. Chalosee had climbed higher and was hiding in the branches.

In the center of the village, Cota stopped, and the people spread out in a circle around him. Kaho and Mi-sa stood in the inner part of the circle. Cota waited for the crowd to quiet before he spoke.

Mi-sa felt the eyes of the crowd upon her, but something from behind pulled her attention. Discreetly she turned and looked at the cypress. She saw nothing unusual there, just a tall cypress. Still, she shivered.

Chalosee climbed down from the tree and walked into the back of the crowd. She waited to hear Cota, a scared, sick feeling in her stomach. Naska came and stood next to her. He let her know that he was staring at her, watching for her reactions.

Chalosee edged around the back of the circle, moving away, but Naska followed. Finally she stood her ground and ignored him.

"You should thank me," he said to her.

Chalosee looked at him with a puzzled expression.

"If I had not detained you, you would have been right there on the bank when he arrived. I have spared you humiliation."

"She does not walk beside him. Do you not see?"

Naska's lips turned up into a patronizing smile. "He has not asked for you yet, has he?"

Chalosee quickly looked away from him as Cota began to speak.

"The journey was safe. I have seen no signs of A-po-la-chee." A sigh of relief echoed through the Kahoosa. "I have brought back the Tegesta woman called Mi-sa. We found her village, but the storm had destroyed it. There is nothing left. This village will become her home, and we will welcome her."

Olagale stepped forward. "If I may," he began, asking for Cota's approval.

"We will profit from the words of Olagale," Cota said.

"Mi-sa is a Tegesta shaman. Difficult as that is for us to understand, we will all make the effort. The ways of the spirits should not be questioned. This woman must be treated with the respect you give a man of the spirits."

There was silence, then whispering. Some nodded in agreement, and others expressed their doubt in their faces.

Cota asked the men, "Who will help to build her shelter?"

Naska quickly stepped forward, staring squarely at his brother. "I will," he said.

Others followed, offering to help.

Kaho entered the center of the circle. "This is good. In another day this woman will have a shelter."

"But who will provide for her?" Naska asked.

Cota hesitated. This was a question he had hoped to delay. If he was too quick to offer, Chalosee would be embarrassed. He did not wish that for her.

"I will provide," Naska said.

Ursa stood in the background. Her heart sagged within her chest. Naska had been good to her while Cota was gone. The return of Cota and the Tegesta woman made her ache inside.

Hala walked away quietly so as not to cause a disturbance. She sat beside a collection of flat rocks where in the spring she had placed berries to dry in the sun. The small fruits she had put whole on the rock. With her woman's knife she had sliced the larger fruits before laying them out to dry.

Her head was full of sad thoughts and wanderings. Cota had returned with the Tegesta woman. And though he had not indicated it, she had lived long enough to see things in a person's eyes. Cota had looked at Mi-sa no more than was absolutely necessary. Perhaps it was that purposeful attempt to keep his eyes from Mi-sa that struck her. Still, when he did glance at the Tegesta woman, Hala saw his eyes soften. Only an old woman would notice, she thought to herself. An old woman's imagination, perhaps.

Hala took her knife and ground it on one of the stones. She tested its edge, drawing the knife along her thumb. But her concentration was elsewhere, and the knife slit the base of her thumb. She slung the knife aside. Hala put her thumb to her mouth and sucked on the cut.

She looked up to see Cota standing with Mi-sa.

"She will stay with you," Cota said to Hala. He had decided that since Mi-sa had stayed with the woman before, if he suggested she should stay with someone else, it would arouse suspicions. The people would know soon enough that he had chosen Mi-sa to be his woman. But Chalosee should be told first—at the proper time.

"Hala, you have hurt yourself. Let me see," Mi-sa said, squatting next to the old woman, taking the cut hand from Hala's mouth so that she could examine it. Mi-sa supported Hala's hand in hers. "It is not so bad," she said. "But I will prepare a medicine so that it will heal quickly."

Hala drew back her hand, and Mi-sa looked at her.

Hala knew.

CHAPTER
— 23 —

The heat of summer would soon mellow. The days would stay hot, but the nights would become more tolerable. The steam that carried the smell of the high pines wafted in the air above the coontie grounds. But near the river the steeping rot made the air musty.

The women headed for the high ground where the coontie grew. Mi-sa had offered to help gather the starchy root.

The trip was a long walk in the heat. They wandered through the heavy foliage, following trails away from the river to the sandier soil that supported pines and palmettos. Mi-sa pinched a twig off a tree that resembled the mulberry that grew around her village. This tree was much smaller, though, and there were no berries to compare.

She lifted the torn stem to her nose. The rank odor made her grimace. This was not like the mulberry she knew. She looked at the end of the broken stem. The plant did not bleed milky sap like her familiar mulberry. Carefully she tore a shred from a leaf and tasted it. The stringent taste made her wince, and she spit it out.

The others had continued on, making their way down the trail. Mi-sa rubbed the stem between her fingers. This plant was a new medicine. She tucked it inside her pouch to take it back with her so she could study it later. Maybe Olagale could tell her about it.

She looked up the trail. The others had disappeared, and so she ran along the path to catch up to them as they began their work.

With their digging sticks, the women pried the starchy coontie roots out of the soil and put them in their baskets. Digging in the ground, gathering coontie, was hard work. When their baskets were full, they sat on the warm ground, talking and laughing. The coontie was bountiful, but they had been careful to leave many roots behind so that there would always be more.

Hala was the first to stand. "Come here, Mi-sa," she said. Hala touched a ball of resin that had oozed out of an injury on a slash pine. "Take this," she said.

Mi-sa snapped the pitch off. It was amber and smelled bad but reminded her of pine.

"My supply is low, see if you can find more." Hala told her. "I need pitch for my baskets. And I will give some to Cota."

Mi-sa wandered over the pinelands, checking the trees for scars, stopping to take the resin balls. Some of the scars were deep, and she could see that a lot of pitch had run down inside the gashes. She withdrew her knife and sliced out some more of the valuable resin.

Suddenly she felt someone behind her. "Hala!" she said, startled. "You frightened me."

The old woman leaned on her walking stick, her bony hand cupping the worn tip. "You are jumpy. That tells me you are nervous."

"No, Hala. You surprised me. That is all."

The old woman cleared her throat and made a sound that meant disagreement. "Chalosee has not said anything."

Mi-sa felt herself tense, though she tried to keep it from showing on her face.

"Hala, do you know the story of how coontie came to be?" she asked, putting her knife away.

Hala hesitated. She knew the Kahoosa story, but was curious to know if the Tegesta told the same tale. "Tell me," she said, knowing that Mi-sa would make another point when she related the story.

"The Tegesta know the story this way. A long time ago, when our ancestors walked this land, there was a great famine. The People became sick and weak and prayed to the Great Spirit to help them. The Great Spirit took pity on the People and heard their cries. He sent his son down to the earth. He walked through the pinelands, and everywhere his heel pressed into the soil, the coontie grew. The Great Spirit had provided food for the People."

Hala nodded. "The Tegesta story is the same as ours."

"The Great Spirit watches over all the People. He does not let things happen; he makes things happen, even though we do not always understand his reasons. Do you not think the People wondered why the Breath Giver had sent his son to walk on the earth? Do you not think they wondered why he had not sent food? But as the story tells us, the Great Spirit takes care of the People in his own way."

Hala took a hard ball of resin from Mi-sa's basket. She held it up to the sunlight, then gave it back to her. "It is time to leave."

Hala sat at her hearth. With two sticks she picked up hot stones and dropped them into her new basket with several balls of pitch. She held the basket in her lap and began to rock it, swirling the hot rocks and pitch around and around. The stones heated and softened the pitch, and as it rolled around, it formed a waterproof seal inside the basket.

"That is a fine basket," Mi-sa said, stopping in front of Hala.

"Yes, it is," Hala agreed. She picked up several sticks with pitch on the end; she had rolled them in the dirt to keep them from sticking together. "Wait," she said, afraid that Mi-sa would leave too quickly. "Here." She held out the pitch sticks. "Take these to Chalosee. She will give them to Cota."

Mi-sa reluctantly took the sticks. Her own platform had been completed, and she spent much of her time there. Often she had seen Cota with Chalosee, and the memory of her own night with him was fading. Perhaps he had not meant what he said. Maybe he was never going to tell Chalosee how he felt because he thought there was nothing significant to tell her.

She saw Chalosee in the distance, standing with Cota. At the same time, Chalosee saw her. Mi-sa would have preferred to wait, but now she had to proceed.

"Hala asked me to give you this," she said, handing the pitch sticks to Chalosee.

"These are for you, Cota," Chalosee said, passing them on to him.

Mi-sa's eyes stayed on the pitch. She could not look at Cota or Chalosee. She felt a hand on her shoulder and turned to see that Naska had come up behind her. "I have brought you some fresh venison." He spoke to Mi-sa, but he was smiling hard at his brother. "Come," he said. "I have already prepared it. The skin is for you also."

As much as she disliked Naska, he had a way of helping her salvage her dignity, and she was grateful. Somehow, Naska knew what happened between his brother and her, and he knew her feelings.

She walked away with him.

"I have seen your eyes on my brother. I know what you want. You are stubborn, woman."

"No," Mi-sa objected. "That is not true."

Naska laughed. "I like your defiant spirit."

As she approached her hearth she saw that he had put the meat on a grate and started a smoking fire. The deerskin lay on the ground; she would have to prepare it. "Naska," she said, "I do not feel well, but I do appreciate your gift. I hope you understand."

"This is not a gift. I said that I would provide for you."

"And I truly am grateful. I need to go into my platform."

"Go and rest, Tegesta woman," he said. "The meat will smoke on its own, and the skin will wait."

Mi-sa climbed her ladder and found shelter in the dark shadows inside. She sat in the far corner and held her medicine bag tightly in her hand.

She watched the shadows change inside her platform as the sun sank in the sky. She did not want an evening meal. She removed her skirt and covered herself with a light skin, curled up on her sleeping mat, and closed her eyes.

Chalosee stood in her platform overlooking the village. Cota had not been with her, as a man is with a woman, since he had returned. She attributed that to his many obligations.

Cota passed the central hearth in the twilight, which made him appear mystical.

"Cota," she called softly.

An owl began his eerie melody as Cota looked toward Chalosee. She beckoned him with her hand.

As Cota climbed the ladder, Chalosee drew back under the thatch roof, becoming a shadow. She stood still, waiting for him to reach out to her. She longed to be with him again.

Deep purple and indigo tinged the sky as darkness fell over the village and the earth gave itself over to creatures of the night. Yellow and red eyes lurked in the brush, voices cried for mates, slinky bodies slithered under rotting leaves, and padded feet stalked prey. The chorus of crickets filled the night air, and the People settled in to sleep.

Mi-sa, startled by a dream, sat up, looked around her shelter, and then lay back on her mat. She stared up at the roof. The palm thatch was fresh and green, and instead of rustling like dry brown thatch, it swished in the small bursts of breeze.

She heard the ladder creak beneath someone's weight as it leaned against the opening of the platform. She stiffened, daring to move only her eyes. Again she heard the movement of the ladder. A silhouette appeared in the opening, rising above the edge of the flooring.

"Who is there?" she called, sitting up, holding the blanket against her and scooting backward, deeper inside the platform.

The silhouette moved into the darkness of the shelter.

Mi-sa's voice trembled. "What do you want?"

And then she felt his hand on her cheek as he knelt in front of her, close enough for her to see his outline and his face.

"Cota," she said with a sigh. "Why did you not answer?"

He pulled her to him so that he held her head to his chest, stroking her hair. She could hear the thumping of his heart. "I have told Chalosee," he said, his voice low.

She turned her head so that her lips touched his chest in a soft kiss. "Is she all right?"

"She will be," he answered, lifting her face to his. His mouth fell heavy on hers, and his hands were eager to touch all of her.

"I was afraid," she whispered through his kisses.

Cota nipped at her bottom lip as he held her face in his hands. "Shh," he murmured, leaning back, pulling her along with him, until he lay on the floor. The light weight of her body against him made him quake. His arms went around her, firmly, roughly, turning her beneath him.

The power of him shook her. Suddenly he was arched over her, looking down, watching her face.

She reached around his neck and pulled him toward her. His mouth began a hot trail at the hollow of her throat until he found her breast where he teasingly paused to explore.

"Cota," she whispered, her eyes closing, her body aching for him to be everywhere on her. She remembered the vision on the dune and twisted her fingers in his thick hair as he probed and tasted all of her, making her groan with want and need.

He raised his head to see her face flushed and awash with desire as his hand sought those places that needed his touch. He slid against her until he could reach her mouth with his.

His hands moved along the damp path his tongue had blazed, slipping into secret folds and warm valleys. A roaring started in her ears, that same sound that had obliterated everything else once before. She knew she stood at the brink of that wonderful, overwhelming, spiraling gift a man could give a woman. Instinctively she pulled away, wanting to give *him* more.

"Let me touch you," she whispered breathlessly.

They moved so that they lay on their sides, facing each other. His large hand tenderly held her soft breast as he looked into her eyes.

Mi-sa touched his thigh, feeling the strong cords of muscle beneath his skin. She ran her hand across his buttocks and up to his waist, fumbling with his breechclout, finally releasing it and letting it fall free. Her hand moved along his stomach, feeling the tautness and the small quivers that flowed through him at her touch.

The feel of his body, the sensation of him straining against her, fed the fire inside her, a slow-burning flame that was about to rage out of control—a blaze only he could extinguish. His hand was on hers, guiding her touch, directing her where he most urgently needed her. She heard him gasp as she encircled him, then caressed him. His arm went over her, pulling her closer as he moved against her.

Mi-sa moved back, allowing room for her to press her mouth to his chest and sweep her lips down over his ribs and across his stomach. His responses taught her what pleased and excited him most. His hand tangled in her hair, and a low, ragged moan came from him as he felt the warmth of her mouth embrace him. Her own arousal grew as she knew he so desperately wanted her.

Suddenly he pushed her away and rolled on top of her, holding her still and tight against him. She could feel his breath coming fast and hard against her neck, his hands in a panic to touch her, to take her.

The rough maleness of him pressed against her. Mi-sa

parted her legs, and Cota blindly, in a frenzy, sought out the smooth warm passage.

An incoherent cry escaped Mi-sa as he drove deep within her.

Cota slid his hands beneath her, lifting her hips as he dropped his head to her shoulder and softly bit her neck.

The dark thatch shelter echoed with their cries of hunger and then their whimpers of repletion. Cota fell against her, his body still shaking.

Mi-sa drank in the air in thirsty gulps, running her hand down his back. This was the design of the spirits. Nothing else could be so divine.

As the moon made its journey, Mi-sa slept until she felt Cota moving away from her side.

"Why do you leave?" she asked.

"Chalosee will be the one to tell the others that I am with you. I cannot stay until morning. I would be seen. The darkness will help keep our secret."

"I understand," Mi-sa said. She put her arms around his waist, laying her head against him. "Let me feel you once more before you leave. Hold me," she whispered.

Distant thunder rumbled, and veins of lightning crossed the sky.

"Even the spirits protest your leaving," she said, pressing her lips to his chest.

Cota crossed his arms behind her. "Soon," he said into her hair.

She watched him descend the ladder and then disappear into the night, as he did in her dreams of him, coming out of the darkness, out of nowhere into her life, consuming her, and then disappearing.

Cota stopped at the central hearth and pitched a stick into the fire before journeying on to his own platform. He climbed the ladder and stepped inside. He heard the heavy breathing before he saw her and stopped in the entranceway.

"I have been waiting for a long time," Chalosee said.

Cota cocked his head to try to see her in the dark, puzzled by her presence here.

"You have been with her," she said.

Cota was not sure if she was asking a question or making a statement. Whichever it was, he heard the challenge in her voice. "Yes," he said.

"But you told me that you would not shame me—let me lose my pride. You said that I would be the one to tell."

Cota moved in the direction of her voice, which sounded peculiar and strained. "No one else knows, Chalosee," he said, taking another step.

"Everyone knows!" Her voice rose to a shout and ended in a whisper.

Cota moved closer, seeing a vague outline of her rocking back and forth as she sat on the floor. "No one, Chalosee."

Cota squatted in front of her and reached to touch her arm. Chalosee swung at him, batting his hand away. She balled her fists and pounded on his chest.

Cota grasped her wrists. "Stop," he said. "Do not do this."

"Let go of me," she said, jerking her hands free. "No, Cota. Tell me that you did not mean it. Tell me you have not left me and chosen Mi-sa. Please." Her face twisted as she started to cry. She threw her hands over her face and sobbed into them, slumping forward.

Cota cradled her in his arms, letting her cry, stroking her long, flowing hair. Finally she straightened up, swept back her hair, and dried her face with her hands, looking more rational.

"I did not want to cause you pain, Chalosee," he said.

"But you have," she retorted, rising and struggling to regain her dignity. "Yet I will find a way to live with this. Promise that you will give me time."

"Of course. I have already told you that. Did you fear that I was not being truthful? Is that why you came here in the night and waited for me?"

Chalosee's face was hidden in the shadows so that Cota did

not see her strange expression. She hesitated and then turned
away from him. "Yes," she answered eerily, "that is why."

"Chalosee?"

She carefully made her way down the ladder so that the
woman's knife stuck in her waistband did not cut her.

CHAPTER
— 24 —

"Give it to me!" Chalosee said. "Make me the solution!"

Olagale touched her hand. "I have told you, that balm is for a married woman. She uses it to regain the affections of her husband."

"Please, Olagale." Chalosee was now pleading rather than demanding.

Olagale shook his head. "The herbs alone are no good. Incantations are needed to make them potent. The prayers are for those who are married. The magic words speak of a husband and his woman. You have no use for it."

"Make the solution anyway. Perhaps it is not for me at all. Maybe it is for someone else who does not want anyone to know she fears the loss of her husband's affections."

"Chalosee, you have already told me that you want this elixir for yourself."

"I was lying. Please prepare it and tell me what to tell my friend."

Olagale's face showed that he did not believe her. "Wait here," he said, retreating to his platform to collect the ingredients. In a moment he reappeared, carrying a special pot he used when he brewed magical mixtures.

Chalosee watched him blend the plant parts with water in

the bowl. He added hot stones and suspended the pot over the fire that burned at his hearth.

Olagale began his soft chant, first getting the attention of the spirits, and then saying the magic words to give the concoction its effectiveness.

"Eat no fish for the next four days," he said as he poured the mixture into a plain bowl. He skimmed the top, taking out the floating bits and parts of the plants he had used. "After bathing in the river, rub this all over your body." Olagale looked up at her and corrected himself. "Tell your friend how to use the solution."

When she took it from him, Chalosee raised the bowl to her nose and sniffed. "But I do not smell a perfume. There is not much smell," she said, looking up at the shaman.

"I did not make a perfume."

"How will it work if it cannot be smelled? I do not understand."

"I have made you what you asked for. Do as I have said."

Chalosee nodded and turned to hurry off, but she ran squarely into Naska. Her precious medicine sloshed and threatened to spill.

"Naska!" she said angrily. "You almost made me spill this."

Naska's curiosity was aroused. "What is it?"

Chalosee stumbled over her words. "It is . . . from Olagale—a medicine. A woman's medicine."

"Mmm," Naska mumbled, studying her, noting her nervousness.

"May I pass?" she asked.

Naska stepped aside and watched her as she left. He looked back at Olagale who quickly made himself busy.

"You prepared her a woman's medicine?" Naska asked Olagale. "Does Cota know that his woman has troubles?"

"It is not my business," Olagale said.

Naska cocked his head, staring at the shaman. "What kind of woman's medicine?"

Olagale kept on with his task of disposing of the leftover

mixture, cleaning his bowls, and doing other mundane chores. He did not look up at Naska.

"What trouble does she have?" Naska asked, probing farther.

"Nothing serious. She will be fine. Your brother has nothing to worry about."

Olagale had not convinced Naska. "The cacique would not want to take a woman who had health problems."

Olagale finally stopped and looked at Naska. "Since when do you look out for your brother?"

Naska rolled his head back and let out a hearty laugh. "There is more to this than you and Chalosee want to tell me. I think I have struck a sore spot."

"Do you need my help today?"

"No, Olagale. I need nothing from you."

Olagale waved him off. "Then go about your business," he said.

Naska still smiled. He nodded and walked away.

"How is Chalosee feeling?" he asked Hala as he passed her.

Hala grumbled.

"Speak more clearly, old woman. I could not understand what you said."

Hala pushed on her walking stick and hoisted herself up. "Always poking where you do not belong. Be gone," she said. She shook her walking stick at him. "Get."

"You make a mighty protest just because someone asks about your daughter's health." He smiled at her, knowing he had made her angry. She had confirmed that there was more to this than just woman troubles.

He saw Ursa at her hearth. She was fleshing a rabbit skin he had given her. She was quite beautiful to look at, he thought. Taller than most of the women of the village. Long legs. Large breasts, but not too large, nor did they droop. They were perfect, he decided, wanting to touch them right now.

"Women talk a lot," he said to her, standing behind her and massaging her shoulders.

Ursa put down her fleshing tool and rocked back her head, feeling the wonder of Naska's strong hands. "What do you mean?" she asked with her eyes closed, enjoying the rub.

"Women," he said, moving in front of her, stopping the massage and sitting down. "They talk to one another, more than men I suspect. What do you think?"

"I suppose," she said.

"You discuss private things, like illnesses that afflict women. You know, woman troubles, problems—a woman's cycle and things like that."

"Naska," Ursa said, wrinkling her nose, expressing her embarrassment at the broaching of such a subject.

"Do I not know you well? I know every part of your body intimately. Nothing should embarrass you when you are with me."

Ursa looked down shyly.

Naska lifted her chin and swept her hair aside just long enough to catch a fleeting glimpse of one of her breasts before her hair fell back into place.

"Do you ever have these troubles—these woman problems?" he asked.

Ursa shook her head.

"But if you did, what kind of medicine would Olagale make for you?"

"I do not know," she said quietly, still uncomfortable with the talk.

"Do you know anyone who is having those problems now?"

"No," she answered.

"What about Chalosee? Have you heard?"

"No, I do not think so."

"Would you know if she were?"

"Possibly. As you said, we women talk among ourselves."

"If the sickness was bad enough for her to seek Olagale's help, would you know?"

"Probably. Before women seek Olagale's help, they ask other women if they have experienced the same problem."

Naska leaned back, lifting his head to look at the sky, and a powerful smile broke across his face.

"Why do you ask these things?"

"Just curious. Olagale made some medicine for Chalosee, and she said it was for woman troubles. I thought not." He paused a moment before he spoke again. "You keep listening to the women. See if you hear something about Chalosee."

"Are you concerned because she is your brother's woman?"

"Yes. A cacique cannot be too careful about whom he chooses to carry on the bloodline."

"I will listen," she said.

"Good."

Chalosee stepped out of the river. She took the bowl Olagale had given her and began to sprinkle some of the mixture on her naked, damp body. She rubbed it across her skin and then waited for it to dry. Nearby she spotted a vine with small sweet-smelling white flowers growing in clusters. She knew the fragrance. She picked some blossoms and crushed them in her hands, then spread the residue on her body. Now she had to find Cota.

Pa-hay-tee took the twig from Cota and held it in his small brown hand. A ball of heated pitch stuck to the end of the twig.

"Touch the pitch to the notch," Cota said.

Pa-hay-tee followed his directions, touching the hot, sticky pitch to the notch in the arrow shaft. He rolled it around, coating the notch, letting the pitch ooze inside the slot.

"Good," Cota said, leaning close, inspecting the notch. "Now wedge the point in."

Pa-hay-tee took the treasured chert bird point that his

mother had given him. It had been his father's. He looked at Cota with admiration, gratitude, and love.

"Like this?" he questioned, carefully putting the point down into the notch filled with pitch.

"Hold it in place while it cools. Do not let it wiggle." Cota put his large hand over the boy's. "Steady."

"What was the Tegesta woman's village like?" Pa-hay-tee asked, passing the time while the pitch set.

"Smaller than ours. But I could not tell much more than that. Everything had been destroyed or washed away by the storm."

"But they did not live near the Big Water or on a river. I do not think they lived a good life."

"They are surrounded by water and they go to the sea. Their oarsmen must be very good. They hunt and fish in the shallow water and on the hammocks. There is much wild game on the hammocks."

"I have never seen the land where the sun goes down. I am curious," the boy said.

"I will take you there sometime, to where the river disappears and the saw grass stretches as far as you can see."

"I would like that," Pa-hay-tee said.

"I believe the pitch is cool enough," Cota said, setting a bowl of water in front of his young friend.

"You will show me how to bind the arrowhead to the shaft?"

"Here." Cota took a string out of the water. "Wrap the sinew tightly around the base of the arrowhead like this," he said as he demonstrated. "Keep binding down the shaft a bit. That way it will not split when you use it."

Pa-hay-tee took over, his wrapping less expert than his teacher's.

"When the sinew dries, it will shrink. The pitch and the binding will hold the point securely in place. In another day, if we do not have rain, the sinew should be dry. Then I will help you kill your first bird. Your father will watch you. He will be proud."

Pa-hay-tee's little mouth quickly turned up into a wide grin.

Chalosee walked up and stood behind Cota. He caught a glimpse of her and looked up.

"Go and show your mother the arrow you have made," Cota said.

Pa-hay-tee took off at a sprint, whooping, mimicking the cry of the men after a successful hunt.

"He would not have the life of a man to look forward to if it were not for you. He would do the work of a woman for the rest of his life," Chalosee said.

"Someone else would have taught him," Cota said, standing up and preparing to leave.

"There is no need to rush away. I will not embarrass myself or you again. I must apologize." She stepped a little closer, but still left a comfortable distance. She wanted Cota to catch the scent of the flowers, but more importantly the magical mixture she had splashed over her body needed to ride on the air to him.

"No apology is necessary. I have hurt you. I am the one who needs forgiveness."

"What does Mi-sa offer you that I do not? That is what I do not understand. I lie awake wondering what it is." Again she moved closer.

Cota wanted to stop her from going on. "You are not less appealing than she. The spirits direct the heart, that is all. We cannot stop the will of the spirits. You understand that."

He thought she had been listening, but apparently she had not.

Chalosee stepped closer—uncomfortably close, crowding him.

"You joined with her while you were on the journey. I know you did. There is some way that she pleases you in joining that I do not. Why did you not just tell me? I would do whatever pleases you."

Cota put his hands on her shoulders. "Chalosee, do not go on. You torture yourself needlessly."

Chalosee shook his hands off her shoulders and glared at him. "Yes," she said, her tone and expression suddenly becoming meek. "I do not mean to rattle on. I suppose there are things I need to settle in my own mind. And now I have made you angry."

"I am not angry, but you must accept—"

"Accept?" Chalosee's face contorted, and angry lines formed gullies in her forehead. Then, as if she realized how she looked, she deliberately changed her outward appearance, relaxing the small muscles in her face, recapturing her composure. She took a deep breath, lifted her head, and said, "Such an easy word to say and so difficult to do." She turned and walked off.

She had smelled heavily of flowers, he had noticed. She had not accepted that his heart belonged to someone else. Cota watched to see where she headed. He was relieved when she stayed clear of Mi-sa's hearth.

Naska saw Chalosee hurrying across the mound. His curiosity was piqued. She was going to see Olagale again. She had too much strength to be ill. His instincts were right. There was something going on, and he would find it out.

Naska slipped behind the platforms so that he would not be detained by anyone. When he drew close to Olagale's hearth, he stopped and ducked into the cover of the trees. He did not have a clear view, but he could not risk moving closer and possibly being discovered.

Chalosee's voice was sharp and loud—loud enough for Naska to catch parts of the conversation.

"The elixir is no good," she said.

Olagale kept his voice low. "Chalosee, the mixture is good."

"But it has not worked!"

"You must use the medicine for four days. Do not eat fish during those days. Bathe and splash the mixture on your body. That is what you must tell your friend."

"Yes," Chalosee said, suddenly realizing her mistake. "I will tell her."

"Remember that the medicine is only good for regaining the affections of a husband."

"That is what you told me. My friend needs it for that reason."

"And what makes her think she has lost her husband's affections?" Olagale recognized her apprehension. "Sit and talk with me. Perhaps I can help your friend. If she does not want to come to me, maybe I can help her through you."

Chalosee looked about the village, then sat by the shaman. "She fears that her husband has lost his heart to another woman," she whispered, leaning forward to be sure Olagale could hear her.

"Maybe the balm seems not to work because nothing is really wrong. Maybe your friend's husband still loves his wife."

"No!" Chalosee said explosively through clenched teeth. "She knows he has turned to another woman. She knows it!"

"And how long have they been husband and wife?"

Chalosee shifted nervously. "Why should that matter?"

"Can you tell me?" Olagale asked.

"No," she said, standing up. "If I told you that, then you might be able to think of who she is. My friend would not want that."

Olagale also rose. "Chalosee, tell your friend that if she seeks the help of the shaman, she must be honest with him." He stared at her a moment, hoping that she understood what he was trying to say. "Tell her that all secrets stay with me."

Chalosee scored her bottom lip with her teeth and blinked back tears. "I will," she said, turning and walking away quickly so that Olagale would not see how upset she was.

Naska had heard enough of the conversation to know there was no friend. The medicine had been for Chalosee. Olagale and Naska both knew that.

Naska approached Olagale, coming through the trees. "Chalosee must be very sick. She comes to you again."

Olagale ignored him.

"I think either you or I must tell my brother. What do you think, holy man?"

Olagale spun on his heel. "I think you tend to someone else's business. I think you are up to no good."

Naska cracked a smug grin. "How can you say such a terrible thing to one who is only concerned about his brother's well-being, the cacique's interests, the future of the tribe?"

"Do you not have something else to do? Should you not prepare for the black moon festivities tonight?"

Olagale could hear Naska's laughter as he walked away. He grew angry and spat on the ground.

"Cota," Naska called as he left Olagale.

Cota turned to see his brother take a piece of fruit from one of the women and bite a chunk off it, then give the woman a big smile.

Naska's arm went around his brother, and his hand rested on Cota's shoulder.

"I love women, do you not?" he said, the juice of the fruit succulent in his mouth. "They are so mysterious. Have you noticed?"

"What do you want, Naska?"

"Sometimes I think there are too many women to choose from. Each of them has something special to offer a man. Some have large . . ." He used both hands to draw imaginary curves at his chest. "Others are gentle and consoling. Sometimes a man needs that. And some know the ways. You know what I mean," he said, thrusting his hips back and forth. "Do you ever think there are too many women to choose from, brother? Do you ever think of other women besides Chalosee?"

Cota moved his brother's hand off his shoulder. "You have something to tell me—some point to make. Get on with it."

Naska took another bite of the juicy fruit. "No point, brother. Just man-to-man talk." His mouth was full of pulp and juice. "I know you look at the women. The Tegesta woman, Mi-sa . . . what special gift does she offer a man, do you think? I think she is good at the ways." Again he thrust his hips and grabbed his crotch.

Cota seized Naska's face, pressing his thumb into one

cheek, his index finger into the other, and clamping the palm of his hand over his brother's lips. Juice oozed out of Naska's mouth. Cota squeezed hard until Naska's back teeth cut into the flesh on the inside of his cheek. He pushed back sharply on Naska's face, jarring him, then let go, turned his back, and walked away.

Naska laughed and spit out the piece of bloody fruit.

CHAPTER

— 25 —

The night was as black as burned-out coals, and the People celebrated the end of the moon's trip across the sky. The stars twinkled; the flames of the spirits' and ancestors' hearths changed colors as they lapped at the night sky so far away.

Olagale stood at the blazing central hearth, opening the festivities, waving his arms like a large graceful bird, seeming to nearly rise off the ground. The People watched, bewitched by his words, the pulse of the drums, the blackness of the night, the flames of the fire.

Mi-sa watched from the cover of darkness. The sounds and sensations brought back so many memories and stirred a need that had been born in her. She did not know Olagale's words, but the rhythm and the rise and fall of his voice were familiar. They penetrated her like a magical painless knife, cutting deep to free her own birthright.

As the Kahoosa were drawn to the central hearth, Mi-sa slipped farther away into the darkness, aching to sing her own songs. She stared into the black sky. Quickly she was enlightened by the celestial fires. She could feel the spirits rush through her, making her lighter than the air, giving her their gift of magic. From inside her, the blood gift of her ancestry rose to the surface. She began her quiet chant, then her song. The melody was simple, an ancient tune that flowed dreamily from her.

Cota searched for her in the crowd as he danced to the drums and the shaman's songs. The People had painted white moon crescents on their cheeks and black circles around their eyes. Their shell necklaces and beads winked in the firelight, and the bands of feathers coasted on the same wind that carried Olagale's voice throughout the lush, steamy forest.

Chalosee joined in the dance, passing the bowl of cassite on to Hala, who also took a small sip of the ceremonial tea and passed it on. Too much and she would lose touch; bright colors and lights, strange sounds, and ghosts would appear in the night. The strong tea was fine for the younger people. Taken in just the right amount, the tea could sharpen perception and loosen a person's inhibitions. But Hala's body was too old and too quickly succumbed to the medicine of the spirits.

Chalosee danced closer to Cota, feeling the initial effects of the drink lighten her head and make her more daring. As she moved past him, her shoulder brushed against his.

"Dance with me," she whispered.

Cota moved next to her as they proceeded around the circle.

"Closer to me. Touch me," she said.

"That is the dance of lovers," he responded.

"If you do not, everyone will be suspicious. They will know we have parted if you do not dance with me."

"The dance would be a lie. The People trust me. Chalosee, not dancing together would be a subtle way to tell them, an easy way. You will not have to say anything."

Chalosee suddenly moved in front of Cota, stepping into his path. Her hands encircled his neck. "Please," she whispered as she touched her forehead to his mouth. "I cannot bear the humiliation, Cota. Do not do this to me."

Cota gently unwrapped her hands from his neck. He held her wrists by her sides. "You cannot carry on a lie, Chalosee.

Let it go. You are young and desirable. Let the other men see that you are free."

Chalosee jerked her hands clear. "You are not the man the People think you are. You are cruel," she said, raking her fingernails down his chest.

Cota flinched as she drew blood. Chalosee appeared stunned at what she had done. She touched her palm to his chest and said, "I am sorry. I am so . . ." She did not look at him before she ran off and passed Naska as he danced with a woman.

Naska followed her with his eyes. As the evening wore on, he danced with several women, teasingly touching them, rubbing himself against them, going as far as he could without inviting too much trouble; he continued to watch for Chalosee's return.

He did not see Chalosee enter the celebration again, but he did see Mi-sa come out of the shadows.

Ursa finally had her turn to dance with Naska. She touched her lips to his chest. "Do you want to leave?" she asked.

Naska saw his brother make his way over to Mi-sa. "Yes," Naska answered, feeling Ursa move her body provocatively against him. He wanted to stay and watch what happened with Chalosee, Cota, and Mi-sa, but Ursa had a way of distracting him. All the cassite and the touching and fondling of the women had intensified his arousal. He needed a woman tonight. Now. Ursa had come to him at just the right time.

She took his hand, and they made their way out of the circle of dancers. As they walked together in the darkness, Ursa ran her hand inside his loincloth, pleased to find that he was unquestionably ready for her.

They walked on a little farther, Naska feeling his need to have her reach every part of his body.

At the base of Ursa's platform, he abruptly turned her and pressed her back against the ladder.

"Let us go up," she whispered, pulling back from him.

Naska wanted to have her there, against the ladder, with only the darkness to hide them. He eagerly bit into the soft curve of her neck and grasped her buttocks as he thought of the dangerous excitement of someone passing by. He ran one hand beneath her thigh and lifted up, but Ursa did not cooperate. He grumbled his disappointment and followed her up the ladder.

The music slowly faded, only the occasional sound of laughter recalling the earlier festive assembly. Naska squatted by the last coals burning at Ursa's hearth. He stirred the hearth with a stick, and the last glowing flickers sprayed into the darkness.

"Ahh," he said, lowering himself to sit, feeling the warmth of the drink that continued to flow through him. He felt relaxed, still bathed in the slowly abating heat that Ursa had satisfied. Sometimes he was certain that he led a better life than Cota, even if he was not the cacique. He indulged in earthly pleasures that demanded little responsibility. Surely, he was convinced, he led a life filled with much more fervor and zeal than his brother's. He lived from the gut.

Naska let the dwindling fire settle and kicked some dirt over the last gray coal after he stood up. Indeed, life was good, he thought again as he made his way across the village to his own platform.

Nearly there, in the solid black night, he stopped. A peculiar noise caught his attention. The sound was not loud, but not natural. It sounded like a scraping, and then a human sound, like a grunt, followed. He strained to hear it again, to determine which direction it was coming from.

Again he heard the abrasive rubbing noise. He followed it into the trees and brush close to the river, where there was no path. He quietly stepped through the brush, cautious but resisting the desire to make enough noise to drive out snakes. His hands stretched in front of him, feeling for branches that he could not see without the light of the moon, silently moving them away or ducking beneath them.

He stopped to listen again. The noise was close. Very close. He approached, taking one small careful step at a time.

The grunts now sounded like muffled crying. He stepped on a dry twig, and it cracked.

Chalosee looked up, her muscles tensing. Hard as she tried, she could not see much in front of her because the night was too dark. She made every effort to keep her breathing soundless, but the crying made that difficult. Her nose was stuffy and her throat full. The animal that approached could already smell her, she thought. If she ran, it would immediately know where she was and would chase her. She would be safer if she just remained still and quiet.

Naska listened for the sound again. He was sure it had come from close by. Someone was out here, in the middle of the night, wanting to be hidden. He must have been heard, he decided when the noise was not repeated. He hunkered down in the brush to wait.

Chalosee tilted her head, listening intently, not moving. A spot on her neck itched, but her fear prevented her from scratching. The time passed slowly and nearly painfully, but after a while, when she heard no other noises, she decided she was probably safe. First she tossed a stone into the brush, then sat quietly and listened. Nothing. She threw another stone and waited. When nothing happened, she loudly rattled the brush near her, then shrank back. Nothing. Chalosee was convinced that she was safe.

The stone landed so close to Naska that he could hear it roll in the leaves as it settled. The first noise had not come from the same place. Someone had thrown the stone to draw his attention elsewhere. But he was not fooled.

He also heard the second stone. He sat so still he was sure that whoever it was would soon decide there was no one or no animal there. Soon after he heard the thrashing of the brush, the original noise returned. He decided to continue his stalk, but first he would be patient and wait just a little longer. A patient hunter was always rewarded.

Soon he rose and moved toward the noise. The vocal sounds had become louder. Someone was speaking but he could not understand the words. They were mumbled and sounded like a woman crying.

If she had not moved, he probably would not have seen her in the darkness, even as close as he was. "What are you doing, woman?" he asked her.

Chalosee was startled. He crouched in front of her, close so that she could see who had spoken.

"Go away, Naska," she said, hiding her hands first in her lap and then behind her.

"What are you doing out here? What do you have in your hands?"

"Nothing, Naska," she said, sniffling, finding herself off balance as she tried to stand up with her hands behind her.

Naska rose up in front of her. "Show me what you have," he said, reaching out and taking her arms.

Chalosee twisted her shoulders, attempting to free herself. "Let me go!"

"You must have something you do not want me to see," he said, pulling one of her arms to the front. "What is this?" he asked, unfolding her fingers. He could not see it clearly in the dark. He felt inside her hand. She held a flat, smooth stone.

"Only a stone," she said, beginning to wrestle out of the grip he had on her other arm.

"What is in your other hand?"

Her resistance became more violent. She twisted sharply, jerking her shoulders and torso. "Leave me alone, Naska. Why do you always bother me? Go away!"

He finally pulled her other arm to the front. He fumbled with her clenched fist until he could feel what she was holding. Suddenly he felt a quick sting across the palm of his hand. A knife.

He knocked the weapon to the ground and drew his injured hand back. Immediately he forced her to her knees, holding her firmly by the shoulder. "Explain," he said.

Chalosee refused to answer.

"You sit out here in the dark, in the middle of the night,

sharpening your woman's knife. I do not . . ." He was going to say that he did not understand, but suddenly he did. "This is for Cota, is it not?"

Chalosee did not answer.

"You are no longer his woman. Mi-sa is," he said, the whole mystery becoming clear to him.

"Yes!" she suddenly shouted, looking up at Naska.

"And you were going to use your knife on him? Has your mind become addled? What is the matter with you?"

"Did you see how he refused to dance with me tonight? Everyone did. Did you not hear the laughter, see the gleaming eyes that stared at me? He has wronged me." Chalosee began to sob again. "He humiliated me. He deserves this," she said, picking up the knife. "I cannot bear the shame!"

Naska loosened his grip on her shoulder and stooped in front of her to see her face. He was jealous of his brother. He even resented him, but he did not want him dead—did not want Chalosee to kill him. "Chalosee, you do not want to do this." He took the knife from her and stuck it in his sheath alongside his own.

Chalosee rested her face in her hands. "I love him. He should not have turned against me," she cried.

Naska sat with her as she wept, listening to her express self-pity one moment and rage the next. He sat with her until she was spent and exhausted, comforting her when she would allow it. Maybe if she released all of her tension, she would give up this idea of killing Cota. She needed to be watched.

"Come with me," he said when she finally appeared to have calmed down. "It is good that you have let all your misery out. Thoughts of Cota will not obsess you anymore."

Naska helped her to her feet and walked her back to the village, stopping at the central hearth to tweeze up a hot coal with two sticks. "You will stay with Ursa," he said, leaving her at the base of Ursa's ladder while he climbed up with the coal. In a moment she saw a light inside Ursa's platform, and he told her to come up.

Naska held a burning cattail firebrand. In the dim light

Ursa could see Chalosee's tearstained face. She unrolled another sleeping mat, covered it with a deerskin, and handed Chalosee a bowl of water. "You will feel better in the morning," she said.

Chalosee sat on the mat and sipped the water. "I am ashamed. Do not tell Hala. I would shame her also."

"No one will tell anything, Chalosee," Ursa said. "All you need is some rest."

Naska took the light to the ladder and tossed it down onto Ursa's hearth. Keeping a fire inside a platform would be dangerous. The thatch could catch from a tiny spark, and the whole platform would go up in flames in moments.

"I am glad that you stopped me," Chalosee said to Naska.

He descended the ladder. Ursa followed. He extinguished the firebrand, covering it with dirt and ash as he explained how he had found Chalosee sharpening her knife. Ursa stood next to him in the dark and listened as he spoke softly so that Chalosee could not hear.

"Take care of her," he said.

CHAPTER
— 26 —

Chalosee rolled up the mat and handed it to Ursa. "I am embarrassed," she said, squinting as she stood in a shaft of bright morning light that splashed inside the platform.

"I know what it is to love a man," Ursa said, putting the mat away. "But you cannot let it destroy you."

"I know that. It is a terrible burden to charge someone else with being responsible for your own happiness. I know that I have to put the hurt away and move on."

"I am glad to hear you say that, Chalosee. I was afraid for you."

"Not for Cota?" Chalosee laughed.

Chalosee's humor showed she had begun to heal—a good sign. "You could never have hurt him, though I know you must have wanted to."

Chalosee looked down. "No, I could not have killed him," she confessed. "But it gave me satisfaction to think I could, to prepare as if I could." Chalosee abruptly looked back at Ursa. "Are you certain that Naska will not tell Cota? I do not want him to think of me as someone who lost her mind and thought about doing something so terrible."

"If he said he would not tell, then he will not. Naska is

many things, but he honors his word. Good or bad, he keeps his promises."

Chalosee gave a short laugh, then asked, "How do you stand the way he teases with other women?"

"That is the way Naska is. I cannot change him. If I try to do that, I will lose him. Naska is not like other men. He needs more freedom. If I tried to take that from him, I would no longer be a part of his life."

Chalosee shook her head, finding that hard to understand. "But he does take other women. I have seen that happen. You know it is true."

"But whose bed does he always return to?" Ursa said with a curious smile. "As I said, Naska needs to be free. I will take whatever part of him he gives to me. I have enough for now."

"But one day, Ursa, you will find yourself old and still alone. A burden to the clan, people will say. Your brother is much older, and when he crosses to the Other Side, no one will provide for you. You will have no husband."

"I cannot think of that now," Ursa said, finding something to busy her hands.

Chalosee stood mute, knowing she had said enough. Finally she thanked Ursa again and left.

"Chalosee," Ursa called down, "if you need someone . . . If you need to talk . . ."

Chalosee waved up to her, thanking her. She hoped she would not need to accept Ursa's offer. She never wanted to feel so desperate again. How shamelessly she had behaved.

"Father," Naska called, making Kaho look up from his morning meal. "May I sit at your fire?" he asked.

Kaho nodded. "Some morning tea?"

"It is good to share tea with my father," Naska said, dipping a shall ladle into the pot.

"What brings you to me this early?" Kaho asked, noticing how eager Naska seemed.

"I just want to spend some time with my father. We do not

sit together much anymore. We have not done so since I was a boy."

Kaho nodded, but his expression remained guarded as he waited for Naska to go on. Eventually the real meaning of his visit would become clear.

"I think my brother has had his heart taken," Naska began.

Kaho did not respond. So this was what Naska's visit was all about.

"He has given up Chalosee, a good Kahoosa woman. A sad thing it is."

Naska waited for his father's reaction, but Kaho did not oblige him.

"What do you think of Chalosee?" Naska asked.

"She is a good woman, as you said. Young, beautiful. Strange that you are so concerned for her."

"Spurned women can be dangerous, do you not think so?"

"Women endure unrequited love all the time. Is Ursa dangerous?"

Naska cracked a smile. "I understand why you were such a great leader," he said. "You instinctively go straight to a weak spot. Tell my brother to watch his back, to be careful, and to be gentle with Chalosee."

Kaho's forehead furrowed with worry. What was Naska trying to say? "Do you have reason to say that?"

"No," Naska said. "No reason. I believe that Chalosee is going to be just fine. I am sure of that. I just wish to offer some good basic and general advice. My brother is sometimes too trusting. He thinks everyone is like him."

"Why do you not tell him this yourself?" Kaho asked.

Naska stood up, preparing to leave. "The tea was good." He hesitated, then said, "Cota will listen to you. This is important."

"Is Mi-sa the one who has taken his heart?" Kaho asked as his son turned to leave.

"I am not sure why that pleases you," he answered, hearing the rise in his father's voice. "Yes, she is the one."

"It is destined," Kaho said. "The great design unfolds."

"So you have said before."

Naska left his father's hearth and wandered through the village. Smoke was rising from Mi-sa's hearth. He decided to visit her. He would do as his father had taught him—find the weak spot, Mi-sa's vulnerable spot. If he was observant enough, he would be able to do that. Certainly he was resourceful and shrewd. The task was not impossible. He was determined to have the Tegesta woman. If he could take her from his brother, the game would be a good one. Kaho would see how clever he was, and Cota would have to respect him even if he did not like him. His brother should know what it felt like not to get everything he wanted. He deserved that.

"Chalosee will get over it," Naska said, striking up a conversation with Mi-sa. He knew that statement would get her attention.

"What are you talking about, Naska?"

"The situation is becoming quite clear to everyone. Cota has chosen you over Chalosee."

Mi-sa was not sure if he was suspicious and trying to trick her or if he really did know.

"I talked with Chalosee last night. She told me. She told Ursa. There is no need to hide it."

"You are always in the middle of other people's business, are you not?" Mi-sa asked.

Naska sat close to her, reached out and touched her thigh. "I think you have chosen the wrong man. I would not be surprised if I creep into your dreams when you sleep. You wonder what it would be like with me." Naska gave her a vain smile.

Mi-sa brushed his hand off her thigh. "You are amazing," she said.

Naska was intrigued that he had not flustered her. Her lack of response only made him more determined. He saw Hala approaching. This was going to be interesting.

"I am not surprised to see you here," Hala said to Naska in her gravelly voice.

"But I am surprised to find you visiting Mi-sa's hearth," Naska returned.

"Ah, you have it right. I have come to speak with Mi-sa,

not with you. So get away," she said, swinging her walking stick close to him.

"Grouchy old woman," he said, grinning. "Take control of your dangerous weapon before you hurt someone."

Hala swatted at him with her stick in earnest this time. Naska jumped back. "Every day I realize more and more that women can be dangerous," he said, an evil smile spreading across his face, settling in his eyes.

Hala was not simply annoyed now. She was furious. "Shut your mouth," she said.

"I am leaving. Relax, old woman, before you make yourself sick. My remark about women being dangerous has really brought sourness to your face and tongue."

Hala looked hard at the man who snooped into everything. "With a mother's eyes and ears, I observe what happens to my daughter." She leaned on her walking stick, her old back hunched with age. "Few secrets can be kept from a mother. Do you understand me?" Hala's face grew red with anger as she pointed her long bony finger at him.

"Calm yourself, old woman."

"Arghh," Hala mumbled, turning away from him.

As Naska backed away, Mi-sa could see that his face was creased with a disgustingly conceited victorious smile.

Hala slowly lowered herself onto the ground. She grunted, and as her strength, her knees, and her control gave way, she flopped onto the ground. "He is an affliction on our clan—a pestilence."

"He does have his vexing ways," Mi-sa agreed.

Hala squirmed, trying to find a comfortable position in which to sit. It seemed there was none—too much pressure here or there, the ground too hard. She must not sit for too long. She ran her tongue over her dry lips before she spoke, feeling them sting with her saliva.

"I cannot stay. I do not want to, and my old, aching bones will not let me. I will not hint at things, and I ask that you give me some respect and be forthright. Do not waste my time. I am a miserable old woman who does not have time to play games. Have I made myself clear?"

Mi-sa smiled. She admired Hala's straightforward manner. "Quite."

"Do not bother to deny that Cota has taken you. The talk has started around the village. You cannot hide the truth from me."

Mi-sa watched Hala's piercing eyes as she spoke. "I will not lie to you, Hala. You are my friend."

"Do not look for sympathy. You will find none in me."

"I have no reason to ask for sympathy."

"I want you to talk honestly with me. I am not happy about what has happened, but I do believe that you will tell me the truth."

"I will speak the truth with you, Hala. Tell me what you wish to discuss."

The old woman fidgeted and pulled her walking stick onto her lap. "What would it take?"

"What do you mean?"

"What would it take to make you go away—return to your own kind?"

"My own kind?" Mi-sa asked, her eyebrows arching, taking offense.

"Your own people—the Tegesta."

"I have nowhere to go, Hala."

Hala looked about and nearly whispered, "I could arrange to have you taken to a Tegesta village somewhere. Admit to me that you would like to do that. As a shaman you need to serve your people."

"Do you think strangers would be willing to accept me? And what about their own shaman? Who would provide for me?"

"I have many things and could acquire more. You would arrive with many goods. The other Tegesta would be envious. They would listen to a woman with such wealth."

Mi-sa rubbed her forehead.

"What would it take? What kinds of things do you desire?"

"Hala, I am not going anywhere."

Hala took a deep noisy breath and pushed herself up with her staff. "Think about it," she said, taking her first step to leave.

Mi-sa noticed Hala was moving in pain. "Why do you limp?" she asked.

Hala pushed, rubbing her hip, ignoring Mi-sa.

"Your hip is paining you," Mi-sa said, walking up to her.

"It always hurts."

"Not like this." Mi-sa placed her hand over Hala's as it pressed her hip, then closed her eyes and made the sounds around her fade.

"What are you doing?" Hala asked.

"Move your hand," Mi-sa said softly, without opening her eyes.

Hala slipped her hand from beneath Mi-sa's.

"Close your eyes, Hala," Mi-sa said.

Hala cooperated, feeling she had no other choice, as if Mi-sa controlled her.

The woman shaman began to hum, and Hala felt a strange vibration begin inside her hip. She could feel the heat pass from Mi-sa's hand through her skin and down into her joint. The incredible warm vibration worked its way through her, easing the pain like a deep massage.

"There," Mi-sa said, opening her eyes and taking her hand away.

Hala realized that all the pain was gone. "Olagale was not able to help me. He made many potions and said many prayers."

"I will teach him," Mi-sa said. "I will show him a medicine you can drink that will also help."

"You are a confusing woman," Hala said. "You know that I am angry with you. I have made my feelings clear."

"As you said, a shaman must serve."

Hala stared at the strange woman. "You are not leaving. I can see that."

"No, Hala, I am not."

"Then put everything in the open. As long as you and Cota keep secrets, the Kahoosa will gossip. Your secretiveness also keeps Chalosee bound to the past. She clings to hope. She cannot sever the tie. Be kind enough to do it for her. Set Chalosee free. Let her hate you. Let everyone hate you. It will pass."

Mi-sa nodded. The old woman was full of wisdom and love for her daughter.

"You will have done two good things for me. One day I will repay you," Hala said.

"It is done," Mi-sa said. "And there is nothing to repay."

Hala turned and walked away, slowly but without a limp. The only pain she felt now was the hurt that resided in her heart for her daughter. But when the break with Cota became known and final, when Chalosee saw that there was no hope, she could begin to heal.

Mi-sa watched Hala leave. She would teach Olagale how to help her. Mi-sa leaned her head back. How she missed her own mother. A sick feeling welled up in her. She had helped Hala. Why could she do nothing for Miakka and the rest of her people? Foul, rotten guilt made chills run down her spine. She crossed her hands over her chest and briskly rubbed her upper arms.

Suddenly she felt someone else's hands rub her arms. Bigger, more powerful hands.

"Cota," she said, so glad to see him.

"Come to the river," he said and walked away.

Mi-sa waited a few moments and then followed.

From out of the brush he grabbed her by the arm and pulled her aside. Almost in the same motion he firmly planted his mouth on hers. Mi-sa felt him flex his knees, then press against her.

Suddenly he pulled away and spun around, throwing his head back. "I cannot take this any longer," he said in a husky voice, pacing.

"Why do you turn away from me?" she asked.

"When I want to be with you, need to be with you, I must guard myself, wait. I do not think I can do this much longer, woman."

"I need to tell you something," she said. "I spoke with Hala this morning."

Cota turned around and touched his fingertip to her lips. "Does Hala make this more difficult?"

"No," she said.

"Good." He sighed with relief.

"Have you seen Chalosee?" Mi-sa asked.

"Not since the dancing last night."

"It would be inconsiderate to flaunt our love for each other in front of her. But it is best that Chalosee see that we are together. Letting go of you, accepting this new situation, is difficult for her. I think it would be kind if we followed Hala's suggestion."

Cota wrapped his arms around her, pulling her closer. "What does Hala say?"

Mi-sa spoke into his neck. "She knows that Chalosee suffers. And, Cota," she said, pushing out of his arms to face him, "Hala feels that we should bring our secret out in the open. She feels that will make Chalosee face what has happened. She wants us to make the break clean and swift. The secrecy has dragged on too long."

"Chalosee does not want to believe that I do not love her. Even last night she begged me to dance with her as a lover."

"Then we must be honest and reveal the truth . . . for her. She is too weak, and the longer this goes on, the more she holds on to hope. We are being unfair and dishonest. You have given her time to save her pride. The village is whispering. Now it is time to end the gossip and her false hope. That would be the kind thing to do."

"Hala said this?" Cota asked, appearing surprised.

"She loves her daughter. She is not happy that we are together, but she wants her daughter to begin healing."

"You know this will invite hard feelings toward you?"

"I can accept that, as long as I have you."

Cota's arms bound her tightly. Then he backed up and took her hand and led her down the path to the river.

"Get in," he said, holding the bow of one canoe.

"Where are we going?" she asked.

The Big Water crashed on the shore, white crests riding blue waves. Cota held her hand as he led her along the beach.

Mi-sa felt the sand cave in under her feet as the retreating wave swept past.

"I am sorry," he said, realizing that he was rushing her. She was from the west. The Big Water was still a new experience for her. He stood beside her, smiling as the wave took away the sand beneath their feet.

"Now we can move on," she said, running out of the water and onto the hot sand that burned her feet.

Cota grabbed her hand as he ran past her. "Hurry, woman, or your feet will cook." He held her hand as they ran up the beach, their heels kicking up sand.

"This is what I wanted you to see," he said, stopping on the top of a high dune. He bent down some sea oats and other beach grass, giving their feet a less uncomfortable place to stand. "Look there." He pointed to the Big Water, then put his arm around her.

Mi-sa stood motionless, again in awe of the vastness of the sea. Stretching out in front of her as far as she could see was the clear blue and turquoise of the ocean, colors she knew existed nowhere else. And the wind was crisper here, blowing steadily and noisily. The sound of the roaring ocean could only be compared to thunder. Indeed, seeing, feeling, and hearing the Big Water was an extraordinary experience. She turned and looked at Cota. "I have seen this once before," she said, remembering that same wonder and astonishment.

"But not with me," he said.

"Oh, yes, with you," she said mysteriously, taking both his hands and backing down the far side of the dune into the shade of a cluster of trees.

Cota's eyes glimmered with puzzlement and arousal.

"I will tell you about it later," she said, pulling him down onto the sand with her.

CHAPTER
~ 27 ~

Mi-sa snuggled closer to Cota. She was glad to be back from the isolation platform. She thought the Kahoosa custom strange: when a woman had her moon cycle, she was considered unclean and had to stay in an isolated platform until her cycle was complete. She knew that the Tegesta men would not let a woman come near their weapons during her cycle, but the woman was never isolated. This was one of the many small differences between the Kahoosa and the Tegesta.

She had missed being near Cota. The nights and mornings had grown cool, and the warmth of his body comforted her. She lay there as the sun began to rise in the east, slowly trickling through the thatch. Mentally she made a list of things she had to do today. First she must gather the plants she would need to make the special medicine to keep a baby from growing inside a woman. The medicine was not perfect, but she hoped it would be effective. She swallowed the bitter elixir every day. This was not a good time for a child to grow within her. She was informally Cota's woman, but not his wife. And she needed to be ready to help rescue Cherok if the time came.

There were other things on her list as well. The dreams had to be dealt with. She needed to find a secluded spot, where

no one would interfere, where she could be alone and speak
with the spirits. The dreams were horrible. Cherok was suffering, and the spirits punished her by making her witness it
over and over again.

Cota lifted his head and bent over her. "You are awake," he
said, seeing that her eyes were open. He slithered one hand
along the length of her slender body, feeling the cushion of
her flesh and the waves of curves and depressions ride beneath his fingertips. Finally his hand came to rest on her
breast. He closed his eyes, letting the scent and feel of her
envelop him.

"You feel even softer when you are fresh from sleep," he
said.

She wanted to close her eyes again and drift off. The
dreams had been robbing her of sleep, and dark circles had
started to form beneath her eyes. She had not enjoyed a night
of complete peace in a long time. Maybe she would prepare
some sleep medicine. But Cota would not like that, she
thought, reaching behind her to rest her hand on his hard
thigh. Sometimes he wanted her in the middle of the night, as
if he also had been awakened by a dream. But his dreams
were pleasant, and she wanted to be there to satisfy him. She
did not want to take the medicine and be too sleepy to answer
his touch when he needed her.

Mi-sa sat up and looked at him, her hair spilling onto his
shoulder. "Turn over," she said.

Cota rolled onto his back. She smiled when she could see
all of him. He smiled back, proud of his arousal. She leaned
forward and teasingly kissed his belly.

Suddenly she was standing, taking the warmth of her body
away. She gathered the skin that had covered them in the
night and wrapped herself in it. Cota groaned.

"I will start the fire," she said, looking out at the pale yellow morning.

"You already have," he said. "But you are a poor fire
keeper. You leave it unattended," he said, standing next to her
and reaching through the wrap to touch her naked body again.

Mi-sa slapped at his hand. "I will heat some meat and tea," she said, dropping the skin blanket. She put on a freshly made moss skirt, shook her hair back, and combed her fingers through it. "While it heats, I will bathe in the river," she said.

Cota watched her descend the ladder. He ran his fingers through his hair and picked up the deerskin from the floor. He could never have enough of this woman. Every time they joined there was something new and adventurous. She kept him hungry.

The river water was cold and shocking as she stepped into it. Several other women were behind her, moving slowly, as if not yet fully awake. But the temperature of the water awakened them quickly. She recognized a voice.

"Good morning, Mi-sa," Chalosee said, leaving the group of women she was with and moving closer to Mi-sa.

"Good morning, Chalosee."

"The water is very cool this morning," Chalosee remarked.

"Yes, it is."

The conversation was formal and stiff, but it was the first they had had since Mi-sa had become Cota's woman.

"I am glad that you have spoken to me this morning," Mi-sa said. "I hope we can be friends again."

"I believe we could be friends," Chalosee answered. "I will see you again," she said, walking up onto the shore, wringing out her hair.

When Mi-sa had finished and dressed, she wandered off the path, picking a few plants, stripping leaves, breaking stems, gathering roots. She remembered that the fire was heating their morning meal, but she still needed one more plant for her medicine. She would have to find it later, she thought, returning to the path.

When she reached her fire, Cota was standing there holding the blanket. "Are you cold?" he asked.

"I feel fresh," she said. "The water was cold but tolerable. The sun is warming me."

"I could do a more thorough job," he said, his eyes gleaming with mischief like a boy's.

"Perhaps the cold water would do you some good," she said, putting her plants down, then stirring the tea. She ladled some out and sipped it. The tea was ready.

"I will bathe in a while, when the sun is higher," he said. "I do not like the cold. I much prefer the heat."

"Here," she said, handing him a skewer of raccoon meat and then a bowl of tea. "This will warm your belly."

Cota looked at her as the morning light fell on her face. "You look tired."

He did not mention the dreams. He had asked her about them once, the first time she had awakened crying and shaking. He had held her and quieted her until she calmed down. Then he had asked her what the nightmare was about. She had looked at him, then buried her face in his chest and started to cry. She had begged him not to ask her about it, and he never had again. But this morning he saw the dark circles under her eyes. Every night she had those terrible dreams that awakened her sometimes three or four times. He went back to sleep easily, but obviously she could not.

"I am worried about you and the dreams," he said. "Mi-sa, you are not sleeping."

"I am fine," she said, taking a sip of tea. "Do not bother yourself. I have never been a sound sleeper."

"I will listen if you want to tell—"

He did not get to finish. "There is nothing to tell," she said, clearly agitated, ramming the skewer into another cube of meat and resting it on the hot hearthstones.

"The Council of Men meets today. Best that I do not fill my stomach. It would make me lazy," he said, standing and stretching.

Mi-sa ran her hands up the sides of his thighs. "Never," she said. "You live the life of a good cacique, always leading, always fulfilling your obligations."

Cota looked down at her. "Touch me no more this morning, woman, or the cacique will be late to arrive at Council."

Mi-sa smiled and looked away.

"You delight in the power you have over me," he said, squatting in front of her, turning her head by cupping her chin.

"I have no power," she said.

"A shaman with no power?" He grinned. "You have special powers. I envy the men of your village who had the pleasure of watching you for so long." Again he made her look at him, tipping her head back a bit. "I am sure they would have been envious of me."

Mi-sa pulled away. "It was not like that, Cota. You are the first man."

He held both her hands. "I know that I was the first. A man knows. But the men of your village must have fought for your attention."

Mi-sa's black eyes stared into his. She remembered how difficult her life had been. When she became a woman, the doubts, the mistrust because of the Gift, had followed her. No man had ever pursued her. The spirits had seen to it that she was this man's alone.

"My heart has always been yours, Cota," she said.

"And mine is yours," he said.

Mi-sa wandered through the woods, farther and farther from the village, looking for the plant she needed. The white-flowered plant was small and grew close to the ground. It had hairy leaves and preferred soil a little drier than what lay close to the river.

She knew the medicine might fail and that Cota's seed might grow inside her. Lightly she touched her abdomen, wondering what that would be like. The time would come. After Cherok was home.

Just in front of her, in a bright patch of sunlight, she discovered a cluster of the plants. All she needed was the flowers. She gathered as many as she could. With these and the others she would make a batch of medicine that would last a long while.

Suddenly, as she straightened from plucking the last flower, a hand grasped her shoulder, making her jump. Cota had followed her, she thought. He had certainly let her know that he wanted to join with her this morning. He was persistent, she thought. Before she turned, she laughed, dropping the flowers so that her hands would be free to touch him.

"Cota—"

But as she completed her turn, she saw who the man was.

"Did I frighten you?" Naska asked.

"I thought you were Cota," she said, backing away.

"What makes you wander the woods, Tegesta woman?"

"I need plants for special teas."

"What special teas?" he asked.

"Tegesta teas that I prepare for myself." Mi-sa shrank back as he moved closer. His face was serious, his eyes alive with unprincipled energy.

"I make you nervous," he said, his voice steady and smooth—too self-assured.

"Why are you out here?" she asked.

"Do you really want me to tell you? I think you must know," he said, raising one eyebrow and holding his own flat breast with one hand, rubbing it as if it ached.

Mi-sa felt her skin crawl and her stomach ball into a hard knot.

"I followed you," he said, taking several steps closer, making her back into a tree.

"Well, I have what I came for. I am going back to the village. Cota is waiting for me." She attempted to move past him, but he blocked her.

"No, he is not," he said, putting both hands on the tree, locking her head between them. He leaned in. "He is at Council."

Mi-sa stiffened. She hoped her voice would not tremble and give away her fear. "Why are you not in Council?" she asked. "Cota will see that you are not there. You should return."

"I have better things to do," he said, sniffing her hair, brushing his nose and mouth back and forth in it.

Mi-sa pushed on his chest with her hands. "Stop, Naska. You are making me uncomfortable."

Naska drew back his head so that he could look at her. "Good," he said. "I want you to tremble when I am near. I want you to shake inside." He pushed away from the tree so that he did not crowd her anymore, but he held a fistful of her hair in his hand. "You should not be afraid. What I want will be pleasurable. I have no intention of hurting you. But I will have you, Tegesta woman. I will."

Naska dropped her hair and ran his hand down the front of her body, swerving to touch her breasts, stopping at the juncture of her thighs. He grinned, removed his hand from her, then turned and walked back toward the village.

Mi-sa picked up the flowers she had dropped, feeling the ground for them with her hand so that she did not have to look down. She continued to watch Naska until he disappeared in the thick cover of the forest. But still she watched the way he had gone, making sure that he did not change his mind and come back. When she finished retrieving the flowers, she also made her way back to the village, but she kept close watch out of the corners of her eyes all the way.

She heaved a sigh of relief when the woods grew thin and the village came into sight. Quickly she hurried to her hearth and began to prepare her medicine.

She stirred the brewing elixir, still looking about for Naska. She decided not to tell Cota. Nothing had happened, and things were already difficult enough between the brothers. She did not want to be the cause of more dissension. She sipped her tea and set the medicine aside to steep for the rest of the day.

Darkness unfolded and slipped over the village. The full moon hung in the sky, coating the land with a glimmering silver patina. The cold, crisp air dried the throats of the people as they slept.

Mi-sa huddled against Cota, pulling the blanket over them. She was extremely tired from the lack of undisturbed sleep.

Tonight, when she had first lain next to him, Cota had touched her and kissed her neck, letting her know that he wanted to join with her. But even as he nuzzled her neck, he heard her slow even breathing and knew that she had fallen asleep. He had rolled away, disappointed, but glad that she was able to sleep. He did not like the gaunt look of her face, the drawn exhausted lines. It was good that she was sleeping.

As narrow pillars of moonlight pricked the thatch, Mi-sa fell deeper into sleep. Cota felt her flinch next to him. He opened his eyes, expecting her to waken upset from one of her bad dreams. But she relaxed again.

The dream came later, ripping her out of her contentment. Cherok! His swollen lips were a deep purple. His face was misshapen and bloody, and he lay in the dirt in the center of a circle of men. Several boys were standing in front of some of the men. Each held a club with a large conch shell bound to the end.

"No more blows to the head," one of the men directed before saying, "Go," and shoving a young boy toward Cherok. The boy screamed a war cry as he swung his club and struck Cherok in the shoulder with the pointed end of the shell. Cherok's body doubled up. His bloody lips moved, and Mi-sa heard him whisper her name.

She sat straight up out of her sleep, panting and crying, her body soaked with sweat, then tossed the cover off and moved to the corner of the shelter. Sitting in the dark with her arms wrapped around her legs, she rested her head on her knees. She did not want to go to sleep again. Not ever!

As she sat whimpering, she promised Cherok that she would try to save him. She would not desert him. "I promise. I promise," she whispered.

Cota opened one eye and saw her deep in moon shadow. He ached to go to her, to comfort her, to share whatever pain she suffered. But he knew she would not let him. All he could do was love her and hope she would soon let him carry part of the burden.

At the first hint of light, Mi-sa slipped beneath the cover and curled up next to Cota. He welcomed her, sleepily draping his arm over her.

As the sun came up, Cota stirred. He knew she had not slept most of the night, and he was worried about her.

"Can I help?" he whispered, knowing that her eyes were still open, staring. She had not closed them for even a quick rest. Now it seemed she was afraid to sleep. He wanted her to know that he cared, but he did not want to upset her or intrude on her privacy.

"No," she answered.

"Mi-sa," he said, moving closer and breathing into her hair. "I want you to become my wife."

Mi-sa sighed. "I cannot," she answered, still not turning to look at him. "A shaman takes no mate."

"I spend most nights with you."

"But you do not live at my hearth."

"Mi-sa," he argued, "you are no longer with your people."

"But one day I will be. And this is my destiny. I cannot break the will of the spirits. A shaman takes no mate. It does not matter if he has lost his people."

Cota swept his fingers over her profile. "You say 'he.' "

Mi-sa took his hand and pulled it to her mouth, kissing his palm. "I spent most of my life thinking of all shamans as 'he.' " Mi-sa held his hand to her cheek. "Both of us were born to a special destiny. Yours is to keep the peace. You cannot change that—would not change that. It is part of you. You must understand that I was born to serve my people. I cannot change that. I would not. I will never not be a shaman. I do not have a choice." She tilted her head back to look into his eyes. "Do you understand?"

Cota pulled her close but did not answer.

CHAPTER
— 28 —

Olagale fed fuel to his fire and sat close to it. The warmth of his hearth radiated to him, taking the bite out of the air. Many of the People had been sick, and he was tired. The cold air always brought sickness. The Kahoosa were not used to cool weather; they spent their lives dealing with heat. But the winter would pass soon. It never lasted long.

"Fix my hip," Hala said, walking up to him, casting a cool shadow over him as she blocked the setting sun.

"Have you used all the medicine?" he asked.

"Yes, but your elixir is not enough," she complained. "I need the healing touch. The cold air has done this to me."

"Hala, your joints always hurt. When the weather is hot, you grumble. When the weather is cold, you grumble."

"You are supposed to help me," she said, poking him with her walking stick. "Get up."

Olagale stood up, shaking his head. "Old woman, you—"

"Give me your hand, Olagale." It was Mi-sa. She had come up behind Hala.

"Take a lesson from this Tegesta woman," Hala said. "She told you how to prepare the medicine, but she can do much more than that."

267

Mi-sa took Olagale's hand in hers, then placed his palm on Hala's hip.

"I do not need to feel the old woman's joint," he said. "I believe her when she says it hurts."

"Olagale, please be quiet," Mi-sa said. "Close your eyes."

"Yes," Hala said haughtily, "do as Mi-sa says."

Mi-sa began to hum softly, and immediately Olagale could feel the strange vibrations pass through his hand. Hala also felt it and smiled.

"Clear your mind, Olagale. Stop trying to figure out what is happening. Just let it happen. Let go of all other thoughts," Mi-sa said.

She began a chant. Olagale knew some of the words, the special words of a shaman, but not all of them. They were not Tegesta and not Kahoosa. They were from the old, old language that the ancient ones had used when they talked with the spirits.

"Say the words with me," Mi-sa whispered.

Olagale struggled to make his tongue and lips form some of the words. The cadence was peculiar, unpredictable. He knew many chants, formally taught to him by his predecessor, but this one was different.

"Again," Mi-sa said. "Concentrate."

"But I do not know what the words mean, and they are difficult to say."

"Shh," Mi-sa said. "Do not fight it. Close your eyes, Olagale. Let the healing happen."

Mi-sa began to hum again, and Olagale hummed with her. The vibrations seemed stronger, perhaps because the two of them were working together, he thought.

Then she began to chant the ancient words, the peculiar melody. He concentrated on the chant and nothing else. Soon he was surprised to find that the music came easily from deep within him, as if the song had been buried inside him all the time. He still made mistakes, but as he and Mi-sa repeated the chant over and over, he found it easier, more natural, until he was lost in the sound.

Suddenly he felt heat pour out of his hand and into Hala's hip. He heard the old woman sigh with relief. Her pain seemed to float out of her and ride away on their words.

What wonderful magic, Hala thought gratefully. In a moment all the pain was gone.

The remedy complete, Mi-sa opened her eyes and retracted her hand. It took Olagale a moment to collect himself, to bring himself back from the dimension to which she had taken him.

"See, Shaman?" Hala said. "She should teach you more."

Olagale nodded as Hala walked off, her limp gone.

"Continue to give her the medicine I showed you how to make," Mi-sa told him, "but her pain is stubborn. She needs your healing touch."

Olagale sat down. The experience had left him exhausted. His whole body had been involved. Most remarkable, he thought.

"Did you hear me, Olagale?" Mi-sa asked.

Olagale nodded. "But I did not do the healing. It was you."

"But you can, Olagale. I have taught you how. Practice. Let yourself go so that you can find the spirits' help. The words can only lead you. You have to be willing to let go, to believe."

"Where did you learn this?" he asked, still amazed at what had just happened.

"I carry the blood of my father. The healing comes from inside me."

"How did you know the words? How did you even know that you could do it?"

"The same way you know that you can walk or talk. The way you know that if you want to raise your hand in the air, you can. It is the same."

Olagale pinched the bridge of his nose.

"Healing will leave you tired at first," she said, seeing his weariness.

"You do not look drained."

Mi-sa sat in front of him. "This was harder work for you because you had never done it before."

Olagale felt the need to defend himself. "But I have performed many feats."

"Of course you have. This was just new and different. That is all."

Olagale leaned out to look around Mi-sa. She turned to see what he saw.

"Pa-hay-tee, what do you do there?" Olagale asked, seeing the boy peek out from behind a bay tree.

The boy stepped out. "I wanted to see. I heard the chants. I heard Mi-sa. I wanted to watch."

"Sneaking about is not the way a man should behave," Olagale said.

"I did not mean to sneak around. I just did not want to interrupt."

"That was wise of you, Pa-hay-tee," Mi-sa said. "You used a man's judgment. The healing would not have happened if you had disturbed us."

Pa-hay-tee grinned. He liked this Tegesta woman. He was glad that she was Cota's woman.

"Go now," Olagale said. "Leave us."

Pa-hay-tee bowed his head in respect, then turned and ran off. Mi-sa was wonderful, he thought. He had never seen anything like what had just happened with Hala. The very air had been alive. What magic! He wanted to see more.

Someone grabbed his arm as he ran past. It was Naska.

"What is your hurry?" Naska asked, seeing that Pa-hay-tee was leaving Olagale and Mi-sa. He was curious.

"You should have seen!" Pa-hay-tee cried. "The most wonderful magic! Mi-sa taught Olagale how to heal Hala's hip. It was wonderful! You should have seen!"

"A boy gets so excited over a healing?"

"You should see," Pa-hay-tee said as Naska let go of his arm.

"Perhaps I will," Naska said, looking at the two shamans in the distance.

"No, it is over now," Pa-hay-tee said.

Naska affectionately slapped the boy on the back and walked away.

"Do you think she will do more?" Pa-hay-tee called to Naska, but he did not answer. Naska blended in with the shadows and the trees.

The darkness was setting in, and Olagale again fed his fire. "What brought you here to me?" he asked. "It was not Hala."

"No," Mi-sa said. "I need the help of a shaman." Suddenly Mi-sa shivered. She turned to see who was watching. The feeling was strong, but she saw no one.

"You need my help? You are a shaman."

"I need the help of a Kahoosa shaman. I need a friend," she said.

"Tell me what it is that you want of me."

Mi-sa again turned and looked behind her. Now darkness had completely fallen, and only the light of the moon lit the village. She scanned the area around them and again saw no one.

"I have dreams. Terrible dreams." She paused. "They are more than dreams."

"Are they visions?" Olagale asked.

"Not exactly. They are Spirit flights." Mi-sa realized she was going to have a difficult time explaining. Olagale had not had an easy time with Hala's healing. This was going to be even more difficult.

"Tell me what you mean," he said.

"My brother and our friend are being held by the A-po-la-chee. My dreams take me there."

"No, no, that is impossible. You may have dreams, perhaps visions, but you cannot go there."

Mi-sa took a deep breath. "But I do," she said.

Olagale stirred his fire, shaking his head.

"I can take you there," she said, almost afraid of what his reaction would be.

"Take me where? To your brother and the A-po-la-chee?"

"Yes," she said softly.

Olagale looked into her eyes. He felt frightened but titillated. "You can take me on a spirit flight like the legendary flights of the ancient ones—the pure shamans?"

"I am from a pure line. I have the blood-gift."

"You are sure you can do that?"

"I have never tried to take someone with me before," she said, "except my brother, who shares my blood. You would have to try hard, Olagale. You would have to believe in the spirit flight and want to come with me."

Olagale looked away from her, out into the darkness. He thought about what she had said, and Mi-sa did not hurry his decision. Finally he turned back to her. "Take me there," he said.

Mi-sa reached into a pouch and took out some special plant parts and fungi that she had collected.

"What are those for?" he asked.

"This journey will take a lot of power."

"Do you need to use these plants every time?" he asked.

"The spirits will not come and get us. We will have to go to their world. You purify yourself for vision quests. This is almost the same."

Olagale handed her a wooden bowl and pestle. "What plants do you use?" he asked.

"Lacca, orange fruit of the charantia, milky sap of the moonvine, a small tuber of nut grass, and these," she said, holding out some mushroom caps.

Olagale poked at the mushrooms. "Those are poisonous. We do not ingest them."

"I will dilute them. I know the right amount."

Olagale shifted, not certain he had made the right decision. He watched Mi-sa grind the ingredients, then put them in a bowl. He felt more and more apprehensive.

Mi-sa added water and stirred, then dropped hot stones into it until the water steamed. "The elixir will be ready in a moment. It does not take long. The heat quickly leaches the medicine out of the plants."

Olagale peered at the stained water in the bowl. The residue of the plants rose to the top and floated there.

Mi-sa scooped up the floating debris and tossed it out, then lifted the bowl to her lips, taking a small sip. She held it out to Olagale.

"How much?" he asked before taking the bowl.

"A small sip to start. Let that settle first, then another."

Olagale lifted the bowl to his lips, hesitated and then sipped. He closed his eyes, sure that he would feel something—something terrible. To his surprise, the elixir slid down his throat and landed in his stomach without incident.

Mi-sa took the bowl and sipped again. This time she filled her mouth with a little more. This was the medicine Atula had taught her, the medicine he said every shaman needed. She handed the bowl to Olagale. "Just a little more this time, and that is all. Put the bowl down when you are finished."

As she handed him the bowl, she felt the first sign. The medicine rushed hotly through her, making her flush. "Hurry, Olagale," she said.

Olagale took his drink and set down the bowl. He, too, quickly felt the effects.

Mi-sa reached out and took both of his hands. "Clear your mind. Let all the thoughts tumble out, Olagale. Leave yourself open to nothing but the spirits. Hear only my voice."

Olagale nodded and closed his eyes. The heat that flowed through him made him break into a sweat, and he was suddenly overwhelmed with a wave of nausea.

"Wait it out," Mi-sa said, knowing what he was feeling. "The sickness will pass. Concentrate on what I tell you."

Olagale breathed deeply, relaxing his body, feeling the heat and the nausea subside, experiencing a new and strange sensation of losing contact with his body.

"Collect yourself in the top of your head. Find the place. Gather yourself there," Mi-sa whispered.

Mi-sa wrapped her hands around Olagale's head, resting her thumbs over his eyes. He could feel the power, drawing all of him there, beneath her fingers, tightly compacted, centered, nearly exploding out the top of his head.

Suddenly he felt himself burst through the barrier, free of his body, sucked through a tunnel, traveling like the wind. There was white light at the end, and he felt himself stretch out into a thin wisp as he sped toward it. Quickly he reached the end of the dark tunnel, bathed in the light, surrounded by a white mist.

"Olagale."

He heard her voice, soft and echoing somewhere. He moved through the mist toward the voice.

"You are free, Olagale. Do not be afraid."

Olagale realized that he was frightened, and with each fearful thought he felt himself slip away, back toward his body. He put those thoughts away and concentrated on reaching Mi-sa.

"Here," she said. Her hand reached out through the mist, and then her whole body appeared to him. "Come with me," she said.

Olagale heard the sudden violent rush of hot wind, heard the roaring in his ears. And then they were suspended above the A-po-la-chee village, floating down until they hovered just above a man who was tied to a post, his head back, his eyes and lips swollen, lash scars across his chest and legs.

"He is my brother," Mi-sa said, "and that is my friend, Talasee." She indicated the man tied next to Cherok, his head slumped forward.

Olagale heard voices grow louder.

"Come away," a woman said, tugging on a young woman's arm.

"No, Mother," the young woman answered, kneeling in front of Cherok and swabbing his wounds.

"These men are our enemies. Your father will punish you. Come away," the woman said again.

"Go away, Mother, if it worries you, but I am staying."

The young woman continued to clean Cherok's wounds. She wiped away the dried blood and covered some of the wounds with leaves to keep the insects off them. Then she rose and put her hand around the back of his head, tilting it so that he could see her.

"Drink this," she said, holding a ladle of liquid to his lips.

Cherok sipped. "Help Talasee," he whispered.

The young woman lifted the other man's head. "Drink," she said, helping him sip from the bowl.

"Kyla," a loud male voice called. "Get away!"

The young woman dropped the ladle. "Father," she said, startled.

The man held a long piece of braided rawhide. He drew it back over his head, ready to strike her with it.

"No!" the older woman cried, throwing herself around the man's ankles.

The man kicked her off. "Get away, Kyla," he said to the young woman again, stepping closer.

Olagale heard the whoosh and smack as the man cracked the whip across Cherok's chest. Cherok threw his head back and bared his teeth in pain, but he did not cry out.

"Father, stop," the young woman pleaded, stepping in front of Cherok.

"If you want me to beat this man until he dies, then continue with what you have been doing. If you want him to live, then leave them both. Do not interfere."

"But how can they work for the A-po-la-chee if you—"

"Woman," he said, addressing the older woman, "take your daughter and keep better watch. Teach her more respect, or you will find your back scarred."

The older woman looked defiantly at the man with the whip. "She is your daughter, also."

"So you wish a beating, too?" the man asked.

The older woman kept her head bowed as she stood up. "Come, Kyla."

The younger woman followed her mother. The man spat on both Talasee and Cherok, his spittle running down their faces.

Olagale looked at Mi-sa. Tears were streaming down her face. "Oh, Cherok," she whispered.

The rush of the wind returned, and Olagale felt himself soaring through the air, above the A-po-la-chee village, back through the mist and the tunnel, and abruptly he found himself back at his fire.

He sat for a moment, shaken, unable to speak, trembling, the hair on his body bristling, making his skin tingle. He was amazed at how composed Mi-sa was, slowly opening her eyes, seemingly at peace.

"Now you must believe," she said.

Olagale was still stunned at what had just happened to him and sickened by what he had seen in the A-po-la-chee village.

"You see how my brother, Cherok, suffers."

"It was gruesome," Olagale said.

"I must save him, Olagale. I have no one to help me. My village and my people are gone."

"Then it is out of your hands."

"No," she said. "The spirits keep taking me there because they want me to help Cherok and Talasee. And I cry inside for my brother."

"I do not understand what you want me to do," Olagale said, squinting into the fire.

"I need someone to help me."

"You have Cota."

"Olagale, I cannot tell Cota how I despair. If I did, he would be torn. He would feel he should offer to make war on the A-po-la-chee to save Cherok and Talasee. But he has explained to me the commitment he carries as the seal of the peace. His whole purpose is to preserve the peace. I could not ask him to betray that. But, Olagale, I must do something. I have to leave, and I must ask you to convince Cota that it is for the best; otherwise he will not allow me to go. I need him, or someone, to take me to a Tegesta village. I pray they will believe me and take pity on me. I do not know the way or I would go alone. I am not afraid."

Olagale shook his head. "No, I do not think you are afraid of anything. But I cannot be part of this deceit."

Mi-sa stood up and angrily paced about the fire. "I have no

choice. I need your help, Olagale. There is no other way. I cannot go on like this. My brother cannot continue. You see what they have done to him."

"But there is a woman who cares for him."

"She can do nothing more. You saw that. Please, Olagale," she said, squatting across the fire from him.

The firelight danced on her face as the flames flickered in the night. Olagale could see the circles under her eyes, the need for rest in her eyes.

"A shaman must be trustworthy. Would you betray your cacique?"

"My brother is my cacique, and I betray him every day I do not help him." Mi-sa stood again, wringing her hands. "Think about it, Olagale. Cota will listen to you."

She did not look at him, fearful that he would deny her again. She turned her back and walked out of the firelight.

Just as she passed into darkness, where Olagale could no longer see her, Naska stepped behind her, flung one arm around her, and clamped his other hand over her mouth, then forced her into the forest on the perimeter of the village.

CHAPTER
~ 29 ~

Mi-sa struggled against her abductor, trying to scream through his hand, but the effort nearly gagged her. She fought to turn her head, to see who it was, but his grip was too strong.

Finally Naska stopped, satisfied that they were well hidden. "Do not move," he said. "Do you understand?"

Mi-sa immediately recognized his voice. She nodded.

"I am going to take my hand off your mouth, but do not scream."

Mi-sa nodded again. She would comply.

"Good," he said close to her ear. She could feel his hot breath break through the barrier of her hair.

"I am not going to hurt you. I only want to talk," he said, moving around in front of her. "Do not be afraid."

"If you did not want me to be afraid, why did you do this?"

"I saw what you did with Olagale—the spirit flight."

"You hid in the darkness?"

"I watched and I am impressed with your abilities."

"I told you that I am a shaman. Why are you so surprised?"

Naska smiled. "You are as defiant and full of spark as you were the day I found you across the river."

Mi-sa did not want to participate in Naska's games. He had tried to frighten her, make her anxious, when she was gathering plants. Now he had taken a more drastic measure.

"What do you want with me, Naska?"

His expression became serious. "Nothing is more important to you than your brother. Am I right?"

Mi-sa hesitated, trying to decide what Naska was up to. "Nothing is more important."

"You would do anything for him—to have him rescued?"

Mi-sa nodded. "My brother is a part of me. I do not expect you to understand that. You do not seem to have any love for your brother."

"Shaman woman," he said, remembering the night he had taken Chalosee to Ursa, "you do not know everything."

From the woods there was a noise, like leaves and twigs crunching beneath a foot. Both Naska and Mi-sa looked toward the sound. They waited a moment, but the noise was not repeated.

"Cota will be looking for me," she said. "He will be concerned. If you just wanted to pester me, to make me hurt inside thinking of my brother, you have achieved your goal. Now let me leave."

She took a step to move past Naska, but he grabbed her arm. "I am not finished," he said, then eased his hand off her.

Mi-sa shook her arm and rubbed where his hand had held so tightly.

"The Kahoosa can rescue your brother," he said.

She looked up at him, her eyes wide with question. "How can you do that?"

"We will raid the A-po-la-chee village and bring him back."

"If you were spying on me, watching me with Olagale, then your ears are poor. I will never ask Cota to betray—"

Naska put his hand over her mouth. "You talk too much and do not listen. Quiet," he said, taking his hand away. "You

will not need to ask Cota. I can gather a war party. Cota will
not be involved."

Mi-sa shook her head. "You will challenge your brother. I
will not allow that, either."

"Do you want your brother back? I offer you a way."

"I love Cota," she said. "You will muster a group to rise
against him."

"No, that will not be my way. I promise you that."

Mi-sa searched his eyes for signs of truth. "I will think
about this," she said.

"Does Cherok lead a good life with the A-po-la-chee?
Does he wait in comfort for you and your people to come for
him?"

Mi-sa let out a heavy breath. "He suffers, Naska. You
know that. And because he suffers, I suffer. Have you no
feelings?"

"Why do you think I offer to do this? I could see how an-
guished you were when you spoke with Olagale. I understand
why you do not want to ask Cota."

There was much more to this, Mi-sa thought. "It is not
your nature to do good deeds. What else is there, Naska?
What is in it for you?"

"If I save your brother, you will be grateful, will you not,
Tegesta woman?"

Mi-sa did not want to answer. She did not like where this
was leading.

"I will do something for you, and because you are so
grateful, you will do something for me."

"What, Naska? What do you want?"

"You will be my woman."

Mi-sa took a step around him, leaving this ridiculous, out-
rageous man whom she held in such contempt.

Naska let her pass, but he said, "Picture your brother and
what the A-po-la-chee are doing to him. I know their methods, but then, you have seen for yourself. He is counting on
you."

Mi-sa stopped.

"There is no future here for you with Cota. You will grow to resent him because of what he stands for, because you could never ask him for his help. You know that you must deliver your brother from the hands of the A-po-la-chee. If you abandon Cherok, your decision will eat at you, consume you from the inside out."

Mi-sa turned around to look at him. "I will go to a Tegesta village and ask for help."

"Do you believe that will be easy? I offer you my help here and now."

She feared that if she did go to a Tegesta village the people there would not believe or accept her. They would wonder what a woman was doing on a Big Water journey. Mi-sa stepped back toward Naska.

"You could not gather a war party so quickly," she said.

"It would take time, but only because you do not wish me to openly challenge Cota."

"No, I do not want you to do that."

"The sooner you become my woman, the sooner I can begin—the sooner your brother will be free."

"What will become of Ursa?" Mi-sa said.

"I have no commitment to her."

"I will not have you as a husband," Mi-sa said. "That is forbidden."

"I want no wife," he answered.

"I will not be your woman in my heart. My heart will always belong to Cota. Can you live with that?"

Naska laughed. "To possess you—something my brother cannot have? I can live with that very well. I look forward to it."

"This will be hard for me, Naska. You ask me to hurt Cota."

"Do not feel so bad for him. He has always had what he wants. And he will have Chalosee. His grief will be short-lived. Remember the pain your brother suffers."

"What makes you think I will lie in your bed when you return Cherok and Talasee?"

"I suspect you will not. But you will not be Cota's woman either. You will want to return to your home with your people, search for others, and rebuild. Just as Cota is the peacekeeper, you are a shaman. Neither of you can betray your destiny. Is that not so?"

Naska was right. "Then until my brother returns, I will be your woman," she said.

"When you break with Cota and you lie beside me, then I will begin my work."

Mi-sa walked off, the pact completed. Naska watched her leave. What good fortune Pa-hay-tee had stopped him. He had found her weak spot.

Mi-sa made her way through the dark village. This was the only way. She had had her moment of happiness. Now she would give Cota up, rescue Cherok, and return home. The spirits had let her have the man in her dreams for a short while. Now it was time to sacrifice her own happiness for that of others.

The fire keeper had banked the central hearth for the long, cold night. The flames slapped at the darkness as she passed. Her own coals had gone out. The wood of the ladder was cold on her feet.

"Mi-sa," Cota said, coming out of the night. "I looked for you."

"I went for a walk," she said, standing on the ladder.

"In the dark?"

"I needed to think."

"Mi-sa, come down so that we can talk," he said.

She slowly stepped down to the ground.

"Tell me what troubles you," he said, slipping both hands up under her hair, cradling the back of her head.

"I am very tired, Cota," she managed to say without her voice trembling.

"I will hold you until you fall asleep," he said, touching his lips to hers.

"Not tonight, Cota," she said, finding it hard to take her mouth from his.

Cota lifted his head away. "What is wrong, Mi-sa?"

"Nothing is wrong. I just need to be alone. I am tired."

Mi-sa saw the hurt, the confusion, in his eyes, and her heart was heavy. If he did not leave soon, she knew she would cry.

Cota slid his hands out of her hair. His eyes explored hers, probing for an explanation, assessing her feelings.

"Tomorrow," Mi-sa said, turning away from him and climbing the ladder. She gripped the rungs tightly, closed her eyes, and bit her bottom lip.

Inside the platform, she sat on her mat, holding her medicine bag, rocking back and forth. She reached into the pouch that hung around her neck, withdrew the dream-catcher, and pressed it to her lips.

Mi-sa hummed softly, praying to the spirits. Soon she was chanting, asking the spirits to come this way and touch her, give her the strength to do what was right, reaching into their world until the energy inside the platform crackled and sparked.

Olagale could not sleep, so he climbed down and sat by his hearth. He looked across the village and stared at Mi-sa's platform. Until tonight he had never known her kind of sorcery was possible.

His thoughts were interrupted. Behind the fire, where he could see only shadows, silhouettes, he observed a small figure running, staying low, as if not wanting to be seen. Olagale stood to get a better look, but Pa-hay-tee's fleeting image disappeared in the dark shadows.

The night passed slowly for Mi-sa, for Cota, and for Olagale, but not for Naska. He was deliciously ebullient. That was what kept his eyes open at first, but once he drifted off, he entered a deep, contented sleep.

When morning came, Naska awakened easily, eager for the day to begin. He was going to enjoy watching his plan played out. This would give him great satisfaction.

Mi-sa was already at her fire. She had slept little, and her eyes felt as if they were filled with grit. Her head ached, and she had no appetite. The only good thing was that even in her short spells of sleep, there had been no dreams. It was the first night in many, many moons that the dreams of Cherok had not awakened her, terrorized her. Maybe that was a sign from the spirits that she had made the right decision.

She saw Chalosee taking something in a basket to Hala. She watched the gathering of the Council of Men begin. Cota stopped at her fire on his way. She saw Chalosee stop and try to discreetly watch them. Mi-sa looked down at the tea that brewed above the hearth.

"Look at me," Cota said, squatting next to her. "Let me see your eyes." He turned her head with a gentle touch. He did not like what he saw. The light that always flashed in her eyes was gone; they looked sad and dull.

Mi-sa resisted his touch and turned back to the fire.

"Why can you not tell me what is troubling you, Mi-sa? Why do you carry this burden alone?"

"I have just been thinking about us together. I am not certain that it is good."

Cota rocked back and then sat on the ground. "What do you mean?"

"We have no future together. One day I will return to my people."

"When that time comes, we will think about it."

Mi-sa stood up as if to walk away. "No, Cota. I think about it all the time. I am a Tegesta shaman, and you are a Kahoosa cacique."

Cota took her hand in his. "I do not understand."

Mi-sa pulled her hand out of his and stepped back. "The Council gathers," she said, looking toward the central hearth, feeling her stomach tighten into a sick, nauseated ball.

Cota rose and took her hand again. "We will talk after Council," he said. "Wait here for me."

Chalosee was still standing there, but she looked away when Mi-sa turned toward her. Mi-sa watched Cota enter the

Council, his golden brown skin shining in the morning light, his long black hair flowing over his shoulders and down his back like black water, the white eagle feathers that dripped down the side of his hair caught in the breeze. How glorious he was to look at, how wonderful to touch.

She watched him take his place in Council and saw how the other men treated him with great respect and honor. Giving him up had already become painful. But then, her happiness was not important. She was a servant of the spirits.

As Naska passed her, he hesitated so that she would notice that he was looking at her.

Mi-sa cringed. He smiled and moved on.

She finished her morning tasks, gathered some basketry materials, and walked out of the village and down to the river. Council would end soon, and she did not want Cota to find her. She moved along the bank, ducking under the overhanging branches, smelling the wet earth and decaying leaves. The aroma was not unpleasant, just natural. She felt more at home here than in the Kahoosa village.

Deciding that she had walked far enough, she sat by the river and watched the current move the water in deep sheets and whirl it in eddies. She had not felt this peaceful in a long while. She leaned back onto the soft bed of leaves, closed her eyes, listened to the song of the river, and drifted into sleep.

When she awakened she was surprised to realize that she had slept. Again her sleep had not been interrupted by horrific dreams. She knelt by the river and cupped her hands in it to get a drink. Suddenly she let the water splash out of her hands. She saw a reflection in the rippling water.

"Pa-hay-tee!" She laughed, turning to face him. "I did not hear you come."

Pa-hay-tee smiled. "I am learning well the ways of a warrior," he said, pulling something out from behind his back. "Look," he said, holding up a dead little blue heron. "I killed it with my father's bird point. He traded for it before I was born. It is mine now."

"Is this your first kill?" she asked.

"No, Cota helped me with the first, since I have no uncle and no father. It was a gallinule. My mother keeps those feathers. She thinks the gallinule is beautiful." The boy held the fresh kill by its long greenish legs, lifting it up to admire it more closely. "It is a grand bird, do you not think so?"

"Yes, Pa-hay-tee. It is a fine bird. You will provide well for your family."

Pa-hay-tee plopped himself down on the ground next to her, resting the dead bird in his lap, a few of its slate-blue feathers sticking out at angles from all the handling. "Would you like this bird?" he asked.

Mi-sa smiled at the boy. "I would be honored to accept it," she said.

"Will you come with me when I show it to Cota and my mother?" he asked.

Mi-sa looked at the boy who was so proud of his accomplishment. He had offered her his kill. She could not refuse to go with him, even though she wished to.

"Is something wrong?" Pa-hay-tee asked, noticing her hesitation.

"No," Mi-sa assured him. "Just let me get my basketry."

As Mi-sa gathered her things, the boy girdled the feet of the bird with a narrow piece of rawhide and then tied it to his waistband at his side. "Do you love Cota?" Pa-hay-tee asked.

The question startled Mi-sa. "Let us go," she said.

Pa-hay-tee did not ask again. Mi-sa kept him busy in other conversation as they walked back to the village.

"Mother!" Pa-hay-tee shouted, starting in a trot toward Nakila. "Come, Mi-sa."

She followed behind. Mi-sa watched Pa-hay-tee's mother tousle his hair and bend her knees so that she was face to face with him. "You will be a great hunter," she said with a mother's pride.

"I have offered the bird to Mi-sa. She says she would be proud to take it. That is all right?" he asked, suddenly wondering if his mother might object.

"That is a noble gesture, Pa-hay-tee." The boy's mother

ooked up at Mi-sa, her face showing how pleased she was
hat Mi-sa had accepted.

"I want to show Cota," he said.

"Of course," his mother said.

"Come on, Mi-sa," Pa-hay-tee said excitedly. "Help me
ind him." He grabbed Mi-sa's hand and tugged her along as
e took off.

"There he is," Pa-hay-tee said, springing across the village.
"Look! Look!" he shouted, getting Cota's attention as he ran
up to him, dragging Mi-sa along.

Cota looked at the boy, but his eyes darted to Mi-sa. Even
as he spoke to Pa-hay-tee, he was looking at Mi-sa.

"What is this?" he asked.

"I have killed it, as you taught me," the boy said.

Cota looked away from Mi-sa and took the heron from Pa-
hay-tee's hand, inspecting it.

"A good kill—clean, neat. The bird did not suffer. You
have honored the bird's spirit with your skill, and now he
gives his substance to you." Cota spoke to him with respect.

Pa-hay-tee was grinning. "I have offered the bird to
Mi-sa."

Cota found Mi-sa's eyes again. "And what does the woman
say?"

"She is proud to take it. I have provided for her."

"So you have," Cota said, patting the young boy on the
head.

Pa-hay-tee looked at the two of them as they stared at each
other.

"Take the heron to her hearth," Cota said.

Pa-hay-tee obeyed his teacher.

"How does a small one find the woman I have looked
for?"

"I was by the river," Mi-sa answered.

"You hide from me, Mi-sa."

"I needed the solitude. The river is a comforting sight and
sound. You must find it that way also."

"Why do I feel this sudden distance between us?"

"Things change," she said.

"I do not believe what you say," Cota said. "It sounds to me as if you are saying your heart has turned from me. This has to do with your dreams. Let me help. Do not shut me out."

Mi-sa felt her throat tighten, and she fought back tears. He would suffer more if she dragged this on. She had to tell him now. She had to make a clean kill, like Pa-hay-tee's.

CHAPTER
— 30 —

Cota saw the look on her face. He did not want to hear what she was going to say. Something in her dreams had driven her away from him. She did not want to tell him what was troubling her, and he could not help her unless he knew about her dreams.

"Come with me," he said. "We will walk quietly to the river together. Leave your basketry."

Mi-sa dropped her materials and followed him. She thought perhaps it would be better if she told him in a more private place.

They passed Chalosee as they left the village. Mi-sa saw her staring. Chalosee must have sensed there was a problem.

The path through the forest was wider now that the grasses and ground cover were dying back in the cold weather.

At the edge of the river, Cota took her hand and led her down the bank. The river cut deep into the land. He led her to a shelf that jutted out from the bank below them.

He held her face in his hands and touched his mouth to hers, lightly first, and then hungrily. He pulled her close, reveling in the feel of her smooth skin against him.

Mi-sa savored his touch, his scent, his kiss. "No, Cota," she whispered, objecting, but not strongly enough. His mouth pressed ravenously, voraciously, against hers. She felt herself weaken, and then her body gave in to his embrace and her mouth searched for him.

As she closed her eyes, faltering, relenting, Cherok's face appeared in her mind, and she pushed herself away. "No, Cota," she heard herself say. "I am no longer your woman."

Cota shook his head in disbelief, stepping close to her. "You say that, but your body betrays you." He attempted to embrace her.

"No, Cota," she said again, moving out of his arms.

"I do not believe you," he said, his heart in his throat. His mouth was again suddenly on hers, then on her neck as he whispered to her. "Tell me you do not want to be with me. I feel your body yield to mine. You are my woman."

"Stop," she said, fighting the urge to succumb to him, to confess that he was right.

"I need you," he whispered, his voice full of passion. He kissed her shoulder and moved in to the crook of her neck, his hands searching her. He let out a soft groan as his mouth suckled her breast before he went to his knees, pressing his face against her belly.

Mi-sa's hands held his shoulders as she stepped back, trying to get her breath. "Do not make this any more difficult," she said, then turned and ran off.

"Mi-sa," he called loudly, but she did not turn around, and he did not see that her cheeks were covered with streams of tears. He could not see her tormented expression as she held back the sobs.

Naska saw her run into the village, hiding her face with her hands, desperately trying to reach her shelter without being noticed. His mouth turned up into a roguish smile.

Mi-sa sat alone at her hearth during the evening meal. She had stayed inside her platform all the rest of the day. She did not want to see Cota. She could not endure Chalosee's stare or Naska's victorious glance. And Hala would have gone straight to the heart of the matter if she had stopped to talk.

But, she decided, her continued absence would invite questions.

Naska approached, and Mi-sa felt a mixture of anger and a need to cooperate.

"Your eyes are swollen," he said.

"It is done," she said.

"You have broken with Cota?" he asked.

"Yes," she answered.

"So soon? I am surprised, woman."

"I want my brother back," she answered.

"When you become my woman," he said, smiling and moving on.

"Naska," Mi-sa called. "Let it begin now," she said. "Sit close to me."

Naska turned around, his eyebrows arching in doubt. "Cota will be watching."

"I know," she said.

"I never knew that you were so callous," he said, seeming to be pleased with this new discovery.

"This is the kinder thing to do. Let Cota begin his new life as soon as possible. He deserves more days of happiness. I have already robbed him of one. I will take no more than I must."

"Interesting," Naska said, finally sitting at the fire with her. He surveyed the village. Many eyes were watching them, and he was filled with satisfaction.

Mi-sa pressed her thumbnail painfully hard into her palm, her fingers moving constantly, which revealed her distress. "Do I go to your platform, or do you come to mine?" she asked.

"Which do you prefer?"

"I have no preference," she said. "Only my body will be there; my spirit will be elsewhere."

Naska sat back, displeased by her comment. "Then maybe I will wait until you can bring all of yourself to me." He pitched a fallen twig into the fire.

"You will have a long wait, Naska."

"And so will Cherok," he said, the corners of his mouth slightly turned up. He knew his barbed comment would hurt her.

She did not want Naska to know that he had alarmed her, and so she turned to face him squarely. She glared at him as she spoke. "You only made me promise to be your woman. I told you that my heart would never be yours."

The small muscles of Naska's face kicked up into an expression of false surprise. "Oh, I never would have agreed to that, woman. When I join with you, I want to know that you are there with me."

"But I will not be. And you did agree to that," she argued.

Naska plunged a stick into the ground so that it stood on its own. "Perhaps you need more time to think." He moved, as if to leave. "I have time. Too bad your brother may suffer even more while you wait. But think of the best thing that could happen: He could die and not have to suffer anymore."

She was not able to hide her feelings this time, and Naska saw her face blanch.

"I think I see now how you most differ from your brother," she said. "You cannot help it. I feel sorry for you. You were born without a heart."

Naska rose and looked down at her. "Ursa will be happy to gratify me until you change your mind," he said. "Your decision may come too late. If I am without a heart, I may change my mind if someone else attracts me. You do understand, do you not?"

Mi-sa did understand. She touched his calf as he took his first step to walk away. She found it hard to speak.

"You want something?" he asked.

"All right, Naska," she said. She would pretend that she enjoyed being touched by him, joining with him. She would make him believe her act. She could do that, she thought. She could do anything—for Cherok.

"If you let me, I can please you. I am good at satisfying a woman."

Mi-sa had no response. What she wanted to say would not have served her purpose.

"We do not have to be together tonight if you need more time."

"No," Mi-sa said, standing beside him. "It will be tonight. That is what is best for Cherok, and that is what is best for Cota. The quicker this is done, the better for all."

"As you wish," he said. "My platform, then. Let the villagers see you walk with me, and then go inside with me. The word will travel fast."

She walked next to him, feeling his hand crawl onto her shoulder. She flinched at his touch, but made herself accept it. She stared straight ahead, unable to look at the villagers, especially afraid that she would pass Cota.

"Cota will be suspicious," Naska said.

"He must not know my reasons," she answered. "You must let the gossip out so that everyone believes I have left Cota for you, and not for any other reason."

"I can do that," he said as they reached the ladder that led up to his platform. "Why do we not sit at my fire for a while. The night air is cool, and the fire pleasant."

He would have been pleased if even more of the Kahoosa had noticed that Mi-sa was with him. "Maybe if we just talk awhile before we go up, you will find this easier."

"Nothing will make this easier," she said. "Let us get it over with."

Mi-sa took her first step up the ladder. Naska looked about. Many people were watching.

Chalosee was one of those who stared. Immediately she searched for Cota. Finally she saw him leaving the central hearth, heading for his platform.

Many of the men had gathered to talk about the hunt they planned, and they stood around the hearth discussing what needed to be replenished. Cota had listened, but he had not concentrated on the men's talk. He was thinking of Mi-sa, and then he had seen her with Naska.

The shock of seeing her with his brother had nearly taken

his breath away. He continued to try to participate in the discussions, approving when others voiced their agreement, laughing when someone told a humorous story, but concentration became impossible. After a short time, he excused himself.

He stood in the shadows, unable to keep from staring at Naska's platform. He could not allow this to happen with no explanation from her or from his brother. Cota approached Naska's ladder. He would confront them both.

Mi-sa moved out from under Naska and sat up. "When will you begin to ask the men to attack the A-po-la-chee?" she asked.

"Tomorrow," Naska said, his voice still rough. "I will keep my word."

Mi-sa stood, grabbed her skirt, and wrapped herself in a skin.

"Where do you go?" he asked.

"To the river to bathe," she said.

"It is dark, woman. Wait until the morning."

Mi-sa turned to the opening and was shocked to see Cota standing at the head of the ladder.

"Naska!" Cota said, looking past Mi-sa, seeing his brother sprawled naked on his mat.

Naska sat up, the moonlight bright enough to show his wide smile. "Brother, you should not enter a man's platform without announcing yourself. You can never be sure what you might walk into. It could be embarrassing. Is that not so, Mi-sa?"

Even in the dim light she could see the muscles in Cota's jaw clench as he reached for his knife.

"No, Cota," she said, grabbing his hand. "He is your brother."

"I have no brother," Cota said, stepping closer to Naska, his knife drawn.

"Come on, brother, mighty cacique," Naska taunted.

"Come and cut your brother. Show us how you value the peace."

Cota sheathed his knife. "You are right, Naska. There is something much greater than you." He turned to Mi-sa and glared.

She nervously crept down the ladder, feeling Cota follow her to the river. When she reached the bank she stopped and turned to face him.

"Why have you done this, Mi-sa?" Cota asked, grabbing her upper arm through the wrap. "Why have you left my bed for my brother's?"

Mi-sa pulled away. "I do not want to discuss this with you."

"Do you not think you owe me an explanation? You suddenly grew cold to me, and then in nearly the same heartbeat I see that you sleep with Naska."

"I have come to the river to bathe," she said, turning away from him.

Cota pulled at her again. "Is he rough with you when he joins with you? Does he treat you in his bed the way he treats everyone? Is that what you like?" he asked, gripping her arm until the tender flesh burned. "Is that the Tegesta way?" He yanked her toward him and the deerskin fell away from one shoulder.

"You are hurting me, Cota. Let go," she said.

Cota released her.

"Leave me alone," she said, adjusting the wrap, then rubbing the pain out of her arm. "Leave me alone."

"When I think of him touching you, I become so angry!"

"Go back to Chalosee. That is what was meant to be. I am Naska's woman."

"No, that is not what is meant to be. It is what you have made it to be. Why, Mi-sa? Tell me why."

Mi-sa knew she had to get him to leave. If he did not go away quickly, she was going to cry. The pain inside her was so intense she found it hard to speak.

"I love him," she lied. "I have chosen Naska. I am his woman."

Cota stepped back and looked across the river. Finally he turned to her and stared for a long time.

Mi-sa held her breath, afraid to move.

"I will not bother you again," he said.

She watched him go, and when he was out of sight, the deer-skin drape fell down her back to the ground as she wrapped her arms around her middle, muffling her scream by holding it in the back of her throat, bending over, and finally dropping to her knees.

Cota entered the village, stunned and destroyed by Mi-sa's words. He did not notice that Chalosee followed him, keeping her distance. She waited until he was inside his platform, then climbed up the ladder.

"Cota," she called.

At first he thought it was Mi-sa's voice, but quickly realized that it was not.

"What do you want, Chalosee? I am weary and ready for sleep."

"May I enter?" she asked. "I wish to speak with you."

He did not answer right away, and Chalosee took advantage of his hesitation, stepping inside and walking up to him. He sat on his mat, and she moved behind him, placing her hands on his shoulders, massaging him gently.

"What brings you here?" he asked, leaning his head down to better enjoy the massage.

"You are still my friend, are you not?" she asked, her fingers rolling over his tensed muscles.

"Yes, of course."

"Then I have come to comfort my friend," she said softly. "I have seen Mi-sa with Naska."

Cota moved one of her hands off his shoulder. "Perhaps you should leave," he said.

Chalosee knelt behind him and touched her lips gently to

the back of his shoulder. "I can make you forget her," she said softly.

In his mind Cota saw the image of Mi-sa going inside Naska's platform. That was what all Mi-sa's dreams had been about—his brother. That was why she would not tell him what troubled her. He wondered if she had been with Naska in the woods while he was searching for her this afternoon. Suddenly he could see Naska's mouth touching her, his hands groping and feeling. He could even hear Mi-sa whisper Naska's name. His heart pounded, and he could feel his blood rush through him.

Chalosee ran one hand around him, holding him as she touched her lips to his neck. "I have always loved you," she said.

Cota twisted his head over his shoulder, reached around, and grabbed the back of Chalosee's head, pulling her to him.

His kiss hurt, bruising her lips as he pulled her down onto his mat. His roughness frightened her a little, and she pulled free.

"Touch me here," she said, leading his hand to her abdomen. "The spirits approved when we joined—before you went away with Mi-sa—and they have brought us back together. Your child grows within me."

Cota sat up, releasing the harsh grip he realized he still had on her arm. "A child?"

"Yes, Cota," she whispered in his ear. "I carry your child."

The days passed, and to everyone it became evident that Mi-sa had become Naska's woman. Chalosee quickly spread the news that she carried the cacique's son. But Cota seldom joined with her, and when he did there was little tenderness, especially if he had been around Naska and the Tegesta woman. He was sometimes apologetic afterward, but offered no explanation. She constantly tried ways to keep him interested in her, to stir his passion.

Mi-sa prayed for visions and for strength to tolerate Naska. The spirits were kind enough to show her the Kahoosa at-

tacking the A-po-la-chee, so she knew that it would come to
be, if she could just continue to honor the agreement she had
with Naska. The visions convinced her that she had made the
right decision.

Each time Naska came to her, she asked him how many
men he had spoken to about the raid on the A-po-la-chee.

"Be patient," he would tell her. "If you do not want an uprising against my brother, then this must be done slowly, with
subtlety and finesse. That is what you want, is it not?"

Mi-sa would agree to be patient.

The men prepared for the hunt. They gathered at the central hearth.

"You will accompany me," Cota said to Pa-hay-tee. "We
will hunt deer."

"And Naska hunts the alligator?" Pa-hay-tee asked, seeing
the pointed pole he carried, the length of two men.

"Yes."

"That is a dangerous choice," Pa-hay-tee commented.

"All hunters must be careful. Naska enjoys enticing the
alligator, and when the alligator comes for him, its mouth
agape, thinking that it will fill its belly with the man, Naska
will ram the pole down the alligator's gullet. It is like a game
for Naska."

Pa-hay-tee looked at all the men, the weapons, and equip-
ment they carried. One man had laid his gear and trappings
on the ground. Pa-hay-tee bent down to look at it all—nets,
weights, spears, hooks, barbed bone harpoons, and poisons to
coat the tips of the weapons. Pa-hay-tee looked forward to
the day when he would go to the Big Water.

Over the boy, Cota draped a deerskin with head attached,
adjusting it as Pa-hay-tee stood up.

"Keep your face hidden as best you can," Cota said. "If
you walk slowly the way I have taught you, and keep the dis-
guise, you will find yourself very close to a deer. Do not
rush."

The deer head bobbed as Pa-hay-tee nodded.

"Now we will say our prayers," Cota said. "Each hunter must pray to the spirits of his quarry to ensure the rebirth of the animal."

Cota began to speak the words of the prayer. Pa-hay-tee repeated every word and phrase, knowing the importance of this ritual, which guaranteed continued abundance for the People.

When they finished praying, the men dispersed. Kaho and some of the older men chose to fish in the river. They carried their labyrinths of weirs woven from reeds. Kaho looked back at the village before following the path to his canoe. The women wished their men good fortune and quick return. He saw Naska wrap his arm around Mi-sa and Chalosee embrace Cota. This was all wrong, he thought.

Naska hoisted his pole and carried it over his shoulder. "So, Ockla, we will hunt the alligator together," Naska said as they made their way to the riverbank. "You enjoy the danger also."

Ockla slapped Naska's back. "We will be a good team."

"Yes," Naska agreed. "We are much the same." Naska paused, and they tramped through the thick brush along the edge of the river. "Sometimes I think the Kahoosa have grown weak."

Ockla looked up. "What do you mean? The Kahoosa are a strong tribe."

"But not as powerful as they were when my father was the young cacique."

"Things change, and the Kahoosa are wise to make changes. We cannot stand still with our feet mired in the mud of the past."

"No, Ockla. I do not mean that we should not make changes. But we must balance things. We must remain proud and strong even though we stand for peace."

"You do not think the Kahoosa are proud and strong?" Ockla asked, sounding a bit annoyed.

"If one of our people was taken by the A-po-la-chee and held captive, do you think we would go after him?"

"We would be upon them like water on fire!"

"Think, Ockla. Cota is the seal of the peace. His mission is to keep the peace. The Kahoosa no longer make war."

"It would be a dilemma, then. I see what you mean."

"But there are those of us who could go after our brother without feeling that we had broken the peace. I feel that you are one of those strong warriors among us."

Ockla nodded, listening carefully to Naska.

"Can I trust you?" Naska asked, feeling he had prepared the bed of Ockla's mind to receive his suggestion.

"Of course," Ockla answered.

Both men stopped their trek to continue the conversation.

"The woman, Mi-sa, who lives with us—she is Tegesta, and we are one with the Tegesta. Her brother, cacique of her clan, and another man were stolen by the A-po-la-chee. She will not ask Cota to go to war, for she understands that he cannot. I believe the A-po-la-chee think we are a weak tribe of old men and boys. If we do not strike, what will the enemy and the other tribes think of the Kahoosa and the Tegesta? They will call us women!"

"We cannot break the peace," Ockla said. "We are a people of our word. And we must never take such action without the approval of the Council and the cacique."

"Perhaps you are not the man I thought you were," Naska said, moving ahead of Ockla.

CHAPTER
— 31 —

The moon turned in its cycles, and the cool air vanished. The streams and rivers were alive with the flashes of silver and gold scales of breeding fish. Birds nested, and dormant cypresses burst forth with lacy pale green buds. Hala's old bones did not seem quite as stiff. Winter had retreated back to the land to the north.

Mi-sa sipped her medicinal tea. She had made it especially strong since she had been with Naska. She prayed that no child would come from this.

She remembered hearing about Chalosee from Hala.

"The union is good," Hala had said. "A child grows inside my daughter." Soon after that, Cota had taken Chalosee as his wife.

Mi-sa had tried to appear happy when Hala told her about the baby, but it was difficult.

"Olagale prepares a medicine for her," Hala had said. "I want to know what you think of it."

"Tell me about it, Hala."

"It is an herbal concoction made of gumbo-limbo bark, cones of the pine tree for health and a long life, and spines of the prickly pear so the baby will jump down when it is time."

"It sounds like a good medicine."

301

"Is there anything else she should do?" Hala asked. "Something the Tegesta know and we do not? I believe in your medicine. I have seen for myself what you can do."

"Tell Chalosee not to wear anything around her neck; the cord might wrap itself around the baby's throat. She should eat no spotted fish or the baby may have birthmarks. I cannot think of anything else."

Mi-sa had continued to watch Chalosee's belly swell. She sipped her bitter medicine. Suddenly she had a flash of a memory—a vision she had had of Chalosee a long time ago. She shuddered.

In a few more cycles of the moon the baby would be born. The thought made Mi-sa go to find Naska. She would ask him again, hoping this time he would tell her that all was set, and that the men had planned a raid on the A-po-la-chee.

"What do the men say?" she asked. "When will you go for Cherok?"

"This takes time," he said. "Perhaps you want me to incite the men, have them take the matter to Council—to Cota. An uprising? No," he said, "I know that is not what you want. Be patient, woman." Naska smiled at her, then moved her hair so that he could see more of her. "Do I not bring you pleasure?"

She wanted to tell him no. She wanted to tell him that she only made him believe she enjoyed being with him, but really she hated it. If she had not had continued visions of the Kahoosa attacking the A-po-la-chee, showing her that she had made the right decision, she would have ended the agreement with Naska.

"I am anxious to have my brother and Talasee delivered from the A-po-la-chee. Each day they remain, they suffer more."

"The time is coming."

Mi-sa walked away from Naska. If he did not do something soon, she was going to back out of this arrangement. When Naska had proposed this scheme to her, she had not realized that it would take so long. When she had accepted, she had thought she could tolerate anything for a short time. She knew that Naska could indeed incite the men to rebellion at the idea that the A-po-la-chee had taken two of their Tegesta brothers. And if she did not go along with Naska, he would do just that. But she did not want to see Chalosee every day, her belly protruding with the fruit of Cota's seed. She did not want to be here when Chalosee's baby was born. She wanted Cherok and Talasee to return, freed from the torture and enslavement, and then they would leave together.

"Mi-sa!"

She heard her name being called. It was Olagale. He was trotting up to her.

"What brings you in such a hurry?" she asked as Olagale reached her.

"It is Chalosee. She does not do well. I fear for her and the baby. Her belly tightens even as we speak."

"It is too early for the child to be born."

"I have given her my medicines and said my prayers, but still she suffers. Can you help?"

Mi-sa stepped away. "No, Olagale. I do not think Chalosee would want me to. And if something went wrong—"

"She will do anything to save this child."

Mi-sa paused and looked across the village to Cota's platform where Chalosee lay. "Let me get some things," she said.

"Come quickly," Olagale pleaded.

"Yes," she said, "I will be there."

Inside her platform she searched for plant parts she had collected for medicines. Suddenly a shadow fell over her, and she turned to see Cota standing in the entrance.

"You will help her?"

"Yes," Mi-sa answered, unable to take her eyes from his.

"If the baby comes now, it will be too small."

"You love her," Mi-sa said, seeing the sadness in his eyes.

"She is my wife," he answered.

Mi-sa went back to searching through the plants, but she could not concentrate on what she needed.

"Can I help you?" he asked, leaning over her, grazing her, making her close her eyes.

She fumbled through more baskets and pouches, finally coming up with some leaves that were still green and pliant.

"They are fresh enough. I will not need to brew them into a tea."

"Mi-sa," he said softly as she passed him.

She stopped and turned to face him. Their eyes met, and the silence inside the platform became profound.

"Nothing," he finally said.

Mi-sa moved to the ladder and descended. Cota followed. Pa-hay-tee trailed behind them. Something important was happening. There was a lot of commotion. The boy called out to Cota.

"Not now, Pa-hay-tee. Chalosee's baby wants to come too early."

Pa-hay-tee continued to follow them. The boy's voice was filled with excitement. "Are you going to do magic like you did the night you helped Hala with her hip?" he called to Mi-sa. "That kind of magic? Will you take Olagale on a spirit flight like you did that night?"

Mi-sa stopped and turned around, recalling that night—the night Naska had offered his terms. Pa-hay-tee had confessed to hiding and watching while she healed Hala, but then she thought he had gone away.

"Pa-hay-tee, you came back? How much did you see?"

Pa-hay-tee hung his head in shame. "I did leave after I saw you heal Hala's hip. But then I saw Naska," he said, defending himself. "I could tell he thought you were going to do more, so I went back and watched."

"You stayed hidden all that time?" Mi-sa asked, disappointed in the boy.

"Yes," he admitted, "even after the spirit flight, when Naska stopped you and said he would rescue your brother if you became his woman."

Cota's eyes shot to hers.

Mi-sa looked back at Pa-hay-tee. Perhaps Cota had not understood what the boy had said. But the way he just looked at her made her believe he had.

"You should not have done that, Pa-hay-tee," Mi-sa said.

"I am sorry. I meant no harm. You do such wonderful magic. I had never seen anything like that before."

"There is no place for you at Chalosee's bedside," she told him. "It would be rude for you to spy on me that way again. Do you understand?"

Pa-hay-tee looked ashamed and nodded his head.

Cota and Mi-sa walked on to the platform. At the base of the ladder she could hear Olagale chanting inside and Hala crying and saying prayers.

Cota watched her climb up and into his dwelling. He decided to stay below.

Mi-sa looked at Chalosee, her hands in fists as they gripped the edge of the mat. Olagale sat next to her cross-legged, his voice gravelly from chanting so long.

"Mi-sa," Chalosee said frantically, lifting her head, "the baby wants to come. It is too early. I am frightened. Please help me! Please!"

Mi-sa knelt next to her. "Chew on this," she said, slipping one of the leaves she had brought into Chalosee's mouth.

Suddenly Chalosee squinted her eyes, arched her neck, and pulled up on the edge of the mat. Mi-sa lightly put her hand on Chalosee's belly and began whispering words.

"Make it stop," Chalosee grunted.

"Chew the leaf. Feel the warmth of my hand," Mi-sa said.

In a moment Chalosee relaxed. "They are birthing pains. I know they are. Do not make me go to the birthing hut," Chalosee pleaded, grabbing Mi-sa's arm.

"I will not make you go there, Chalosee." She understood the woman's fear. If she did enter the birthing hut, her worst fears would be confirmed. If she could deny what was happening, then maybe the pains would stop.

"Here," Mi-sa said, putting another leaf in her mouth. "Now relax. Let the medicine help you. Close your eyes and feel the warmth of my hand as I move it over you. Trace it in your mind. Concentrate."

Mi-sa moved her open hand in small circles over

Chalosee's belly, barely above the skin. She breathed in deeply through her nose and blew the air out her mouth. Four times she breathed this way, cleansing herself, preparing herself to become the receptacle of the spirits.

Hala fidgeted as she felt the air inside the platform change. She could not have explained the difference, but her skin and scalp tingled.

Olagale's eyes grew wide as he, too, noticed the change.

Mi-sa moved her hand in widening rings until she encompassed Chalosee's abdomen in one large circle. She stopped whispering and began a song.

Chalosee kept her eyes closed and, after concentrating very hard, found that she could feel Mi-sa's hand, even though it did not touch her. Then she could picture it—as if she could see without opening her eyes. Remarkably the pains had stopped, and she felt much more relaxed, very tired even.

The sound of Mi-sa's voice filled the platform, and then slowly she lowered her voice so that the song became softer and softer. She moved her hand from over Chalosee, laid it in her lap with her other hand, and slowly opened her eyes. She handed Chalosee another leaf to chew.

"How do you feel?" Mi-sa asked.

"The pains are gone. The baby rests. Thank you, Mi-sa," she said, crying.

Hala moved closer and put Chalosee's head in her lap. "Go and tell Cota that the baby will wait to be born," she said to Olagale.

"I will go," Mi-sa said, needing to leave. She handed Olagale some more of the leaves. "If there is any more pain, give her one of these," she said.

Olagale nodded. "I will stay with her."

Mi-sa climbed down the ladder. Cota sat by his hearth.

"The child will not be born today," she said.

He nodded and gave her a look of thanks. Mi-sa smiled warmly and turned to leave.

"Wait," Cota said. "Is what Pa-hay-tee said true?"

"I am done here now," she said. "Have Olagale call me if there is more trouble."

"It *is* true," Cota said, rising and stepping close to her. "That is why you could never really explain to me. Naska has used your devotion to Cherok against me. But why did you not tell me?"

"Cota," Mi-sa said with a sigh, "I did not want to ask you to do something that is against everything you stand for. I had to do something to save Cherok, but I could not ask you to go to war. You are the peace."

"And so you did as Naska proposed."

"I had to."

"No longer," Cota said.

Hala suddenly appeared at the top of the ladder and began slowly climbing down.

"Mi-sa saved the baby, Cota," Hala said.

"She has told me, and I am grateful," he said, still looking at Mi-sa.

"The baby will not be born today. But I do not know about tomorrow or the next day," the shaman woman said.

"We will take good care of Chalosee," Hala said, looking first at Mi-sa and then at Cota. She stared for a moment. She sensed that she had interrupted something. "I will prepare something for her to eat—to give her strength," Hala said, her words coming slowly and deliberately.

"That will be good," Mi-sa agreed.

"Cota and Olagale will stay with her," Hala said. "Is that not so?" She glared at Cota.

"Yes," Cota answered.

Hala walked away, knowing that there was a piece of Cota's heart that her daughter would never have. She felt distress over that, but harbored no ill feelings toward the Tegesta woman.

"Go up to her," Mi-sa said to Cota. "She will want you to be with her."

"This conversation is not finished," he said.

"There is nothing else to say, Cota."

* * *

Mi-sa searched for Naska. She found him in the shade of
a tall spreading oak. Ursa leaned against the tree. Even
though Mi-sa was considered Naska's woman, he continued
to see Ursa. Mi-sa was thankful for that. She watched them
from a distance. Ursa appeared entranced by every movement
he made and every word he spoke. Mi-sa was too far away
to hear the words, but his flirtatious smile and body movements were overt and unmistakable. She felt a twinge of pity
for Ursa. Perhaps when all this was over and she was gone,
Ursa would have Naska—if any woman could ever have a
man with no heart.

"Naska," she said coldly when she reached them, "I need
to speak with you."

"You are jealous," he said, his grin hard and arrogant.

"I apologize for interrupting your talk, Ursa," she said, ignoring Naska's vain remark. "He is not my husband and is
free to speak with anyone he wishes. It is only that I need to
discuss something with him."

Ursa looked down, embarrassed that she was part of this
confrontation.

Naska playfully tapped Ursa's rump. "Let me settle her
down," he said, addressing Ursa, taking Mi-sa's arm to leave.

"Now, what is it that is so urgent?" he asked, smiling at
her.

"Tell me again about the men you have persuaded to go
with you to rescue Cherok and Talasee. Who are they?"

"I have spoken with many," Naska said defensively. "We
have been over this before."

"I am impatient. Tell me who has agreed to go."

Naska spouted some names, saying he had spoken to each
of them.

"Did Ockla agree? Tell me who has agreed."

"I will convince them. But it takes time."

"There is no more time, Naska. I must ask Cota to provide
an escort to a Tegesta village. I should have done that to begin with. Why did I believe you?"

"I was keeping my word. The men are stubborn. They do not wish to betray my brother."

"As I have done," Mi-sa said, feeling shame and regret.

"Ah, well," Naska said with a sigh. "I have kept you from my brother. He will always think that I won your heart from him. That is enough."

"Cota knows the truth," she said. "I need you to go for Cherok now before Cota betrays everything he stands for."

"So it will be," Naska said. "Tonight you show me how much you want me to save Cherok. Put all your spirit into it. If I am pleased, I am certain I will feel the urgency as much as you do. It should only take a day or so more to get everything ready. I will have had my fill of you by then."

"Get it done, Naska."

"I hate for our understanding to end." He grinned. "Even though Cota knows how you came to be with me, he will always wonder how much I was in your heart," Naska said.

"He is wiser than that."

"He has believed that you were my woman by choice all this time. Those thoughts will haunt him. For once I have won. Even though the game is over now, I have enjoyed every moment of it. And Ursa says she has missed me," he said, looking back at the woman who waited for him by the tree.

"I do not know why she accepts all the things you do."

"Oh, yes, you do, Mi-sa. Our many nights together have explained her affection for me. In the shadows, in the dark, you have known the side of me that Ursa cannot do without."

Mi-sa shook her head in disbelief.

Mi-sa sat inside her platform, looking out, watching the twilight filter through the trees, dreading the moment when Naska would come for her. Swarms of butterflies, their colors subdued in the last light, flitted into the cover of the wood, seeking refuge for the night.

She saw Cota coming toward her platform, moving in the light of dusk. He did not stop to ask if he could come up.

"Do you love Naska?" he asked as she backed into the shadows, letting him step inside.

"It does not matter," she answered.

"Do you love him?"

"No, Cota."

Cota rammed his fist into one of the support posts made from the bole of a Sabal palm. "You did this so you would not have to ask me to rescue your brother?"

"Naska said he would not challenge you, and he would go for Cherok."

"Mi-sa," he said, his voice low and soft, his hands coming to rest on her shoulders. "If only—"

"You should not be here, Cota."

"And you should not have kept the truth from me." Cota's hand swept over her face, his fingers tracing her bottom lip. "You will never need to return to his bed," he said. He stepped closer and wrapped his arms around her, pressing her close to him, recalling every curve and swell of her.

Mi-sa felt the ruggedness of him in contrast to her softness. "Go home, Cota," she whispered even as she clung to him.

"Let me hold you just a moment longer," he said. "Then I will be gone."

Mi-sa buried her face in his chest. She hoped that he would be the strong one and move away first. Somehow, even though she knew this had to end, she also knew that she would not be the one to step away.

Suddenly he stood at the ladder, his hands at his sides, his body so far away. "You will have your brother," he said.

Mi-sa watched him leave as nightfall swiftly cloaked the village. She watched until he was swallowed by the dark.

CHAPTER
~ 32 ~

Cota stood before the Council of Men. He looked upon the faces of the oldest men. Lines of age and sun, wisdom and responsibility, rolled over their faces in bony prominences and carved channels. Their once clear and gleaming eyes were now haloed with a hazy gray rim. They did not see so well anymore, and their teeth were worn down, some to the gums. But they were perceptive, knowledgeable, and sagacious.

With their shining black eyes and smooth brown skin that was yet to rumple with such deep creases and folds, the younger men studied the older ones, watching for small twitches, dipping brows, smiles, and grimaces that would provide clues to their opinions.

"We are Kahoosa!" Cota began, thrusting one arm into the air, making the men cheer. "The power of the spirits is with us!" Again the crowd broke into whoops and cheers.

Cota waited until the men settled. "And we are brothers of the Tegesta," he said. "The Kahoosa and the Tegesta have led the way in a lasting peace brought to the People by the Kahoosa cacique—my father, Kaho—and by my Tegesta mother, Teeka."

The men in the crowd mumbled their agreement. Cota paused, allowing them to fuel each other's morale and ardor.

"Never could we permit the A-po-la-chee to destroy the peace by attacking the Kahoosa or the Tegesta."

"No!" some of the men shouted. "Never," others said, the spirit rushing through them already.

"We have heard the tragic tale from the Tegesta woman, Mi-sa. As she has lived among us, we have heard how the A-po-la-chee enslaved her brother and her friend. The storm destroyed her village, and so there are no Tegesta warriors to fight for them."

"Then the Kahoosa must free them," Ockla shouted, shaking his fist in the air.

Naska had actually planted the seed for Cota's appeal by speaking to the men one at a time. Even though he had thought he was working against Cota, his efforts had worked in the cacique's favor. The men were zealous and receptive.

"We must ensure the peace! We will show the A-po-la-chee that we will not tolerate their warlike ways!" Cota said.

"Yes, avenge the Tegesta!" someone called out.

"The A-po-la-chee must be stopped!" another bellowed.

Cota looked beyond the Council. He saw Mi-sa with Hala, watching and listening. "It will be done!" he roared.

Pa-hay-tee watched in wonder as Kaho dipped a thorn into a finely powdered black soot mixed with a small amount of fat, then pricked Cota's chest, leaving a permanent black dot in his skin. The tattoo was a series of black dots in the shape of a *V*, extending from his shoulders to just below his sternum. Kaho filled in some of the spaces with solid black. He followed the same pattern that he had had tattooed on his own chest before his last war party.

All the warriors had their chests and arms tattooed with different designs, but all of the patterns meant the same thing: They were going to war against the A-po-la-chee.

Cota painted diagonal lines on his face from beneath his eyes to his neck. He was the leader, and the lines were the symbolic path of his tears as he cried during prayers for the success of the venture. After fasting, prayers, and orations that went on through the day, the warriors passed a large conch shell filled with black drink. Each of the men partook several times.

Olagale held the bowl to his lips for the third time. He felt himself break into a sweat, and his stomach turned. He passed the ladle on, watching to see if there was any man who could not keep the drink down. Such a man would not be entrusted with any responsibility during the raid; he would be considered too weak.

All of the men swallowed the black drink proudly, feeling it travel all the way to their empty bellies, and no one was unable to keep it in his stomach. At the end of the ritual, Cota assigned three scouts to find the A-po-la-chee and report back.

"May your legs be as swift as the deer's and as agile as the panther's, your eyes as sharp as the eagle's, your body as strong as the bear's," he said to the scouts. "We wait for your return."

The next morning the scouts left before the others arose, the furtiveness beginning at the onset of their mission.

The days passed, and the Kahoosa waited for the return of their scouts. The men hovered over prayer sticks and toiled over the creation of new weapons. Cota assigned tasks. They hardened their bodies by sitting close to the central hearth, letting the heat of the fire draw all the fluids from them. At dawn they sprinted through the woods, running a great distance, then turning and running back into the village. This increased their endurance, which would be an advantage in battle. The days passed quickly and torturously.

Cota sat by his fire, tempering the end of a wooden spike, hardening it. Naska sat nearby, his eyes closed, saying prayers as he sweated in the scorching heat.

"I am surprised that you intend to go with us," Cota said.

"I am a warrior. Why would I not go?" Naska asked, not even looking at his brother.

"You are an able and powerful warrior, Naska. I am certain that we will see your ability and power in battle also. I have no doubt about that."

Naska finally looked at him. "I have done what I set out to do. I took something from you that you wanted. Now I go about the business of the Kahoosa. I have felt all along that we cannot allow the A-po-la-chee or any other tribe to become stronger than we are. I am happy to go into battle. I anxiously await it!"

"We go to war to defend the peace—to enforce it. The Kahoosa will not be intimidated. What we do is a good thing."

Naska made a sound like a doubtful laugh.

There was a sudden commotion in the village. Pa-hay-tee came running, carrying the message. "The scouts return!"

Kaho handed his son his war whistle made from the bone of an eagle's wing. "It has been a long time since this whistle was used to signal our warriors." The whistle made such a shrill sound that it could be heard easily above the noise of battle.

The men gathered and practiced responding to the commands of the whistle. The sound from one end was the signal to attack. The sound from the other end would signal them to retreat. Certain rhythms meant to turn and wheel during the attack.

They practiced speeding toward the enemy, coordinating their ambushing methods, and rescuing fallen warriors.

"We must surprise them," Cota said to the assemblage. "They must be confused as to our number and location. The scouts say the village is large, and the A-po-la-chee outnumber us. Their village is on a lake. Some of us will come out of the water, and the rest will approach from two other directions. We must be patient and cunning, waiting until all of us have arrived at our stations. We will make noise from all sides. If we can cause them to panic, confuse them, the battle will be easy. We must strike quickly and accomplish our mission swiftly, then get out. There will be no time for error. If we linger, then we lessen our chances of success."

The mumblings in the crowd were sounds of agreement.

Kaho told of his first war party. "I will not forget it," he said. "I was young and eager. I was so proud the day we slipped quietly out of our village. We wore no bright paints, only dark lines that would help us hide in the shadows of the trees. We carried nothing except our weapons and our prayers."

The other old men also spoke, giving advice and telling stories. The younger ones listened intently, anticipating the day when they would participate. Pa-hay-tee's face contorted with a variety of expressions as he listened and watched.

The night before they were to leave finally came. The day had seemed exceptionally long, and all of the Kahoosa knew they would have little sleep overnight.

Mi-sa lay on her mat listening to the hum of the crickets and the sound of wind blowing through the thatch. The men had gone to their platforms early to be with their women, and the sounds of their joining seemed to echo in Mi-sa's ears.

She had watched as Naska led Ursa away and as Cota had strolled across the village and up to his platform where Chalosee still rested. Since the threat of the baby's premature birth, Chalosee had not been seen about the village very much. On the advice of Hala and Olagale, she rested most of the day.

Tonight Mi-sa was afraid to close her eyes, afraid to sleep. If she did dream, if the spirits brought her a vision, she might see something she did not want to. She might see the attack as unsuccessful, see people injured, see Cherok killed, see

Cota dead. She sighed and turned to her side, staring out into the starlit sky.

Suddenly she heard the thud of footsteps, someone running up to her platform.

"Mi-sa," Pa-hay-tee called breathlessly. "Come down!"

Mi-sa rushed to the side of the platform. "What is it?"

"Come down. Cota wants you!"

"Tell me!" she said as she went down the ladder.

"I was too excited to sleep, and I sat at the central hearth pretending I was a warrior. Then I heard the noise and went to see. Cota has sent me for you. Chalosee's baby is coming," he explained, tugging on her arm.

Mi-sa followed the boy across the village to Cota's shelter.

"She is afraid, Mi-sa," Cota said.

Mi-sa scrambled up the ladder and knelt next to Chalosee. She touched Chalosee's belly, and that flash of a vision she had before returned, making her shudder.

"Move the light closer," she told Hala, who carried a torch.

"Relax, Chalosee." Gently she urged Chalosee's legs apart and reached inside. Mi-sa sat back on her heels and wiped her hand on the deerskin at Chalosee's side.

"I am cold," Chalosee said, her knees shaking.

Mi-sa covered her with the skin.

"Chalosee," Mi-sa began, "I know it is still too soon, but we must move you to the birthing hut. The baby is going to be born."

"No!" Chalosee cried, squeezing her eyes closed.

"There is nothing else that Olagale or I can do. The child wants to come," she said, stroking Chalosee's cheek.

Olagale moved behind Chalosee's head and hefted her shoulders. Mi-sa moved to the side to help her up. Suddenly Chalosee looked down.

"Blood! All the blood!" she cried, throwing her head back against Olagale. "No, no, no. Please!"

Olagale and Mi-sa helped her to the ladder.

"Where is Cota?" Chalosee asked. "Where is he?"

"He is below, Chalosee."

"Send him away," his wife said.

Mi-sa looked at Olagale, confused.

"This is bad blood. If it contaminates him, he might die in battle!"

"He will not touch you," Hala said.

"Send him away, or I will not leave," Chalosee said, resisting their urgings.

Hala crept down the ladder. "Back away, Cota. Back away. Chalosee is afraid you will be contaminated by the blood." A moment later she called up to them, "He is gone."

Chalosee moved down the ladder. When she touched the ground she bent over in pain and waited for it to pass. Cota's hand steadied her. She looked up.

"I am not afraid," he said. "You are my wife, and this is my child."

"The blood is dirty," she said, grunting the words as she suffered.

Cota ignored her warnings; he lifted her and carried her to the birthing hut.

"You must wait outside," Olagale told Cota. "I must also."

The men exited, giving Hala the torch. On the way out, Cota touched Mi-sa's arm in a desperate plea. "Can you help her?"

Mi-sa shook her head.

Cota stepped outside and listened to Olagale's prayers.

"When the next pain comes, hold the pole and push," Hala told her, putting the torch in the ground so that it stood up and she did not need to hold it.

But when the next pain came, there was another gush of blood and Chalosee fell over, her head spinning, her whole body shaking.

Mi-sa moved Chalosee onto her back. "We will do it this way," Mi-sa said to Hala. "She is too weak to stand up."

"I am so cold," Chalosee said, her legs jumping and twitching, her teeth chattering.

Hala leaned over Chalosee, covering her daughter's body

with her own to keep her warm. She looked at Chalosee's face and wiped heavily at her forehead, sweeping her hair back. "Be strong," she kept saying, but Chalosee's eyes closed, and when her stomach tightened again, she did not respond.

The small baby slid into Mi-sa's hands, entering the world quietly. So very tiny, Mi-sa thought, noticing the incredibly miniature fingers and toes. The baby did not cry.

The flood of blood increased, pooling around Chalosee. Hala's and Mi-sa's knees were red as they knelt close to her.

Suddenly Hala sat up, no longer feeling the shallow breaths of her daughter. "Chalosee?" she said, softly at first. Then again she said her daughter's name, only louder this time. Chalosee did not answer.

Hala turned to Mi-sa, tears rolling down her cheeks. She looked at the very small body in Mi-sa's hands that lay as still as her mother.

Hala moved closer, and with a fingertip she gently touched the baby's delicate hand. "She would have looked like her mother," she whispered through her tears.

"Yes," Mi-sa said, handing the still child to her grandmother. "I am sorry, Hala."

The old woman cradled the infant and began to sing a lullaby, her voice breaking with the crying she fought. "This is all I can give this little one," she said. Then she pulled Chalosee's arm out to the side and laid the baby there, nestled against her mother.

Hala was singing to them both as Mi-sa left the birthing hut.

"The baby does not cry," Cota said.

"No," Mi-sa said. "She did not cry."

Cota heard Hala's song that was racked with grief. "Chalosee?" he asked.

Mi-sa looked at him, aching inside for his pain. "I am sorry."

Cota turned away for a moment and then faced Mi-sa

again. "Olagale will leave with the warriors in the morning. Chalosee and the child need a shaman. Mi-sa, will you prepare them to meet the spirits? Can you lead them to the Other Side?" he asked.

"I will," she answered.

CHAPTER
~ 33 ~

At dawn the warriors began to gather. They took the smaller canoes into the Big Water, but stayed close to the shore, away from the waves that could have swamped them. For two days they traveled on the sea, stopping to fish and camp on the beach.

When they reached A-po-la-chee territory, they dragged the canoes ashore and concealed them in the brush beyond the dunes.

They broke into three groups, each led by a scout. "Go as planned," Cota told them. "When we meet again we will smell the enemy's blood!"

Cota's group felled a pine, cutting the trunk into pieces to make small rafts on which they could kick their way across the lake. The enemy would not expect to see them come from there. Only Cota's group would come in from the water. The others would come from two other directions.

The warriors made their last loud war cries. From here on out they would move quietly and carefully, like shadows in the woods, the way they had been taught even as boys.

They advanced through the thickets, following crooked paths where the sunlight found entrance through bright openings in the canopy. The scouts led them through the forest, closing on the enemy from three directions.

At nightfall the warriors camped. They built no fire. Cota's group huddled beneath large live oaks, sucking the juice from fresh berries and eating from the small stash of food they had brought along. Naska's group and Ockla's party would gather moss and keep it as dry as the small burning coals they carried. They would make good use of the moss when they met the enemy.

When dawn arrived, the men prepared to leave.

"Today we will be upon them," the scout told Cota.

As the sun climbed in the sky, the men came upon a rill. "It flows from the lake?" Cota asked.

The scout nodded. It was time to take precautions. They crept through the wood, their golden bodies well hidden by the dense palmettos and withering grasses.

"Here," Cota whispered to those near him. He made a sound like a bird to get the attention of those far away, then waved for them to come.

The men gathered, crouching to see a small, cold hearth and fauna bones scattered by it.

"We are close," Cota said, looking through the wood.

The scout felt the hearth and stirred it with a stick to see if any warmth remained underneath. "All cold," he said.

"The hearth of one of their sentinels. I hear that they constantly move them about."

"Cota," a man called. He stood at the edge of the brook where the soil was moist. Impressed in the wet earth was a footprint. "He walks heavy on his heels," the man said. "He was not on the hunt."

Cota looked at the track and agreed, then waved them on and made the sound of the bird. It was the call they had decided upon in Council, and he waited to see if there was an answer. In a moment, far in the distance, he heard the return call, and then another. The groups could not see one another and depended only on their sense of hearing to keep them organized and in formation.

Soon the smell of the A-po-la-chee fires wafted to their nostrils. Cota held up his hand, telling his troop to stop. They could not see them yet, but the enemy was close. Somewhere nearby there could be a sentry.

The large lake came into sight. Cota stood steady as a pine, peering around the tree that hid him. Trodden paths wound around the lake.

"Stay off the trails," he warned.

They posted their own watchmen.

"We will stay here until dawn and cross the water just before it is light," Cota told them. "The others will also be positioning themselves."

Just after dark they heard the brush rustle. Cautiously the men hunkered down amid clumps of palmetto, the saw-toothed stems grazing their skin. Others shinnied up trees and watched below.

A stout A-po-la-chee warrior ambled down one of the paths. He stopped to relieve himself. He was so close that Cota could hear the splatter of the man's urine.

Cota could feel his heart pounding in his chest and was sure his breath sounded like the wind.

Soon the man moved on, and the Tegesta warriors came out of cover and waited for dawn through the long night.

No man slept. Their muscles twitched with alertness, and their eyes stared in the darkness.

When the eastern horizon softened from the bleakness of night to dark blue, Cota motioned for the men to begin their passage.

Each man carried his tree-float, stopping briefly to cut a reed near the water. Cota blew through his reed, clearing it out, and then stripped it of leaves. Silently they entered the water and stretched out on the rafts, keeping their legs straight behind them, kicking quietly beneath the surface, propelling themselves across the lake.

Dawn was coming quickly. The men hid their floats in the tangle of great reeds and rushes along the shore. They waited for the clear daylight, hiding beneath the water, breathing through their cut reeds, only surfacing to catch fleeting glimpses of the village.

Cota left his group, moving under the water to where the A-po-la-chee canoes were beached. Carefully he crept up the bank beside a dugout and pushed it out into the water. Concealing himself behind the canoe, praying that it would not be noticed, Cota guided the dugout to the stand of reeds where his band waited. With their help, he pushed the canoe up into the rushes. They would have need of it when they made their escape.

When daylight came, he knew that all of the warriors would be in place. Cota rose out of the water and made the bird call. Naska's party and Ockla's group quickly answered, confirming that they were ready.

Cota took the eagle bone war whistle and blew, setting the attack into motion.

Naska's band swept in from the east and Ockla's from the northwest while Cota's group rose up out of the water and entered the village from the south.

Sudden shrieks and cries could be heard as the A-po-la-chee realized what was happening.

Naska found the beached canoes and waved his men on. They loaded the tips of their arrows with moss and set them afire with the coals they had brought. The arrows streaked through the sky in arcs like many fiery red stars. As soon as the A-po-la-chee canoes were ablaze, Naska and his group moved on into the village whooping loudly even as Ockla and his group came from the other side, confusing the A-po-la-chee.

Cota and the scout slipped away from their band, which drew the A-po-la-chee in their direction. The two men moved through the pale yellow light on the outskirts of the village to the place where Cherok and Talasee were kept.

Suddenly a pair of ferocious eyes glared at them through the bushes, and an enemy warrior charged at them. The A-po-la-chee swung his club over his head, shouting a war cry. Cota ducked and swerved as the warrior struck, barely missing. The scout used the moment while the A-po-la-chee was off balance to plunge his knife into his adversary's chest.

Immediately the warrior fell to his knees, his war club still raised. Red blood spilled from the wound and bubbled out of his nose.

Cota stared as the man fell forward, one hand clawing desperately at the empty sky as if he could hold on to it. The outstretched hand finally surrendered as he toppled face down.

"Just there," the scout said, pointing. "That is where we saw the Tegesta."

A sudden screech made the two men turn around. A boy no older than Pa-hay-tee tore the knife from its sheath at the fallen warrior's side. The boy shrieked and bolted at them.

Cota grabbed the young warrior's wrist and wrenched the knife from him. That was when he saw the stream of tears roll down the youth's face. The boy continued to scream at him. Cota could not translate the A-po-la-chee words, but he understood the terror and the pain. The warrior who lay dead was someone special to this boy—his father, his uncle, his friend.

Cota stared at the small one, his feeling of triumph quickly mingled with sorrow. The moment was a stern reminder of the importance of peace.

Cota released the boy, whose countenance displayed his surprise. His eyes wide, the boy dropped down beside the A-po-la-chee warrior. Cota and the scout waited a moment, then turned and entered the far end of the village.

"Where is the other one?" Cota asked, seeing only one man tied to a post.

"There were two before," the scout answered.

The sound of war blared through the early morning light. The cries of women and children, the bold whoops of the warriors, echoed.

A woman's voice, closer than the rest, made Cota and the scout dive to their bellies in the coarse grass.

An older woman was pleading with a younger A-po-la-chee maiden. Cota watched as the younger woman ran to the man tied to the post and cut him free. The older woman was protesting and frantically watching in all directions.

The man fell to the ground, and the woman helped him up, putting his arm over her shoulders.

Cota made a decision to move in. If the woman took him into the village, he and the scout might not be able to get to him. The Kahoosa had been told to distract the A-po-la-chee, to draw them away from this spot.

Cota and the scout rushed forward. The old woman bellowed hysterically, but the younger woman only looked up, the continued on, holding tightly to the man.

Cota put his knife away and ordered the scout to do the same. He quickly glanced behind them to watch for the enemy, and then turned back to the young woman.

Cota moved close and looked at the bruised and swollen face of the man the woman supported. "Cherok?"

The man looked up at him, but then his head slumped to his chest.

Cota put the man's other arm over his shoulders. The woman nodded, and they began to drag the weak man, following the scout who checked their trail, leaving the screaming and crying older woman behind.

The smell of fire filled the air; the crackling and hissing were loud in their ears. The black smoke began to filter through the village. The bright light of the fires could be seen, radiating into the sky. The village was ablaze.

"Hurry," Cota said, hoping the woman understood.

A skirmish ahead stopped them.

"Take Cherok," Cota said. "I will meet you at the canoe."

The scout moved into Cota's position, helping the woman support the Tegesta man.

"Go!" Cota ordered the hesitant scout, seeing that they had been noticed.

An A-po-la-chee hurdled the brush in the scrub timber, coming at Cota, his ax cleaving the sky as he swung it overhead.

Cota drew his knife and took a defensive stance, legs

spread for balance, then bent forward to make a smaller target, his weapon extended in front of him.

The warrior leapt at Cota, howling his war cry as he swung the ax at his enemy. Cota darted to the side; the ax missed his head but grazed his shoulder. He tossed his knife to his other hand, then reached up, grabbed the A-po-la-chee's arm, and twisted it on the downswing. In the same fluid movement, Cota jabbed his knife into the warrior's side, feeling it glance off a rib before finding its way deep inside the flesh. Quickly Cota changed the angle of his wrist and thrust the knife upward.

The warrior staggered back as Cota pulled his knife free and swiftly turned to see another A-po-la-chee. The warrior had seized Naska and was wrestling him to the ground. Cota held his injured shoulder as he made his way to his brother.

The warrior swung his knife high as Naska fought, then plunged it down. Naska rolled to the side but not fast enough, and the knife hit him at the collarbone. Again the A-po-la-chee had the advantage and pinned Naska beneath him, his knife at Naska's throat.

Cota quickly grabbed the man's hair, yanked back, and reached around his neck with his knife. With a firm, deft stroke, he drew the blade through the throat of the A-po-la-chee.

Naska had been wounded earlier, and blood poured from the side of his head. He fought to sit up, to free himself of the dead man, to rise to his feet and fight again, but he fell to the ground, his head spinning.

Suddenly the A-po-la-chee were everywhere, whooping, screaming, threatening.

Naska was sure that he would die sprawled on the ground before his enemy, weak and unable to fight to the end. For the first time in his life he felt vulnerable. A sour taste rose in his mouth. He would not die nobly in battle; the last blow would come as he lay disabled. There would be no glory.

Cota lunged at the attacking warrior, stabbing him in the

belly. Then, grunting and groaning with strain and pain, he lifted Naska and heaved him over his good shoulder.

Part of Ockla's band arrived, screeching, drawing the attention of the A-po-la-chee away from Cota.

Naska dangled over his brother's shoulder, their blood mixing.

Cota finally saw the edge of the lake and the tall reeds that hid the canoe that would carry them away.

The scout bounded up the path and took Naska from Cota, carried him onto the shelf in the water, and then dumped him inside the canoe with the Tegesta man. Cota followed, passing the young woman, who stood at the edge of the lake.

"Come," he said to her, motioning with his hand, then grabbing his shoulder in pain.

The woman did not know the words, but his meaning was evident. She shook her head.

Cota struggled aboard the canoe, the scout helping him inside, then both of them taking up the paddles. Again Cota motioned for the young woman to join them. He knew her punishment here would be serious if not deadly.

The woman looked back toward the village. There was a sudden rush of movement and noise as a small company of the A-po-la-chee came toward them. She stood in shock as the tip of an arrow embedded itself in her back, making her sink to her knees.

The A-po-la-chee began shooting their arrows at the canoe as Cota and the scout paddled away. Some of the arrows came so close they could hear them pass.

The enemy stood infuriated on the bank, the other canoes burned out. There was no way to go after the Kahoosa.

When Cota was at a safe distance in the lake, he sounded the eagle bone whistle and began to paddle less furiously. The others would meet them back at the Big Water after leaving the A-po-la-chee village in two different directions so the enemy would not know which group to follow. The plan had been executed well, and their venture was successful.

"Brother," Naska whispered from the bottom of the canoe.

Cota turned from the bow and looked back.

"You risked your life for me," Naska said.

"You are my brother," Cota answered, seeing that Naska's scalp had stopped bleeding. The other injury was superficial also, though the collarbone was probably broken. He had lost a lot of blood, but now the bleeding had stopped. He would be sore, but he would heal.

Cota looked at the Tegesta man, also lying in the bottom of the canoe. He appeared alert but very weak, some scars from torture still red and raw, others white and old, evidence of long suffering.

"Cherok," Cota said. "Your sister, Mi-sa, awaits you at our village."

The man stared up at Cota, his lips slowly moving to form words.

"Talasee. I am Talasee."

CHAPTER

— **34** —

"They are coming! They are coming!" Pa-hay-tee hollered, running through the village. He had kept watch ever since the warriors had left, just as he had watched for Cota's return when the cacique had escorted Mi-sa to her own village.

Hala pushed herself up on her walking stick and began to hobble toward the river. Mi-sa heard Pa-hay-tee and began in a trot, passing Hala, her teeth scoring her bottom lip in apprehension.

Cota pulled his canoe onto the bank, the scout helping because of Cota's injured shoulder. Ursa was at the side of the canoe already, helping Naska. He leaned on her.

Mi-sa hurried toward Cota, rejoicing in her heart that he had returned, and looking for Cherok. Suddenly she stopped, remembering that she was no longer Cota's woman. She looked past him to find her brother.

"Talasee!" she called joyously, seeing him disembark. She embraced her old friend. Quickly she turned to Cota. "Thank you, Cota," she said, then turned back to Talasee. "Where is Cherok? Where is my brother?"

Talasee shook his head, thinking that he might cry as he had when he was a very small boy. "A woman set him free, just days ago. The A-po-la-chee went after him, and I have

329

not seen him since. I heard them tell the woman who helped him—the same woman who helped me—that he is dead and that they showed no mercy, that for the rest of her life she should know the agony they made him endure, that his death and suffering were her fault."

Mi-sa felt her head become light with dizziness. "No!" she said. "It cannot be."

"I am sorry, Mi-sa," Talasee said.

Cota watched as Talasee told her the terrible news. He saw her face and knew her anguish. He watched as she and Talasee walked off, arms about each other's waists for support.

"We are destroyed," Cota heard Mi-sa say, her head leaning against Talasee.

Mi-sa sat inside her platform applying medicine to Talasee's wounds.

"I feel stronger already now that I do not breathe the stench of the A-po-la-chee."

"You will be yourself again soon," Mi-sa said, offering him a bowl of food. "We will put some flesh on your bones," she told him.

"May I come up?" Pa-hay-tee called from below.

Mi-sa went to the edge of the platform.

The boy carried another bird. He held it up for her to see. "I have provided food."

Mi-sa nodded and thanked him. "Leave it by my hearth," she told him.

Pa-hay-tee set the large bird on the ground, then looked back at Mi-sa. "I want to see the Tegesta man."

"He is just a man," Mi-sa said. "He looks like any other man. You saw him when he arrived."

"But not up close," Pa-hay-tee said.

Mi-sa looked back at Talasee who nodded at her.

"Come up, then," Mi-sa told the boy.

Pa-hay-tee quickly climbed up and went inside the platform.

Talasee sat up to greet the youth. "I am Talasee," he said. "I heard you say that you had provided food. You must have good hunting skills."

Pa-hay-tee smiled. Already he liked this Tegesta man.

"I am sorry about your brother," Pa-hay-tee said, turning to Mi-sa as if he had been inconsiderate.

"It comforts me to know that you care," Mi-sa said.

Pa-hay-tee looked back again at Talasee. "You do not look any different from the men of this village. It is true that the Tegesta and the Kahoosa are one."

Talasee smiled.

"Have you seen her do magic?" Pa-hay-tee asked. "I did once."

"Olagale does good magic, too," Mi-sa said.

"But Olagale was lost in the battle," Pa-hay-tee was quick to tell her.

Mi-sa felt her stomach sink. "I did not know."

"Will you be our shaman?" he asked.

"I do not think so. I am Tegesta."

"But the Tegesta and the Kahoosa are one."

Mi-sa smiled painfully at the young boy. "I am pleased that you asked."

Pa-hay-tee looked at the last fading light. "My mother will look for me. Good-bye, Tegesta man," he said before leaving.

"He thinks you are wonderful," Talasee said, reclining on the mat with a few groans.

"The young do not have their minds already fixed. It does not matter to Pa-hay-tee that I am Tegesta or a woman shaman."

"That is how we should all be," Talasee said, closing his eyes.

"You are tired," she said.

"Will the Kahoosa accept that I sleep in your platform? Will it bring disgrace to you?"

"It does not matter. This is the best place for you. I can help you heal."

Mi-sa left her platform so that Talasee would rest. It was

dark, and only a few stragglers wandered the village. She sat by her hearth, letting the coals burn very low so that no one would see that she wept.

She heard her name whispered. Cota stood behind her. She looked up at him, wiping away her tears.

"Let me see your injury," she said, standing, seeing the bandage he had applied to his shoulder.

"It is nothing," he said.

"I have heard that many were wounded, Cota. I did not wish for your people to suffer. And Pa-hay-tee tells me that Olagale fell in battle."

"It is true, but we have defended the peace. You should not carry a burden of guilt."

"I feel I have brought misery to the Kahoosa. Especially to you," she said, turning and looking in the distance. "Chalosee and your daughter rest in the charnel house. The spirits will recognize them. I said the prayers that I know. They are not Kahoosa prayers, but they ride the same wind to the same Great Spirit."

"And you have lost your brother," he said. "I know how much he meant to you and the sacrifices you have made for him."

"I had to, Cota. I hope that you will one day forgive me for the lie."

"Knowing that you did not really give Naska your heart makes it easier."

"My heart has always been yours, Cota. I was yours long before I came to this village. But the spirits will not let me have you. I am to be punished forever."

"Why would you think that?" he asked.

"Because I did not heed their warnings, read their signs, and deliver their message to the People as a good shaman would have done. I did not warn them of the storm because I did not understand the spirits' message. I was afraid that the men would see me as a weak woman. The spirits gave me great power, and they gave me wonderful visions of you, but now they have taken my people and you away from me. They have stripped me of everything, even my most beloved brother."

"But they have never taken me from you," he said, his arms reaching around her. "I have always loved you."

Mi-sa melted in his arms—his strong, comforting, powerful arms. Cota lifted her chin and brushed his lips over hers. Then, without saying anything, he let go of her and backed away into the night.

She was a woman of the spirits, and that was where all her answers would come from, Cota thought.

In the next few days Talasee grew stronger, though it would take him a long time to regain all his strength. Ursa waited on Naska, anticipating his every need. Something had happened to Naska while he was gone. He had returned a different man, and she loved him even more.

Cota's shoulder began to heal with medicine that Mi-sa prepared for him. They had not spoken of the night by her hearth. She was afraid that the spirits would rip him from her again if she gave in to her heart, and she was not ready to face another loss.

She was seated by her fire preparing food for Talasee when Hala appeared at her hearth.

"Go to him," the old woman grumbled as she sat.

"What?" Mi-sa asked.

"Go to Cota. I see the way he broods. Chalosee would not like that. She would wish him to be happy."

Mi-sa turned away.

"Look at me, Tegesta woman. I have lived a long time. If you love him, then go to him."

"I cannot," she said.

"I do not see any tethers," Hala argued.

"I am afraid. If I go to him and then have to give him up again—"

"No proper shaman is afraid. Show the spirits your strength—the fiber from which you are made. They will give you their respect, just as they give you their power."

Mi-sa looked toward Cota's platform.

"The man laments. That is no good. Go now so that I can feel I have fulfilled my daughter's wishes. Go!"

Mi-sa obeyed Hala, but she approached Cota's platform unsurely. She did not stop at the bottom of the ladder and call up to him. If he did not answer her, if he turned her away, she would not be able to bear it. Instead she climbed inside, where she saw him sitting in a shaft of sunlight.

Cota looked up, but did not say anything. She would have to speak first.

"I love you," she said. "I have never loved another."

Cota reached up and took her hand, pulling her down to him.

Mi-sa lay nestled in his arms, holding the dream-catcher up to the light so that it glinted and sprayed prisms of color inside the platform.

"This crystal catches your dreams," she said. "It is how I first knew the man who would love me—you."

"It showed you the truth," he said, looking at the crystal shell.

Mi-sa snuggled against him. "I need to go home, Cota. I need to put everything behind me. When you took me to the village, I should have stayed longer and said the prayers, done the things a shaman should do."

"Returning to your village would be too painful for you. I will not let you go," he said, kissing her bare shoulder.

"Please, it is important for me to go home. I have left things undone. This is the last thing I can do for my people. Will you take me there?"

"If I do that, will it mean that you can be my woman without reservation?"

"Yes," she said. "It will also mean that I can live with myself."

"Then I will take you there as my wife."

Mi-sa sat up. "How can that be? As a shaman I am forbidden to marry."

"Woman," he said, pulling her back down. "The spirits must find you most stubborn. They have united us. They showed me to you with this crystal shell. The times are changing. Your father told you that you were the new river. Together we can unify the tribes. We will do the work of the spirits."

Mi-sa sank into his arms. Suddenly she realized that Cota was right. The spirits had certainly given her signs—taken her to the man, sent her visions of him, let her see him with the dream-catcher. Maybe she was again ignoring the spirits, misinterpreting their message out of fear.

She sighed and turned to rest her face against his chest.

"My husband will take me home."

Naska bent over Ursa as she lay sleeping. "Wake up, woman," he said, taking her breast and meeting it with his mouth. "I wish to see my brother and his new wife off."

Ursa turned onto her back, sleepily opening her eyes. "It is too early," she said. "Cota and Mi-sa do not leave at dawn."

He led her hand down across his taut belly so that she could feel his hardness. "But I am ready," he said, kissing her neck.

"You are never satisfied," she whispered, a contented smile crossing her face.

"It is your fault," he said. "The way you move, the way your body curves and dents and swells."

"The way I sleep?" she said, laughing softly.

Naska enfolded her, groaning as he moved the shoulder with the broken collarbone.

Ursa slid out from under him. "You will hurt your shoulder this way," she said, helping him onto his back. She straddled him, and this time his groan was one of pleasure.

"I love you, woman," he was barely able to say.

Cota and Mi-sa prepared to leave the Kahoosa village in the quiet of the morning. Hala patted Mi-sa's hand. "Do what you must, Tegesta woman," she said.

Naska grasped Cota's upper arm. "Go safely," he said.

There was a serious smile in Cota's eyes. "Brother," he said.

"It is as it should be," Kaho said as Cota helped Mi-sa into the dugout. She had brought peace to his sons.

"Safe return," Talasee said. He had thought of going with them. He yearned to touch the soil of his home, but he knew that this was Mi-sa's journey. To her it would be more than a trip up the river into the grassy waters of the Tegesta—it would be a spiritual journey.

They traveled during the daytime, Mi-sa sitting in silence, absorbed in her thoughts much of the time. They camped on a small hammock. There they also saw the damage done by the storm. Some of the largest old trees lay toppled on the ground, brown and leafless now, vines and brush already climbing over them.

"The Great Spirit puts the storm behind him. I will also," she said.

Cota spotted the small hammock in the distance. Mi-sa stood next to him, her head resting against him. He banked the canoe and helped her out.

"I will go alone," she said.

"No," he answered, stopping her. He moved beside her, turned her head to him, and touched his lips to hers. "I will go with you."

Suddenly Cota stopped and pulled back on her arm.

"I smell fire," he said.

Quietly they crept through the brush, Mi-sa gladly feeling the sharp edges of the saw grass, smelling the musty scent of the damp muck, sensing everything that meant she was home.

As the brush began to clear, Cota motioned for her to stay back. "It could be A-po-la-chee," he said.

She started to protest, but the look in Cota's eyes made her yield to his wishes. Mi-sa dropped back a little, and Cota soon disappeared. She waited silently, nervously.

"Come with me," Cota said, reappearing.

She followed as he led her into the village, ducking beneath low branches, brushing the spiderwebs aside. The vines and brush had taken over already, covering what was left of collapsed platforms and hearths, as if her people had never been there.

At the crest of the mound, where a fire had once burned perpetually in the central hearth, a small, weak spiral of smoke curled into the air.

Mi-sa turned and looked at Cota in question.

He nodded.

She approached cautiously, stepping over debris, barely seeing reminders that her people had once called this home. But in her mind she could hear their voices, see the fire of the central hearth leap into the night air. The spirits of her people had waited here for her. It was good that she had returned.

Mi-sa knelt next to the dying fire. A curious Tegesta must have stopped here in passing not long ago—maybe even a survivor from her clan. She knew the emotion that must have choked in the man's throat, seeing that all was gone, disappeared. Perhaps she had been right—maybe the People would suffer the same fate as that ancient animal she had wondered about so long ago. Maybe one day all that would be left of her people would be their old bones.

She covered the fire with dirt and wandered over the mound, finding it difficult to move through all the brush that had grown there. At the place where her mother's platform had once stood, Mi-sa knelt and touched the earth. Miakka's spirit rested here, no matter where the storm had taken her body. Mi-sa leaned forward and pressed her ear to the ground. She could hear her mother's soft song.

"I am here to set you free," she whispered. "I will guide all of you. Take with you part of my heart."

An unusual cool breeze whistled through the trees. The fallen leaves swirled in small dances and then quickly fell back to the ground.

Mi-sa opened her medicine bag to take out those totems

that she needed to sanctify this ground, to help send her people on to the Other Side. She lifted the cord over her head, then shook the bag. All the honored articles tumbled onto the ground.

Suddenly she was blinded. The dream-catcher had caught the sun and burst with its light. Mi-sa reached for it and held it up, seeing the rainbow of colors.

Within the radiant brilliance, something moved. She lowered the crystal shell so that she could see past it, blinking as her eyes adjusted.

From out of the gray shadows of the trees, Cherok moved into the rays of light.

"Cherok!" Her voice caught as she dropped the calcite shell and rose to embrace him.

When she was finally able to pull herself away and speak, she said, "You are alive!"

"A woman helped me escape."

"I thought you were dead. Talasee heard—"

"No, Mi-sa," he said as they held each other again.

Behind her, Cherok saw Cota. He drew back and looked into Mi-sa's eyes. He smiled when he saw the glimmer within. "He is the one," he said.

Mi-sa stooped and picked up the crystal shell, watching it glitter in the sunlight. She held it up so that Cherok could see the incredible sparkle.

"What is it?" he asked.

She looked at Cota, and then back at her brother. She had seen both of the men she loved in the light of the crystal.

"A dream-catcher," she answered.

EPILOGUE

The rays of the morning sun, hot and yellow, percolated through the filter of leaves. Gently the sunlight swaddled the Kahoosa village with its warmth. Mi-sa greeted the day in her way, thanking the spirits for their patience, their confidence in her, their kindness to her.

When she had finished, she felt the palm of Cota's hand against her shoulder.

"I have been speaking with your brother," he said.

"And do the two of you enjoy each other's conversations?"

"Cherok is a man I am glad I have gotten to know."

"He is worthy of another cacique's friendship," she said, taking Cota's hand.

"And of your devotion. But you must also know that he cherishes you. You have a remarkable bond."

"If I had not been able to turn to Cherok in my early life, I do not know what I would have done. He was my strength, as you are now."

Cota wrapped his arms around her, feeling the softness of her skin. "Your brother is healed. He feels much stronger. The days you have spent with him, the ways you've tended to him, have made him healthy."

Mi-sa turned her head against Cota's chest. "Cherok bears many scars. He suffered so long."

"But he suffers no more. He is strong in his head and his body."

"Yes, I am very fortunate to have him back."

"Mi-sa," Cota said, tilting her head back by lifting her chin. She looked so fragile and delicate that he found his next words difficult to say. "Cherok and I spoke of many things this morning."

The angle of Cota's brows and the slant of his lips as he spoke gave Mi-sa a warning.

"What did you discuss?" Her contented expression suddenly gave way to lines of confusion. "Tell me," she said, her voice anxious.

"Speak with your brother," he answered, touching his lips to her forehead.

Pa-hay-tee's mother ran her fingers through the boy's hair, adoring and treasuring the feel of its thick silkiness. Soon he would come of age. Someday she would lose him ... but strong women had to let go of their sons. The boys belonged to the tribe, not to their mothers. Flashes of memory spun in her head of how she had held him at her breast as a baby, how she had beheld in his face the image of his deceased father, how she loved him beyond anything.

"I want to talk to the Tegesta cacique," the boy said.

His mother nodded, fighting off the urge to tell him no, to stay with her for a while, and to reach out and hold him.

Pa-hay-tee ran off, turned once to see his mother, then sprinted on.

"Cherok!" he called to the man sitting and talking with Talasee.

Cherok lifted his hand in welcome to the boy.

"When are you leaving?" Pa-hay-tee asked.

"And how is it that you know this?"

Pa-hay-tee hung his head. "I was not trying to listen when you talked to Cota, but I could not help overhearing because

I was so close." Pa-hay-tee looked up to see Cherok's expression. "You do believe me, do you not?"

Cherok grinned, and Pa-hay-tee's face lit up in response, his heavily lashed black eyes sparkling. "I want to go with you."

"This is not a boy's journey," Cherok answered, and Talasee nodded in agreement.

"But I need to learn the ways of men. I have no father, no uncle. I will learn more from this journey with you than—"

"I like your spirit," Cherok said, witnessing the enthusiasm in Pa-hay-tee's voice and on his face.

"I am a good hunter . . . and I fashion fine weapons. Ask Cota. My eyes are keen, and my body does not tire easily. I eat little."

"There is still time for you to become a man. Cota is teaching you."

"But I have never seen the land where the sun goes down, the land of the shallow water," the boy said.

"Can you fish?" Talasee asked.

"I can perch on any rock and spear a healthy fish, and I build strong traps and make sharp hooks from shells."

"And can you start a fire?"

"I have a fire drill and know the wood to choose." Pa-hay-tee saw the doubt in Cherok's eyes, and so he kept on. "I can catch game and cook the food. I have provided for Mi-sa. I can repair weapons, and I am small enough to be a good scout. I climb trees, and I can swim. My eyes are sharp, and I can see a long way."

"I will think about it," Cherok answered just as Mi-sa came up behind him.

"Cota tells me you have something important to talk to me about," she said.

"Sit down, Mi-sa."

Talasee put his arm around the young boy. "Come. Show me your best weapon and demonstrate your skills for me."

Pa-hay-tee smiled with his whole face, took a skipping step, and walked away with Talasee.

"I have a feeling of dread," Mi-sa said. "Cota would not tell me what you discussed."

Cherok took both of her hands in his. "I believe that some of the People survived the storm. They huddle alone on islands or on the hammocks with other clans."

"Do you really think so?"

"I heard the rumors of the A-po-la-chee, and Atula's voice comes in my quiet daydreams. He tells me to go and gather the People."

Mi-sa studied her brother's face. "You must leave." Her voice was soft and strained.

Cherok nodded. "You know I must go. If any of our people live, we must find them and come together again."

She bowed her head, and Cherok knew what she was thinking.

"You have two great loves in your life, your people and Cota."

Slowly she looked up. "I serve the People."

"Not yet. Talasee and I will search for our people. When the clan has gathered, no matter how great or small in number, we will begin to rebuild our village. That is when we will need our shaman. I will come for you then."

Mi-sa leaned forward and wrapped her arms around Cherok. "I will be ready," she said, her voice trembling as she choked back the tears.

Mi-sa stood on the bank watching the early mist rise from the warm water of the river into the cool air.

Pa-hay-tee ran along the bank, keeping up with Cherok and Talasee as their canoe moved upriver. "I am Pa-hay-tee, a boy of the Kahoosa! A friend of the Tegesta!" he cried. "When you return, I will be a man!" He lifted his head and sang out, his young voice pitched high, imitating the cry of a warrior and hunter.

Cota comfortingly put his arm around Mi-sa's shoulders. Briefly she touched his hand, then reached inside her medicine bag and withdrew the dream-catcher. The early morning sun caught in the crystals. She held it up so that she could see Cherok within the radiant light as the canoe carried him away. Pa-hay-tee still followed the departing canoe, and his voice rang out in the distance.

Cota held her close to him, lending her his strength.

She turned to look at him. "I will not cry," she said, holding out the dream-catcher. "You and Cherok are forever inside its light, and I keep it against my heart."

Cota cupped his hand beneath hers.

"This shell is the keeper of my dreams," she whispered, turning away from the water as the last vision of Cherok and Talasee faded beyond the bend in the river.